The Smallbeef Chronicles

Book Three

Nothing Stays the Same

Stephen Edwards

Nothing Stays The Same
Copyright: Stephen Edwards 2015

All rights reserved

This story is a work of fiction. All characters are fictitious, and any resemblance by name or nature to real persons, living or dead is purely coincidental.

Edwards and Edwards

Cover illustration by Clean Copy

For some reason, Jennie Harborth does not want to be mentioned for her invaluable technical assistance, formatting and how to write more gooder English, but it was her, Jennie Harborth.

1

Do you ever have dreams? Inspector Alan Orange does. He is a mallard and he leads the Armed Response Ducks, better known as ARDs. For the past few years he has had a nasty demon following him about, mostly in his head but sometimes showing up for real. We join him in one of his nightmarish dreams in which he is standing alone down an alleyway. He is outside a shabby building. It's dark and raining lightly:

The lone mallard, Al Orange, faces the stout door of planks hewn from tight grained oak, their age betrayed by occasional splits proudly pronouncing their time-served duty done, their colour greyed by Nature's hand. A solitary latch is all that stands between him and his probable Armageddon. He warily ascends two steps of heavy oak before clutching the wrought iron ring to release the door from its jamb. He gives the door a gentle push, it does not move. Its sheer weight firmly grips the hinges and refuses to budge.

He feels friendless; he has done for most of his life. His inner self gropes blindly in the hope of finding a hand-hold among the realms of delirium now whirling around inside his head. His sense of self-preservation hangs by a thread. Life has become extremely difficult, polluted by vile thoughts which were never meant to dwell inside a duck's head, filling him with paranoia and causing him to hate himself at every opportunity.

'How did I get here?' he whimpers.

Such is his low regard for himself that he doubts his ability to fend off whatever nasty presence awaits him on the other side of the door. He thinks this is the end; perhaps this night will bring things to a conclusion. Maybe

1

his tormentor has finally finished playing with him.

He turns askew, leaning his shoulder against the door, building pressure until it yields without a sound. He sidles inward, partnered by the door as if in a slow waltz. The room is now open to him.

He is very confused. 'What is this place? Is this in my head or is it real?'

Through the musty twilight of the dimly lit room he can see no lanterns or lamps, yet there are faint shadows lying across the dark floorboards born of the same oak as the door which stands sentry to this most unwelcoming of places. The cream-painted walls have long since been yellowed by the breath of its occupants.

'Will my shadow join theirs, is this to be my end?'

While the mallard's nightmare continued, the Sun moved into position just below the horizon, preparing to bring the dawn light into the water birds' world once again. Mother Nature tenderly bathed the land in warm mist, wiping things clean and lovingly stirring the creatures of the day into life.

Four days had passed since Abel Nogg had returned to Fort Bog with his select crew. The crew's mission had been to rescue a missing Beast of Grey who had somehow slipped through the ether into the world of the humans. Sadly, their mission had failed. The Beast of Grey was still missing.

Mother Nature continued caressing the remains of the fort which had been left in ruins following the savage storm a fortnight earlier. The Sun warmed the roof of the make-shift dormitory in the centre of the bailey before peering in through the windows to wake those inside.

Sergeant Bob Uppendown, a Canada goose of the Mounties, was first to rise. He slowly swept his gaze over the others in the room, all of whom were mallards. Inspector Al Orange and his three Armed Response Ducks were resting along one side of the room while along the other side were four constables of the

Flying Squad.

The mallards continued their slumber for a few more precious moments, floating among thoughts of returning to Smallbeef where their loved ones were waiting.

A quiet mumbling wrestled with the peaceful ambience. One mallard in particular was having a troubled sleep – Inspector Al Orange. The light of a new day teetered on the window sill waiting for Mother Nature to give the nod, but she was beaten to it by a scream.

'No!' cried Al Orange. 'No – where is this?' He shouted as anyone would when they have just woken from a troublesome nightmare.

'Steady, Inspector, steady,' said Bob Uppendown, putting a reassuring wing around the mallard's shoulder.

Al Orange sat up on his bed of hay bales, swaying back and forth. He looked around the room, dazed and bewildered. Uppendown comforted him with kindly Canadian tones. 'That sure must have been some nightmare you were having, sir.'

Orange tried to unscramble his thoughts before replying, 'A door…a big heavy door…I went through it into a strange room.' He tried to remember what he could before the images faded. 'It wasn't a room I recognize.' He shivered with staring eyes before forcing the words out. 'I think there were humans in the room…humans.' His voice struggled to keep going while he drew support from the closeness of the goose. 'They weren't little ones like we have here, they were as big as me, like the ones we saw on the other side of the timbered wall.' He peered around the room again with a worried look on his face. 'Are they here, are the humans here?' He pressed himself into the strong chest of the Mountie. 'Tell me it was just a dream, please,' he sobbed.

By now the entire squad had been roused by his ramblings.

3

They were surprised and embarrassed in equal measure by the blubbering inspector who was normally known for his stalwart constitution.

'You were having a nightmare, Inspector,' Bob Uppendown repeated. 'It sure sounds nasty though, but just a nightmare all the same. There are certainly no humans here.'

Al Orange fell back onto his bed and stared up at the rafters. It was clear to those in the room that he was not himself, his eyes could not see past the stuff that filled his head, most of which was not of his making.

Bob Uppendown straightened his Stetson on his immaculate black and white head and then he turned to the constables. 'Keep an eye on him, guys. I'll go and fetch Inspector Hooter.' He closed the door behind him, leaving a concerned silence in the room.

The constables shared their gaze between Inspector Orange and each other, none of them quite knowing what to say.

***

Just beyond the remains of the fort walls lay a small cemetery bordered by a dilapidated picket fence. Two Beasts of Grey stood looking down at the headstone of a newly filled grave. The elder of the two was Abel Nogg, and the other was Eeland Ross, son of the late Beeroglad whose grave they were standing next to.

Standing head and shoulders above young Eeland, Abel read the epitaph in his gruff tones. Here lies Beeroglad, leader of the Beasts of Grey. A dark heart that turned bright and did good things – forever in our thoughts.

'He was a good soul – wasn't he?' asked Eeland.

Abel replied, 'Your father was not always good, but he learned it is never too late to reach out for help – never too late to change your ways and take the right path'.

Eeland looked up at Abel's eyes and said, 'But he always taught me that physical strength was the most important thing. He also told me never to show my emotions to anyone.'

'Fear commands only fear, young Bog,' Abel replied. 'Your father offered only aggression for much of his life, but towards the end of his days he learned from the heart of a Suffolk Punch that love is the stronger of a soul's emotions...' After a brief pause for thought he continued, 'Tell me, Eeland, who would you gladly risk all for, the one who strikes fear into your heart, or the one who shows you love and compassion?'

'But love and compassion cost him his life in the end,' replied Eeland with a tear waiting in the corner of his eye.

'The important thing is that your father saw the light and changed his ways before his passing,' said Abel.

'But the mission to rescue one of our own kind failed, and my father was killed by something in that other world, something evil; surely that's nothing to be proud of.'

'Pride is so often the downfall of those who put themselves above others. They then have to spend their entire lives struggling to stay there; pride is a self-inflicted millstone which some refuse to cast off.'

'But a leader has to be strong to lead,' said Eeland, now feeling more at ease in the eyes of his senior.

'You confuse strength with aggression, young Bog. It takes a very strong person to be meek, humble, or caring,' replied the huge pterosaur.

Eeland's eyes asked for more; his young mind, like any youngster's, was like an empty sponge gladly soaking up Abel's wisdom.

Abel obliged: 'Consider Inspector Hooter of the Flying Squad for example; he has never raised his voice in anger against any of his constables even though they have at times committed some dreadful blunders, as ducks are prone to do.'

Eeland smiled at the thought of Hooter's absurd appearance and the occasional bizarre behaviour of him and his constables.

Abel continued, 'The inspector always supports and guides those around him as best he can, although he himself has sometimes gotten things very wrong. But there is nothing his constables would not do for him…because they repay his love with their love.'

'But isn't love a sign of weakness, sir?' asked Eeland.

Abel carefully curled his large clawed hand over Eeland's shoulder. 'Love is born of the heart; aggression is born of the mind. Minds can be changed like the wind, but the heart will always stay true.'

Gathering comfort from Abel's embrace, the youngster let go another innocent thought. 'Surely my mind and my brain are where my strength comes from.'

'And what if your heart stops – what good is your brain then?'

'Well, yes, but that's different,' replied Eeland, sensing he had been outwitted.

Abel rounded off the conversation by saying, 'All life comes from the heart; without your heart you have nothing and are nothing; be guided by it without the millstone of your mind to weigh—' something suddenly alarmed him before he had finished what he was saying. A certain smell jarred his senses; a smell out of place and unwelcome. He looked up to the sky and drew a troubled breath and held it firmly inside him.

'What is it, sir?' asked Eeland, wondering what had disturbed his mentor so abruptly. 'What's the matter?'

Something was not right – a smell, an entity. Abel had smelt it before, in this world and in that of the humans. A hint of decay tinged his nostrils. His attention was drawn by Bob Uppendown standing among the ruins of the portcullis. Abel expelled the foul air he had gathered, and spread his wings wide. Mother Nature lifted him from the ground high enough for him to glide effortlessly towards the goose.

Uppendown called out with a concerned look in his eye. 'Mr Nogg, sir, I think Inspector Orange is unwell. He seems very distressed. He's talking of dark rooms and humans, very weird fer sure. I'm looking for Inspector Hooter to let him know.'

The huge pterosaur landed immediately in front of the goose before replying, 'You will find him in the remains of the barn; I believe he is talking to young Dick Waters-Edge and his horse.'

'Thank you, sir.' Uppendown hastily continued towards the barn, leaving Abel to search for the source of the smell. 'If you are here, show yourself,' he said quietly. 'You have no place here – I shall not allow you to spoil this world as you have others.'

A few moments later, Sergeant Uppendown passed by again, this time with Inspector Hooter by his side, heading back to the dormitory.

'I shall join you in a minute,' said Abel, his eyes still scouring the land.

Uppendown and Hooter entered the dormitory to find Al Orange prone on his bed, staring blankly while a teardrop or two slipped down his cheeks.

Constable Robert Roberts reported. 'He hasn't said a word since you left, Sergeant.'

Inspector Hooter made his way to the bedside. 'My dear chap,' he said, 'what seems to be the trouble?'

Al Orange turned his head just enough for his eyes to find Hooter's. 'Trouble?' he sighed wearily and his face contorted with utter despair. 'Why can't this be over?' More tears joined the race down his glistening cheeks and dampened the sheet beneath him.

Hooter had always regarded Al Orange as the hard-duck of the police force, the one you did not mess about with if you knew what was good for you. It was clear that the mallard now lying before him did not want to be here anymore.

The door creaked. The birds turned to see Abel Nogg crouching under the doorway; he shuffled his way across the room prompting Hooter to make way for him next to the bed where Al Orange lay.

Abel, in his pterosaur guise, towered over the sick mallard. 'My dear Inspector,' he said in as soft a tone as he could. 'I know of your suffering and I know it is not of your doing; we have spoken of it before.'

Orange managed the weakest of nods to acknowledge Abel's regard.

'You must rest now.' Abel cast his gaze about those in the room. 'You are in good company, you are among friends.'

With his eyes now closed, Orange sank submissively into the mattress of hay.

'Oh dear,' a familiar female voice carried across the room; Moira Maywell, a most likeable moorhen, stood in the doorway with her husband and chick close behind. 'Can I do anything to help?' she enquired.

'You are just in time, my dear.' replied Abel. 'Would you watch over Inspector Orange for a while? We have certain arrangements to make.'

'I will be glad to.' Moira bustled past the other birds and settled down next to the bed. 'Take as long as you like, Mr Nogg,' she said, gently stroking Orange's iridescent brow.

Abel and his assorted crew took their leave.

Moira cast a compassionate look across her patient's face; the green-blue sparkle was still there but his bill was uncommonly dull. She spoke to his closed eyelids, 'Just you rest, my dear Inspector – everything is going to be fine, you'll see.' But she could not see what Al Orange could see – the eyes lurking inside his head, never letting him rest; eyes not belonging to him.

2

Punch stood stoutly in the middle of the barn, looking as impressive as a Suffolk Punch could look. 'Good boy,' said Dick, running a firm brush over the horse's broad chestnut back while his father, Harold Waters-Edge, filled the water bucket.

The beaten barn door opened and Abel Nogg entered with a line of birds following. 'Good morning, Mister Waters-Edge. Good morning, Master Waters-Edge.'

'Good morning, Mr Nogg,' father and son replied.

'I am sorry to interrupt you,' said Abel, 'but we need somewhere to gather our thoughts. May we prevail upon you for a while?'

Punch lifted his head high as if to show everyone his freshly groomed coat. He welcomed the group with a hearty huff from deep within his chest to encourage Harold's reply.

'That's no problem, sir,' said Harold. He then put the water bucket down in front of Punch who eagerly began to sup and slurp while keeping a beautiful eye on his guests.

'Please gather round.' Abel gestured with a half-folded wing. The mallards and the goose eagerly shuffled about to settle in a circle, keen to hear what the pterosaur had to say.

Abel looked in Hooter's direction. 'I have no wish to interfere with the running of your police ducks, Inspector, but I am sure you will agree that Inspector Orange is in need of a rest from his duties.'

'I agree,' Hooter replied sympathetically. 'We must do all we can for the poor chap.'

Constables Lock, Stock and Barrel of the Armed Response Ducks glanced at each other while wondering what would become of them while their leader was out of action.

Inspector Hooter reassured them. 'Don't worry, Constables, you will be drafted into the Flying Squad under my charge until your inspector is well again.'

Unsure of how they would be welcomed, Lock, Stock and Barrel cast a wishful eye in the direction of the Flying Squad constables. Their concerns were immediately greeted with keen smiles and a quick bend of the legs in proper police fashion, down and up again.

'Thank you, sir,' Constable Lock replied to Hooter.

Constable Stock nodded towards Hooter's constables and said, 'Thank you, too.'

Hooter then adopted an unusually firm tone in his voice. 'However, there is one thing which I must insist on.'

Abel Nogg raised an eyebrow, thinking, Please don't say anything embarrassing, Inspector.

'Raise your wings, please,' said Hooter, leading the way by raising his. The three Armed Response Ducks did as they were told. A muffled hush filled the room at the sight of the flintlock pistols concealed beneath. 'You won't need those while you are in my squad, Constables, so you can jolly well take them off and I shall store them under lock and key until further notice.'

'Yes sir,' all three ARDs replied enthusiastically.

Abel's eyes smiled.

Lock, Stock and Barrel removed their holsters and gladly put them to one side. The three of them then spoke up in unison, 'That feels better.' They paused for a moment before raising their other wing to reveal their truncheons. 'Should we still keep these, sir?' asked Barrel.

'Of course you should, Constable.' Hooter clarified the situation to ensure uniformity. 'Your helmet shows others that you are a police duck; your whistle is to attract someone's attention – and your truncheon is handy for pointing the way when giving directions.'

Abel was both charmed and amused by Hooter's nature, but felt it necessary to intervene. 'I am sorry to interrupt, Inspector, but could I ask that you continue your lesson later, we really do have some very pressing matters to discuss.'

Hooter gladly deferred to the pterosaur's authority. 'Of course, Mr Nogg, please go on. You have our full attention.'

Abel remained on all fours, needing only to straighten his neck to rise above those around him so that all could see and hear him. 'Inspector Orange is suffering from a very troubled mind; he is almost completely incapacitated.'

'But what could cause such an affliction?' asked Hooter.

Abel replied, 'Such troubled minds rarely exist in your world, and that is as it should be. During your brief mission into the other world you saw the chaos and anger within the humans' society, did you not?'

'Oh yes, dreadful behaviour.' Hooter spoke for all in the room. 'They had no manners, they were suspicious of every one and they were very aggressive, even to people they didn't even know, how tragic is that?'

'Quite so, Inspector,' Abel nodded. 'From the beginning of their time, the humans of that world have brought strife upon themselves. Not one generation has known what peace is.'

Hooter rubbed his bill. 'But why? Surely it's easier to live peaceably than it is to fight all the time.'

Abel answered Hooter's question with a question. 'You have watched the tiny humans in your world, Inspector; what do you make of their behaviour?'

Hooter stared up at the ceiling for inspiration while rubbing his bill yet again. 'Hmm, they're always bickering and they never make any attempt to integrate with other animals. They seem to think they're superior and special. I'm just glad they're as small as they are or who knows what they would get up to. I've never really gotten close enough to look one in the eye, but I bet they'd have a shifty look if I did.'

The others in the room nodded in quiet agreement while muttering, 'Mmm – yes, very shifty – no doubt about that.'

'Sadly, you might be right,' said Abel.'

Bob Uppendown joined the debate in his soft Canadian tone. 'Are you saying that in the other world, where humans are as big as us they have no natural threats, and so spend their time making up threats of their own?'

'Yes, Sergeant, and not just against others; they quite often fight against themselves. Man fights man – woman fights woman, children are taught to fight children. They have designed tools specifically for killing.' As the words came out of Abel's mouth his heart hurt more and more. 'And quite often…man fights women and children.'

Every jaw in the room dropped. The entire ensemble looked horrified. They simply could not believe what they were hearing. Bob Uppendown felt obliged to speak up. 'I'm sorry, sir, I must have misunderstood you – you didn't say grown-ups fight children and women, did you?'

'Yes, Sergeant, I am afraid I did,' replied Abel, his voice clearly distressed.

'No, sir. You mustn't say that,' Uppendown insisted. 'You must be mistaken, such an act just isn't possible.'

The mallards in the room nodded in support of the goose who was now very upset, tears pooling in his eyes.

13

Abel explained, 'Despite their incredible intelligence, humans have one weakness.' He paused for the mumbling to subside and then said one word…'Greed.'

Hooter replied firmly, 'But if someone has enough, how can they want more? That just doesn't make sense, no sense at all.'

'We shall talk more on the subject later,' said Abel. 'Now we must arrange for Inspector Orange to be taken back to Smallbeef where he can convalesce and be looked after.'

'He's in no fit state to fly, sir,' said Bob Uppendown, now regaining his composure. 'Perhaps we can prepare a wagon to take him.'

'That is a good idea, Sergeant,' said Abel. He looked around the room and realized that one of his select team was absent. 'Does anyone know where our orangutan friend is?'

Hooter answered, 'I assigned Mr Grunt to tend to the few donkeys that are still here; he's seeing to them as we speak.'

'Here I am,' a well-spoken voice called from behind them. 'Have I missed anything?' Aano Grunt stood in the doorway, an orangutan by nature and a farrier by trade. His silhouette highlighted his bizarre proportions comprising a stout rotund body with overly long arms which never seemed to be where you might expect them to be, but usually above his head.

'Ah, Mister Grunt,' Hooter greeted him warmly. 'We were wondering if you could prepare a team to pull a wagon to Smallbeef.'

'Certainly,' Aano replied with a huge apish grin. 'If Sergeant Uppendown can spare two of his Hanoverians, I'm sure they will do fine.'

'Fer sure, Mr Grunt, take yer pick,' replied the Mountie.

***

Meanwhile, in the world of the humans, the mid-morning Sun

warmed the shop fronts and cafes of Davidsmeadow.

'Good morning, madam, tea or coffee?' asked the barista behind the counter in one such café.

'Regular coffee, please,' replied Kate Herrlaw.

Davidsmeadow was still busier than usual with gongoozlers keen to see where the giant flyers from another world had made landfall. Kate took her coffee and sat at a table outside Café Hero. The barista followed her outside to clear the table next to her. 'It's nearly back to normal,' he said, looking at two television vans on the far side of the town square with their dishes pointing into space.

Kate replied with a polite smile, 'It will be nice to get back to normal.' She picked up a newspaper left behind by a previous visitor. 'It's still on the front page I see.' The pair of them gazed at the artist's impression of a gigantic pterosaur with a snarling expression and outstretched talons about to grasp a mother and toddler from the shore of the pond.

'Where do they get these ideas from?' Kate sighed. 'It would be nice if a newspaper would print what actually happened for a change. As far as I'm aware, the only aggressors by the pond were the men in the crowd – and the police.'

The barista was happy to extend the conversation a little longer. 'Yes, but you know what they say, never let the truth get in the way of a good story. After all, it's not every day you see a pterodactyl the size of a bomber plane flying overhead.'

Kate looked up, her eyes held the young man while he balanced a pile of crockery on his arm. She added to his difficulty by smiling again and replying teasingly, 'I think you'll find the creature in this picture is a different kind of pterosaur altogether. A pterodactyl was just one type of pterosaur, often little bigger than a crow, I believe.'

The barista listened dreamily. 'Ah, not what we had here

then.' He put the crockery back down and piled it up again more carefully. 'Better press on,' he said, reluctantly retracing his steps with a very warm feeling inside.

Alone with her thoughts, the events of the last few days left Kate unclear as to what she should do next. She knew her purpose in this world was to observe and report; only in special circumstances was she to lend a helping hand. She knew she might not be called on again for many a year, but she also knew that things could not rest as they were. She had revisited the site of the arch beneath the bridge where she had met Abel Nogg's select crew. She had also travelled the route she thought Inspector Hooter and Aano Grunt most likely to have taken when returning to the timbered wall, but she had found no evidence of them ever having been there.

She opened the second-hand newspaper and perused the inner pages. Photos of young children in far off lands depicted the effects of drought and famine. "Thousands suffer and die" exclaimed the heading. "No end in sight." The editorial told of the effects of the longest drought in living memory cutting a swathe of suffering across the entire African continent. The editor's comment asked, "Is this our own doing? Has the west brought this upon those who can least help themselves?"

'Hollow words,' Kate murmured. She continued reading the article which typically pointed the blame at others without daring to suggest the solution.

After a while Kate sighed and put the newspaper down on the table, taking a few moments to study the general goings-on around her. While her attention was elsewhere a gentle breeze ruffled the newspaper, leaving it open on the puzzle page. She thought nothing of it but soon found herself casually browsing the clues to the crossword. She would occasionally look up from the paper to catch a passer-by studying her as he walked past;

the onlooker would quickly look away, blushing at having been caught out. Despite the rich mix of colours among the people milling about and the colourful window displays behind the sun-kissed panes, Kate would always stand out. Her lightly tanned skin and her long black hair contrasting with her crystal blue eyes ensured that she never blended into the background.

'Difficult or hard?' she mused, looking closely at the crossword clues. 'I think I'll stick to the easy ones today.' She looked up at the blue sky which was empty save for the faintest wisp of white on its way to meet others of its kind beyond the eastern horizon. She imagined Abel Nogg soaring high above, hand in hand with Mother Nature, each enjoying the other's company. She remembered Abel's clever disguises, one as a pterosaur and another as a human acting as a chauffeur. *How did I take so long to realize who you were?* She took a pencil from her clutch bag and set about the first crossword clue: *A collection of sorts – nine letters.* She paused briefly…*Anthology.*

She sipped her coffee while continuing to people-watch. *Always too busy in their own worlds to see what is going on around them,* she thought. *So busy trying to keep one step ahead of time that they don't appreciate the moment they are actually in.* She glanced all around her, studying the faces of all those milling to and fro. *Fifty people, but so few are smiling. Who are the blind ones, those who smile in ignorance or those who cannot see anything to smile about?*

She returned to the crossword: *Two down, a cryptic clue – a commotion in the centre.* She smiled and filled in the squares as another passer-by sneaked a sideways look. *Hubbub.*

And so the town of Davidsmeadow went about its business while Kate Herrlaw waited patiently for the next time she would be called upon, by someone also not of these parts.

3

Back in the world of the water birds, Constables Thomas Thomas and James James stared out of the police station window. They had returned to Davidsmeadow ahead of their fellow squad members to keep an eye on things in and around the town. It was now autumn. Rainwater dripped idly from the blue sign hanging above the door, the words "Davidsmeadow Police" were clearly written in gold as it swung merrily in the wind.

Thomas, still gazing into space, spoke up, 'If I live to be a hundred I'll never understand those humans.'

'What humans?' replied James.

'The ones who live on the other side of the timbered wall,' said Thomas.

'I know what you mean,' replied James. 'We were only in their world for a couple of days and they broke both our laws a hundred times over. Even their police officers broke the rules; they tried to arrest us for no reason and then they shot Inspector Hooter and locked him up just for being a big duck.'

Thomas continued the discussion while his eyes followed a mother mallard hurrying past on the other side of the road with a trail of four ducklings waddling eagerly in her wake. 'Abel Nogg told me they have shelves full of books, and the books are full of laws, and the laws cover every single thing that can be done.'

'Who have?' said James.

'The humans of course.'

'Did he say how many laws?' James asked, thinking as many as ten might be possible.

'Thousands,' replied Thomas.

James let forth a raucous volley of laughter as only a duck can. 'Thousands? Don't be daft, Tom; there aren't that many things that can be done, so how can they have thousands of laws to tell them how to do them?'

Thomas felt a little embarrassed for saying something that did indeed sound absurd, but the teller of such things was Abel Nogg and, as far as anyone knew, he never lied. 'I'm only saying what Mr Nogg told me.'

'Really?' replied James, cutting his laughter short.

'Yes, really.'

They continued looking out the window while discussing their recent adventure into the world of the humans. Their mission had failed and the loss of their new-found mentor, Beeroglad, had struck a blow right to their hearts. Neither Thomas nor James could understand how or why one living creature should seek to do away with another for no good reason.

'Who do you think killed Beeroglad?' asked James.

'I don't think it could have been the humans, they were no match for a pterosaur like Beeroglad....' Thomas paused for thought. 'But they did have guns; perhaps that was how they did it.'

'Perhaps,' said James, 'they also had that helicopter thing; that was really weird, all that noise just to stay in the air, and it never did catch anyone. I ask you, how can something that noisy expect to creep up on someone without being noticed?'

'No, but its all-seeing eye might have captured our image,'

replied Thomas with a tremor in his voice.

'Our image?' James was puzzled. 'How can something capture an image, I mean, an image is just a reflection in a window or in a puddle; surely no one can take it away.'

'No, you're probably right, James. I just thought I overheard Mr Nogg telling Inspector Hooter – that's all.'

'Well I've still got mine,' said James, glancing across at the station mirror.

After a short while the mother mallard hurried past again, going in the other direction with her four children still faithfully following close behind. The little chap at the front turned to his brother and said in a new voice, 'That's what I'm going to be when I grow up.'

'What is?'

'One of them, they're the Flying Squad, and Mum says they're wonderful; I heard her telling Mrs Waddleforth in the park.' The youngsters looked across at the two police ducks who in turn were looking out at them.

'What makes them so wonderful then?'

'I think it's because they're heroes, that's what Mum said. And they wear hats.'

'What's a hero?' asked the second duckling, soaking up all the information as any new brain would.

'I think it's to do with making eggs,' replied the first youngster.

'Making eggs?' said number two, now very puzzled.

'Yes,' said the first, very confidently. 'I heard Mrs Waddleforth saying that her daughter, Fay, was going to marry one of the police ducks and then they were going to make some eggs.'

'Oh…our dad made a wardrobe, does that count?' asked number two, not entirely sure how eggs were made.

'Err, it's probably the same sort of thing,' replied his brother, older by all of thirty seconds and therefore quite a bit more knowledgeable.

The mother mallard looked across at the two police ducks and gave a wave.

Thomas and James waved back and called out in unison, 'Good Morning, Mrs Bottoms-Up.'

Despite being married herself, Betty Bottoms-Up could not help but admire the officers' good looks, each enhanced by their police helmets adorned with shiny chrome badges.

The last of the ducklings soon disappeared around the corner leaving the two constables to continue pondering.

'Do you think we'll have to go back again to find the missing Bog?' asked Thomas, watching the water wend its way along the joints in the cobbles outside.

'Hmm,' replied James, rubbing his bill. 'Mr Nogg did say that because we were the ones who put him there, we would have to go and get him back; that's the way of the world – that's what he said.'

'Let's go and walk the beat,' said Thomas, 'that should help clear our heads.'

'Good idea.' James adjusted his helmet to be sure it was perfectly straight.

Thomas closed the door behind him and the two of them made their way along the narrow side street towards the town square. The rain clouds were doing their best to hide the Sun, but that didn't stop Thomas or James calculating the time of day by the varying shades of light and dark.

'About eleven thirty.'

They emerged into The Square adjacent to the coffee shop on the corner. The rain didn't bother the ducks sitting at the tables outside. The water simply ran over their well-oiled plumage without ever touching their bodies beneath; perfect in every way.

The birds, mostly mallards, would nod and bid the handsome young constables good morning. Thomas and James would acknowledge with a light touch on the brim of their helmets.

All was as it should be, nothing out of place; various creatures enjoying the day for its true worth and thankful for every breath they took.

'Hey, look at that,' James whispered, not wanting anyone other than Thomas to hear him. He gestured with a sideways glance at the female mallard sitting alone outside the café.

'Ooh,' remarked Thomas, trying equally hard not to be heard by anyone else.

The lady duck looked up just as both constables were sneaking one last glimpse of her plumage. They both looked away with brightening yellow bills. She smiled at them and nodded slowly to let them respond equally slowly and enjoy the exchange.

The constables walked on, not daring to risk another quick look over their shoulder; that would be very unprofessional, but they both felt her smile follow them down the road.

'I don't remember seeing her here before,' said Thomas.

'Me neither, and I'm sure we would have noticed her if we had, crikey.'

***

At Fort Bog, the wagon carrying Inspector Al Orange began its journey back to Smallbeef where he would be looked after until he was better. Aano Grunt sat up front on the plank seat while Inspector Orange lay in the back, covered with a soft blanket and supported on each side by hay bales to prevent him rolling over. Two handsome Hanoverians pulled the wagon with a knowing look in their beautiful eyes. Following behind the wagon were two more, each with a Canada goose of the Mounties sitting astride them. The blue numnahs with gold edging contrasted beautifully with the horses' rich brown coats and saddles. A red and white pennant atop the lance carried by one of the escorts provided the finishing touch.

Inspector Hooter watched the wagon disappear into the distance. 'I still don't understand why Inspector Orange is so troubled.'

Abel replied, 'I think his constables know him best, they have seen how he has constantly fought his demon from within.' Abel looked at Lock, Stock and Barrel, inviting them to join the discussion.

Lock cleared his throat and said, 'He used to be fine. He was really nice, just like Inspector Hooter, but over the last year or so he's not always been himself.'

'That's right,' Stock added, 'after a while we could tell what sort of mood he was in just by the change in his eyes.'

Barrel then had his say. 'It would only be slight, but his face would drop just enough for us to notice, and his eyes would narrow and his cheeks sag.'

'Yes, and his bill would go dull, almost with a tinge of grey in it, not right at all,' said Lock. 'And he tended to keep himself to himself when he wasn't well, as if he was keeping something from us. He would look as if he was in pain – but not in pain, if you know what I mean?'

Inspector Hooter rubbed his bill. 'I feel so selfish for not helping him sooner, but we all thought he was just being horrible for the sake of it. I should have known there was more to it than that, after all, why would a mallard be nasty of his own accord?'

'You could not have known, Inspector,' said Abel while

23

beckoning all to sit and listen. 'You are blessed with beautiful minds, my dear birds. You live by only two laws.'

Hooter could not help butting in. 'That's right. Love Mother Nature and be good. What more is there?'

'Quite right, Inspector,' Abel replied. 'There need be nothing more than that.'

The crew settled, knowing that Abel's deep tones were about to enlighten them a little more. 'You know that Mother Nature likes things to be balanced; for every high there is a low and for every warm there is a cool. You believe in your hearts that angels walk this world, they do not make themselves known to you but you believe they are there none the less. They are Nature's friends. They warm your hearts and guide you in your thoughts, but there is one who occasionally ventures into your world with ill-intent; he is uncomfortable in the presence of such purity as yours and so he rarely stays for long.'

Hooter could hold back no longer. 'An angel with ill-intent? Are you sure, Mr Nogg?'

Abel smiled as much as his beak would allow. 'Yes, Inspector, but your heart casts out any sway from him, and so he leaves in search of easier prey.'

'Do you mean he actually finds a place inside some creatures' minds?' gasped Hooter in disbelief.

'Yes, Inspector. He is devious and thrives on spite and suffering. He has corrupted a world close to this one, and I fear he is now looking for a new playground.'

Bob Uppendown added to the conversation. 'Is this bad guy free to move about wherever he wants, sir?' The Mountie's eyes showed a hint of anxiety which quickly spread to the mallards around him.

'Angels are able to enter and leave your world at will, but no mortals can pass through the timbered wall with them unless the

24

Amulet is close by.'

Lock, Stock and Barrel blurted out together, 'That was the stone our inspector took from Harold Waters-Edge.'

'That is correct,' said Abel.

'I remember now,' said Constable Stock. 'When we found Inspector Orange in that smelly bunker in the woods, we thought we heard voices. We didn't see anyone, but there was definitely someone else in there, and since then Inspector Orange's condition has gotten worse.'

'You might not have seen anyone else,' said Abel, 'but he was definitely not alone.'

The three ARDs gulped as one, realizing just how close they had been to such an awful presence.

Abel continued, 'Your inspector was in such a state of despair and anguish through the torment of his demon that he would do anything to be rid of him.'

'Do you mean he gave the Amulet away?' said Hooter.

'Yes, in the hope of regaining his soul,' replied Abel.

'Did our inspector know the purpose of the Amulet?' asked Lock.

'He was not sure, Constable. He was confused and had given up caring.'

Harold Waters-Edge, who up until now had listened quietly, thought it time to add his part to the story. 'When I was hiding from Inspector Orange in the back of a lorry, someone else was in there with me, in the dark.'

Abel gave Harold an encouraging look.

Harold went on, 'He sounded familiar, so I let him hold the Amulet for just a moment, that was all, but he gave it back to me and then the back door of the lorry flew open and Inspector Orange was there with his constables. I didn't realize until later that I'd lost the Amulet as I escaped.'

'And that was the Amulet that Inspector Orange gave to the Dark One,' said Abel. 'Unknown to him it had been exchanged for a fake when you, Harold, let the stranger in the lorry handle it.'

Stock interjected, 'So that's why the timbered wall didn't work for the angry soldiers when they tried to cross. We watched them from the bushes when they arrived in their lorry. There was a well-dressed man in a hat with them; he got very angry.'

'I'm sure he did, Constable,' replied Abel.

'Now I see,' said Hooter with one of his rare but charming looks of understanding. 'That nasty man was going to follow the wagon through the ether with all his soldiers – it was him chasing us across the common, too.'

'You are almost right,' said Abel in his soft, gruff tone. 'The stranger you speak of would not be seen to get his own hands dirty, but he gladly encourages others to do his evil deeds.'

Hooter replied, 'But what happened to them? They didn't come through the wall with us did they?'

Abel stared through the broken roof into the sky above, saying in a deliberately slow and deep voice, 'They were reckoned.'

'All of them?

'All but one,' replied Abel.

The birds were not too sure what Abel meant by 'reckoned', but whatever it was, it sounded rather final. They knew he had more to say and they knew their mission was not yet over; there was still the body of the deceased Bog to be retrieved from the world of the humans, a world almost too terrible for the hearts of such honest birds to comprehend.

4

With her evening palette in hand, Mother Nature washed the undulating horizon in mauves and dusky pinks. The Sun was nearing the end of its duty for the day, gently touching the far off hills to bid the day-dwellers farewell.

In the fading light the wagon party carrying Inspector Orange approached a small bridge over a sparkling narrow stream. Constable Justin Case looked around. 'What d'yuh think, Mr Grunt, will this do fer the night?'

Aano replied, 'I'm sure it will do fine, Constable.' Holding the reins between his fingers he eased the two-horse team off the track and onto the firm grass by the side of the bridge. 'Steady now, steady,' he called. He was unsure of the correct terminology but the horses obliged by coming to a halt just where Aano had wanted.

'They seem to have taken to you, Mr Grunt,' said Constable Case with a smiling voice.

'They are lovely horses,' replied Aano, 'it's a good job they know what to do.' He tidied the reins before springing down to the ground and taking a stretch.

The two Mounties watched as he reached high above his head and then down to his toes. No matter which way he stretched, he never seemed remotely in proportion; *Weird*.

Constable Stan Duprite looked into the wagon from atop his horse. 'How is the Inspector doin'?'

Aano replied, 'He's been very restless; a good night's sleep under the stars might help.'

'Fer sure.' Constable Duprite dismounted and led his horse towards some light scrub where he formed a simple rope corral to contain all four horses. Once ushered in, the horses were groomed, fed, watered and settled down before the Mounties tended to their own needs.

Duprite and Case unpacked a few more blankets from a side locker on the wagon and handed them to Aano.

'Thank you,' said Aano, folding them into a pillow for his patient.

Having made sure the inspector had some water to drink, the Mounties nestled on the lush grass in the lea of the stone bridge. They watched Aano with amusement while he gathered up his favourite ferns and a few strands of long grass. With his adept flick of the wrist and a quick twist he produced what seemed to be a bouquet of greenery, he then turned the ensemble upside down and placed it on his head. 'Perfect,' he said, 'not as smart as your Stetsons, but it will do just fine.'

'Well I'll be darned,' said Case, 'it's a hat.'

'Just in case it rains,' said Aano.

'Fer sure,' replied Duprite, turning his head and snuggling into his plumage alongside his fellow constable. 'Goodnight, sir.'

'Goodnight, Constables.' Aano carefully climbed into the back of the wagon where he looked upon Inspector Orange and wiped the troubled mallard's brow. 'Goodnight, Inspector.'

The inspector had barely heard the conversation through the confusion and disorder inside his head. He closed his eyes, fearful of what was awaiting him in his sleep.

***

In Davidsmeadow, the creatures of the day had retreated into

28

their beds leaving the way clear for the incoming tide of those of the night.

'How about one last stroll around the town?' said Constable Thomas.

'Okay,' replied James, 'at least the rain's stopped.'

The unique smell of wet cobbles greeted them as they stepped out into the mild night air. At first there was no one to be seen, but they both knew they were not alone.

'How do they do that?' Thomas asked, looking at the bats flitting around the Town Hall roof. 'How do they fly so silently? I mean, when we fly you can hear us coming a field away.'

James rubbed his bill in youthful contemplation. 'Hmm, well for a start they're a lot smaller than us so they don't displace as much air when they go along.' James always was the technical one among the squad. Thomas listened contentedly as they waddled slowly across The Square with just the moonlight to show the way.

James continued, 'And then of course the noise we make is caused by the air sweeping through our feathers, whereas bats don't have feathers.'

'That's true,' Thomas joined in. 'When you think of it, bats are very similar to pterosaurs but in miniature.'

'But bats haven't got beaks.'

'Hmm, they don't lay eggs either.'

'Can you imagine Abel Nogg, or any Bog being related to a bat?' Their laughter echoed around the nearby buildings.

An owl hooted from atop a nearby signpost. Thomas looked up. 'Good evening,' he said respectfully.

'Ooo – oo,' replied the owl before taking to the air in search of his supper.

'You see,' said James, 'you could hear him taking-off because of his feathers, he was just a lot quieter than us because he's only got a wingspan of three feet, not fifteen like us…and I have a feeling his wing feathers are especially soft and fine.'

After strolling down one side of the High Street and back up the other they returned to The Square and passed the café, now closed.

Thomas cast an eye at the empty tables outside. 'Who do you think she was?'

James did not have to second guess who his friend was talking about. 'You mean that lady mallard we saw earlier.'

'Yes,' Thomas replied wistfully. 'I know all lady mallards are beautiful, but there was something very special about her, don't you think?'

'I think you should be grateful for your Fay, she's lovely and you're lucky to have her.'

'I know,' Thomas replied without hesitation; a warm feeling grew inside him.

When they arrived back at the police station they paused quietly outside the door and listened to the motion of the world itself. Everything sounded as it should. They closed the door behind them and were soon settled down in their beds for the night.

'The others should be here tomorrow,' said Thomas, curling up beneath his blanket.

'I hope so,' James replied. 'It will be good to see them again, but somehow I don't think things will get back to normal any time soon; I don't think we're going to get off that lightly.'

'Hmm…goodnight,' said Thomas.

'Goodnight,' replied James.

**

All was quiet by the stone bridge, save for the gentle tinkling of the stream as it continued its way to join the River Rother a few miles away; from there its waters would be carried onward to join the River Arun just outside the mystical town of Arun Dell, a few miles from the south coast of England.

Mounties Duprite and Case had slipped into a light sleep while Aano remained curled up in the back of the wagon beneath his fern hat. He kept one eye half open, keeping watch over the troubled Inspector Orange.

Nightmarish thoughts quickly gathered in the inspector's mind; thoughts with no basis in truth. The presence within his mind presented heavily cloaked skies shutting out the moonlight behind his eyes. Nature's palette had been snatched from her and the land likewise painted in an unearthly darkness. His dream had started again….

The room in which he now stands is small, no more than ten paces square with cream-painted walls long since yellowed by its occupants' breath. Six heavy wooden tables, each with four equally heavy chairs, take up much of the floor space. Most of the chairs are occupied – by humans; Al Orange assumes they are male, not because of their faces but because of their demeanour and stature. He strains but is unable to gather any detail in the poor light. The faces are grey, devoid of eyes, nose or mouth, or anything that might identify them. Some hair is short, some well over the shoulder and some not there at all. But their flesh is all the same colour as the floor – ashen grey.

The figures wear full length unbuttoned coats the colour of earth, their hems relaxing on the boards beneath. It is impossible to gauge how many people are in the room, many are standing. A dull hum emanates from the crowd, but no words can be sieved from the soil of utterances. One by one the conversations end. The silence grows and the lone duck becomes aware that all in the room are all facing him. He is frightened.

He finds it difficult to look any one of them in the face. To look into another's eyes is to risk them seeing into yours, and should not be done with anyone other than those with whom no secrets exist. But these people have no eyes. Without eyes they can yield no secrets – no true emotion and no lies.

At the far end of the room is a bar as you would find in any tavern, but there are no beer pumps or taps. The counter is empty and the wall behind holds no optics or spirit bottles. The mirror into which might be thrown the chair during the pub brawl is not there either, but there is a barman, his upper body visible above the otherwise inert counter. He is a large portly man with no face. He turns his head towards a particular table. Al Orange follows his vague aim to a table to his left.

A lone figure sits there; his hands are clasped with interlocking fingers.

A warm flush races through Orange's brain to press against the backs of his eyes. He can see nothing but the seated figure – he is sure he knows him. His mind succumbs to a certain dire fate which this hell's offspring has sought to serve. Al Orange had never hated anyone in his entire life, but he knows he hates with every ounce of poison he can muster from his soul this man who shows him his back.

The room starts to quake; the figures in the room tremble.

Al Orange mumbles to himself, 'Be strong. Courage don't desert me now for I have little time left. For the Great Duck's sake let me see what is to be done. Please let this fog lift from my heart and from my eyes that I may put this aberration to the floor and sever him from my world once and for all.'

The entire room trembles violently.

'No, no; please!' shouts Al Orange.

'No, no; please!' Al Orange shouted from the back of the wagon.

'Oh dear, Inspector, calm down,' said Aano wrapping a long arm around the mallard in an attempt to subdue his thrashing. With a curled finger the ape wiped the tears from the inspector's cheeks.

Constables Case and Duprite quickly appeared and leaned over the side of the wagon to help steady the distressed inspector. 'Easy sir, easy.'

Orange said nothing and slumped back into the confines of the wagon. He stared up at the sky. The clouds were now parting to let a little moonlight reach down to help them all see.

'Oh boy, that sure must be a humdinger of a nightmare, sir,' said Case.

The inspector paused in the constable's eye for a moment and then said in a broken voice, 'I was back in that room – the room full of humans. It was as if I was sharing someone else's nightmare; I didn't belong there but I was seeing it through someone else's eyes.'

'There, there.' Aano stroked Orange's forehead. 'Don't upset yourself, Inspector. Such nasty thoughts have no place in a duck's head, they truly haven't.'

Orange struggled to slow his breathing. 'I don't understand what's happening to me,' he fought to hold back the tears while describing more of his dream. 'The room was full of strangers again. They were all faceless apart from the nasty one sitting alone at the table. I could tell he hated me just by looking at him, but I wasn't the only outsider in the room. There was someone else there. I think he was a human man, but not grey like the others. I don't think he belonged there either. He was lonely too, like me – it was so real.'

When the inspector mentioned the word "human" the Mounties turned their gaze to Aano; he was an ape after all, and apes were almost human in the eyes of a bird.

'I don't suppose you can offer any suggestions, Mr Grunt,' asked Constable Case. 'You seem to be a creature of the world, is there anything we can do to help the inspector make sense of this?'

'I think the most important thing to offer right now is love and support,' Aano replied. 'We must show the inspector he is among friends and is not alone.'

'Fer sure,' said Case. He and Duprite nodded and helped straighten the inspector's blanket and pillow. 'We'll soon have you back at Smallbeef, sir,' Case added. He then whispered light-heartedly in the inspector's ear, 'Just think of all those pretty ducks wanting to fuss over you to make you better again.'

Sadly, the inspector's head was still reeling from his nightmares; he was no longer sure of what was real and what was not. He closed his eyes and rested against Aano Grunt's ample chest.

The group settled down for the last couple of hours before sunrise in the hope that the new day might bring some peace for the troubled inspector.

5

In Fort Bog, Dick Waters-Edge wiped a wing across his face having been rudely awakened by a slobbery kiss and a snort from Punch.

The rain in the night had refreshed the air and nourished the flora; thin shafts of dawn light reached in through the gaps in the barn's planking.

Punch gave Dick a hefty nudge with his broad muzzle.

'Okay, mate; I can take a hint.' Dick laughed and dozily got to his feet. He stroked the side of Punch's muscular neck and lingered in his hazel eyes for a few moments. The horse gladly returned the look of friendship before nudging the young mallard again towards his empty feed bucket.

While Dick was filling the bucket with oats and pellets the barn door creaked open.

'Good morning, Son,' said a welcome voice. 'How are you today?' Harold waddled over and gave Dick a loving hug. 'Oh, my boy, it feels so good to hold you again.'

'Likewise, Dad,' replied Dick.

'I didn't think I was ever going to see you or your mother again you know.'

'I know, Dad, we all thought you were lost forever, like all the others who went missing.'

Despite his best efforts, Harold could not conceal the worried look on his face. He had something on his mind. He gave another squeeze before releasing Dick from his grip. They briefly looked each other in the eye before Harold lowered his gaze.

'What is it, Dad? What's troubling you?' asked Dick.

Harold took a deep breath. 'I'm concerned about you and your mother.'

'Me and Mum?' said Dick, puzzled. 'What about me and Mum?' His innocent smiling eyes reflected the light of the new day. 'We'll soon be together again, Dad. Can you imagine how thrilled Mum will be to see you again?'

Punch huffed and looked up from his feed bucket. He cast a spontaneous look across the room at Dick, a look which Dick had seen before; the horse was telling him to listen to his Dad.

Harold spoke quietly, choosing his words carefully. 'Your mother has been alone for over a year now.'

'Yes,' said Dick.

'It's just that I've heard things said – you know, whispers that weren't meant for my ears and certainly weren't meant to cause upset.'

The smallest of thoughts entered Dick's mind, like a seed not yet open, one which would inevitably burst forth to show its contents to the world. 'What do you mean, Dad?' he replied, still keeping his cool.

'Well, Son,' Harold forced his words out. 'I have heard that in my absence…and I can quite understand why…I mean it's not every day that your dad or your husband just disappears.'

The seedling opened in Dicks mind.

Harold went on, 'I wouldn't blame you or your mother if…if,' the words could find no way past the lump in his throat. He tried again. 'If you had….' A teardrop rolled down his cheek, glistening over his brilliant blue-green face.

'But Dad—'

'No Son,' Harold interrupted. 'I have heard things, and I have seen the look in Inspector Hooter's eye when he is around you; please, tell me, was he…?'

Harold's plea halted when the door creaked again to announce the arrival of another mallard. The silhouette, complete with officer's cap, was that of Inspector Hooter.

Father and son looked across at him. 'How long have you been there?' asked Harold.

'Just long enough,' replied Hooter with a hint of sadness in his voice. 'May I come in, please?'

Harold didn't answer at first, worried about the outcome of any ensuing debate.

'Please, Mr Waters-Edge,' said Hooter, 'we need to talk, for all our sakes.'

Harold warily nodded and shuffled backwards, taking his place next to his son. Inspector Hooter waddled in, leaving the door to come to rest slightly ajar.

An uneasy silence hung in the air. Hooter stopped as close as he dared to Harold. The two mallards looked each other in the eye. Dick didn't know what to expect next, surely his father wouldn't take on a police inspector. *Surely not Inspector Hooter.*

So engrossed were they that another figure standing silently outside the door went unnoticed. The stand-off continued for a full minute, neither mallard quite summoning the words to start a dialogue.

However hard Harold tried, he could not think of a word to get him started, so he did the only thing he could think of. He stretched his legs and neck to gain the height advantage. He fully expected the inspector to do likewise, and so did Dick. But the inspector remained unmoved. Harold then did the only other thing left, short of striking a blow. He fluffed up his chest feathers to present as imposing a figure as he could. His thoughts briefly recalled the last time he did such a thing when he and Inspector Orange came to blows by the timbered wall. Never the less, he held his provocative stance.

An eye of crystal blue peered through the gap in the door, waiting to see the outcome of this confrontation.

Harold took a deep breath, inflating his chest as much as a duck ever could. Such was his exertion that his eyes were on the brink of becoming blood-shot. Harold had never looked so menacing in his life.

Dick was about to step in between them when Hooter made his move, but rather than strike out, he slowly held out his wing. His eyes held no temper, letting his heart shine through them and rest against Harold's chest as surely as if a hand had been placed there, consoling and caring.

'Please,' said Hooter softly. 'Dick is your son, and Marion is your wife; and you rightly love them both.' Hooter's cheeks wetted. 'I was privileged to briefly be a part of Dick's life in your absence.'

Harold struggled to reply while keeping up the big chest. 'And what of my wife?' he asked in a strained voice.

Dick listened intently, not knowing exactly what it was that his dad was questioning.

Hooter replied, 'Your wife tended to my injuries after the battle of Smallbeef...we talked a lot over the following days, about Dick...and about you.'

Harold tilted his head, thinking, Is that all you did? Did you only talk, really?

'I can assure you, Mr Waters-Edge, we only ever talked. I would be lying if I said I had not hoped that Marion and I might have had a future together.' The pools deepened in his eyes. 'But I know that will never be; not now that you have returned to your rightful place.'

Harold let his chest down and relaxed to his normal height. He reached out and held Hooter's wing and they shook in friendship.

Abel Nogg silently moved away from the door, unseen, smiling in his heart and ever more respectful of the hapless Inspector Hooter. *One day Inspector, one day.*

***

While all this had been going on in the world of the water birds, the new day was also beginning in the world of the humans. The Sun had thrown its morning light across the pond on the heath; the endless gold tipped ripples jostled softly against one another, all fitting perfectly within the confines of the shoreline, Mother Nature is clever like that. The heath was still enduring a far greater footfall than normal; people came from far and wide to see where the monstrous pterosaurs and giant ducks had dared to invade their world.

Kate Herrlaw stood at the water's edge imagining Inspector Hooter confronting the humans on that very spot. She pictured Hooter innocently debating with the local police. *My dear Inspector, you could never have known what they are capable of, or of their limitations.* She noticed a vacant table at the drinks kiosk and made her way over. 'An Americano, please,' she called softly to the young lad behind the counter.

The barista hastily set about her order. He would look up at every opportunity to check she was still there, glad of another glimpse.

'Here you are, madam,' he said in his best diction, having first made sure his shirt was properly tucked in and his hair smoothed down.

'Thank you,' said Kate, teasing his eyes momentarily. 'It's still very busy down here.'

The young lad's libido muddled his words causing him to fluff his reply. 'Yes, lots of ducks too, but I don't think they're here because of what happened.' He instantly realized how stupid that sounded. *What am I on about, they're only little ducks, and they live here you idiot.* He retreated to the refuge of his counter, frustrated at his blundering, holding Kate's image easily in his mind.

Kate smiled at him to let him know he had done just fine. She still had the newspaper from the day before and so, taking her pencil from her bag, she settled down to have another go at the crossword.

'Hmm, three down, another cryptic one – Dick and Tom at odds perhaps?' She rested her chin between her fingers and thumb for a moment. 'Dichotomy – that should do nicely.' While pencilling in the answer her attention was caught by a fit looking man with military cut dark hair, probably in his thirties, walking along the shore. He seemed to be studying the water birds, the Canada geese in particular. 'And who are you?' Kate hushed under her breath.

Her attention was snatched suddenly from behind, 'Good morning, my dear.'

Kate turned to see a smartly suited figure of a man in a hat standing over her, slightly closer that she would have preferred.

'I am sorry if I startled you,' said the man.

'Mr Helkendag.' Kate gathered her composure. 'I didn't expect to see you again so soon.'

Helkendag held his gaze on her, just long enough to make a point. 'May I join you for a minute,' he had already begun pulling the chair out from the table.

Kate folded the newspaper and put her pencil back in her bag.

Helkendag's eyes held hers again. 'I wondered if you had

made any contact with your friends since they disappeared.'

Kate always felt that Helkendag knew more than he let on whenever he asked a question. His scent wafted towards her, she deliberately quietened her breathing not wishing to make anything of it.

'If, by friends, you mean our visitors from another world, no I haven't,' she replied. 'I've been out looking each day but I've found no trace of them.' She was glad to be able to tell the truth without giving him any information that might be of use to him, unsure as she was of his motives.

His eyes let her go and peered over her shoulder focussing on the dark-haired man at the water's edge.

Kate turned her head and followed his sight. 'What is it?' she asked, trying to draw Helkendag's attention back to her. But his eyes were fixed firmly on the very lightly tanned stranger who was still single-mindedly studying the Canada geese.

'It's rude to stare,' said Kate.

Helkendag ignored her, remaining fixed on the newcomer. 'Where have I seen you before?' he growled just above a whisper.

Kate could not think why, but she knew it would not be in the young man's interest to look up and catch Helkendag's eye. She leaned across into Helkendag's view and stared straight at him. 'Why did you sit down at my table only to ignore me?'

Helkendag moved to one side to catch the stranger again, Kate moved with him, her brilliant blue eyes reaching into his. Their eyes played cat and mouse for a few moments. As much as Helkendag enjoyed the game, he was annoyed at her for interrupting his scrutiny of the stranger. He finally shook his eyes from hers and cast them back to the shore – but the man was gone.

Kate waited for Helkendag's stare to land back on her, which it quickly did. She was ready with a wry smile and a raise of one eyebrow. 'Why the interest in a total stranger?' she asked. 'Do you find his looks nicer than mine?'

Helkendag rose to his feet and returned the smile. 'I shall find you in a day or two,' he said, showing no emotion. 'Perhaps you will have some news for me then.'

'Perhaps,' replied Kate. She doubted the sincerity of his smile, knowing that she had probably pushed her luck further than she should have.

***

In the water bird's world, in Fort Bog, Sergeant Uppendown had just finished preening himself when Abel Nogg called across the bailey to him. 'Sergeant Uppendown.'

'Good morning, Mr Nogg,' replied the goose.

'Good morning to you, too.' Abel always found the sergeant's aura calm, measured and thoughtful. 'Would you be so kind as to gather all of the crew from the last mission and ask them to join me in the barn?'

'Certainly sir, right away.'

Inspector Hooter and Harold were still in the barn after having settled their concerns with each other. Now they were content to sit on the hay bales side by side watching Dick give Punch a good brushing down.

Standing four-square with a slight forward lean, the horse looked truly impressive as his eye followed the brush working its way back towards his massive thigh.

The barn door creaked, announcing the arrival of the rest of the crew; in waddled four constables of the Flying Squad, three of the temporarily Unarmed Response Ducks, and Sergeant Uppendown the Mountie.

'Excuse me, sir,' said Uppendown to Hooter, 'but Mr Nogg

asked us to join him in here. I think he has something to say to us all before we leave.'

'Oh, right, thank you, Sergeant.' Hooter jumped up from his seat and straightened his feathers and put his cap on. 'Line up, everyone, nice and smart if you please, helmets on straight.'

The crew duly lined up for parade. Hooter hastily cast his eye over them, sure as always that he would find no cause for complaint. 'Well done, Constables, very smart. Well done, Sergeant, immaculate as always.'

'Erm, excuse me, sir,' said a tentative voice from the doorway. 'It's me, sir, the bobby from Davidsmeadow – remember me?'

'Of course I remember you.' Hooter greeted the young constable with a hearty gesture encouraging him to come in and join them. 'We are hardly likely to forget you and your bicycle in a hurry, why, who knows what might have become of my squad if you hadn't come to our rescue when you did.'

'Thank you, sir,' replied the bobby. 'I was just wondering what I should do now…should I head back to Davidsmeadow Police Station?'

'Hmm, not right away, why don't you wait in here with us until we hear what Abel Nogg has to say, then we'll make a decision, how does that sound, Constable?'

'Fine, sir, thank you, sir.' The bobby sidled his way next to the other constables. He had always admired them, and had thoroughly enjoyed his recent flight with them after accidentally on purpose depositing his bicycle in the grave of the now missing Bog.

The light in the barn faded when Abel Nogg entered, momentarily blocking the daylight from the doorway. 'Thank you all,' he said in his ever-deep gargle of a voice. 'Please relax your squad, Inspector.'

'Squad, stand at ease – stand easy.' The birds relaxed their stance and waited patiently for Abel to begin.

'I will not keep you long, my friends. I know you are keen to return to your duties in Davidsmeadow, not to mention your loved ones and friends in Smallbeef.'

Hooter's gaze fell wistfully to the floor. Not for me a loved one waiting– not any more.

Abel continued, 'The task of returning the deceased Beast of Grey to this land is still outstanding. At the moment the whereabouts of the body is unknown. However, I am quite certain it will be found, and when it is I shall come to you, Inspector Hooter, for your help in the matter.'

A few days earlier Hooter would have dreaded the thought of leaving his beautiful homeland again, but since losing any hope of renewing his association with Marion he felt numbed and empty.

Abel spoke in his softest possible tone, 'Inspector.'

Hooter raised his head and his eyes fell into Abel's. Neither of them moved, but Hooter could feel something sailing through his mind, searching without disturbing anything. A hand as gentle as a mother's touched his heart and squeezed him gently.

Abel released him from his ethereal grip. 'You should go about your business as usual. I shall be in touch as soon as I have news.'

With that, the pterosaur swept his gaze across all the birds in the room, ending in the eyes of the horse. They shared a few moments, dabbling playfully in each other's minds before Abel shuffled his way to the door and left them all to gather their thoughts.

Uppendown tipped his Stetson to the back of his head. 'Phew, that was something,' he said. 'That guy sure has a way of saying a lot without saying much at all.'

'He certainly has,' replied Hooter. 'We must waste no time in getting airborne and on our way to Smallbeef. With any luck we should overtake Mr Grunt and the wagon and get there before them.'

'What about Punch?' asked Dick, stroking the horse's cheek. 'Could I ride him back?'

'I think you should fly back with us, young duck,' replied Hooter. 'You and your father should arrive together; your mother will be relieved to see the pair of you back safe and sound.'

Sergeant Uppendown lent some weight to Hooter's argument. 'I think the guys here could do with Punch's muscle to help put this place back together.'

'Quite right, Sergeant, thank you.' Hooter turned to Dick. 'Perhaps you can come back for him in a few days, when his work here is done.' He then turned and addressed all in the room. 'Right then, let's have you all outside ready for take off in two minutes.'

Dick looked Punch in the eye. Punch kissed the top of Dick's head in response, more of a big suck than a kiss, but Dick enjoyed it all the same.

In those two minutes Hooter tracked down Moira Maywell and asked if she would be willing to care for Punch during his stay at the fort, a duty she was all too pleased to accept. 'That's very kind of you, my dear,' said Hooter. 'Thank you so much.' He then turned to join his squad only to find himself bill to bill with the bobby who had followed him outside, still wondering what he should do next. 'Ah, of course, Constable,' said Hooter, 'as you know, I shall be leaving very soon for Smallbeef and then on to Davidsmeadow. It would be a great help if you stayed here to provide support and a little authority along with the Mounties who are also staying behind. Once you are satisfied that you have helped all you can then you may make your own way back to Davidsmeadow to resume your normal duties.'

'Yes sir,' replied the constable, trying in vain to straighten his helmet on his head.

Hooter could not help but comment on the issue. 'I don't think I've ever seen you with your helmet on straight, Constable. Is there something wrong with it? We can always get you another one.'

A concerned look beset the constable's face while he tried to hold his helmet upright on his glistening blue-green head. His words did not come easily. 'I'm sorry, sir.' He carefully moved his wing away from his helmet and stood as still as he possibly could.

Hooter watched the constable's delicate stance and then raised an eyebrow as the helmet slowly slipped to one side coming to a halt at about five degrees off-centre.

'There is obviously something wrong with it, shall I have a look at it for you?'

The bobby replied through an expression of humility, 'No sir…it's not my helmet that's crooked.' With that, he raised his wing and slowly removed his helmet altogether. He stood quite still, eyes straight ahead, waiting for the inspector's response.

Hooter tilted his head one way and then the other while studying the constable's head. He didn't really want to stare, but how else was he to assess the matter? 'Oh…I see,' he said, immediately diverting his gaze into the constable's eyes.

'I'm sorry, sir; I can't help it. I was born like it, but it—'

'Don't worry yourself, Constable.' Hooter put his wing around the young constable's shoulder. 'I have to ask – does it hurt?'

'No, not at all, sir.' The bobby was still unsure as to whether he should expect some sort of disciplinary action for not being perfect. 'Does this mean I can't be a police duck anymore, sir?'

Hooter's eyes smiled, stopping just short of becoming embarrassingly wet. 'My dear Constable, you seem to forget I have seen you in action. I can assure you I have no doubts as to your bravery and niceness – both very fine qualities.'

'Thank you, sir.'

'Did it happen when you were inside your egg?' Hooter asked, softly.

'That's what I was told, sir. Apparently my mum didn't turn my egg as often as she might have. I suppose my head got kind of squashed against the inside of the shell when I was still soft. But it's not too out of shape – is it, sir?'

'Not at all, young fella.' Hooter patted the bobby reassuringly on the back. 'It's what's on the inside that matters anyway, I'm sure you know that – my constables certainly do.'

'Yes sir, thank you, sir.'

'You don't need to keep saying thank you, you know.'

'Oh, right, sir. Er…right, sir.'

'Now then, put your helmet back on and set about helping the Mounties. I shall see you in Davidmeadow in due course, all right?'

The bobby stood to attention as straight as he could and gave a firm salute –with his helmet five degrees off the perpendicular. 'Yes sir.'

Within a few minutes Inspector Hooter and his squad were in the air. Those on the ground looked up in admiration at the wonderful sight as they chased the Sun towards Smallbeef, with their helmet badges glistening in perfect vee formation.

The bobby also looked up, his helmet not quite straight, but with a good mind inside it.

6

Hooter led his squad in a west-southwest direction. In reality, compass points meant nothing to any of the birds, none of them had a compass. They had the Sun, the horizon, and their hearts to unfailingly guide them home.

The long balmy days of summer were gone; now a little more effort was needed to maintain altitude, but Mother Nature would offset their labour by cooling them and thereby helping them to conserve water. Onward flew the beautiful birds, in perfect harmony with the one they depended upon.

***

'Good girls, lovely girls.' Aano Grunt grinned, wondering why he bothered holding the reins at all; the two Hanoverians seemed quite capable of hauling the wagon without any input from him. The horses kept up a brisk walk following the gravel track alongside the trees, their nostrils twitching and caressing the smell of pine, birch and oak. Mounties Justin Case and Stan Duprite maintained a regulation two-horse length behind the wagon, keeping a watchful eye on things from atop their equally fabulous, vibrant steeds. The song of small birds in the trees accompanied them as they went.

'How much further, Mr Grunt?' Duprite asked.

'Only half an hour,' replied Aano. 'It will be a relief to get the inspector into a comfortable bed.'

'Fer sure, sir,' replied the Mountie.

The trees about them suddenly shimmied; the oaks had heard something. The horses' ears pricked up and turned this way and that way. Their hazel eyes widened.

'They've heard something fer sure,' said Constable Case, turning his head almost all the way round.

'I hear it…it's very faint.' Duprite studied the far off horizon behind them. 'Something's sure comin' up fast.' Their anxiety soon waned when the reassuring honk honk of Hooter's horn grew louder.

'Well, look at that,' Duprite called out.

Inspector Hooter and his squad came rapidly into view and, upon seeing their friends below, Hooter gave the order, 'Follow my lead – descend.'

The squad banked and swooped, presenting a brilliant blue, green and silver delta formation. The trees joined the celebration by waving their branches in the air, hoping for the gentlest touch of the birds' undersides.

Hooter honked his brass horn once more for good measure while they passed low and fast over the wagon. The sound of eleven pairs of wings singing harmoniously in the air stirred the hearts of those below. All too quickly the squad had passed but Sergeant Uppendown, at the rear of the display, could not resist a honk of his own, without the aid of a horn. 'Honk, onk,' he called to his comrades.

'Honk, onk,' Duprite and Case called back, waving their Stetsons in the air.

'See you guys soon,' Uppendown hollered before disappearing hastily over the treetops.

'Don't they look magnificent, Inspector,' said Aano to Al Orange. 'I'm sure you'll soon be mended and up there with them again.'

Al Orange heard Aano's words, but they were very distant and did not register above the voice taunting him constantly from within.

Onward they went, four beautiful horses, two brave Canada geese, a mallard with an unwanted demon, and a bright ginger ape not sure where he fitted in, but glad to be of help.

***

A little while later, in Smallbeef Caravan Park, a lady duck called out while staring into the distant sky, 'Look, I think it's them.'

Within seconds all in the park had joined her, hoping that the birds flying rapidly towards them were the heroic constables of the Flying Squad. Marion Waters-Edge stood among the crowd, hoping for news of her son, Dick. *Has he been arrested? Perhaps he is still on the run. Oh, I do hope he is all right.* And what of her new-found love, Inspector Hooter, had he prevailed? Had he kept Dick safe as he had promised? She did not dare think of the alternatives. Her heart beat longingly, willing the incoming birds to be bearers of good news.

'I can just about make out their shapes,' Mrs Dabblemore called excitedly. 'They're definitely mallards.'

'Yes,' her neighbour, Mrs Waddleforth shouted, 'and look, they're wearing police helmets.'

The whole park erupted euphorically as the squad came clearly into view.

Very quickly voices in the crowd began to mumble, 'But who are the extra ducks? There were only seven when we last saw them. Now there seem to be ten mallards, and a Canada goose?'

The spectators moved aside to give the visitors room to land. Inspector Hooter touched down first, quickly stepping aside. One by one his constables followed him down and promptly lined up smartly. It was not until all the constables had landed that the remaining two mallards touched down, not wearing police helmets.

Marion was thrilled to see Inspector Hooter safe and sound. She wondered why he had not come straight over to see her, but her attention was quickly drawn by the last two mallards to land. 'Dick,' she cried, waddling hurriedly towards her son; she cast a grateful eye towards Hooter as she ran, to say thank you for bringing him home – but then her heart recoiled when she recognized the last mallard in the line. 'Harold?' She gasped. 'But how?' Her words stifled in shock.

'Mum,' shouted Dick, throwing his wings around her.

Harold stood motionless, watching the outpouring of a mother's love for her child.

'Oh, you're safe.' Marion wept with relief. She looked across the yard again to find Hooter among the crowd. He hesitantly steered Marion's eyes back towards the mallard waiting nervously next to her. Her emotions were in turmoil, she had never expected to see her husband alive again. He had been missing for over a year, and now Inspector Hooter of all people, had brought him back to her.

'Marion,' Harold whispered while a voice inside his head wondered, *Perhaps I shouldn't have come back…perhaps I've been gone too long.*

Marion rested a wing on Dick's shoulder; they looked into each other's eyes and then they both turned to Harold.

'Oh, my dear Harold,' sighed Marion.

'Oh, my dear Marion,' Harold responded, tears now rolling down his cheeks. 'Do you want me back?' His eyes begged her to say yes. *Or do you love someone else now?*

Marion's feelings for Inspector Hooter were real; he had touched her heart with his naïve honesty and courage. But Harold was both her husband and Dick's father, and he had

51

always been a good duck. She slowly raised her head and settled her eyes in his. 'Of course I want you back, you silly duck.' She wept openly as the three of them huddled together, a family once again. The crowd shared their joy, cheering, loudly.

Marion cast her eye fleetingly in the direction of Hooter; his eyes smiled at her, then he mingled with the crowd and slipped from view. The trees rustled a quiet welcome to him and bade him rest beneath their cover for a while, so he settled down by the hedge outside number seven, away from the hustle and bustle and celebrations.

With the hedge and the trees and the occasional squirrel for company, Hooter began reminiscing. He recalled his pursuit of Dick and the Suffolk Punch horse. He remembered tracking the two of them down to this very caravan park before discovering that Marion Waters-Edge, the mallard with whom he was falling in love, was actually Dick's mother. That seemed so long ago now, so much had happened in such a short time. He had fallen in love for the first time in his life, quite a long life for a duck, and would probably never find another like Marion. *But Marion is not mine, she never was.* A wave of sadness broke over him. *I was such a fool to think that I could ever have such a wonderful lady duck.* He refused to weep for fear of falling apart, but he could not stop his eyes hurting from the overwhelming sense of loss.

While the sound of rejoicing and laughter echoed around the park beneath the permanence of the sky, Hooter sat with his dreams in tatters – alone, or so he thought. The hedge shivered uneasily.

***

'At last,' Aano called out from atop the wagon. 'Smallbeef is just around the next bend.' He fidgeted on the unforgiving seat. 'My bottom is definitely not made for sitting on a plank like this.'

The trees thinned out, discreetly beckoning the team onward with a subtle wave of their branches. Duprite and Case were not familiar with this neck of the woods but the ambience was kindly and the trees welcoming.

'I reckon you'll be glad to get down from that seat, Mr Grunt,' said Duprite with a smile. 'I have to say, you sure handle those horses mighty fine.'

Aano gave a grin that could only come from an orangutan. 'To be honest, Constable, I feel a bit unnecessary up here, these lovely horses seem to know what to do before I even ask them.'

'Fer sure, Mr Grunt, but that's because they like you sitting there.'

Aano thought sideways into the sky for a moment. The two horses in harness turned their heads just enough to show him their eye.

'Yes, I love you too.' Aano grinned at them.

The track grew more substantial and the trees moved back a little. The gentle downhill slope had the horses holding the wagon back steadily until they were almost at the entrance to the caravan park.

Duprite and Case passed by each side of the wagon to take up the lead. All four horses now strode in perfect time with each other, line abreast with red pennants flying high.

Such a splendid sight as the Mounties and their steeds turning into the park brought the merriment within to a temporary halt.

'Oh my,' exclaimed the lady ducks.

'How magnificent,' they all agreed.

'How you doin' ma'am?' said Duprite, tipping his Stetson in the direction of the first mallard he came across, who just happened to be a female.

The duck in question blushed and tittered that the Mountie

should notice her at all, let alone greet her so warmly. *Oh, he's so handsome.*

The horses came to a halt in the centre of the yard, their eyes soaking up the convivial atmosphere, their coats glistening in the late afternoon Sun.

Duprite and Case promptly dismounted. No sooner had they loosened the girth on their horses when they were greeted by two Mounties unknown to them. 'Hi there, you guys, and you too, Mr Grunt,' said one.

'Oh, hello,' Aano grinned, recognizing them as Sergeant Jolly's constables. He attempted to flatten the hair on his head with a licked hand, to no avail of course. He then gestured with his hands to introduce the constables to each other. 'These two chaps are Constables Duprite and Case, they have escorted me and Inspector Orange on our journey from Fort Bog…And this is Constable Dune, and this is Constable Nutt, they helped me when I got into trouble with Inspector Orange a while ago.' Aano took on a more worried expression when he added, 'Did I tell you I had been arrested…for murder?'

Duprite and Case tipped their heads to one side, unable to conceal their surprise. 'You, Mr Grunt?'

'About that incident, Mr Grunt,' said Constable Dune, pointing in the direction of Sergeant Uppendown. 'The sergeant says he wants to see you right away.'

The worried creases on Aano's forehead deepened. 'Me? Oh dear.'

'This way if you please,' said Constable Dune politely.

Aano stole a brief glimpse from his team of horses as he passed. One of them gently placed her lips on top of his thinly haired head and deposited a warm kiss on it.

'Thank you,' said Aano nervously, still not sure if he was about to be arrested again.

Sergeant Uppendown stood tall with the brim of his Stetson perfectly level. The glint in his eye immediately put Aano at ease. The goose put a wing around the ape's shoulder and drew him to his ample chest. Aano was unaccustomed to such close contact with a creature not of his own kind, but in this instance he found the experience warming and reassuring.

'I had no idea what you had been through, Mr Grunt,' said Uppendown. 'Constables Dune and Nutt have filled me in with all the details about how you were wrongly pursued by Inspector Orange.' Uppendown gave another firm squeeze; Aano grinned with relief. Uppendown then continued, 'It sure looks like someone wus trying to set you up for killing Constable Burr; the question is who and why?'

'Thank you, Sergeant,' Aano squeezed his words out through the Mountie's embrace.

The Mountie relaxed his hold.

'Phew, thank you again, Sergeant,' Aano said, catching his breath.

Uppendown looked around. 'Where is Inspector Hooter? I need to talk to him about yer situation.'

Mrs Watertight answered from the crowd, 'I think I saw him waddling towards number seven. On his own he was.'

'Thank you, ma'am,' replied the sergeant. 'Come with me please, Mr Grunt.'

***

Hooter lay curled up beneath the laurel hedge outside number seven with his eyes closed. The hedge had tried in vain to get his attention, but a hedge can only shake so much, so the trees took up the cause, rustling as boldly as they could but also to no avail. The jackdaws were glad of the warning however, and promptly took to the air.

Eyes as black as pitch peered through the hedge; they did not belong there but they had ambition and aspirations, they were seeking a despondent mind in which to sow a seed or two of discontent.

Hooter ached from his insides out; his head hurt and he felt confused. *Perhaps it's time to hang up my cap and my whistle.* Alien thoughts began racing around inside his head. *I'm not as young as I was. I'm sure they're all laughing at me; everyone's laughing at me. They probably think I'm stupid because I try to do things properly all the time.* The trees watching over him let a couple of leaves float tenderly down and settle in the hollow between his curled up neck and his side. This was all they could offer, but it was enough to prick Hooter and bring him out of his disturbed muddle. He looked up. 'Thank you,' he said under his breath, unaware that he was being watched. He shook his head to eject the bitterness that had tried to find a foothold within him. 'I can't think what that was all about,' he mumbled. He swept his head feathers smartly back and sat upright, not realizing what a narrow escape he had just had. His soul warmed him from within. He was just picking up his cap when a familiar voice rose above the accompanying sound of webbed feet.

'Inspector Hooter, are you there?'

The evil eyes that did not belong quickly faded, taking their foul hatred with them. The hedge and the trees shook *good riddance* as the entity took its leave.

'I'm up here by the hedge,' Hooter replied. 'Is that you, Sergeant Uppendown?'

'Yes sir. I have Mr Grunt with me. I wus hoping to have a quiet word with you.'

Hooter stepped out from the shade of the laurel. 'You didn't pass anyone on the path did you?' he asked.

'No sir, not a soul,' replied Uppendown.

'No one at all?' Hooter enquired further.

'No sir.'

Hooter rubbed his bill, staring at the hedge. 'That's strange, I could have sworn there was someone else here. Perhaps I was just dreaming. Anyway, what was it you wanted to talk to me about?'

Uppendown explained the matter of Constable Burr being killed by an unknown assailant, right where the inspector was now standing. Hooter listened uncomfortably and shuffled to one side, not wanting to stand on the very patch of grass on which the poor Mountie had died. Aano Grunt squatted down on his haunches with his arms in the air as if hanging from an invisible branch, glad of being cleared of any wrongdoing, but also hurting for the murdered Mountie and his friends.

***

On the other side of the park, the resident mallards busied themselves converting the storeroom into a dormitory for the constables to stay in overnight. A situation the young police ducks had fond memories of.

'I don't think Inspector Orange should be billeted with the constables, do you?' said Marion Waters-Edge to Constable Dune.

'I guess not ma'am,' Dune replied.

Marion called to Dick who was still enthusiastically reminiscing with the rest of the squad; they all had a lot to look back on and were glad of a little respite in which to share their thoughts.

'Dick,' Marion called.

Upon hearing his mother's call, Dick promptly made his way across the yard. 'Is everything okay, Mum?'

'That depends on you, my dear,' said Marion. 'Inspector

Orange needs somewhere quiet to rest – away from the hubbub of the rest of you.'

Dick was not quite sure where this conversation was going, but it was his mum talking so he listened like a good son should.

'We were wondering if you would let him stay in your home with Mr Grunt to look after him,' said his mum.

'But where will I stay?' Dick replied.

'Well, you seem to be getting along with the constables rather well, perhaps they would let you billet with them.'

At that moment Inspector Hooter appeared and spoke on behalf of his squad. 'I'm sure that will be fine,' he said.

Thrilled at the prospect of spending more time with the Flying Squad, Dick offered no objection and eagerly waddled off to tell them.

Within the hour all was quiet in the park. The residents had retired to their homes while the Flying Squad, along with Dick and the Mounties, were nicely accommodated in the dormitory.

***

In Marion's caravan, Harold felt decidedly awkward. 'Perhaps I should sleep on the sofa, tonight,' he said, unsure of how Marion really felt about his return.

'Don't be silly, Harold. You'll spend tonight in your own bed where you belong,' Marion insisted. 'We have a lot to discuss, after all.'

Before long they were side by side in bed enjoying each other's closeness, but Harold kept one leg hanging out the side with his foot resting on the floor, to avoid any misunderstanding.

***

Meanwhile, in number seven, Aano pulled a blanket over Al

Orange. 'Are you comfortable, Inspector?' he asked. 'I'll be in the other room – just shout if you need anything, anything at all.' He patted Orange on the shoulder and then left the room, leaving the door slightly ajar.

Sleeping on a sofa was the utmost luxury to an orangutan. He curled himself up into a roundish hairy ball with his hands over his eyes. The aches and pains of the journey soon filtered from his body and he slipped into a light sleep with one ear half-cocked towards the inspector's bedroom.

***

Hooter lay silently in his bed in the corner of the dormitory, relegated to sleeping with his squad. He knew he could not ask for better company but he yearned for another. His heart-ache slowly dulled as tiredness washed over him and he drifted into sleep, his last conscious thought, one of sadness.

7

In number seven, Inspector Orange lay tense and hurting. The endless battle in his head gained momentum, crushing his mind into submission. He sobbed quietly in his bed, but Aano did not hear. Hostile visions soon came crashing into his mind once again, his nightmare continued where it had left off. He was back in the dismal room of faceless figures.

Be strong; courage don't desert me now for I have little time left. For the Great Duck's sake let me see what is to be done; let this fog lift from my heart and from my eyes that I may put this devil to the floor and sever him from my world once and for all.

The man with the sickening smile is still sitting at the table. He leans forward and motions to stand up. Al Orange cringes when massive gushes of fear heave up from his stomach into his throat; his nerves quickly surrender their stand and leave him fear-stricken.

Before the man has risen to his feet, the mallard turns for the door; "I am too gutless, worthless, all is lost," he cries. He reaches the threshold and steadies himself on the door frame trying one last time to gather any vestige of courage to turn and face his demon. A hand, cold and rough, strokes the side of his head from behind. The mallard feels sick. He cannot see the man's face and there is no sound, but he knows the man is laughing at him – he always laughs at him. Coarse fingers toy with his feathers; around his head and probing his ears, mockingly. He feels utterly pathetic, his misery is total. He fixes his gaze on the wall across the alleyway – crying for his torment to be over.

The rough hand now spreads out against his rump and fires him from the building – he is ejected. The heavily planked door slams shut behind him with a malevolence driven by pure hatred.

Al Orange is now outside in the dark chilled air. His bones are in agony, his muscles cramped hard and his breath white, suspended in the air, assuming an entity of its own for a few short moments until it disappears back into the world from which it had come.

Every part of his body competes to scream the loudest, yet not a sound is to be heard as is often the case in nightmares. His eyes chill, his pupils dilate desperately trying to plot a safe course through the dank shadows cast by the clear moonlight. The pale silvered light reflects off shallow puddles and high wet walls between which he hurriedly and pitifully waddles. The reflections are disrupted only by the contours of lost souls as destitute and lifeless as the granite flags on which they lay. They no longer raise their heads in Orange's presence. They fully expect him to join them before long, for he has passed this way many times before.

He hurries onward, unsure of his footing on the steely uneven ground. His speed is agonisingly slow for the effort he is putting into his escape; the harder he tries, the slower the walls pass.

The alley ahead forks to the left and to the right. He takes the left fork – he always takes the left fork. He becomes aware of a distant wailing getting louder and closer; a falsetto changing in tone many times per second.

The shrill voice catches up with him. Ahead is light, brilliant white light. The wailing voice becomes his, he is screaming into the night silence at the top of his voice. 'No, no, please leave me!'

'No, no, please leave me!' Al Orange jerked up in his bed, his eyes bulging. He stared through the darkness at the bottom of his bed. A human shape stood there. Was this his demon in the flesh? Was this the tenant who kept on and on at him, making him feel sick and sad at every opportunity? Orange shouted out again, 'Please stop it!'

The bedroom door flew open and Aano rushed in, but the silhouette at the bottom of the bed was gone.

'Inspector – shush, shush,' said Aano rushing to his aid. 'You're having a bad dream.'

Orange looked over Aano's shoulder. 'Where is he?'

'Where is who?' replied Aano, gently patting the inspector on the shoulder.

'There was someone at the end of the bed, a man, I've seen him before.'

'There hasn't been anyone else in here, I promise you.' Aano held a cup of water to the inspector's bill.

The inspector took a clumsy slurp and then slumped back onto his pillow. 'I was back in that room again,' he said in an obvious state of exhaustion. 'Then I was thrown out, but I'm not sure if it was me or not; it was as if I was looking down on someone else.' He struggled to keep his thoughts together. 'It was a human – what's happening to me?' Orange wept openly against Aano's chest.

Aano ventured a reassuring smile. 'I'll stay in here for the rest of the night, that way I can keep an eye on you. Rest assured nothing will come in here that shouldn't be in here.'

The inspector settled into the bed; his eyes stared blankly at the ceiling. His mind fell deaf to all sound from without, but eyes other than his were still looking out from within, watching the ape…and measuring him.

***

Meanwhile, in the world of the humans, a small cottage sat among the modern boxy houses in the village of Longford. If this were the world of the ducks it would be but a few miles from where Al Orange currently lay with his troubled head. Sadly, this was a world where many people lay with such troubled heads.

The cottage was once the village blacksmith's shop, but that was when the society of Longford was far more rooted; before commuters had been invented. The blacksmith had long since gone, so had the butcher, the baker and the candlestick maker, along with the identity of the village itself. The cottage was now home to Mr Jones and his dog, Polly.

The moonlit night was quiet and still, but Mr Jones was sleeping a bad sleep. His face betrayed his inner thoughts; he too was having a nightmare not of his making, just like Inspector Orange…

The alley ahead forks left and right. He takes the left fork. He becomes aware of a constant wailing getting louder and closer; a falsetto changing in tone many times per second.

The shrill voice is with him now. Ahead is light, brilliant white light. The falsetto voice is his, he is wailing into the night silence. 'No, no, please leave me!'

'No, no, please leave me!' Jones cried out from his bed, disrupting the quiet of the small room. 'Oh Lord,' he whispered, feeling utterly alone. He rested his body into the bed and looked around the room. The rural night air loitered all around him; shades of subdued moon blues and greys darkened into the corners, all at ease. His emotions hung in the balance, teasingly see-sawing between tears of sadness and anger. 'Just another nightmare,' he whispered to himself.

His legs slid from under the bed covers, his feet homed in on the slippers always in precisely the same spot. His left hand reached towards the bedside table and engaged the empty cup. Slowly and silently he left the bed and then the room, not bothering to put a light on. He carefully meandered through the gauntlet of shallow steps up and down from one room to another. He knew the dog would be hiding along the route, waiting until the last minute to make his presence known.

He was a beautiful dog; some would call him a mongrel with Alsatian features, much slimmer and more muscular, probably of Alsatian and Greyhound origins.

Now in the kitchen with his master, the dog sat by the doorway to block the exit. He watched as the same routine unfolded: Jones puts the kettle on, prepares the cup, washes hands, goes to the loo; washes hands, always washes hands; then back into the kitchen just as the kettle gives a resounding click to confirm its job done.

Having filled the cup, Jones made his way into the living room and sat down in his armchair with the dog at his feet. Quietly they both sat, the dog not wanting to be anywhere else. Jones, so sad, did not want to be there at all, wishing things were different.

Being over a hundred years old, the windows of the cottage were small, but the casement doors allowed the moonlight to reach in to end its long journey by stroking the dog before smoothing the carpet and coming to a halt on the floral pattern on the sofa. The oblique light highlighted the uneven walls and low ceiling built in a time when straight edges for country folk were not compulsory.

Part way through his coffee, Jones rose to his feet and made his way to the doors wondering if he might catch sight of the badger wending his way across the lawn, snuffling and pawing the soft earth in search of a lush worm or two.

The balance of light reflected Jones' image in the glass pane; average height, average build, quite fit; once blonde but now more ash than blonde, and as much bald as not. What hair he had was softly back-combed, resting comfortably on his ears and collar. The well-'ard bouncer look was not for him. He stared briefly into his own blue eyes searching for a shadow, a reflection of something he knew was there but never showed itself to the outside world. Bound by years of crying and screaming without anyone knowing, the rare occurrence of a smile would give rise to many lines across his brow and below his eyes.

He switched the radio on before lying back on the sofa with his coffee on a small table beside him and the dog's head resting next to his. The dog would have dearly loved to join his master on the sofa, but he knew dogs never got on sofas – not when anyone was looking. Instead, he leaned inward with his head warming Jones' shoulder, enjoying the hand gently stroking his ear.

The radio news spoke of the famine laying most of the African continent to waste. No prospect of any harvest whatsoever and little hope of planting new crops, due in part to the weather but also to the presence of many armed militia who would kill and plunder those who dared to try to help themselves. The peoples' plight was made all the more unbearable by outbreaks of cholera and other water-borne diseases.

Getting back to sleep proved difficult, but eventually Jones drifted off with the voice of the news reader speaking of a nuclear arms build-up in Asia. *That's just what we need*, he thought, *more weapons. If they spent a fraction of their weapons budget on food there would be no hunger in the world. But that would never do...*His mind skipped across the surface of sleep, waking several times before morning, each time taking a sip of cold coffee to moisten his lips.

Six o'clock eventually arrived. Jones woke without the need of an alarm, all part of his routine. The dog was now flat on the floor with one eye open. He had no calendar, nor a copy of his master's rota. All he knew was devotion and his best mate's habits.

Jones' thoughts wandered while he stared up at the ceiling. Like Inspector Orange, his thoughts were also not of his own making. Woe betide him if he should commit even the most minor error, however human or trivial. He had a tenant, a demon equipped with an armoury of the most vile and spiteful hatred, borne of incessant bottomless evil, all aimed inward at himself. There was neither rhyme nor reason to his feelings of despair, sometimes many months apart, but when they came there was no escape. He would endure days, weeks or months imprisoned in the darkest, loneliest place on Earth, a place created within his own mind, but not by his own hands.

Whether asleep or awake, nasty visions such as the night-time dreams would constantly flood his mind; a black mire drowning any chance of hope, obscuring the daily rituals of normality which he would negotiate sub-consciously. He would do this without exposing to others the anguish and turmoil of the situation within his mind – for his eyes had learned to cry on the inside as well.

The sofa had become uncomfortable, his neck and back ached, and so he stood up and stretched.

Polly did likewise, almost like a shadow willingly articulated to his master's existence. The dog arched his back and exuded a long satisfying groan as he prepared for a new day, hopeful of a good romp in the woods or across the common.

With his forlorn sadness firmly registered, Jones sat in the living room with a bowl of cereal on his lap. The dog sat upright in the corner with ears erect and eyes alert for the first sign of his master making for the exit. No matter what sneaky plan or trickery Jones employed, the dog would always get to the door first, not wanting to be left behind. Was it guess-work? Could he read minds? Did he keep a log of Jones' activities? Did he already know what he would be doing next Thursday? If one were to look under his dog bed would there be a pencil and paper, or a diary perhaps?

Summer was over, but the wood pile still needed topping up for the winter. The dog probably had that in his diary as well. He had come from a rescue centre at the age of two and was very much in his prime; very fit and very fast. He came with the name Apollo, but Jones considered that to be a little too ostentatious, so he was renamed Polly. Although somewhat unusual for a male dog, Polly didn't mind, especially if it was followed by the words, 'walkies, dinner, or pussy cat.'

Jones had finished his cereal, and the game was about to start. The dog knew it and fixed his eyes on him. Jones leaned forward to ease himself out of the chair; Polly leaned slightly towards the door. Jones relaxed back into the chair, teasingly; the dog straightened up. Jones leaned forward again; Polly leaned towards the door again. Jones straightened up, so did the dog. Jones pretended to look out into the garden to divert the dog's gaze, but Polly was not fooled that easily, but he had one weakness; he loved to chase cats. He would never catch them but loved the chase. If he should find himself getting too close he would deliberately miss a step or change course just to prolong the game.

Jones suddenly jumped from his seat. He lunged for the French doors and flung them open, saying, 'Pussy cats.' The dog leapt through the gap in the doors like a dart. Jones now raced through the house to get to the front door first. He reached for the handle and opened it swiftly, but Polly was already there, sitting outside with his tail sweeping the doorstep and his tongue hanging lazily from one side of his mouth. His eyes were bright and eager, daring Jones to try it again.

How do you do that? Jones wondered.

Present score, Polly hundreds, Jones nil.

8

Three horizons away from Mr Jones and his dog, in Davidsmeadow, a fine layer of mist lay over the pond on the heath like best Egyptian cotton. Water birds dabbled and foraged among the reeds while the young barista opened up his kiosk for business; he wondered if the beautiful woman who had muddled his head the day before would be back. His thoughts were soon answered.

'Good morning, young man,' said Kate, rounding the corner of the kiosk.

'Oh, good morning, madam,' the barista jumped with surprise.

'Sorry,' said Kate, 'I didn't mean to startle you.'

'Your usual?' asked the young man, trying to conceal his delight in her company once again.

'Yes please.' Kate's attention was quickly drawn by a lone figure standing at the end of the nearby jetty. Although his back was to her, she was in no doubt that it was the same well-groomed man she had seen the day before. *This time I'll keep my eyes on you.* She continued to watch him discretely until Art Helkendag's voice caught her unawares.

'Good morning, Kate. I see that young man is here again. Intriguing isn't he.'

'Maybe,' Kate replied, sounding almost nonchalant.

'Oh, I think I detect more than a passing interest.'

Helkendag's voice had that unnerving edge to it. Kate knew he was prying, trying to search among her thoughts.

The barista brought Kate's coffee and placed it on the table. 'Can I get you anything, sir?' he asked of Helkendag.

'No, thank you, I won't be stopping long,' he replied.

The barista retired to his kiosk and busied himself while stealing the occasional glance of the woman who had filled his head all night long.

Kate had made a point of sitting facing the water, leaving Helkendag to sit with his back to it, and thereby depriving him of a view of the stranger on the shore.

Helkendag studied her instead. 'Do you have any news for me?' he asked, watching her eyes veer past him.

'No, nothing,' said Kate, pausing for thought and changing the subject. 'Do you ever dress down?' she asked.

Helkendag smiled subtly. 'Do you?' he replied.

Kate kept her eyes in his. 'I certainly don't wear suits all the time.'

'Does it bother you that I do?' he said, enjoying the small talk.

'No, but I would have thought you might try to blend in a little more with the locals – incognito so to speak.'

'Hmm,' he toyed. 'Maybe I shall change my appearance next time, just for you.' He noticed her attention straying beyond him once again.

The handsome stranger had made his way from the jetty to the kiosk, and was now heading towards the table next to Kate's, that being the only other one presently set out.

'Is he nice?' Helkendag quietly asked.

'Who?' Kate replied.

'The young man behind me.'

'I'm sure I don't know what you mean,' Kate replied.

Helkendag rose from his seat and reset his hat. 'I shall be in touch soon, perhaps you will have news for me next time; there is much unfinished business here.'

'Perhaps,' said Kate.

Helkendag turned and addressed the stranger directly, 'Goodbye, young man. I'm sure we have met before.' His tone required a response.

'I don't think so,' said the dark-haired stranger politely.

Helkendag released him from his gaze. 'Goodbye, Kate,' he said in a louder voice than was necessary.

Kate acknowledged with a subtle nod. Both she and the newcomer then watched as Helkendag climbed the slope and disappeared beyond the brow.

At that moment a couple of mums, each with a young child in tow turned from the kiosk in search of a table to sit at. The dark-haired stranger, noticing there were no spare tables rose and offered his.

'Thank you, are you sure,' said one of the mums.

'Yes, that's fine,' replied the man.

Kate then caught his eye and gladly beckoned him to join her at her table. He returned her smile and sat facing her. The void across the table was instantly breached. Nothing was said for a full minute while their eyes soaked up the other's aura.

'I beg your pardon,' said the man, 'I'm Walter – Walter Haker.'

Kate's eyes never left his. 'Kate – Kate Herrlaw,' she replied.

Walter knew this was the Kate he had been told to look out for. He had yearned to find one of his own kind for so long. They sat for many minutes, hands together and eyes swimming in each other's. Kate, too, felt a warmth she had only previously known when close to Abel Nogg.

Walter gathered his thoughts and carefully put his words

71

together knowing that no matter how absurd they sounded, Kate would not doubt him. He leaned across the table and whispered, 'A few days ago I witnessed something I have never known before.'

Kate gently squeezed his hand for him to continue, which he did...

'In all the time I have been in this world I have seen the most atrocious acts one creature could inflict upon another, just as you have, I'm sure.' Kate's eyes held him as surely as if she were holding him in her arms. Walter continued, 'But in all previous conflicts it has been mankind against the rest, the stronger beating up on the weaker, striving to make their point by wreaking death and destruction upon their foe.' He drew a breath. 'But I have recently seen beings not of this world; above our standing in the order of things, magnificent beings standing tall in the face of mankind's hatred.'

'These beings,' Kate asked softly, 'what did they look like?'

Walter gave a tenuous smile while holding tight to her hand. 'They were...Canada geese.' He chuckled in disbelief of his own words. 'Canada geese the size of very tall men – on horseback. Some wore Stetsons, others wore pith helmets – and some carried lances with pennants flying high.'

'Keep going,' Kate encouraged with another squeeze, her heart racing.

Walter could not believe he was telling such a tall tale to someone he had only just met, but he was sure that the beautiful creature facing him already knew much of what he was saying. 'The horses stared across the moorland at the rifles which they knew were seeking to kill them – and then they just walked straight towards them without flinching.'

'And?' said Kate, her delicate hands keeping a firm hold on his.

'The bullets flew one by one. Straight through their targets and around the world and back again – straight into the backs of the men who had fired them; each one felled by his own evil hand.'

'What of the horses?'

'They were untouched. Each round of gunfire was greeted by an increase in the horses' speed; the more the men fired at them, the harder the horses charged. They rode straight over them, raising the land in their wake. When the dust settled, the men were buried deep beneath the earth without any sign of them ever having been there. Nature had swept them under the carpet, quite literally.'

'And where did the riders go after the battle?'

'They cantered back to the far side of the moor and waited for their leader.' Walter's eyelids each cradled a tear. 'They were so beautiful, immaculate, it was as if no dust from this world could touch them.'

Kate knew the answer to her next question. 'Their leader, did you see him?'

'Yes, he—' Walter replied.

Kate finished the sentence for him. 'He was a huge pterosaur by the name of Abel Nogg.'

Walter's eyes widened. 'You know of him?' A smile of relief eased his expression.

'Yes, I've also met him.' Kate stroked the back of Walter's hand, adding, 'On several occasions in fact.'

'Oh, thank heavens,' said Walter. 'I wasn't sure if I was going mad.'

'He has also appeared as a man,' said Kate, 'a human, but that is not his true identity, he is no more a man than he is a pterosaur.'

'That explains the aura about him.' Walter's voice settled as the truth sank in. 'Despite his horrendous looks, I felt no need to fear or doubt him.'

'Did you see where any of them went after the battle?' Kate held her composure and remained the picture of cool. She tilted her head to one side and raised one eyebrow. 'There wasn't a timbered wall involved was there?'

'Yes,' Walter nodded and smiled broadly, almost breaking into a laugh, 'on the far side of the common; I could only just make it out at the time, and there was a big chesnut horse pulling a wagon, that's what the nasty looking soldiers were chasing and shooting at. It was difficult to see properly because of the dust, but when the air cleared, the horse and the wagon were all gone.' He paused, the reflection of his eyes resting happily in hers.

Kate's eyes wetted with relief. 'So they made it, those big lovely creatures – they made it back to their world.' She snatched a breath before eagerly asking, 'And what of the hundred horses – and Abel Nogg?'

'The last I saw of the pterosaur was him taking to the air in the direction of the horses. I turned away for a moment to see if I could see any of my squad – to see if they had witnessed it, when I looked back the moorland was empty.' He looked deeper into Kate's eyes for support. 'I honestly wondered if I had imagined the whole thing.'

'You hadn't.' Kate raised her hand and touched Walter's cheek. 'This is why we are here, to witness and to help where we can, but you already know that.'

Walter put his hand to hers lest she would let him go. 'You are the first of our kind I have ever met. Through all the troubles of the past I know I have come close, but have never actually met another before.'

Kate replied just above a whisper, her voice as gentle as her touch. 'Perhaps there is something ahead that needs the two of us working together to achieve.'

'I think you're right. All we can do now is wait for a sign, or a word, I suppose.' Walter looked into his cup of now cool coffee. 'Would you like a fresh cup?' he asked, a smile settling amiably among his features.

'Why not,' replied Kate, 'perhaps we can finish this crossword together.'

Walter returned to the counter. 'Two more coffees, please.'

'Yes, sir,' replied the young barista, turning to the coffee machine. *He's a bit like her.* Images of their eyes lingered in his mind. *I wonder what country they're from.* He turned and placed the two fresh cups of coffee on the counter. 'That's four pound fifty, please sir.'

Walter sorted the exact money from his wallet. The barista's eyes fixed on his hands. *Strong, definitely man's hands – but not a blemish, blimey.*

'Thank you,' said Walter returning to his table.

The barista got on with his chores, casting the occasional glance towards the twosome whose images would remain at the forefront of his thoughts for some time to come. *I've never seen anyone so beautiful, not actually perfectly beautiful – but they both are.*

Walter re-took his seat. 'That man in the hat you were with when I arrived, is he a friend?'

'Hmm,' Kate replied, 'to be honest I don't really know what he is. He has helped me in the past, but I can't help thinking he has an ulterior motive. He's very powerful.'

'What's his name?'

'Art Helkendag.'

'Unusual name.'

'Unusual by name and by nature,' Kate replied.

'And by smell,' said Walter.

'You noticed that too.'

'Yes,' said Walter, staring to the heavens. 'I don't like to say it, but it reminds me of death, or decay perhaps.'

Kate visibly shivered at the thought.

'How are you getting on with that?' asked Walter, changing the subject and nodding at the crossword.

'I've hardly started; I've only answered three clues, they're very easy though. I reckon we could knock it out by the time we finish this drink.'

'Sounds good,' Walter replied, 'what's the next clue?'

'Let's have a go at one across; I've got a few letters in place.' Kate read the clue verbatim: 'No dark horse this, but The Dark Angel is not to be trusted.'

They both sat with a hand to their chin in thought.

'That's strange,' Kate said, softly.

Walter glimpsed her eyes.

Kate went on, 'The words, "The Dark Angel," have capitals.' They each stroked their lips with their forefinger while they unravelled the letters. 'The Dark Angel must be an anagram,' Kate added.

Walter scanned the crossword, uttering the letters Kate had already got. 'A, H, D.'

Kate joined him in muttering various possibilities just above a whisper. 'Aft, arm, ark – art.' The table fell silent as the letters fell into place.

'The Dark Angel,' they said. 'Art Helkendag.'

Walter studied the top of the page. 'The Tribune, dated the sixteenth.'

'Yes, two days old,' said Kate, 'that's when I picked it up from the table outside the café on The Square, someone had left it there.'

'Where is the Tribune's office?'

'In the High Street, a brisk five minute walk,' Kate replied, holding Walter's hand to lead the way.

Five minutes later the buzzer sounded in the empty office; a middle-aged lady emerged from a back room. 'Good morning, what can I do for you?' she asked.

Walter answered politely, 'I wonder if you would have any copies of your paper dated the sixteenth.'

The woman nodded towards a bundle tied with string sitting by the doorway. 'You're just in time,' she said, 'the van will be here at midday to take them back.'

'Could we just have a quick look at them?' Kate asked.

'Yes, my dear, just pop them up here on the counter and have a butchers.'

Walter eagerly untied the bundle. He and Kate pulled half a dozen copies at random from the pile and opened them at the crossword page.

'These are all the same as each other,' said Walter.

'Of course they are,' said the woman behind the counter, 'what did you expect?'

'Then where did this one come from?' Walter replied, holding Kate's copy for her to see.

The woman looked from one copy to the other. 'They look the same to me.'

'Apart from one particular clue,' Walter replied, pointing to one across.

'Ooh-er,' said the lady, bemused, 'how odd.'

'Exactly,' said Kate.

'But it is our paper – see here.' The woman pointed out the code at the bottom of page two. 'All copies from that issue will have that number; so it definitely came from the same print run.'

'Then how come the crossword on one particular page is different and yet everything else is the same?' Walter asked.

'It is a puzzle, that's for sure. Is it really important?' asked the woman.

'I think it probably is,' said Walter, holding the door for Kate before both taking their leave.

'Come with me,' said Kate, 'I'll show you where I found it.' She and Walter rounded the corner and walked twenty paces to the café on The Square – Café Hero.

'Here,' Kate tapped the table, 'this is where I sat two days ago. The paper was left on the table, presumably by the previous occupant.'

'Well,' said Walter, 'neither you nor I believe in coincidence, so this paper must have been deliberately put here to be found by you.'

'I've been so dim-witted,' said Kate. 'Not to see it in his name.'

'Not everyone has names like ours,' Walter replied, 'and in any case, you've had so much to deal with lately, you shouldn't blame yourself.'

'Of course I should.' Kate rebuked herself, clearly annoyed and embarrassed. 'I can't believe I didn't see it.' She slipped deep into thought; *Abel Nogg, Leon Bagg. Aano Grunt; and then there's Beeroglad.* 'I know they're all anagrams, so how did I miss Art Helkendag – Oh, I've been so slow.'

They engaged in a subtle embrace. Kate whispered close to Walter's ear, 'Abel has somehow brought us together.'

'I think you're right,' Walter whispered back, not wanting to ever let go of this most perfect creature. 'The question is, why?'

'I'm sure we'll find out in good time.' Kate released her hold and gently lifted Walter's hands from her waist. 'In the meantime, we must be wary of our Mr Helkendag and try not to arouse his suspicion.'

Walter replied earnestly, 'If we are right about him, we are in for the fight of our life.'

'Not ours,' Kate replied. She looked around at the people milling about the town. 'Theirs.'

'Hmm,' Walter pondered the situation. 'If you can meet me tomorrow, I'll show you where the battle took place, and where the timbered wall is.'

'Okay, fine,' Kate replied.

Walter wrote on a page from his pocket notebook. 'Here, this is the map reference; ten hundred hours tomorrow, okay?'

'Okay.'

They held hands briefly before getting up and going in opposite directions, each wondering what the future held in store for the people of this world. Your world.

A deep voice uttered on unearthly breath from beneath a wide-brimmed hat while eyes of pitch stared across The Square, watching the twosome part company. 'As I thought…'

9

Back in Longford, Mr Jones opened the tailgate of his elderly estate car; Polly leapt in and settled down while Jones hitched up the small wooden trailer.

The dog knew his master to be a good man, but he also knew there was something not good within him – dogs are clever like that.

The car started up and they were on their way. Polly sat upright looking straight ahead. Most of Jones' view through the rear-view mirror comprised a pair of pointed ears fully flared to gain maximum reception. The dog's face was a comfort, something warm and loving; dedicated without ulterior motive, apart from food of course. *Why doesn't God make humans like that?* Jones wondered.

Polly grew more excited when the car turned off the road onto a narrow dirt track. He knew where they were, and he knew why they were there. Logging with his bare teeth was his favourite hobby. Jones opened the tailgate and the dog was away and back again with a branch between his teeth before his mate had even donned his gloves. Polly would spend as long as it took to chew the branch into two; if the wood was soft it would be done in seconds; a fresh timber might take fifteen minutes, but he would work vigorously until the job was done.

Having filled the trailer with timber, they took a break; coffee from a flask for Jones, water for Polly which he would drink as it poured from the bottle, his long tongue lapping at it in mid-air.

Their thirst quenched, they walked for a while. Polly busied himself smelling the undergrowth as he went along, conjuring up images of those who had gone before. He ventured into the bushes and retrieved a stick the length of Jones' forearm and about half the thickness. He dropped it at Jones' feet and gave one high pitched bark.

Jones duly picked up the stick.

Polly tensed up, totally focused; nothing else mattered now except the stick. He always knew which way it would be thrown. The world now consisted of nothing but him and the stick.

In one swift movement Jones drew his arm back to full extension; Polly turned his head away. Jones then hurled the stick into the air as far as he could.

Without looking, Polly lowered his hind quarters to the ground and powered his feet into the soil; energy from the Earth's core rose through him and catapulted him to his maximum speed within three strides. He scythed his way through the undergrowth, his body horizontal in perfect balance; dog, air, Earth. Mother Nature cradled him unseen, but the dog knew she was there.

No matter how hard or how far Jones would throw the stick, Polly would always be there before it landed. Occasionally a last second change of direction would be tried to catch Polly out, but the dog would still take off in the correct direction; the stick was the Messershmitt, the dog's ears the Spitfire gunsight.

Leaping into the air at the end of his sprint, Polly captured the stick and landed heavily in the soft sandy soil, his attention was instantly taken by something beneath him. He dropped the stick, his ears forward and his nose sniffing furiously at the ground.

'What is it, mate?' Jones stopped by his side.

Polly dug frenetically with his front paws.

Jones looked down to see what looked like an old piece of pipe, or a tree root perhaps. 'Wait a minute, boy, let me have a look,' he said, easing the dog to one side. The dog's expression and drooling chops told Jones that this was no ordinary find. He knelt down and began carefully sweeping the soil away with his hand. The nearby trees shivered and let loose many leaves, the birdsong fell silent.

A deep voice spoke up from behind. 'I think it better if you leave well alone.'

Jones turned around to see a man of similar age to him, very well dressed and out of place in such an environment. Polly's ears flattened tight to his head, he lowered his rear end to the ground and bared his teeth.

'Polly, behave,' Jones called firmly, concerned by the dog's uncharacteristic attitude. 'I'm sorry, he's normally very docile,' Jones said to the stranger, wondering what could have caused such a change in Polly's temper.

The dog snarled and kept his eyes singularly on the interloper, his instinct was torn between fleeing or throwing all to the wind and tearing the man limb from limb. Never before had he felt such basal hatred for another creature.

The man stood firm, saying, 'You should keep your dog on a lead you know, or he might get hurt.'

Before another word was said, Polly leapt towards the man and set his teeth into his arm just above the wrist.

'No Polly!' Jones shouted in disbelief.

Polly's jaws clamped tight into the man's flesh.

With the dog hanging from his arm, the man turned his back on Jones and stared intensely into the dog's eyes. His own eyes of crystal blue instantly changed to solid orbs of the most inhuman black. Polly stopped growling and fell to the ground with a terrified whimper.

'What on Earth…? Jones knelt by the dog's side, puzzled.

'He will recover in a few minutes,' said the man while adjusting his hat. He then cast an eye, which had now turned blue again, towards the dog's find. 'As I was saying, you will do well to leave that alone. And perhaps you should not come here again.' His voice was cold and sharp, not a hint of compassion showing.

Using his bare hands, Jones hurriedly smoothed over the hollow and then returned his attention to Polly who was now struggling to his feet. 'Easy boy,' Jones put an arm around the dog's body to steady him before looking up to have a word with the man in the hat – but the man was gone.

***

In the world of the ducks, in Smallbeef, Inspector Hooter and Sergeant Uppendown had gathered all the information regarding the killing of Constable Tim Burr. Hooter was satisfied that Aano Grunt had been falsely accused of the crime and had told him so. Hooter was now keen to get back to town, and so to that end he called from the centre of the yard, 'Squad, pay attention. Fall in right away if you please.' He stared sharply upwards to check his cap was on straight and then he puffed up his chest for effect and called out, 'Squad, from the left, call your name.'

The constables duly responded: 'Robert Roberts, Russell Russell, Peter Peters, Howard Howard… Lock, Stock, and Barrel.'

Hooter rubbed his bill briefly before looking at the last constable to report. 'Andbarrel?' he queried.

Constable Barrel maintained a straight ahead look while

replying, 'Pardon, sir?'

'You said your name was "Andbarrel", is that correct?'

Barrel paused, he desperately wanted to rub his bill to help him think, but that would be poor etiquette while on parade. 'No sir, it's just Barrel.'

'Justbarrel?' Hooter replied, still a little puzzled. 'Your name is Constable Justbarrel?'

Oh no, thought the constable. He so wanted to make a good first impression like his comrades, but now it all seemed to be going horribly wrong.

Noting the concerned look in Barrel's eyes, Hooter said with a hint of compassion, 'You may rub your bill if it will help, Constable, surely you know your own name.'

'Thank you, sir.' Barrel eagerly rubbed his bright yellow bill before continuing, 'You see, sir, with the three of us being Armed Response Ducks we were named after parts of our pistols. One was named Lock, after the firing mechanism, one named Stock – that's the butt or the handle; and the other…that would be me, sir, named Barrel, after the barrel.'

The expression of puzzlement which so often adorned Inspector Hooter's face remained unmoved. He too rubbed his bill for good measure.

Barrel added, 'I suppose it's because of the old expression – lock, stock and barrel – meaning the whole lot.'

Hooter's eyes smiled. 'Oh, I see – Lock, Stock **and** Barrel, a very old saying indeed. Well, I thank you for clearing up that confusion, Constable Barrel, well done, I think we've all learned something there.'

Barrel breathed a sigh of relief and returned his wings smartly to his sides.

Hooter continued to speak aloud for all to hear. 'This morning the Flying Squad, including Constables Lock, Stock

and Barrel will return with me to Davidsmeadow to conduct our normal policing duties. I have no doubt we shall hear in due course from Mr Nogg in respect of the Bog who is still missing in the world of the humans. Until then it will be business as usual.' He paused briefly for thought. 'I realize some of you have made new friends here at Smallbeef, and I dare say you will use your off-duty time to keep up your acquaintance.' He scanned the line of young mallards; most of them exhibited a certain twinkle in their eye and very bright bills. 'I know I can trust you to be on your best behaviour and not bring our breed into disrepute.' He struggled to keep the image of Marion from entering his mind. *This won't do*, he shook his head to clear such thoughts and continued, 'Mr Grunt will stay here to tend to the donkeys in need of his farrier skills. Sergeant Uppendown will also remain behind for the time being to offer support until the migration from Fort Bog dies down.' Hooter then looked along the line and asked, 'Any questions?'

'No sir,' replied seven mallards eager to get on with their job.

'Excellent, you may stand down for thirty minutes to say your goodbyes, please be back here promptly for take off.'

Lock, Stock and Barrel could remember a time when their inspector, Al Orange, was like Hooter in his demeanour, but that was before someone or something had got inside his head.

***

'How is our patient this morning?' Marion Waters-Edge stood in the doorway of number seven with a tea trolley in tow. 'I've brought you both some breakfast.'

'Oh, thank you,' Aano replied, spying the apple and banana on a willow pattern plate.

'And for you, Inspector Orange, I have a bowl of soaked pellets and a nice cup of tea.' Marion wheeled the trolley up to the side of the bed. 'Would you like a cup too, Mr Grunt?'

Aano grinned widely. 'Yes please, that's very kind of you.'

Al Orange swung round and sat on the edge of the bed rubbing his head. 'Why are you being so kind to me?' he asked of Marion, his voice croaking from a night of troubled groaning. 'Is your husband here…is he back now?'

'Yes, Inspector; he arrived yesterday with my son Dick.' Her eyes beamed with joy. 'Inspector Hooter has returned to Davidsmeadow with his constables, but the Mounties have stayed behind for now.'

Orange slurped his tea, too tired to sip properly. 'I still don't understand why you are doing this for me; by rights your husband should be baying for my blood. He does know about my behaviour towards you, doesn't he?'

'Yes he does, Inspector. I've told him everything, and from what he tells me, you were quite horrid to him as well.'

Tears gathered in Orange's eyes; despite his poor condition, his feathers still shed water, allowing the tears to slip down his cheeks unhindered.

Marion put her wing to Orange's head and gently swept his ruffled feathers back into line. 'There there,' she said, 'don't worry yourself about me or my husband. You have enough to contend with. We look forward to getting you better so that we can get to know the real you.'

Al Orange fell back onto the pillow and let his eyes dwell in Marion's for a few seconds, he then turned to Aano, saying rather bluntly, 'I think you are the weirdest looking animal I have ever seen, but I think you are also the cleverest…and possibly the kindest.'

Aano didn't know how to react to such a compliment from a mallard who, just a few days earlier, had been brandishing a pistol in his face and hitting him with his truncheon.

'I shall leave you both to have your breakfast,' said Marion. 'I'll leave the door ajar to let some air in.'

'Thank you, Mrs Waters-Edge,' said Aano.

'Thank you,' the inspector croaked.

Aano deftly peeled the banana while Orange took a spoonful of the tasty pellets to his bill. The two of them set about quietly enjoying their breakfast and tea, occasionally casting a glimpse at the other, giving respect a chance.

***

A low overcast sky stood sentinel over Davidsmeadow. The residents welcomed the rain as much as the Sun and the wind. Their hearts knew it was heaven sent and that Mother Nature knew what was best. The Square, being the centre of the town, was as busy as usual. The majority of the birds milling about were mallards, with the occasional Canada goose and perhaps a few migrants from Europe passing through.

'Look up there, Mummy,' a duckling called out, pulling on his mother's tail to get her attention.

'Oh, how wonderful, my dear,' the mother replied enthusiastically.

Seven constables and Inspector Hooter circled just below the cloud layer, surveying the scene before coming in to land. Their helmet badges somehow caught the grey light of the day and brightened it, showering the town with silvered rays of sparkling gossamer.

These were the first police ducks the duckling had ever seen, him being just a few days old. The two feet tall ball of grey fluff looked up in awe, his bill agog. He didn't know what he was looking at, but the admiration in his mother's eyes told him these were special mallards.

Hooter sounded his horn for good measure, honk honk.

Those on the ground moved aside. One by one the constables landed with pinpoint accuracy and promptly took their place in the line-up. Hooter was the last to touch down with a customary short runway. He shook his plumage straight and then waddled smartly to take his place in front of his squad. The crowd looked on from around the margins. Hooter returned the onlookers' gaze until one duck in particular caught his attention; a very fine lady mallard sitting at a table outside Café Hero. *She's looking straight at me, I mustn't stare.*

His constables were now standing smartly to attention with helmets perfectly in line and bills six degrees above the horizontal. Hooter couldn't resist another quick look across the cobbles, but the table was now empty, *She's gone – what a shame.*

The town looked on while the inspector addressed his constables. 'Well done,' he said, 'now we shall make our way to the station.' He raised his voice. 'Squad, right turn, in single file, quick waddle.' The seven police ducks turned and briskly marched in duck-waddle fashion across The Square and down the side road to the police station with Hooter keeping pace by their side and one eye hoping to spy the attractive newcomer again.

Having heard Inspector Hooter's horn, Constables Thomas Thomas and James James were standing outside the police station waiting eagerly for his arrival. As soon as the squad rounded the corner the two of them stood smartly to attention. Their dazzling plumage and glistening helmet badges were not lost on a couple of young lady ducks who happened to be passing by. The young females giggled and cast a furtive eye across the road at the handsome young police ducks who were determined not to be distracted.

The two females did a little shimmy and a shake to show their curves. Thomas and James shut their eyes tight. The young ladies giggled as young females do, and then, upon seeing the inspector appear with the rest of his squad they whispered saucily, 'Farewell, brave drakes.'

Thomas opened one eye to see the young females disappearing down the road, tittering merrily to each other.

'Phew, they've gone.'

'Good job too,' said James, 'a right couple of corkers, though.'

'Never mind that now, look smart,' said Thomas.

'Squad halt,' Hooter called. The seven mallards came to a firm halt in front of the station. Hooter turned to Thomas and James. 'It's good to see you again, I hope you've managed all right on your own, anything to report?'

'No sir,' replied Thomas, 'all quiet and peaceful.'

'Good,' said Hooter, 'let's hope it stays that way.' He looked along the line to catch the eye of each and every one of his young squad. 'I have a feeling we shall soon be called upon to go back to that strange world of the humans. Abel Nogg will be in touch soon enough. In the meantime you are to refer to your rota and go about your business as usual…any questions?'

'No sir,' replied nine young voices.

'Excellent, squad dismiss.'

The mallards turned and made their way into the station. Thomas, being the last in line, turned to see the inspector staring up the road in the direction of The Square.

'Is everything all right, sir?'

'Mmm?' Hooter replied, vaguely. 'You haven't noticed any new faces in the town, have you?'

Thomas thought carefully before replying, 'Well sir, we did notice a new female outside the Café Hero, never seen her before.'

'Can you describe her?'

Thomas looked up to the sky while he gathered her image. 'All the colours of the Earth in her plumage, very soft looking.' He recalled a little more. 'Super fine chest feathers, sir. I couldn't really say how old she was, adult for sure…and very beautiful.'

'They all are, Constable.' Hooter saw a hint of something else in the young constable's eye. 'Is there something else, young duck?'

'Well sir, you'll probably think I'm going daft,' Thomas replied, 'but…'

Hooter interrupted. 'After all that we have been through and endured in the last couple of weeks, I doubt if anything would surprise me, so come on, out with it.'

'It was her eyes, sir…they were the most brilliant blue, really piercing; not what you normally get in a mallard's head, if you know what I mean, sir.'

'Yes,' said Hooter, rubbing his bill. 'Thank you, Constable, you may join the others now.'

Thomas joined his comrades, leaving Hooter outside alone with his thoughts. He waddled back to The Square which by now had returned to its normal state of hustle and bustle. Most of the tables outside the café were taken; couples and singles, mostly mallards, but none with blue eyes that did not belong.

Ten minutes to ten in the morning, overcast skies of battleship grey loitered low over the moorland. The rain in the night had cleansed and smoothed the sand ready for the new day, but Mother Nature could do little hide the occasional plastic drink bottle or empty crisp wrappers left behind by a certain type of animal.

At one minute to ten a black MPV pulled up by the five bar gate at the Golden Hill entrance to the common. A young soldier stepped from his sentry box and walked towards the driver's side of the car; the windows were moderately tinted. He was two paces away from the car when the driver's window slid down to reveal Kate looking out at him.

'Good morning, madam. Do you have business here?' the soldier asked.

Kate was about to reply when a sand-coloured army lorry came to a halt behind her. Looking in her rear-view mirror, Kate watched as Walter jumped down from the passenger side of the cab. Somehow he even managed to make desert-camo battledress look smart. 'Good morning, private,' he called, making his way towards the sentry.

'Good morning, sir,' replied the soldier.

Walter took his identity card from his chest pocket and offered it to the soldier to check. The soldier had never met Walter in person before, but he recalled seeing him from time to time in garrison. 'Thank you, sir,' he said, also noting the familiar insignia on the front fender of the lorry.

'Thank you, sir,' he said again as he returned the ID card. 'You were involved in the bash out here a few days ago weren't you? A weird do that.'

'Weird indeed, Private,' replied Walter. 'If you would let me and the lady in the car through, we have some reconnoitring to do on the far side of Golden Hill…here is her pass.' Walter offered the pass with Kate's image and details all looking very official.

'Very good, sir,' the soldier replied, taking a camera from his tunic. 'Sorry sir, but rules are rules, you understand.' He first snapped a shot of each pass, and then the front of each vehicle. 'Thank you, sir,' he said, handing back both passes and opening the new gate.

Walter caught Kate's eye, 'Follow me'.

The cab door shut with a resounding thud and the lorry awoke with a fulsome rumble. After some brisk working with the steering wheel, Walter's driver led the way through the gate and onto the common in the same direction the horse and wagon had taken a few days earlier. The damp track offered up no dust to hinder Kate's view following close behind.

A couple of minutes later the lorry stopped and fell silent on a promontory overlooking miles of moorland spread out below. Walter jumped down and beckoned by hand. Kate smiled in return and got out of her car. Although not in battledress, her beige cargo pants and white cardigan seemed to add the oneness of their presence.

The pair of them now stood on top of the bunker where Walter had first met Abel Nogg.

'Wow, quite a view,' exclaimed Kate.

'It certainly is,' Walter replied. 'This is where I met Abel

Nogg on the day of the battle.'

'Right here on top of this bunker?'

'Yes, right here where we are standing right now.'

The cool morning air offered no haze to impede their view for miles around. 'Do you see right over there?' Walter pointed to a distant tree line on the far side of the common.

Kate followed his aim and brought a pair of binoculars up to her eyes.

Walter went on, 'Can you see the timbered wall to the right of the trees?'

From such a distance the wall barely stood out, ancient timbers blending in with their surroundings.

'Is that it, is that **the** timbered wall?' said Kate.

'Doesn't look much from here does it,' Walter replied. 'But I think that must be where they all went through, or somewhere near there.'

'You think?' said Kate. 'So you didn't actually see them disappear.'

'Not exactly,' Walter sighed. 'I could see the mercenaries lined out on this side of the common with their rifles aimed across to the far side. I think their leader was a sergeant but I'm not absolutely certain of that. Their uniforms were in such a terrible state it was difficult to see who they were at all.' Walter's eyes scanned near and far to get his bearings. 'The horse and wagon were almost at the wall on the far side. The horse pulling the wagon looked like a chestnut coloured Suffolk type – really heavily built.'

Kate nodded, knowing exactly who Walter was talking about.

The captain added, 'But then a shot rang out from one of the mercenaries…the horse stumbled. I thought he'd been hit, but he got back onto his feet and kept going. An incredibly strong creature.'

Kate stared dreamily into the far distance, images filled her mind, images of the beautiful Suffolk Punch trying to do what was right regardless of the cost to himself.

Walter continued, 'I'm sure one of the mercenaries was about to fire again when our helicopter buzzed along their line, really low. The dust was horrendous, no one could see a thing for a full minute. When the dust settled, the horse and wagon and its occupants were nowhere to be seen.'

'Hmm,' Kate replied, 'Abel Nogg had given them the Amulet, the key to the timbered wall; that is how they passed through.'

Walter gestured with an outstretched arm. 'Do you see the open land between here and the far trees?'

'Yes, two miles away, I'd say,' replied Kate.

'That is where the battle took place. One hundred mercenaries lined out along this side, and one hundred horses lined out on the other side, facing them.'

'And each horse had a Canada goose aboard?'

'Yes,' said Walter. 'Each time a soldier fired his rifle there would be a pause of no more than five seconds before the bullet whistled past me from behind and took down the soldier who had fired it.' Walter drew his breath, knowing that what he was about to say would probably sound too incredible, even to someone with Kate's knowledge. 'I know it's hard to believe, but I'm pretty sure each bullet went right around the world and returned to the breech from which it had been fired; passing through the soldier to get there.'

Kate slid her hand into Walter's. 'We both know that with Mother Nature's help, anything is possible.'

Relieved, but not surprised by Kate's open minded attitude, Walter smiled and said, 'Leave your car here, Kate, we'll take my lorry and have a closer look on the far side.'

Walking back to the lorry, Kate studied Walter's driver who had been waiting patiently behind the wheel. Nature dulled the glare on the windscreen to allow her a good look. *He's young, early twenties I guess.* She climbed up into the cab and settled into the centre seat.

The driver turned and offered a reassuring smile, 'Good morning, ma'am.'

'Good morning,' Kate replied, also with a smile. The air within the cab carried not one atom of discord; it reminded her of when she was in close company with Inspector Hooter and his constables; a comforting air of niceness all around.

'Okay driver, follow the track to the right,' said Walter, 'the timbered wall two miles distant, that's where we want to go.'

'Ay, ay sir,' replied the driver releasing the brake with another smile for good measure.

***

Meanwhile, a few miles away in the little cottage in Longford, Mr Jones called to Polly, 'Come on, boy.' Polly whined anxiously, not wanting to climb aboard the car. 'What's up, mate?' Jones stroked the dog's head reassuringly. Polly groaned and sat firmly on his rear end, adopting the pose of a stubborn donkey.

'You're not hurt are you?' said Jones. 'Let me have a look.' He ran his hands over Polly's sides and back, then down each leg to each foot. Nothing obvious came to light, but the dog sat glued to the spot, refusing to get in the car. Never before had he needed encouragement to go logging, and yet no matter what Jones tried, Polly would not budge.

'Well, we need logs and that's all there is to it, mate, but if you don't want to come you don't have to.'

Polly gave another bark, his voice breaking into a squeal.

Jones got into the car and started the engine. Polly barked repeatedly from in front of the bonnet.

'Out the way, you daft thing.'

Polly barked back, striding back and forth along the front bumper.

The engine stopped and Jones got out. 'Come on,' he said, taking Polly by the collar. 'I guess you don't want to meet that weird bloke we met yesterday. I can't say I blame you. You can wait here indoors, I won't be long.'

The dog stood on his hind legs barking through the lobby window while the car disappeared from view.

A sense of unease filled Jones' head. He would just as soon not return to the common today. 'Besides, there's plenty of time yet to build up our log pile,' he muttered to himself. But the presence within him urged him on, not allowing him to stop and take stock of his own thoughts.

With no dog aboard, the logs could go straight into the back of the car, no need for the trailer. Jones turned off the road onto the track, and needing less turning space than usual was able to travel to within ten paces of where he had met the man in the hat the day before. He switched off the engine and sat for a while staring through the windscreen. There seemed to be no one about apart from the birds discussing the day's topics in the trees above.

He hated being alone. His tenant would come crashing to the forefront of his mind, pounding his head from the inside and taunting him by inducing paranoid thoughts of such strength as to distort his entire outlook on life. He could never confide when in the company of others, but none the less he would usually gain comfort from the closeness of another soul.

With his brain on autopilot he rummaged through the undergrowth, gathering fallen timber until the rear of the car was filled up to the bottom of the windows. *That'll do for today.*

He finished his coffee alone before walking to the top of the rise where the trees thinned out. Staring down at his feet he could see where Polly had uncovered the strange find the day previously. The rain had tidied up after them, leaving little sign of any digging. Jones looked up to the heavens and sighed, 'Please let me go.' No answer came, just the continued birdsong. He lowered his sight and noticed movement on the far side of the common; an army lorry with two people standing in front of it, barely visible. He returned his attention to the soil beneath his feet and dropped to his knees. He was about to start digging again.

'I knew you would be back.' A voice from behind sent a chill down Jones' spine.

***

Walter and Kate trod carefully about the timbered wall. 'There's no sign of any activity here,' said Walter.

'The rain would have erased any tracks several times over by now,' Kate replied.

'But there must be some giveaway, some clue.' Walter held his chin in his hand, deep in thought.

Kate smiled at him, giving way to a brief giggle.

'What?' said Walter, wondering what could have caused Kate such amusement.

'You remind me of someone I met recently,' said Kate, her pupils widening.

'Someone good, I hope.'

Kate conjured up images of Inspector Hooter rubbing his bill in the same way that Walter rubbed his chin. 'Oh yes, very good.'

The driver leaned out of his window and called, 'Sir.'

'Yes?' Walter replied.

'Over there in the bushes, at the far end of the wall,' the driver pointed.

Walter and Kate moved closer. 'What on Earth?' said Walter plucking an extremely large feather from the undergrowth, light grey in colour and as long as his arm.

Kate's eyes lit up, accompanied by a radiant smile. '**That,** if I'm not mistaken, is from beneath a mallard's wing.'

'Look here.' Walter delved among the lower regions of the bush. 'Broken branches and twigs. It looks like there's been some sort of fight here.'

'Harold,' whispered Kate.

'Harold?' said Walter. 'Who is Harold?'

'Harold Waters-Edge is one of the mallards from the other side of the wall, through the ether.'

'What makes you think this belongs to him?' Walter waved the feather in the air. 'It's fantastic.'

'So are the mallards,' Kate replied keenly. 'I remember Harold saying how he and Inspector Orange had fought by the wall, he must have lost the feather in the struggle.'

'Well, if the mallards are to the same scale as the Canada geese I saw, this could easily be his; he must have had a wingspan of five metres or more.'

'About that,' Kate replied. 'If I told you that on the other side of this wall is a police force comprising mallards who stand almost as tall as you, and are led by an inspector who holds his bill whenever he thinks hard about something, in the same way that you hold your chin…would you believe me?'

Walter chuckled a reply, 'You'll be telling me next they were called the "Flying Squad".' He laughed out loud at such a notion.

Kate raised an eyebrow and giggled. 'They are.'

Walter cut her short and reached up to a damaged branch hanging from a neighbouring pine tree. 'If I'm not mistaken,' he said, closely examining the split fibres of the branch, 'there seems to be a bullet buried in here. It must be the shot the mercenary fired at the horse, and missed...so I didn't imagine it.'

'Oh, don't worry, Captain, I have no doubt it happened just as you recall,' said Kate.

'But if it's true, why would they venture through into this world? It can't have been by accident, surely.'

'It wasn't,' said Kate in a more sombre tone. 'They were tricked by the devious act of an evil mind who took advantage of Mother Nature in her moment of need.'

The two of them sat in the sand while Kate explained how the body of the deceased Bog came to be buried in this world, and how it fell to the mallards from the other side to try to recover it.

It took fifteen minutes for them to put together their various pieces of the jigsaw, after which they sat in silence, each building a picture of events in their minds.

'Hand me your binoculars please, Kate,' Walter whispered.

She drew the strap from beneath her long black hair. 'Here you are; what have you seen?'

'I'm not sure,' Walter replied, studying a particular group of trees high on the north side of the common. 'Does that look like someone we know?' he said, offering the binoculars back to Kate.

'It's Helkendag, but who is that with him?'

'Suppose we take a quiet walk up there to find out,' said Walter turning to his driver. 'Take the lorry and get as close as you can to that high ground to your left, see it?'

'Yes sir.'

'We'll walk round to the right and see how close we can get without being spotted.'

'Ay ay, sir.' The driver duly started the lorry and made his way back to the road, leaving Kate and Walter to hike the mile or so using the cover of the trees as much as possible.

***

Mr Jones, still on his knees, looked up at the man in the hat and said, 'It's none of my business, but who are you?'

'Me? I am the one you listen to day and night; this is me in the flesh, so to speak.'

Jones froze to the spot. How could this real person be the entity which had plagued him for almost all his life? But if there was no truth in what the stranger had said, how could he speak of being listened to day and night, how could he know of such things?

'Say something,' said the man. 'We cannot stay here all day in silence.'

'Tell me who you are,' Jones repeated, rather more desperately than before.

'Is a name important?' replied the man. 'All you need to know is that I know all about you. I know about your weaknesses, which let's face it are many. I also know of your needs, which you seem to have no idea of.' The man laughed mockingly.

In an attempt to draw back from confrontation, Jones asked, 'How is your arm?'

The man extended his arm to show his wrist; the teeth marks were very evident and raw looking. 'How is your dog? I see he is not here today, not unwell I hope.'

Jones reeled while trying to sort his muddled thoughts into some sort of order. My mind can't manifest itself like this. They are only thoughts, he can't be real.

'You don't look too well yourself,' the man in the hat sneered.

Jones did what he usually did; he turned away submissively. The adrenaline coursing through his body made him feel sick. His mind filled with thoughts of hatred, mostly for himself.

The man laughed at him. 'This game is so easy, especially with people like you.'

Jones stopped and turned with tears in his eyes.

The man in the hat glared at him with black orbs and a tombstone smile, but his taunting was cut short when a distant twig unintentionally raised the alarm. Cautious footsteps approached on the soft earth.

Jones looked to his right to see a man and a woman appearing stealthily over the brow. Jones kept his gaze on them, glad of the interruption.

The young man and woman acknowledged him with a wave and a smile. 'Good morning,' they called together.

'Hello,' Jones replied.

'You look like you've been busy,' said Walter nodding towards the back of the car.

Jones looked first to the car and then quickly to the rise where the man in the hat had stood.

'Have you lost something?' asked Kate.

'No,' replied Jones. 'I thought there was someone there, that's all.'

Both Kate and Walter noticed the drawn look of anxiety on Jones' face. They moved closer while looking all around hoping to see Helkendag hiding among the bushes, but they knew hiding in such a manner was beneath him – he had simply vanished.

'We thought we saw you talking to someone as we climbed

the hill, has he gone?' Kate asked casually.

Jones paused while a thousand confused thoughts wreaked havoc from within. *How could they have seen him if he's only in my imagination?* He forced his speech onward trying to appear as normal as he could. 'I usually have my dog with me, but he had a bit of bother with a walker up here yesterday and wasn't keen to come out today; so here I am all alone.'

'Well, we won't take up any more of your time,' said Kate, softly.

Her tenderness was not lost on Jones.

'Goodbye, see you again perhaps?' said Walter.

'Perhaps,' said Jones, watching them continue along the narrow track before disappearing among the trees.

Feeling dazed and confused, Jones made his way back to his car and drove off. He barely noticed the sand-coloured lorry as he squeezed passed it along the track. Back onto the road, he would soon be home, his mind not registering any of his journey. At least Polly would have a warm welcome for him.

11

In the world of the water birds, sitting in the front room of number seven, Aano put down the book he was reading and stared through the window. Inky shapes of blue and black slowly trudged across the sky.

Al Orange stirred restlessly in his bed in the next room, never quite managing to fall asleep. He had lain there for an hour or more since breakfast. 'Oh,' he groaned. 'I'm getting uncomfortable in here, Aano. I think I need to get up and walk around for a while.'

'Okay,' replied Aano placing a dried leaf between the pages of his book. *Nice bookmark.*

The inspector swung his legs off the side of the bed and sat upright. The confines of the room did not quite allow a full stretch; his wings spread from wall to wall curling up at each end, narrowly missing the pictures hanging there.

'My word,' said Aano, amazed at the true beauty of the mallard's plumage on full display.

The mallard held his wings open for several seconds to let the air in, each feather a work of art, interfacing seamlessly with the one next to it.

Aano smiled in wonderment, studying the subtle colour changes from greys to whites with sharp blue flashes through each wing. 'All perfectly symmetrical,' he whispered, 'I'm sure no craftsman could ever touch Mother Nature when it comes to making things.'

'Pardon?' said Al Orange.

'Oh, nothing.' Aano replied, 'I was just saying how magnificent your plumage is; your feathers are perfectly perfect.' He then looked down at his own covering of thick ginger hair which seemed to sprout in every direction with no particular plan in mind. 'I suppose I would look silly covered in feathers like you.'

Al Orange managed a smile of sorts. 'They say beauty is in the eye of the beholder.'

'Hmm, I suppose so.' Aano tried in vain to smooth his hair down on his head.

'Thank you for staying with me through the night,' said Orange.

'Don't mention it,' replied the ape, 'it was nice not to need a hat for once.'

'What's that book you're reading?' asked Orange.

'Oh, I found it beside the track on the way here, I can't imagine where it came from. It's a novel about an ape whose parents are killed in a big city somewhere, and he's brought up by a family of humans; it's quite amusing, not that it would ever happen of course. It's called Zantar of the humans.'

'I can't imagine a human doing anything nice for any other animal, at least not from what I've seen of them in their world.'

'I know what you mean. Anyway, enough of that, how are you feeling today?' Aano asked, chirpilly.

'Battered and exhausted,' the mallard sighed. 'I just wish the pressure in my head would ease up for a minute. I really can't remember what it is to have a clear thought of my own.'

Aano put a long arm around the mallard's shoulder. 'You know you can tell me anything if it will help – in total confidence of course.' His sparkling brown eyes exuded honesty which the inspector gladly caught and held on to, knowing as he did the ape to be the truest friend a soul could ever have.

'Thank you, Mr Grunt; but it's so difficult to speak of what is inside me; the words just won't come out.' Orange's voice developed a noticeable tremor. 'You see, even now something is gagging me, pressing against the backs of my eyes, forbidding me from giving anything away. He taunts me even when I'm in others' company.'

'Who does?'

'Him…this thing inside me' Orange replied with wetting eyes.

'There, there, Inspector; don't upset yourself.' Aano patted the mallard gently on the back. 'As far as I can see, you have at least two things in your favour.'

'And what are they?'

'Time and friends,' Aano replied. 'Don't try to rush things, your friends will always be here for you.'

The inspector set his wings tightly and neatly by his sides. 'Could we have a walk around the yard outside to get some fresh air?'

'Of course, I think that's an excellent idea,' said Aano leading the way.

Al Orange waddled while Aano loped with his arms in the air. The yard was peaceful with only the chatter of a squirrel trying to make his point while a small blackbird sang for the sake of singing, to the pleasure of all who could hear them.

The ape and the mallard stood in the centre of the yard enjoying the fresh air.

'Isn't this wonderful,' said Aano. 'Our trip into the humans' world has certainly made me appreciate how beautiful our own world is.'

'But theirs is the same as ours in essence,' Al Orange replied.

'Then why didn't it smell right, and why were they all so angry?'

'And why did every other living creature fear the humans?' Al Orange added.

'Hmm,' Aano rubbed the top of his head. 'It makes you wonder what the little humans here think about us.'

They both stared at the clouds which, still heavily laden with water, were struggling to stay more than three trees high.

'I wonder where Mother Nature is going to drop that lot?' said the mallard. He turned to Aano as if wanting to ask something of him.

'Would you like to walk a little further?' asked the ape.

'Yes,' replied Al Orange, 'that would be nice.'

'Let's just walk up to the top of the road; we can sit on the grass and watch the world go by while we chat about anything you want.'

They covered the first hundred paces in silence before Aano spoke up: 'You are still very troubled aren't you.'

Before Orange could reply, his chest cramped and his throat closed in rebellion. Unable to say anything, he eased a little closer to the ape beside him, the very ape who he had tried to shoot, punch and generally assault on more than one occasion previously, yet now his mind clung on to the very presence of him, a creature who knew no animosity, nor did he bear a grudge of any sort.

The mallard's stomach began to heave anxiously, his chest tightened even more and a lump set hard in his throat. The tenant within him was not happy at the prospect of facing an inquisition of any sort, especially one by an intellectual such as Aano Grunt.

'Here we are.' Aano wandered off the track and sat down on the soft grass. Al Orange followed suit, groaning under the

106

weight of the unrest inside him.

Aano was unsure of what to say, so he put a long arm around the mallard once again. He could feel the trembling beneath the bird's plumage. 'Just relax,' he said quietly.

Orange could contain the anguish no longer; his mind screamed in silence, his soul poured tears into his heart. He looked straight into the ape's eyes and burst into tears, blubbering openly. 'By the Great Duck,' he cried, 'what is happening to me?'

***

In Davidsmeadow, Inspector Hooter peered through his office window; rain fell gently onto the pavement outside, quickly giving it a gloss finish. He looked up at the clouds. 'Hmm, an hour or two's worth of precipitation at a guess.' He took his officer's cap from the hat stand, and after ensuring it was perfectly straight on his head he left his office for the front desk. 'I'm going for a stroll around the town, just to see that everything is as it should be.'

'Okay sir,' replied Constable Roberts. 'Thomas and James are out on their town beat at the moment, you might come across them.'

'Thank you, Constable, I shan't be more than an hour.'

Hooter closed the door behind him and made his way towards the town centre. 'That feels good,' he said, the rain running in beads over his plumage before falling unimpeded to the ground.

He rounded the corner and paused while surveying the scene. On each side of The Square was a café, each with chairs and tables on the pavement for the customers to eat and drink 'al fresco' style, as is the preference of birds. Birds of many kinds could be seen, although mallards were by far in the majority. The subdued light could not dull the drakes' wonderful iridescent heads of green and blue. A group of Canada geese were engaged in idle gossip by the statue in the centre of The Square, while a couple of male gadwall ducks stood window shopping by the furniture store. *They're nice looking birds*, Hooter thought to himself, *similar to us mallards but not as colourful, very delicate plumage though – and nice natured too.*

He took his time to scan the outside tables; one hosted a family of coots and another a couple of moorhens, while around another sat two splendid looking shelducks in their startling black, white and tan plumage. *Probably strayed off course or perhaps looking up old friends before heading overseas.* The shelducks were indeed attracting a lot of admiring glances from the locals, but that was nothing compared to the heart-stopping jolt that hit Hooter right in the chest in the very next moment. *It's her!* He stopped in his tracks when he caught sight of the newly arrived lady mallard sitting alone outside the café nearest him. 'Mustn't stare,' he whispered, casting the occasional glance away in any direction, but quickly coming back to her.

Seemingly oblivious to the inspector's presence, she sat with perfect posture, stirring her tea.

Hooter remained where he was, stealing short glimpses between looking away nonchalantly.

The lady duck turned to get the attention of the proprietor.

Oh dear, she's asking for the bill, she must be leaving. Hooter was unsure what to do, but his heart overruled him and he found himself waddling towards her, not knowing what he would say when he got there.

She looked up before Hooter had reached her table; her eyes rocketed to his heart, spearing him on the inside. Never had he felt so vital, so spirited. He didn't care that he had no idea of what to say, he just wanted the moment to last a little longer.

'Please, sit,' she said, offering a shortened wing.

'Thank you, madam,' Hooter replied, nervously taking the chair opposite her. The proprietor promptly returned and placed a cup of tea in front of him. 'Is this for me?' Hooter quizzed, 'I didn't order one.'

'I ordered it for you,' said the beautiful lady mallard.

'Oh, thank you,' said Hooter, still stumped for words.

Her eyes smiled at him and caressed his anxious brow from across the table.

Hooter's conservative reserve was being tested to the limit. *Oh, please let the world stop and never start again so this feeling can last for ever.* The little duck deep inside him whooped and jumped with delight for only the second time in his entire life.

'I hope I guessed right,' said the female, softly.

'Eh, pardon?' said Hooter, dreamily.

'The tea – I hope it's to your liking.'

'Oh, of course.' Hooter finally came back to Earth and adjusted his cap to ensure it was still perfectly straight. 'Good morning, madam; my name is Inspector Hooter.'

'It's nice to meet you, Inspector – I'm Dana.'

'Erm, I've not seen you in these parts before, are you just passing through?'

'That depends on what I find here,' said Dana. 'I see from your cap badge you are a police duck.'

'Yes,' replied Hooter sipping from his cup and taking care not to dribble.

'Which branch?'

'The Flying Squad,' said Hooter obligingly. 'My squad is stationed here but we travel all over. I'm also Temporary Inspector to the Armed Response Ducks while their leader is on sick leave.'

'That's fascinating,' said Dana.

Hooter had never known a mallard to exhibit such striking blue eyes, finding them very easy to rest in. He was not sure, but he thought he felt something moving gently through his mind, searching without disturbing the furniture, so to speak.

'Well, I'm afraid I must be on my way, Inspector.'

'Of course.' Hooter hurriedly finished his tea and pushed his cup closer to hers. He then rose from his chair and eased Dana's chair away as she got up from the table.

'Quite the gentleduck are you,' she said. 'It's always nice to see a bird with manners.'

Hooter blushed. 'Perhaps we'll meet again, if you're passing this way?'

'I'm sure we shall,' Dana replied. She turned and waddled with a smooth rocking action down the street before disappearing around the corner.

So beautiful, Hooter thought. *And what a strange perfume*; he inhaled quietly until the air had let go of the last vestige of her presence. *So beautiful.*

12

Back at Kate's car, Walter turned and asked, 'Before you go would you follow me for a moment?' They both jumped down from the cab and Walter led her to the edge of the escarpment once again. The pair of them stared in silence across the expanse of moorland spread out beneath them. The sand, the gorse and the heather all seemed at peace; Mother Nature had tended to them to ensure no mere mortal should ever suspect what had gone on just a few days earlier.

Walter spoke in hushed tones. 'Where did those mercenaries come from?'

'And who was their leader?' said Kate. 'Surely not the sergeant.'

'No, there must be someone far more senior than him behind the scenes.'

They looked each other in the eye saying nothing, but one name in particular came to mind.

'I wonder if there are more of them,' Kate mused, 'and if there are, where are they hiding?'

'Let's tot up what we know so far,' said Walter. 'I think we can assume that the horse and wagon along with the orangutan and the mallard did make it back to their world.'

Walter's words went vaguely unheard while Kate's attention hung in the air. She cast her mind back to Walter's earlier account and imagined one hundred horses each with a Canada goose on top, facing one hundred rifles held by one hundred heartless souls. 'And you say no one witnessed the battle?'

'No one except me,' said Walter. 'That was how Abel Nogg wanted it. I was the only one to see the fate of the wrong-doers, as he put it.'

'What about all the animal life? Surely they would have suffered along with the soldiers when the land rose up.'

'That's the strange thing,' Walter replied. 'They were somehow ushered away beforehand and returned after the battle. It was as if they knew what was about to happen.'

'Amazing,' said Kate. She paused with her chin in her hand. 'These events shouldn't really surprise us; after all, we know anything is possible, and to be honest I can't help thinking this isn't the end of the matter.'

'I think you're right,' Walter replied. 'We must remain vigilant for anything out of the ordinary, especially around Davidsmeadow and across the common.'

'It's not easy when we don't really know what we're looking for,' said Kate.

With a creased brow showing his concern, Walter added, 'Above all else we must be very wary of Mr Helkendag; if he is who we suspect he is he could ruin everything.'

'He's incredibly strong, and very devious,' said Kate, 'he always seems to be one step ahead of events.'

Walter gently squeezed Kate's hand. 'We mustn't forget we are here to observe and report. We're not supposed to get too involved with these people; so we'll just see how things work out and maybe lend a little hand if we can.'

Kate smiled, glad of Walter's company and support in what she knew were about to become very dangerous times. She focused on the far side of the common once again. 'The human we met at the top of the rise, what do you make of him?'

'Hmm,' Walter replied, resisting the urge to rub his chin. 'He certainly seemed troubled, but I think he's just another soul who's struggling to find his way; you know as well as I do there are millions of them in this world.'

'There was something about his demeanour though,' Kate pondered deeply for a few seconds. 'He reminded me of someone – the way he spoke, and his mannerisms.'

'He certainly seemed surprised when we asked about the stranger he was with.'

'Yes,' said Kate, 'he didn't deny seeing him, but he didn't want to talk about him either for some reason.'

'If he's a creature of habit, like so many humans are, it might be worth us revisiting the same spot tomorrow to see if he returns. A little more questioning might throw some new light on things.' Walter released Kate's hand and turned towards his lorry. 'We could take another look at the timbered wall while we're there.'

'Okay, sounds good,' said Kate heading for her car.

They parted company, each with a lingering sparkle in their incredibly blue eyes, and a desire to do the right thing.

***

In the world of the water birds, PC James looked across the office desk. 'A right corker if ever I saw one,' he said.

'Who was?' replied PC Roberts.

'The lady duck Tom and I saw sitting outside Café Hero earlier.'

'Really?' Roberts shared his interest with his colleagues, all eager to hear more.

James quickly went on, 'She was a mallard – but she was even more beautiful than most.' He wasn't sure if he should say the next bit for fear of being ridiculed for talking daft, but he couldn't help himself. 'She had the most amazing eyes.'

'Amazing – how?' asked Roberts.

'They were blue, really bright shiny blue.'

The rest of the squad laughed at such a notion. 'Bright blue? I've heard some dopey things in my time,' replied Russell on behalf of his mates. 'But a mallard with bright blue eyes? Come off it, James; we're not that dippy.'

Just then the station door opened and Inspector Hooter stepped in after shaking the raindrops from his plumage.

'I can't believe it,' he said all of a fluster. 'I've just seen the most beautiful lady mallard in the world, right here in Davidsmeadow; sitting at a table outside Café Hero.'

The constables waited with eager anticipation; it had been a long time since their inspector expressed such exuberance. 'Brilliant blue,' he exclaimed.

PC James smiled and nodded knowingly at his companions. 'There, you see, I told you.'

The squad remained silent. Bright blue eyes, on a mallard?

'Not just any old blue,' Hooter added, 'but the most incredible blue you ever did see.'

'On a scale of one to ten, sir, just how blue would you say?' asked Roberts.

'Oh, at least a ten, if not more,' Hooter replied without hesitation. 'In fact I would even go so far as to say twenty out of ten.'

'As blue as Abel Nogg's, sir?' asked Constable Peters.

Hooter had to stop and think for a moment. *Hmm, they really are unbelievably blue.* 'Well, I'm not sure if anything else can be as blue as that, but they were very close; most definitely the next bluest thing without a doubt. And absolutely not normal for a mallard, not even the most beautiful one in the world, which she most certainly is.'

'Wow,' the young constables replied, amazed at their inspector's change of character.

'Do you know where she's from, sir?' asked Russell, keen to keep the inspector's pecker up.

'No, Constable, I didn't get chance to ask before she upped and left.'

'You did talk to her, though?'

'Oh yes,' replied Hooter, sounding like the squirrel that got the nut, 'all in the line of duty, you understand.'

'Oh yes, of course, sir.'

'I hope to continue my investigations tomorrow; you never know, she might decide to stay in the area.' Hooter waddled into his office and closed the door behind him and immediately broke into a jaunty whistle, as much as a duck can whistle that is.

The constables looked at each other, cheered by the obvious joy in their leader's heart.

'Amazing, and him a grown up duck, too,' said PC Thomas.

'On with your work, Constables, on with your work,' the inspector called from behind his closed door, with a twinkle in his eye.

***

Shortmoor was still waiting for the rain from Davidsmeadow to arrive. The clouds above Al Orange and Aano Grunt continued on their way, saving themselves for a distant horizon where perhaps they were needed more urgently. Orange had settled down on the grass with his head partially buried beneath his wing. Aano sat patiently next to him, the soles of his feet turned in and his fingers twiddling as they were prone to do in times of poignancy.

Being an ape of high intellect, Aano tried to analyse the

inspector's dilemma. The world according to Aano was a straight-forward one in which just about everything could be figured out, right down to the very last detail. He could usually see why things were and why they were the way they were and when they were. In his head there were always options, but he could always narrow things down to just one best way. His capacity for always seeing the kindest way and thinking of other's feelings provided the basis for his reasoning. No matter how hard he tried, he could never harbour ill feelings towards another creature, regardless of their breed. So he sat and pondered Inspector Orange's troubles: *Some folk would simply say the Inspector's troubles were all in his head, but that is of no value at all. Of course it's all in his head, after all, everything anyone thinks is in their head, that's what heads are for – thinking. The problem comes when your head doesn't think what you want it to think, but why should that be? How can a person's head not think what they want? I know it happens because I've seen it for myself and not just in the inspector.* Aano was quite satisfied with his reasoning so far, so he continued to think a little more: *I'm quite sure that when a creature is born it has no nastiness in it, none at all, so the question has to be, when and why do things start to turn nasty?* He decided this would be a good time to rub the top of his head to create an artificial pause. His hair, also being of high intellect, rose quite literally to the occasion by standing on end, each strand smiling cordially to the next. After a fruitless attempt to smooth the hair back down he defaulted to his comfort pose. With his chin resting in his cupped hands he found himself drifting off into the land of the fairies, wherever that might be. His pose reminded him of the lovely Kate Herrlaw, *She always held her chin when she was deep in thought.* He recalled the purity of her smile and her homely smell. *Oh, lovely Kate.* A broad grin set on his face while his dreamy eyes stared wistfully into space. *Oh, beautiful Kate.* He very nearly found himself wishing he were a human, *Perhaps then I might have half a chance of getting to know her better.* But the thought of being human instantly sent a shiver down his spine. *Oh dear me no, what am I thinking? They're the last creature I would want to be; covered in bare skin, how daft is that? It doesn't make any sense, what good is bare skin? If you're going to have skin you might as well have feathers or hair growing out of it, or what is the point?* Another grin washed across his face at the thought of himself with no hair, just bare skin. *Oh yuk, that's disgusting.* It took a vigorous shake of the head to banish such absurd thoughts before he settled back down to continue his appraisal of Al Orange's predicament. *I know he doesn't want to feel the way he does, that much is obvious. And I know he doesn't mean to be horrid to others…so why is he?* He turned his attention to himself for a moment. *What could possibly make **me** behave like that?* The ape tried as hard as he could to imagine someone doing something so awful that he would feel obliged to resort to nastiness himself. *It's no use, there is nothing in the world that would make me behave badly, nothing at all.* His mind then went off on a different tack. *Never mind the bad tempers he has, what about the dreadful depression he suffers from, what could possibly cause that? I wonder if the inspector can pinpoint a precise time when his head changed.*

Aano's train of thought was interrupted when Orange slowly opened his eyes and lifted his head from his chest. 'How long have I been asleep?' he mumbled.

'Oh, not long, ten minutes or so, that's all.' After a further minute of silence Aano continued in a gentle voice, 'Would you say you were in good physical health, Inspector?'

'What? Oh, yes, I suppose so, why do you ask?'

'And what about your personal needs, are they satisfied?'

Orange could see where this dialogue was going and did not much care for it, but he knew the ape was only trying to help so he went along with his line of questioning. 'My dear ape, I have

117

everything a mallard could possibly need.'

'Yes, I can see how you might have everything you **need**, but what about what you **want**; do you have everything you would like?'

'If you have everything you need,' Orange replied, 'what more could you possibly want? From the way you're talking anyone would think I was a human being.'

Aano was slightly surprised at the inspector's logical reply. 'But is there something missing that is causing you grief or unhappiness?'

Al Orange gazed up at the sky of many blues, replying dolefully, 'If there is one thing I yearn for it is the company of a good partner.' He stopped short as if there was more he could have said, but decided he had said enough.

Aano knew he hadn't yet got to the bottom of things but thought it time for a brief summation. 'Would you say that not having a partner is the cause of your troubles?'

'Good heavens, no.' The firmness of Orange's answer spoke volumes as he expanded the issue. 'Material things and material doings are nothing to me, they can be thought through and sorted. Life throws stuff at you every day and you deal with it, sometimes with the help of others but sometimes you have to try to sort things yourself.'

Aano was pleased that Orange was at least opening up a little; just a few days ago the mallard would have retaliated in no short measure if anyone had dared to question him on such personal matters, but the ape knew he was getting close to the limit of the inspector's tolerance. 'If you say you have more or less everything a duck could wish for and you are in good health for a duck of your age, how come you feel so awful all of the time?' Aano knew that such a simplistic question was naïve in the extreme and he wished he could retract it before he had even finished saying it.

Orange stared the ape in the face, trying to hide the look of resentment at being asked such a silly question.

'I'm sorry,' said Aano realizing his mistake. He thought carefully before going on. 'If you had just one word to describe how you feel, what would it be?'

A fist not of his making forced its way up through Orange's stomach, making it almost impossible for him to speak, but he so wanted to tell someone, to force this dreadful being out into the world where perhaps it would be consumed by Mother Nature who would be only too pleased to rid her world of one more nasty piece of work. 'There is not a word in our language that comes close to what it's like living inside this head of mine.' Orange rallied one final retort, his emotions now hanging by a thread. 'Tell me, Mr Grunt, what is the most awful, nasty, debilitating, vile, disgusting, foul, heinous, evil word you can think of?'

'Oh, erm,' Aano cupped his chin trying desperately to think of an answer. 'To be honest, Inspector, I can't think of a word any worse than those you've just used.'

'Well there you have it, my friend. Those words piled up together won't even begin to describe how I feel.'

'But you must know why you feel the way you do, surely.'

Orange's eyes finally overflowed. 'That's enough for now', he said. 'I know you are only trying to help, but believe me, there is nothing anyone can do.' The tears ran down his cheeks. 'I am lost and I don't think I will be coming back from this…not this time.'

Al Orange rose to his feet and without saying another word he began the walk back to the park. Aano followed close behind, hoping he hadn't made matters worse by pressing the inspector so.

Before long, the two of them were back in the confines of number seven. Orange immediately made his way into the bedroom and fell onto the bed, hardly raising the energy to make himself comfortable.

***

The sombre light of evening now cosseted Davidsmeadow. Most of the residents had retired to their homes for the night, leaving just a few to take a late stroll in the cooling air. In the police station, Constables Russell and Peters were preparing to walk the final beat of the day while the rest of the squad settled in the dormitory, glad of the chance of an early night.

***

Meanwhile, back in Smallbeef, Inspector Orange had been dozing restlessly for a couple of hours. Aano grew more concerned with each passing hour. I can keep watch over him from without, but what can I do to protect him from whatever is stalking him from within? He carefully lay a blanket over the mallard, loosely tucking it in around the edges. He then stroked the opalescent feathers about the inspector's troubled head, and whispered, 'I think I shall send for Abel Nogg in the morning. I'm sure he'll know what to do. Just rest as best you can tonight, Inspector and don't worry about anything. I'll be right here with you. Sleep tight.'

13

In the world of the humans, the Moon played hide and seek among the passing clouds above Longford. Mr Jones lay in bed, sorely in need of sleep but not of the troubled sort that he knew awaited him behind closed eyes. He could not remember what it was to sleep undisturbed without paranoia and self-loathing keeping him company. Resting on his back, he tried to keep his eyes open for as long as possible in the hope of falling asleep the moment they closed. His bed had room for two, but it had been a while since his partner had taken up with another; younger and more interesting, apparently. *If nothingness were water, I would have drowned long ago. But drowning has an end. Oh Lord, why can't I see an end? A journey is not worth making if there is no end in sight.* Tears loitered in his eyes, queueing eagerly and waiting to spill over, reminding him that he was at least human, although a very poor specimen in his opinion. In silence he waited for his unwelcome dream to come visiting once again.

***

Through the ether and a couple of miles to the west, Al Orange was also having a bad night. He too stared up at the ceiling, not really caring what the night had in store for him; he had all but given up the fight. By the Great Duck, let this be over. If nothingness were water I would have drowned long ago; please let it end. He sobbed in near silence, not wishing to disturb

Aano who was dozing in the next room, doing his best to keep watch. But that which stalked the inspector would not be troubled by the eyes or ears of an ape, not even one as caring and diligent as an orangutan.

The inspector's eyes slowly closed. Mr Jones' eyes slowly closed. Two minds in two different worlds, about to become acquainted in the same dream.

***

The heavy oak door opens again; Jones stands at the threshold staring in to the poorly lit room. The occupants are all the same as the night before, the same shabby coats dragging the floor, the same featureless faces looking nowhere; perhaps they too have given up on life and can see no point in looking anymore. Jones steps cautiously into the room. He peers across to the table on his left, there is no one there, no one nasty with sickly eyes and sour breath. "But he's always there, why isn't he there tonight?" Jones is now standing in the centre of the room. No one acknowledges his presence, he's just another nobody, worthless and not worthy of the briefest glance. But something catches his eye, a hint of colour among the mottled drabs of grey and khaki. A head that does not belong here, "Who is it – and why?"

***

Al Orange is also back in the room. "Who are all these people?" He is hemmed in on all sides by strangers as tall as him if not taller. Their smell offends his senses. He is so close to them and yet no detail is evident; no eyes, no nose or bill or mouth. "What are they?" He jostles against those who stand so close as to make turning round difficult, but with a concerted effort he manages to turn himself about.

***

Jones keeps his eye fixed on the spark of colour, a touch of blue, or green perhaps, but certainly not belonging in this dream. Individuals among the silent mob slowly move apart to reveal the newcomer. "A giant duck? In my

122

dream? What…but?"

***

Al Orange deliberately jiggers from side to side to ease the tight fit of the mob. The bodies around him part to reveal a loner standing in the middle of the room, staring disbelievingly at him. Orange returns the incredulous stare. "A human – a real human in my dream. How can this be?"

Jones holds his stare, also at a loss. "What the heck is a giant duck doing in my dream?"

Having made room for the mallard to step out from their huddle, the lost souls of drabness resume their stance, doing and saying nothing. Al Orange and Jones hold each other's gaze, each whispering, "At least he's got a face with eyes."

Jones remains where he is, not wishing to get any closer to the crowd. Al Orange gladly waddles forward, away from the faceless ones. He stops just inches from Jones. Neither one feels threatened by the other, but rather, a sense of likeness warms their hearts, a sensation neither has felt in a long time. They both look to the table by the wall expecting to see their demon sitting there, but the seat is still empty.

Without trying to figure out the meaning of the dream which they are now sharing, Jones whispers to the absurd giant duck. "There is something I must tell you, quickly." But before another word utters forth, a face rises up from the crowd; unlike the others this face has features, eyes, a nose – and a sickening grin. The demon is something else they seem to share. He stares straight at them with a hateful look in his eye.

Jones turns for the door. "Follow me, hurry."

Al Orange unhesitatingly does as he is bid; the pair of them leap down the steps and into the alleyway outside. As always, the air is dank and depressing. They waddle and run as fast as they can, stumbling in the poor light. Jones takes the same route as always. Past the bodies leaning against the damp walls, their faces crying out for help which would only come with their Armageddon. Always a creature of habit, Jones takes the left fork at

123

the end of the alley. They both dare to look back in the hope of not seeing their demon on their heels. The alleyway behind is empty. They return their attention to the front and are confounded by what they see. Heathland is spread before them. Shortmoor Common, a sight familiar to both of them in their own worlds, but never at the end of an alleyway.

"But this doesn't make any sense," says Al Orange, staring at the welcome sight of sand, gorse and grass, "even the Sun is shining – but it's the middle of the night."

"Why does that surprise you?" asks Jones. "Nothing else in our heads makes any sense, so why should this?"

"I suppose not," replies Orange, feeling a compelling sense of oneness with the human who at any other time he would find utterly revolting.

Jones goes on with an urgency in his voice, hoping that he won't need to repeat anything for fear of running out of time. "I know this is just a dream and I don't even know if you are real or not; I guess you're not, otherwise this wouldn't just be a dream."

"But I *am* real," says Orange, "and that figure we saw back there – he was real as well, or at least he was when he was in my head."

Jones replies, "Whether you are real or not, I've got nothing to lose, so here goes."

At an unnatural speed as is often the case in dreams or nightmares, Mr Jones makes his way up the incline towards the spot where he had previously met the unnerving stranger in the suit and hat. Al Orange somehow keeps pace, whether flying or waddling at some unearthly rate he does not know; all that matters is that he and the human are now standing where Polly the dog had recently uncovered the strange find.

Jones rushes his words. "Buried under here is something that doesn't belong; I don't know what it is, I just know it doesn't belong here."

Recalling his recent mission into the strange world of giant humans, Al Orange soon puts two and two together. "I think I know what it is." Using his bill as a shovel in the soft sand, he takes only a minute to reveal what is hidden beneath.

"What is that?" says Jones, looking down at a monstrous clawed hand.

"You wouldn't believe me if I told you," replies Orange.

Jones laughs a nervous laugh. "But I'm standing here talking to a giant mallard, so how much weirder can things get? Of course I'll believe you."

"All right then, just remember that everything I say is absolutely true...." Orange pauses while getting things straight in his head. He begins to explain the strange events of the last few weeks; of how he and others from his world had ventured through the ether into the world of the humans to retrieve the body of the lost Beast of Grey. His expression saddens when he comes to the part where Beeroglad was found dead in the wagon having been mysteriously swapped for the original missing Bog.

Jones butts in. "Are you saying that this thing my dog unearthed is your missing pterosaur?"

"Yes, I'd recognize those claws anywhere," replies Orange with a concerned eye. "I think there was someone working against me and my companions when we were here last; he must have buried the body here after we'd gone." Faces and voices from the past suddenly fill the mallard's head; his demon in many disguises, the voice in the bunker, the man in the room in his dreams, and the man in the hat who keeps appearing when least expected. "Was it the same person all the time? Is he real? Is it a person at all?"

"Are you all right?" Jones asks, worried by the strained look on Orange's face.

Orange replies, "I must get word to my friends, this is important...Wait a minute, what am I saying? This isn't real is it? This is just a dream; you're not real either."

"Of course I'm real," Jones replies, "but I don't know if any of **this** is." He waves his arms in the air. "I think we're both real – but our surroundings aren't."

"Then how do we get out of this?"

"We'll have to retrace our steps – back to that room with the faceless people in."

"But you know who else will be there, he's the last person I want to meet."

"I know that," replies Jones, "I feel the same; every minute of the night and day he's in my head, screwing me up and hating me…but we've got to go back there to get out of this dream."

Without another word being said, the two of them are running back down the alleyway between the high wet walls and past the lost souls sleeping in their own puddles of tears. In record time they are standing before the door of heavy oak. Jones reaches forward, turning the latch and pushing the door inward. The room is as they had left it, full of faceless grey people huddled in groups.

Jones looks at the table to his left where their demon would normally sit.

Al Orange studies the bodies across the room, they move aside as if making space for him to join them.

Relieved that the evil one is not at his table, Jones looks back to Al Orange, but the mallard is nowhere to be seen, swallowed up by the crowd. Horrified at being alone, Jones runs for the door as he has done so many times before. Away down the alley he goes again, his legs never going as fast as they could despite his effort. Again he turns left at the fork, he is screaming now for fear of what is trying to catch him, gaining on him, the wailing is getting louder.

Back inside the room, the faceless ones part once again, Al Orange jostles his way clear of them; he looks around for Jones, he is nowhere to be seen – but the evil one is now at the table and getting to his feet. Now it is Orange's turn to run for the door. Away down the alley as fast as he can waddle. His beautiful feathers brush the sides of the wet walls; desperate bodies cry out for him to wait for them, but he cannot stop. He hears the distant wailing gaining on him. He cries out, louder and louder. "No, no, please leave me alone."

'No, no, please leave me alone.' Jones woke suddenly, startled by his own voice. It was still dark outside; he sat up in his bed, alone and desperate for someone to talk to. Polly appeared at his bedside with his nose sniffing the bedding, curiously.

***

'No, no, please leave me alone.' Al Orange woke with a start, it was still dark outside his window too; he sat up in bed, shaking.

The orangutan comforted him with a gentle hug. 'There, there, Inspector. It was just another nasty dream, don't worry.'

14

'This is so weird,' said Al Orange with a frantic look on his face.

'Was it the same dream as before?' asked Aano.

Orange struggled to gather as much of the dream as he could before it faded into nothingness, as dreams often do. 'It was in the same place with the same people, but there was another person there.' He stared blankly across the room while an image came to the fore. 'A human – yes, there was a proper human in the room, he was as big as me.'

'Was he like the one who haunts you?'

'No, I think he was lost just like me. I'm sure he didn't want to be there any more than I did.' Orange paused again to get his thoughts into some sort of order. 'He spoke to me…yes, I remember now; we somehow ended up on the common beyond Shortmoor. He showed me where his dog had uncovered something at the top of a slope.' A look of anguish sought to overtake the mallard's train of thought. 'I must be quick, or else I'll forget what it was.'

'Take your time,' said Aano, softly sweeping the mallard's feathers over his perfectly rounded head to calm him.

'But I mustn't forget the detail, I mustn't.' Orange fretted, teetering on the brink of tearful despair. 'Oh, what was it, what was it.'

Aano, using his typical ape logic, suggested, 'Just work your way back from where you were when you woke up. Where were you in the dream when you called out?'

'Yes, of course, think backwards.' Orange sniffed back the tears, and then, helped by a positive bout of bill rubbing, he began to put the pieces together. 'We had both gone back to the building in the alleyway, looking for a way out of the dream. That was after we had been on the common; the Sun was shining and the human had shown me the soft sand at the top of a rise near the edge of a line of trees, mostly pine of some sort.' The mallard's recall gathered momentum. 'Yes, we could see quite a way across the common from where we stood. I remember seeing the timbered wall in the far distance. I shovelled some of the sand away and that is when I found something.' He stopped suddenly.

'What was it? What did you find?' said Aano.

Orange's face lit up. 'A huge clawed hand – or foot. I remember it had three massive fingers with long white claws…it was a Beast of Grey…a pterosaur.'

Aano had heard everything the inspector had said, but could it be real or simply a trick of the mallard's troubled subconscious? 'Do you mean to say this human, whoever he was, showed you in your dream where the body of the missing Bog is buried?'

'Yes,' replied Al Orange. 'I can picture where it was, but I must get word to Abel Nogg before I start to lose it in my mind.'

'But the place in your dream might not really exist.'

Al Orange looked Aano square in the eye. 'How many times have you told me to trust my heart over my head?'

Aano rubbed the top of his head while his eyes tried to look inside himself. He had to admit, Inspector Orange had a point. Aano patted the inspector on the shoulder. 'In that case,' he said reassuringly, 'you must rest until morning and then we will get word of your vision to Abel Nogg. He will know what to do, I'm sure.'

Having recalled all he could from the disorderly remains of the night, Al Orange relaxed into the warm bedding while Aano sat in the comfy chair at the end of the bed with his legs crossed and his hands resting in his lap. Soon the pair of them had slipped into a light but restful sleep which was something Al Orange had not experienced in a long time.

***

Mother Nature presented the new dawn with a scattering of light clouds passing casually from west to east. The ducks and geese of Davidsmeadow would soon be making their way out into the world, going peacefully about their business and grateful for the water that had fallen while they slept.

In the police station, Inspector Hooter was first to rise. The sadness he had felt since the loss of his beloved Marion had been tempered by the arrival of a newcomer in town, a most beautiful and enigmatic mallard by the name of Dana Lethgerk. Watching the ever changing assembly in the sky, Hooter wondered, *Where could she possibly have come from? She is most certainly a bird of quality and breeding. Those eyes…I've never seen a mallard with such blue eyes. In fact I've never seen a mallard with blue eyes of any sort at all.* He continued staring through the window, not really paying attention to what was out there. *I suppose she might be some sort of genetic throwback — no, no, that can't be right; throwback sounds like something that isn't quite up to the mark. One thing is for certain, if looks are anything to go by she's well and truly up to the mark — oh yes, well and truly.*

'Good morning, sir.' Constable Thomas had entered from the dormitory, holding his helmet beneath his wing.

'Good morning, Constable,' Hooter replied jauntily. 'Gather

the squad for muster, if you please.'

'Yes sir.'

As usual, Hooter could find nothing out of place to spoil the immaculate appearance of the squad standing before him. 'Well done, Constables. Let's hope today is a peaceful one, there is no reason why it shouldn't be, of course.' He paused with an uncommon twinkle in his eye. The constables thought it most out of character, but their hearts warmed to see their leader clearly happier than he had been of late. He continued with his morning address: 'There is nothing over and above normal duties today, so please keep to the regular patrols and be of help whenever you can.' He halted again, rubbing his bill slowly. 'Erm…and if you should notice the rather attractive newcomer, please let me know – just as a matter of routine.'

'Yes sir,' the squad replied as one, each constable concealing the slightest hint of a smiling bill.

'That's all then, squad dismiss.'

***

Tap tap tap. Marion Waters-Edge stood outside number seven. Aano Grunt opened the door and offered a huge grin at the sight of the tray loaded with tea, biscuits and toast.

'Thank you so much,' said Aano.

'How was your night?' asked Marion.

'Hmm, things were pretty bad at one point, more bad dreams you know – but the inspector seems to think there was a meaning to them.'

'Really?'

Aano relieved Marion of the tray and gestured for her to take a seat at the dining table. Al Orange was now sitting in the armchair looking surprisingly rested compared to his recent demeanour. Aano offered the inspector first pickings from the tea tray before joining Marion at the table.

'Now then, Inspector,' said Marion, 'Mr Grunt has been telling me about your dreams, why don't you tell me more?'

A sip of tea preceded Orange's explanation through eyes which, though tired, seemed to portray a glimmer of hope. 'It was so weird,' he said, 'but my dreams always are. Much of it was the same as before but there was another person…someone else sharing the dream as if they had been there many times before and yet we had never met until last night.'

'Wasn't he just part of your dream?' Marion replied.

'No, that's just it; he was as surprised to see me as I was to see him. He seemed so real, different to all the other people or things that come into my head.'

'Have another sip of tea,' said Marion, not wanting the inspector to get too worked up. 'Take your time, and don't get too excited.'

'Well, it's like I told Mr Grunt in the night. This other person in my dream, whoever he was, showed me to a certain place on the common where something had been buried – his dog had found it in the sand.'

'But how do you know it wasn't all part of the dream,' insisted Marion. 'We all dream things, but I can't recall anything actually coming true.'

Al Orange deliberately took a moment to ensure he had a firm grasp on his recollections. 'But for the first time in my life, I was able to piece things together. I think a lot of the visions I have in my head actually stem from one person in particular. I think the man in the hat who kept appearing in the world of the humans is the same one who messes with my head from the inside.' He drew breath and continued with gusto, his thoughts seemingly on the run and trying to get out before the tenant within him had a chance to grab him and hurl him back into his darkened hole. 'And I think he was the one who met me in the bunker in the other world, he tricked me into giving him the Amulet.' His speech became more fraught and his demeanour agitated. 'And I remember the very first time I met Abel Nogg by the timbered wall, someone else stalked me in the woods that night and tormented me and wouldn't leave me alone – always tormenting me and mocking me....'

'There, there, Mr Grunt.' Aano put a reassuring arm around the mallard's shoulders and squeezed gently. 'Take a breather before you burst a blood vessel, we're not going anywhere, so just take your time.'

A digestive biscuit and another slurp of tea had the inspector ready to continue yet again. 'But I just know it was real, I grant you I couldn't really have been on the common, and I know the building I always find myself in probably doesn't really exist. Oh, I wish I'd reached out and touched the human, then I would have known for sure he was real. I know the message in the dream was meant for me, and I'm sure I'm supposed to tell someone about it, I can't simply ignore it, it's too important.'

'But what can we do to prove or disprove the reality of a dream?' said Marion.

'I know,' said Aano, giving the inspector another of his squeezes. 'If you are sure you know where this place is on the common, why don't we simply go there and see what we can uncover?'

'Yes.' The inspector's eyes lit up for a split second before his expression fell to zero. 'But my dream was in the humans' world, the one through the timbered wall. How can we possibly check that out?'

'We could check it out in this world first,' replied Aano. 'If we can find the same spot here, that will lend some weight to your story, then we can tell Abel Nogg and see what he says.'

Al Orange felt strengthened by Aano's apparent belief in him. 'Thank you,' he said, wondering why his demon had given him free rein to divulge so much.

***

Mid-morning in the world of the humans. 'This will do fine, driver,' called Captain Walter Haker. His driver duly halted the lorry and switched off the engine. The local blackbirds immediately welcomed them with a full repertoire of their song sheet, not that they ever needed a song sheet to refer to, their hearts providing them with all the guidance needed.

Walter and Kate jumped down from the cab and began the last hundred paces on foot to where they had met the lone human among the trees the day before.

'At least the weather's cleared up nicely,' said Kate, sharing her attention between the sky and the tree tops from where the little birds were still enthusiastically singing to their hearts' content.

'Some of the footprints are still visible in the sand.' Walter took care not to disturb the ground too much, lest Nature's clues might be lost.

'Here, look,' Kate called. 'Another set of prints; so there was a second person.'

'Hmm – the question is, why did the man say he was alone, why would he lie?'

***

Not too far away, but in the world of the water birds, Al Orange called out while on the wing, 'Are you doing all right down there, Mr Grunt?' He and Marion circled above Aano while they made their way to where the inspector's dream had taken place place.

Aano merrily swung through the trees, occasionally resorting to walking when the trees thinned out too much. 'Thank you, trees, nice trees,' he would say each time he left one tree for the next, it would never do to take trees for granted, without them an ape's life would be unimaginable. The trees had taken a liking to the ape, the wind had carried his reputation many days ahead of him. Those that had met him previously had found him to be an extremely amiable fellow and made it their job to let everything else know so.

'It's not far now, Mr Grunt. Less than a mile I'd say.'

'Thank you, Inspector. You and Mrs Waters-Edge can go on if you like, I'll see where you land and catch up with you.'

With that, the two mallards straightened their flight and promptly made for the trees at the top of the distant rise.

***

Walter and Kate had followed a set of footprints from among the trees. 'I guess these belong to the man we were talking to,' said Walter, ending up at a set of tyre tracks where the man had obviously gotten into a car and made his way home. 'So where did the other guy disappear to?' Walter realized he was rubbing his chin again, a habit he had been unaware of until Kate light-heartedly pointed it out to him. He smiled at her and slowly lowered his hand.

Kate took up the narrative. 'Let's start from where the two sets of prints separate and see if we can stick with them.' She carefully made her way back to the edge of the tree line where the tracks were clearly visible. 'Ready?' she said, still with an endearing glint in her eye.

'Ready,' replied Walter, glad of the company of such a warm heart.

***

'I'm sorry to have kept you waiting,' said Aano making his way in leaps and bounds up the heather-laden slope to where Orange and Marion were waiting in the cool autumn sunshine.

Al Orange immediately took up the conversation. 'I'm sure this is where the man in the dream brought me, it must have been in the sand at the edge of the trees there.' The pine trees stood sentinel over the loosely bound flora, knowing, but unable to impart their knowledge.

***

Kate and Walter trod lightly upon the soft earth, following the footprints into the cover of the trees. The composition of the soil gradually changed from a sandy texture to a firmer peat; this was far less helpful in showing the prints of those who had gone before. The birds in the trees abruptly stopped their singing when the pines shimmied from top to bottom, not so harshly as to raise a full bodied alarm but more to point out that something was just a little odd.

***

On his side of the ether, Orange stopped short of the trees and concentrated on a specific patch of sand. 'Here,' he said, in a less than convincing voice. 'I'm sure this is where I dug the earth away with my bill.' The ground he was looking at gave no clue as to having suffered any interference for a very long time.

The three of them stared down at the unyielding ground, trying for all their worth to spot some sort of clue. Their attention was suddenly drawn by the pine trees ahead of them. The trees rustled just as those standing close to Walter and Kate had. If trees could talk they would tell of the ether which separated their world from the next. If the ether could have thinned out for the merest second, perhaps one party would have seen the other standing right by their sides, but that is not how the ether works; those from one world are never supposed to see what goes on in the other. But the trees are cleverer than they are given credit for, they know about the ether; that is why trees cannot speak in any kind of human language.

Aano, being an orangutan and one of the forest, listened acutely to the whispering pines; he knew they were trying to tell a tale. The two mallards watched as he walked over to the closest tree and put his arms around its girth. He squeezed gently, saying quietly, 'Nice tree, lovely tree; don't worry, I know you would tell if you could.' He released the tree from his embrace and patted it affectionately with his chubby black hand. The trees collectively waved their bristled fronds in a passing breeze to thank the orangutan for his kind words. *What a charming chap,* they thought.

***

Walter and Kate were standing precisely where Aano and his group were, but on the other side of the ether, of course. Walter patted the nearest tree, saying, 'If only you could talk.'

The trees waved their arms in the gentle breeze, thinking, *If only you could hear.*

Both Walter and Kate smiled at them, knowingly.

Oops, thought the trees, perhaps they can.

'I keep expecting to see someone behind me, or next to me,' said Walter, looking over his shoulder.

'Me too,' replied Kate. 'I sense there are others here, very close.'

Walter looked up at the trees once again. 'It's all right, my friends, I think I know what you want to say. Perhaps one day we will be privy to your knowledge.'

Kate moved slowly away, looking down at a set of barely

137

visible footprints. She muttered quietly as she went, 'Hmm, they're heading off into the trees.' Walter followed her, paying particular attention to the undergrowth surrounding them. 'I have a feeling it's not just the ether that's playing tricks on us.'

'I feel it too,' said Kate, sensing that they were indeed being watched. After a couple more paces the footprints faded into nothing. Kate repeatedly pressed her foot into the ground around her; her shoe left a faint but noticeable indentation in the soil. 'Strange,' she whispered, 'there's no reason for the prints not to show, they just seem to disappear, as if…'

'As if they simply took to the air?' Walter concluded.

***

'This is definitely the right place, I know I was here and so was the human in my dream,' said Inspector Orange, his tone now carrying an air of certainty. He looked out across the common. 'There, you see, in the distance; it's the timbered wall just like I said. This is where I uncovered the clawed hand.'

Aano came to the inspector's rescue. 'You're forgetting one thing, Inspector; your dream took place in the humans' world, not this one. We may well be in the right spot, but we're obviously in the wrong world.'

'Of course – you're right, I was forgetting the ether.'

Marion could only listen and try to figure out what Aano and Orange were talking about, having never travelled through the ether herself. She had heard through the grape vine of the world which the select crew had visited, but she still felt somewhat bewildered by the direction the conversation was going in. 'Are you saying that this exact spot also exists somewhere else, in another world, MrGrunt?'

'Yes, Mrs Waters-Edge, we know it's true because we've been there, and I can tell you it's most peculiar to see such familiar sights occupied by different beings.'

'So do you agree with Inspector Orange that he really did see something right here in his dream?'

'I'm not certain,' replied Aano. 'I think—

The inspector butted in. 'You must see my point, Mr Grunt, there's no other explanation. I'm sure the man I met is real, so we must have been in his world; you just said so yourself.'

Aano rubbed the top of his head curiously. 'Hmm, I must admit, Inspector, you make a compelling argument…I think we should get word of this to Abel Nogg right away.'

'Good,' replied Orange. 'I think we should get back to Smallbeef as quick as we can.' He looked across at Marion and asked, 'Do you have a carrier pigeon that goes to Fort Bog?'

'I'm afraid not,' Marion replied, 'we only ever need to send them to Davidsmeadow, that being the main police station and the pigeon being for emergencies only.'

Al Orange rubbed his bill while trying to figure out his options.

Not wanting to say something stupid, Aano tentatively said, 'That's something I've always wondered.'

'What is?' replied Orange.

Aano went on, 'Well…I've often wondered why it is that a pigeon is used to carry urgent messages.'

The inspector chuckled, a rarely exposed emotion of his. 'Because they're carrier pigeons, Mr Grunt, that's what they're for; going from one place to another and returning.'

Aano almost didn't want to pursue the matter any further for fear of making the mallards seem a little daft. 'Well, yes; I can see what you mean, Inspector, and I dare say a fit pigeon could make better progress than the likes of me or any other creature restricted to the land.'

'There you are then,' said Orange, thinking he had for the

second time in one day come out on top in a debate with the ape.

'Yes, but you see....' Aano had gone too far to simply abandon the issue, so he continued in as conciliatory a tone as he could manage. 'You can fly.'

'What?' said Orange.

Marion looked first at the inspector and then at Aano, a thought or two growing in her mind.

Aano expanded his thought. 'You are a mallard, as are many of the residents in these parts. You are extremely large birds and your wings are capable of carrying you at far greater speeds than those of a mere pigeon.'

'Good heavens,' said Marion, at a loss for words.

'Erm, what?' said Inspector Orange, sounding more like Inspector Hooter than he would ever have thought possible. 'Yes, well we shall have to get to the bottom of this at a more convenient moment.'

'Of course,' Aano replied, 'it isn't important anyway, after all, your pigeons have proved to be totally reliable over the years, I'm sure.' He swiftly moved things on, hoping he had not embarrassed the mallards. 'I know the way back to Smallbeef from here, so there is no need for you to hang back for me. I'll leave you to make the arrangements to let Abel Nogg know of your concerns, Inspector, and I'll catch up with you on my return.' By leaving Al Orange to deal with the matter, Aano hoped he had gone some way to restoring the inspector's self-respect and not left him or Marion feeling demoralized as a result of his questioning of their emergency pigeon policy.

Within minutes the two birds were in the air and heading for home. Each looked down at the ape who in turn looked up at them and gave a wave of his long arm, accompanied by a sincere, very broad smile. Neither Marion nor the inspector mentioned the matter of the pigeons during their return journey, but they both found themselves admitting within their own thoughts that the ape had a very good point. *Why on Earth **do** we use pigeons?*

15

By late afternoon the weather had settled into a pleasantly warm if slightly overcast affair. Hooter had hoped that one of his constables might have returned with news of the mysterious Dana Lethgerk, but alas, there had been no further sightings.

It was now that time of day when Hooter would walk his own beat just to satisfy himself that everything was as it should be. 'If anyone should want me I will be back in about an hour, or you can always get me by use of your whistles.'

'Yes sir,' replied Constable Roberts from behind the office desk. The remaining constables were busying themselves in the back room, polishing their helmet badges and practising drawing their truncheons from their holsters, just in case they needed to do so in earnest, to point the way for instance.

Turning left out of the station, Hooter made his way to The Square. *Will she be there I wonder?* Were he not such a devoted police officer he would have found it difficult to keep his mind on his work, but even so he could not deny that the lovely Dana Lethgerk had stirred hitherto dormant feelings from deep inside him. *I mustn't allow such thoughts to interfere with my duties; that would be most improper,* he reminded himself. *But I must admit it would be wonderful if we were to meet again – just for a chat, nothing more.*

The little duck inside him grew more exited as he rounded the corner. *Is she there, is she there?* No she was not. Several pavement tables were occupied, but none by the mallard with the amazing eyes. He continued his beat, completing a lap of The Square before making his way down the High Street. Most of the town's folk would nod or bid him good afternoon as he passed, and he, being a duck of the most polite kind, would always acknowledge their regard accordingly. After twenty paces or so, he turned left into a narrow alley of brick pavers, carefully making his way to ensure he didn't touch the wall on either side lest he should spoil his immaculate plumage. The alley widened part way along to make way for a quaint little tea room on the right. The small-paned windows beckoned the occasional passer-by to pop in and savour the intimate atmosphere while enjoying a cup of Earl Grey or perhaps a regular English blend. 'How pleasant,' Hooter muttered as he passed by the open door.

'Is it too late for an afternoon tea?' said a dreamy voice from behind him.

Hooter immediately recognized those sensual tones and turned without taking time to get his head in order. 'Oh, my word, hello again,' he said in something of a fluster while the little duck inside him launched into random handstands and cartwheels.

'I didn't mean to startle you,' said the mallard with the bluest eyes ever seen in a duck.

'Oh, that's quite all right, madam; I was miles away... thinking about police business.'

'Of course,' replied Dana.

Hooter so wanted to say something – anything, but until the little duck inside him had settled down he knew that anything he did say would be gobbledy-gook.

Dana prompted him. 'I'm sure you are a very busy police duck, Inspector, but if you do have the time, perhaps we could share a pot of tea?'

Hooter could not believe his ears or his eyes. *She's really asking me to have a cup of tea with her.* 'That would be lovely,' he said, holding the door for her. 'After you.' Ever the gentleduck, Hooter pulled the chair from under the table and returned it when Dana was ready to sit down.

'Thank you, Inspector,' said Dana with a subtle twinkle in her eye, which Hooter could not help but notice.

The waitress, a very attractive middle-aged duck with white plumage and a yellow bill, jauntily waddled over. 'Hello, honey-buns, what can I get for you?'

'A pot of afternoon tea for two will be fine, thank you,' replied Hooter.

The waitress turned and made her way to the kitchen. Dana carefully watched Hooter to see if his eyes followed her. They did not.

'So, Inspector, are you a busy police duck?'

'Oh, not really, we have our moments, but thankfully things have quietened down a little – at least for now.'

Dana leaned forward in her chair. 'You make it sound as if you've had a lot on your plate recently.'

'Oh…no,' replied Hooter, his head so full of recent adventures and fights and rescues and races and so on. 'Just police things – you know how it is.'

'Not really, Inspector, why don't you educate me?'

The waitress returned with their tea. 'Here you are, my dears.' Humming a tune of no particular name she arranged the crockery etc on the table before waddling her way back to the counter, leaving the twosome to continue their tete-a-tete.

'Well?' said Dana, prompting Hooter to engage in dialogue. 'I'm sure you have lots to tell; it must be very exciting being a police duck, especially a Flying Squad duck, and an inspector to boot.'

Concentrating hard not to sound flustered, Hooter replied, 'I really don't want to bore you with police matters, and besides, some of the things we've been up to lately are best kept secret.'

Dana reached across the table and softly rubbed Hooter's wing. 'I quite understand,' she whispered, 'we would not want your affairs getting into the wrong hands.'

'It's not that I don't trust you,' Hooter promptly replied, 'but I like to keep my work life and my private life separate, if that's all right with you?'

Dana's eyes smiled. 'Of course, Inspector; I think that's very wise. I can see why you are an inspector and not a mere constable.'

'My dear madam,' replied Hooter in defence of his colleagues. 'My squad does not comprise mere constables; each and every one of them is exemplary in every way. They are the finest constables an inspector could wish for.'

'Calm yourself, Inspector; I didn't mean to denigrate your constables, please accept my apologies if that is how it sounded. I was simply trying to emphasize your rightful place as their leader.'

Hooter succumbed to Dana's gentle touch on his shoulder. He found it very easy to sink into her eyes while responding, 'Apology accepted. I didn't mean to snap at you. I've had a very difficult time of it lately – my constables too. I'm sure I just need a day or two to get over recent events and then perhaps I won't be quite so on edge.'

'I'm sure you're right, Inspector....' Dana paused for thought. 'If you should ever feel the need for a compassionate ear I will be happy to listen, but only if it's right with you.'

'Thank you, madam,' Hooter replied, his little duck now feeling quite breathless from all the excitement. 'I think it's time I got back to my beat, thank you for your company.'

'The pleasure was all mine, Inspector,' Dana smiled.

Hooter's heart skipped a beat. 'Until next time then?'

'I shall look forward to it.'

***

Al Orange and Marion Waters-Edge had returned to Smallbeef, and were now sitting at the little dining table inside Marion's front room. Her husband, Harold, had joined them.

'Thank you,' said Al Orange, placing the cup and saucer back on the tray. 'You make a lovely cup of tea.'

'You're welcome to another one if you like,' Marion replied.

Orange hesitated and looked across at Harold, waiting for his approval.

Harold was in the main a peaceable duck, but had found himself exchanging blows with the inspector on more than one occasion during their unintended excursion into the world of the humans. 'Have another cup,' he said, 'have a biscuit as well.'

Al Orange gladly accepted Harold's kind offer. 'Thank you so much.'

'It's only a cup of tea,' said Harold.

'It's more than that,' replied Al Orange, experiencing a rare moment of freedom from his demon who would normally never allow such dialogue with any others; but his demon seemed to be busy elsewhere. 'I mean, thank you for being so patient and caring towards me; everyone knows you both have good reason to throw me out, and I wouldn't blame you if you did.'

Marion was about to reply, but she sensed that Harold had a thing or two to say, so she gave him a look that only a wife can give.

A hint of a smile preceded Harold's words. 'We did have a ruck, didn't we? By the timbered wall – oh dear me, we did have a ruck,' he chuckled.

Al Orange said nothing, but smiled respectfully.

146

Harold continued, 'And when you were halfway through and your constables pulled you back, oh dear – the look on your face. I thought you were going to explode with anger; that was very frightening I must say.'

'I'm sorry if I hurt you,' said Orange. 'I did whack you a good whack with my bill, I remember that.'

'So do I,' replied Harold. He paused and rubbed his bill for a few seconds. 'To be honest, I can forgive you for all that fighting and chasing, you were just doing your job after all, not very well it must be said, but your job none the less. What **does** bother me though is the way you behaved towards my wife, I mean, I don't know what would have happened if Aano Grunt hadn't come to her aid when he did.'

The inspector's eyes welled up. 'I'm so sorry, really sorry,' he said. 'I know there is nothing I can say or do to explain my actions.' Despite his best efforts he began sobbing, his emotions overwhelming him once again. 'The truth is, even I don't know why I behaved the way I did – that honestly was not the real me.'

Harold put a wing around the inspector's shoulder. 'Here,' he said, offering a fresh cup of tea. 'This will help.'

Marion moved the conversation on. 'If your dreams come to fruition, Inspector, you will have a chance to put things right and help to bring the lost Beast of Grey home; then perhaps life will get back to normal once and for all. If you concentrate on that, perhaps your nasty demon, or whatever he is, might get fed up with you and leave you alone.'

Orange knew Marion was only trying to help, but he knew that his demon was also behind the troubles that had beset the world of the humans. Somehow he had to explain his thoughts to others who might help. He knew he could trust Aano Grunt, another soul who had every reason to abandon him and yet had shown nothing but kindness. Above all else he had to get word to Abel Nogg, the only one with the wisdom and the power to help put things right.

***

Here comes that nice chap again, the trees whispered on the gentle breeze. Aano was still making his way back to Smallbeef, expertly swinging his way from one branch to the next, and always taking care to use only those branches which were of such obvious strength as to carry him without straining themselves unduly. He dropped silently to the ground when confronted with a gap slightly too wide for him to leap. 'Not to worry,' he said, patting the tree and making his way on foot to the next nearest. It was between two such trees that he chanced a look up to the sky and spotted a pigeon overhead; a tiny capsule hung from the bird's neck. 'Fort Bog?' Aano called out. The pigeon answered with smiling eyes, timing his reply to fit in with his wingbeats, 'Coo-crooo.' He was soon out of sight beyond the stand of trees. 'Old habits die hard,' Aano whispered to himself recalling his conversation with Marion and Inspector Orange regarding the use of pigeons as messengers. 'I can't think why they don't simply fly themselves, it would be much quicker.' The trees rustled to him collectively. Aano patted the next tree he came to. 'I dare say you know the answer,' he said, shinning up the warm trunk which seemed to open up its bark to make the ape's ascent that much easier. 'Nice trees, lovely trees,' said the ape in perfect harmony with his surroundings.

16

The next morning in the world of the humans, Mr Jones lay on his sofa with Polly's head resting on his arm. It was very early and still dark. Sleep had proved elusive once again, and so Jones got to his feet and made his way to the French doors; he tried to look through the glass into the garden, perhaps the badger would be foraging in the turf. His own reflection looked back at him. He imagined the giant mallard's image overlaid on his, also staring back at him. *Was he real, or was he just another player in my dreams?* He looked down, Polly was now sitting next to him looking up, always his friend. 'What do you see when you look out there?' Jones asked of the dog. Polly mumbled under his breath, he knew barking was taboo at such an hour so he grumbled some more, just a tad louder. Jones gently stroked the top of Polly's head. 'You sensed something in that man we met, didn't you, mate. And you certainly didn't like it.' Polly whined deeply in reply. Jones' voice developed a tremor of desperation as he continued, 'The truth is, mate, I don't know what's going on in my head anymore. It's getting very crowded in here.' Polly listened intently with tilted head while his master added, 'It's as if there's someone else in here as well as my demon – someone working at odds with whatever else is going on. It's getting hard to see who's who.' Polly's grumble broke into a short sharp yelp, the vocal Alsatian coming out in him. Jones rubbed the dog's ears. 'I wish you could talk, mate; I'm sure you'd figure things out better than I can.'

On his way back to the sofa, Jones switched the radio on. The BBC World Service brought more news of others' plight, and of the dire state of humanity. Famine, drought and disease ravaged the entire African continent with no end in sight. From further east came news of the spread of Dengue Fever spreading into territories previously untouched by the mosquito. And as if Nature's onslaught was not enough, added to these reports was news of increasing tension in Asia where those in power sought to wave the big stick at the west in the form of nuclear weapons. 'I honestly think man is the thickest creature on Earth, mate,' Jones whispered while stroking Polly and pulling him closer.

The nearby dawn squirted a tinge of purple along the horizon so as not to take anyone by surprise when the Sun finally arrived.

***

The same Sun lightened Aano Grunt's horizon, warming the roof of number seven. Aano sat quietly listening to the inspector grappling with his unwanted thoughts in the next room.

'Cooee,' a voice called from outside the front door.

'Ah, good morning, Mrs Waters-Edge,' said Aano, beckoning her to come in. Especially welcome was the bowl of fruit that accompanied the pot of tea and biscuits on her tray.

'How is our patient this morning?' Marion asked in an upbeat tone.

'A better night than last,' replied Aano. 'He's still rather disturbed, mind you.'

Al Orange appeared in the doorway from the bedroom, yawning but looking quite smart none the less, having obviously spent a few minutes preening.

Aano ushered him into the room. 'Sit down here, Inspector,'

he said. 'Enjoy your breakfast and then we can sort out what we are going to do today.'

Marion spoke up, 'I don't suppose there is much we can do until we get word from Fort Bog.'

Aano bent his banana and gave it a quick squeeze, the soft flesh popped straight into his mouth. 'Mmm, lovely, you simply cannot beat a banana for breakfast.' He paused and continued on a completely different tack. 'I must confess, I'm a little worried about how long the pigeon might take to reach Fort Bog.'

Both Marion and Al Orange rubbed their bills. Orange spoke up first, 'Don't worry, he has an excellent sense of duty, that pigeon. And he knows the land like the back of his wing.'

Aano stared thoughtfully at the ceiling. The mallards knew there was a question coming. 'Why do their heads go back and forth when they walk?' asked the ape.

'What?' both mallards replied.

Aano continued, 'I was just wondering why it is that some birds, not all, but certainly pigeons – can't walk without their heads going back and forth with their strides.' He paused before strutting across the carpet while mimicking a pigeon.

The two mallards burst into laughter at such an absurd sight. Al Orange had not laughed for such a long time that his face hurt.

'If pigeons weren't flesh and blood,' said Aano, 'I would think they must have a cog at the top of each leg which is connected by a link to another cog at the base of the neck…that would do it.' In his mind he imagined the blueprint for such a device, with measurements and off-sets all quite precise. 'But that can't be right of course, because they are living creatures just like you and me. If they could talk they could tell us why.' After another of his stares at the ceiling he concluded, 'I suppose that's the wonder of life and creation…we are not supposed to know everything, but we each know enough to live by.' He smiled and finished the last bit of his banana.

***

Many miles away, skies of light grey loitered peacefully above the moorland. The pigeon, being an expert meteorologist, knew the clouds had no intention of raining on him, not for the next twenty-four hours at least. Onward he flew, his path crossing the occasional swift busily taking flies on the wing. He knew he was getting close to his destination, and would be glad of a rest and some food before making his return journey.

His forward planning came to an abrupt halt when an unwelcome silhouette appeared in the sky ahead of him. He could not make out the precise shape but he knew it was one of the indigenous birds of prey. Be it a red kite or a peregrine, it made little difference; either one would be only too pleased to include him on their menu. Both were somewhat larger than the pigeon and both sported impressive wings. Such raptors were extremely adept high speed flyers equipped with talons designed for catching and holding their prey to the bitter end. A plump pigeon would be no match for their turn of speed, or their need to eat.

The pigeon instinctively stilled his wings and began losing height in a straight glide, taking care to make no sudden movement that might catch the distant eyes. He knew that if he could spot the hunter's silhouette from that distance, so too would the hunter spot his against the light grey sky behind him. How he wished for the cover of the trees, but the nearest such refuge was almost a mile away. Keeping low to the ground he hoped his soft colours of beige, mauve and grey might serve to disguise his shape against the autumn moorland beneath him.

He turned his head to see if he had been spotted. He had – and it was a peregrine, an especially fast open-air falcon. To the pigeon's horror it was no longer a distant speck, but was most certainly tailing him from on high. No longer concerned with trying to hide, the pigeon put all his effort into reaching the trees as quickly as possible. Half a mile distant, the trees began waving their branches in the air to encourage the pigeon to keep going, and also to distract the peregrine or maybe even frighten him off.

The peregrine was far too wise to allow a clump of trees to muddle his razor sharp constitution. The only thing on his mind was a nice plump breast with wings on. At a height of ten trees the hunter was now immediately above his prey; he stiffened his wings and brought them closer to his body, keen to strike his next meal before the trees could take the pigeon in.

The pigeon focused hard, flying as fast as he could, which when compared to a determined falcon was really not very fast at all. He knew what was coming and he knew he was helpless to stop it. In his heart he felt sorry for those who he would be letting down by not delivering the message tied around his neck. He also thought of his mates who would never know what had become of him, and of the heart that would always wonder.

The trees waved and cheered as trees do when no one else is watching. The pigeon responded, forcing his wings to beat ever faster, singing the characteristic pigeon whistle, but still he was no match for the one who might soon be offering a final embrace.

Like an arrow from a longbow, the peregrine seared almost vertically through the air. Two hundred miles per hour and only two seconds from his victim, his eyes widened and his clawed toes stiffened. The pigeon would soon be his.

The trees took a sharp intake of breath and stilled their

branches, petrified by what they were about to witness. This was Nature, they knew that. This was life as it was intended, balanced and necessary, but the trees always found it heart-breaking to watch. If they could turn away they would, but they were trees, so they had to stand and watch as they had done throughout all of history, bearing witness to life and death through the ages; God's natural witnesses.

Very nearly at the trees, one hundred soft mauve breast feathers flew into the air, no longer needed. The pigeon flapped his wings helplessly, but the talons tightened around his chest and his captor forced him to the ground.

With the pigeon firmly held face down in the sand the peregrine paused for a few seconds to appraise the situation; there was no rush now, the pigeon was his. The pigeon turned his head and looked up at the trees, now only a few paces away – so near yet so far. Those trees that could, let go a solitary leaf or pine needle to announce the imminent passing of one of Nature's own; one who had so often passed an afternoon perched in the shade of their foliage exchanging pleasantries beneath the comforting Hampshire Sun.

The pigeon craned his neck to keep the sand from getting in his eyes. The claws remained tight around his chest, severely constricting his breathing. His feathers floated on the breeze; if he himself could not fly, they would take his place, extending his presence in this world for a few minutes more.

The peregrine had done all the waiting necessary and had regained his composure. He raised his head to deliver the final blow, but a solitary claw, bigger than his entire body, gently curled around him from behind. Such a sight caused the falcon to freeze on the spot; never before had he seen such a thing. He instinctively tightened his grip around the pigeon's body, determined not to lose him. The huge claw gave the peregrine a little tug as if to say, 'Go on, let him go – just this once.' The peregrine slowly turned and looked up, and then up some more to see a creature so monstrous and utterly ugly that he almost vomited on the spot. He had never seen a pterosaur before, and didn't even know what one was. Never the less, he was quite sure that he was about to be firmly crushed by the huge clawed toe that was still wrapped very gently around him while he himself still had the pigeon in his own clawed grasp; now he knew what it felt like. The pigeon managed a sideways look to see the pterosaur towering way above the peregrine who now had a distinctly worried look in his eye.

The pigeon cooed quietly. He was as good as dead, he was sure of that.

The peregrine cheeped nervously, also resigned to a premature end.

The giant claw gave another gentle tug. The peregrine released his grip from the pigeon and then, for some reason unknown to him, he hopped up and perched on the claw which immediately raised him up to the monster's eye.

Standing at over eight feet tall, the pterosaur now took his time to study the eye of the bird of prey. The peregrine found himself gazing back, being drawn in by the spiralling red lines with the amazing blue eye in the centre.

'Perfect', said the pterosaur, 'and beautiful.'

The falcon didn't understand English words, but he sensed they were kindly. He chirped nervously in reply. The pterosaur slowly raised his hand higher still. 'Fly, my friend, but leave this pigeon to live another day, he has earned it.'

The peregrine chirped again and took to the wing, circling twice before straightening his course and flying for all his worth to the south. He didn't know what had just happened, but he knew he would give wood pigeons a wide berth in future.

'Coo croo,' said the pigeon, getting to his feet. *Should I take flight and hope for the best or simply wait to see what this huge monster has in mind.* Before he had time to do either, the clawed hand came to the ground again and waited for the pigeon to hop on, which he duly did. The pterosaur then raised the pigeon high in the air whereupon Mother Nature obliged by bringing a gentle breeze upon the bird to tease the dust from his feathers. The pigeon's eyes widened at such a sensation and before he knew it, he too was sinking into the eye of crystal blue. Without a word being said, the pterosaur and the pigeon engaged in an exchange of thoughts to assuage any fears the pigeon might have had regarding his future. The little bird blinked slowly and cooed again to acknowledge the pterosaur's kindliness.

The sound of approaching hooves interrupted their intercourse. The trees waved fondly as four wagons, each being pulled by a pair of fine Hanoverians, came into view a little way down the nearby track. Each wagon had a Canada goose of the Mounties sitting up front looking extremely smart in their dimpled Stetsons. In the back of each wagon sat an assortment of birds, mostly mallards, moorhens and coots, all being transported back to Smallbeef and the surrounding area where they would be tended to and helped back to good health after their ordeal at Fort Bog. Leading the wagon train was a single rider on horseback who, upon seeing the pterosaur up ahead, broke into a canter to meet him.

'Sergeant Jolly, it's good to see you again,' said the pterosaur.

'The feeling is mutual, Mr Nogg, fer sure,' replied the Mountie, casting a curious eye towards the pigeon who was still perched on the pterosaur's finger.

'This little chap needs a drink and a free ride back to Smallbeef if you would be so kind, Sergeant.'

'That's no problem, sir. Is that a message pouch around his

neck?'

'It is,' replied Abel Nogg, 'let's have a look shall we?'

Using one claw, Abel removed the piece of paper from within the pouch and read it aloud: 'Mr Nogg's presence is urgently requested by Aano Grunt in respect of Inspector Al Orange at Smallbeef. We have important information, please come quickly.'

While pondering the message, Abel hobbled over to one of the wagons where he allowed the pigeon to hop off and perch on the side. 'Hmm,' said Abel, 'I think I should make my way to Smallbeef immediately, Sergeant.'

'Fer sure, sir,' replied Sergeant Jolly. 'We'll see that the pigeon gets home safely; you must make haste, sir. It sounds as though they need yer help. Please say hi to Mr Grunt fer me, I look forward to seeing him again.'

Abel Nogg hobbled a short distance from the group before spreading his wings wide; Nature's breath lifted him from the ground and turned him lovingly until his long beak pointed towards Smallbeef where he was needed. 'Thank you for your help, Sergeant,' Abel called. 'I shall see you again soon.' He then turned to the pigeon and gave a wink, the pigeon winked back, 'Vroo croo.'

17

Abel Nogg soon disappeared beyond one horizon, heading eagerly for the next. The air slipped smoothly above and below him, smoothly that is, apart from a faint whistle caused by the air passing through a small bullet hole in one leathery wing, a reminder of his first encounter with the troubled Inspector Al Orange. Onward he sped, hardly needing to flex his wings such was the care afforded him by Mother Nature.

Meanwhile, many miles to the west, Constables Roberts and Russell straightened their helmets and checked each other over to ensure they were quite immaculate. Roberts then called through the doorway into Inspector Hooter's office. 'Constables Roberts and Russell going on town beat, sir.'

'Right you are, Constables,' Hooter replied. 'I might well meet up with you while you are out; I think I'll do a random patrol around the town centre, just to see what's going on.'

Roberts and Russell smiled at each other, thinking, *To see if a certain blue-eyed lady duck is about, more like.* They pulled the door closed behind them and were soon making their way towards The Square to start their patrol. They had barely waddled five paces when Betty Bottoms-Up appeared from around the corner with her four youngsters following faithfully behind. Still a mere two feet tall and covered in grey fluff, the lead duckling called out the time to maintain some sort of semblance. 'Hup two three four, hup two three four.' Upon seeing the two police ducks coming towards them the four ducklings each took a sharp intake of breath. 'Wow,' said one. 'Cor,' said another.

PC Roberts greeted the mother accordingly, 'Good morning, Mrs Bottoms-Up, your children are coming along well.'

'Thank you, Officer,' replied Betty, trying not to blush.

Remembering the conversation they'd had yesterday, the youngster at the back of the line piped up, 'My dad's making a wardrobe.'

'Is he?' said PC Russell, 'he must be very clever.'

'Not as clever as Constable Thomas,' added the duckling at the front.

PC Russell enquired with a smile, 'And why's that then, young fella?'

'Because he knows how to make eggs.'

Mrs Bottoms-Up blurted out, 'Oh dear, I'm terribly sorry, Officer. I don't know where Bertie got that from.'

Russell and Roberts tried their hardest not to laugh out loud at the youngster's innocent blundering. 'So Constable Thomas is going to make some eggs is he?' said Roberts. He patted the duckling on the head and added, 'I don't think he'll be doing that just yet; not until he's married anyway.'

Mrs Bottoms-Up could barely speak, such was her embarrassment. 'Children do pick things up, don't they; little things they overhear, you know how it is, Officer.'

'Of course they do, madam,' replied Russell.

'Come along, children.' Betty hurriedly waddled onward with her four beautiful ducklings in line behind. The youngsters could be heard chatting as they disappeared around the distant bend:

'Do you think our dad knows how to make eggs?'

'If he can make a wardrobe I bet he can make an egg.'

'That's true, a wardrobe must be much harder to make.'

'Are eggs made of the same stuff as wardrobes then?'

'I suppose they must be if Dad makes them.'

'But only if they're made of wood.'

Roberts and Russell looked at each other until Mrs Bottoms-Up was out of earshot, they then burst into respectful laughter at the ducklings ramblings. As soon as the joviality was out of their systems they continued towards The Square settling into a thoughtful silence as they waddled slowly along, side by side. The Bottoms-Up family had reminded them of their own sweethearts waiting for them at Smallbeef; PC Thomas was not the only one who hoped one day to make eggs of his own – but not out of wood.

***

'Is my cap on straight?' asked Inspector Hooter standing by the police station door, eager to start his own patrol.

'Perfectly, sir,' replied Constable James James.

'Thank you, I shall be back within the hour,' said Hooter, pulling the door closed behind him. Up the road he went with a twinkle in his eye that had not adorned his face for many a moon. *I wonder if Dana will be outside the café.* Her image filled his mind as he neared the corner. *I can't think where she could have got those eyes from, the only others I've seen like that belong to Abel Nogg – and Kate Herrlaw, they can't be related can they?*

A tiny twinge of disappointment tapped his heart when he turned the corner to see the table empty. *She isn't here. Oh well, perhaps she'll be about later.* With his cap in perfect alignment he continued around The Square and then down the High Street.

The rhythm of the town suddenly halted when the cry of a female mallard echoed between the buildings. Her cry of distress was plain to hear. The townsfolk stopped in their tracks and listened intently, all tipping their heads one way and then the other. Hooter instantly moved into the middle of the road, turning his head each way to get a bearing on the call.

'Help me, please, help me.' The cry was easy to trace in the otherwise silent air. 'Please, oh please,' the female called again, clearly in extreme difficulty.

'Stand back!' Inspector Hooter broke into a speedy waddle straight down the middle of the road. Every bird stood well to the side while he, with his wings partly opened to lengthen his stride, urgently made his way to the scene. En-route he removed his whistle from beneath his cap and placed it in his bill, and then he blew for all his worth. 'Quack, quack, quack,' went the whistle.

'What a peculiar noise,' the pedestrians mooted among themselves; strange reminiscences echoed in their most distant memories. *A strange sound indeed.*

The call for help led Hooter from the High Street into the narrow alley where he had met Dana the day before. He looked down the full length of the alleyway, the way was free from pedestrians with the exception of one – Dana Lethgerk lay on the ground some twenty paces ahead. On seeing the inspector approaching she called out, 'Inspector, oh, thank heavens you're here.'

Hooter surveyed the scene as he drew nearer, he could see no obvious reason for Dana's dilemma. 'Did you fall, my dear?' he asked as he settled down beside her.

Dana wept softly as she explained, 'I was walking along the alleyway here when someone jumped from the hedgerow and forced me to the ground.' Tears slipped unhindered from her eyes and sped down her cheeks. 'Thank goodness you heard my calls.'

'There there, my dear, don't worry now. I'll make sure no harm comes to you.'

Dana tentatively eased her wing around the inspector's abundant mass and drew him ever closer. Her scent of nostalgic homeliness filled Hooter's nostrils, rendering his defences useless; for a few moments he forgot he was a police officer and revelled in this beauty's closeness. Her warmth, her breathing, and her smell had the little duck inside him swooning helplessly, falling about within his stomach, intoxicated.

'Inspector, Sir.' Constable Russell called from the far end of the alley, 'What's the trouble?' Constable Roberts followed immediately behind him, looking all around for any sign of a villain, as per his dubious training. He had never actually seen a villain in Davidsmeadow before, and was not sure if he would recognize one if he saw one.

The inspector looked up and replied, 'There must be a bounder on the loose; did you pass any shady looking characters?'

'No sir, we've passed no one,' said Russell looking to Roberts for support.

'That's right, Sir; we haven't passed anyone at all.'

Hooter then helped Dana to her feet, saying, 'Both of you go and take another look in case you missed him. I'll take this young lady duck into the tea room to see that she's all right. Report back to me as soon as you complete your search.'

'Yes sir,' both constables replied and hurriedly waddled around the corner to make further investigations.

'Erm,' Roberts spoke up gingerly, 'what's the difference between a villain and a bounder?'

Russell pondered the question for a few seconds before replying, equally cautiously. 'It sounds to me like a bounder is like a villain but with better manners.' He didn't really know what put that thought into his head but it seemed to sit quite comfortably between his ears, so he settled for his summation and confirmed his thought. 'Yes, I'm sure that's what it is, a villain is just someone who's naughty, whereas a bounder is naughty but says please and thank you while he's doing it.'

'That doesn't really make him any less naughty though, does it?'

'I suppose not,' Russell went on, 'I guess we're lucky there aren't really any bad ducks in Davidsmeadow, so we don't have to worry too much.'

The two of them proceeded to search behind the shops, the backs of which bordered a stream beyond which lay a communal park.

Roberts added another thought. 'The only two ducks who I can recall behaving badly are Inspector Alan Orange and his Constable Lock; they behaved very badly on their first visit to Smallbeef when—'

Russell butted in to put things into perspective. 'Yes, but you can't count Inspector Orange because he wasn't at all well, and as for Constable Lock – he was only obeying orders.'

'That's true,' Roberts agreed. 'And anyway, Lock flew off to avoid doing anything too bad and then he got into trouble for not doing as he was ordered.'

They nodded to each other amiably, having satisfied themselves that they had gotten everything sorted in their blue-green heads.

'But if we both agree that there are no villains or bounders in town and we haven't seen anyone else in the alleyway, who could have assaulted Miss Lethgerk?' said Russell.

'Let's sum things up,' said Roberts. 'We haven't heard any wingbeats, so the villain hasn't taken flight.'

'Right,' said Russell.

'And there are no gaps in the wall or the hedge where someone could have squeezed through to make their escape.'

'That's right too,' Russell agreed.

'In fact, we haven't seen anyone at all anywhere between the scene of the crime and here.'

'That's right, too.'

'The only place we haven't checked is the tearoom.'

'You don't think he would have gone in there, do you?' said Russell.

'Uh-o, that's where the inspector was taking Miss Lethgerk to settle her down.'

'Quick,' Russell exclaimed, 'to the tearoom before it's too late.'

Inspector Hooter slid Dana's chair in as she elegantly sat herself down at a table for two. Her eyes held Hooter's while he took his place opposite her. 'Thank you, so much,' she said, 'you really are my knight in shining armour.'

Hooter's bill glowed bright yellow despite it being out of season. 'Don't worry, my dear; my constables will find and apprehend the culprit in no time.' He rubbed his bill thoughtfully, adding, 'I must admit, I can't imagine who would behave in such a way; I can't recall such an occurrence happening here before.'

'It's not your fault,' replied Dana. 'I suppose there is always a first time for everything – even in your lovely land.'

Hooter was about to reply when the bell above the door pinged and the door urgently flew open. Constables Roberts and Russell rushed in. 'Everyone stay right where you are,' Russell shouted with an unusual note of authority.

Hooter immediately challenged the young constable. 'What on Earth is the meaning of this, Constable Russell?'

'It's the villain, Sir. We've searched all along the alleyway and beyond.'

Roberts butted in, 'And in the air, Sir. There was no one to be seen.'

'Which can only mean…' Russell concluded, 'that the villain came in here to hide.'

Alarmed, Hooter looked all around. There were only two other customers sitting at a table across the room, both female and probably of a certain senior age. 'I can assure you, Constables, there is definitely no one in here who fits the bill, if you'll pardon the pun.'

Everyone in the room cast an eye over each other before replying in unison, 'Quite so, no one at all.'

'But there is nowhere else he could have gone, Sir; not without us seeing him – and we haven't.'

Dana interjected before Hooter could say anything that might prolong the discussion. 'Don't worry, Inspector; I'm sure your constables did everything they could. I suppose the attacker was just a bit too quick for them, it happens; so let's leave it at that. I'm just grateful you were here to help me in my moment of need.' She fluttered her eyelids at Hooter to draw a line under the matter.

Roberts and Russell looked each other in the eye, silently exchanging concerns about leaving things unresolved.

Hooter studied those in the room once more before finishing in the eyes of his constables. 'Thank you, Constables, please return to the station now and write up your report. Perhaps we shall have to formulate a training session to include pursuing villains down alleyways – yes, that's what we'll do.'

The two constables duly left the tea room doing their best to conceal a puzzled expression. Along the alleyway and then a right turn into the High Street and then left at The Square, past Café Hero and left into St Thoughtful Street. The blue lantern welcomed them back to the police station. Neither of them had said a word on the way back, but they each mulled things over in their minds. *One way in and one way out of the alleyway. Nowhere to hide, no sign of anyone having gone through the hedge or over a wall. No one suspicious in the tea room, and no one passed us at our end of the alley. How can that be?*

Constable Peters welcomed them back. 'There's a cup of tea in the mess room.'

'Thanks,' replied Russell, his look of puzzlement was plain to see.

'What's up?' asked Constable Thomas, 'You look troubled.'

'Hmm.' Russell and Roberts rubbed their bills and replied in unison, 'Something very odd has just happened in the town.'

'Odd?' said James. 'How do you mean, odd?'

Roberts took up the tale: 'Russell and I were on our beat, walking along behind the shops by the stream.'

'Yes, then what?' asked Peters, Thomas, James and Howard, as one.

'Well, everything was quiet as usual until we heard a cry for help.'

'Wow,' said Howard, 'a bit of excitement for a change.'

'Yes,' Roberts went on, 'we could tell the cry was coming from around the corner in the direction of the tea room in the alleyway.'

'What did you do?' asked James with considerable enthusiasm.

'Well, it wasn't worth taking to the air, so we waddled at pursuit speed to the alleyway. On the way there we heard the inspector's whistle quacking, so we knew it was something serious.'

'That's right,' Russell picked up the conversation again. 'We stuck to procedures, observing all the way – but that's the strange thing.'

'What is?' said Thomas.

'Well,' answered Russell, 'we didn't see or pass anyone on our way to the incident and yet there was no other way for anyone to leave the scene of the crime.'

'What crime?' four voices enquired impatiently.

'Dana Lethgerk, you know – the lady mallard our inspector's got his eye on.'

'What about her?'

'Well, it seems someone attacked her in the alleyway. When we arrived she was on the ground with the inspector comforting her. She certainly looked a bit ruffled, you know, a few breast feathers missing, that sort of thing.

'Any blood?' asked James, eagerly.

'No,' replied Roberts.

'And you're sure there's no way you could have missed the villain?'

'No, we went back and double checked everywhere.' Roberts paused for a thoughtful moment before tentatively adding, 'It's as if there hadn't been anyone else there at all.'

'Then how do you account for Miss Lethgerk's condition?'

'We can't,' Russell concluded.

All six constables rubbed their bills collectively, hoping that their combined effort would somehow shed some light on the matter. 'Weird,' they said as one.

They continued sipping their tea while pondering matters.

Thomas eventually broke the silence. 'Your first crime in the town and there doesn't seem to be a villain, what rotten luck.'

'The inspector said it might have been a bounder, but either way we failed to find him,' said Russell.

And so the six constables of the Flying Squad poured another cup of tea and pondered a little more while waiting for the return of their inspector.

18

Early afternoon; Al Orange lay staring blankly at the ceiling. Many thoughts tumbled through his mind, refusing to let him rest. Aano Grunt had made himself comfortable in the front room from where he could keep a wary eye and ear open in case the inspector suddenly became troubled again. The confines of the room foiled his ears' sense of direction but he knew something was in the air, quite literally. He rose from the chair and made his way to the front door, opening it and peering out. The thinning canopy of oak and chestnut trees screened much of the sky from where he stood, but he could hear the air being gently parted and then carefully put back in its place. His suspicion was soon confirmed by gasps of astonishment coming from the yard.

'Oh my word!' the residents exclaimed with mixed expectations. The yard quickly filled with resident mallards. All had seen pterosaurs before, gigantic Beasts of Grey, and in the main their experiences had been extremely unpleasant, but word had spread of the biggest of them all with the red face and brilliant blue eyes.

'It's Abel Nogg,' Dick Waters-Edge shouted, stepping out from the storeroom. 'Give him some room to land.'

The look of wonder on the faces of those who had met Abel previously was matched by the look of awe in the faces of those who had not. Either way, every bill was agog and every eye wide open as the huge flying reptile landed softly in the centre of the yard.

As soon as the clawed feet touched the ground the wings folded in half and the equally impressive clawed hands rested on the ground slightly forward of the feet. Abel slowly turned his head, his long beak stopping when Dick came into view. 'Good afternoon, young duck. I hope you are well.'

Dick returned a smiling eye. 'Yes, sir,' he replied, feeling privileged to be the one the pterosaur chose to address before his peers. 'It's good to see you again, sir.'

The last time the residents had set eyes on such a creature was during the battle of Smallbeef; on that occasion an entire squadron of Bogs had cast the constables of the Flying Squad to the ground in tatters. The creature standing before them now was bigger than ever and yet here was the young mallard, Dick Waters-Edge, not only standing up to him but actually having a convivial conversation with him. *How amazing.*

'Steady, young Dick,' said Marvin Plimsol-Line, remembering his last encounter with a Beast of Grey. 'Don't go too close.'

Dick's father, Harold, had now appeared and stood by Dick's shoulder. 'It's okay, Marvin, this is Abel Nogg, the one we were telling you all about, we owe a lot to him.'

Marvin gazed up at the hefty tail swaying calmly behind the pterosaur's head. He rubbed his own head in remembrance of the clout he had sustained from a tail very similar to that one. Abel Nogg held out his hand and waited for Marvin to respond. Marvin was not about to be fooled by such a gesture, but his young son, who until then had been hiding behind him, now stepped out to the side. The residents gasped as they recalled the last time Plimsol-Line junior did such a thing. Marvin ventured to put himself between his son and Abel; he had barely waddled one step when Abel turned his hand palm uppermost on the ground. The duckling, barely knee high to his father, cheerily stepped onto the hand and before Marvin could do or say anything the pterosaur raised the duckling up to his eye. The youngster cheeped. Marvin cried out, 'Put him down this instant, you, you giant thing you.'

Abel bathed in the eye of the duckling for as long as he dared. 'Beautiful,' he whispered just loud enough for all to hear. 'Perfectly beautiful.' He then carefully lowered the youngster to the ground and let him hop off. Marvin immediately drew his son to him and took him under his wing.

Abel nodded respectfully to the father who would suffer any manner of aggression to protect his own son. 'You too are beautiful,' he said.

Marvin stood his ground with his son peeping out from beneath his wing. 'Well, erm,' Marvin blushed, which in his head was not a very masculine thing to do. 'I'm not beautiful actually – but I might be just a little bit handsome I suppose.'

His wife, Penny, cuddled up to him, helping him in his moment of need. 'Yes, darling,' she whispered, their bills touching. 'A very little bit handsome.'

Abel Nogg chuckled and smiled inside. The innocence of mallards never failed to surprise and warm him.

Sergeant Bob Uppendown's reassuring tones rose above the gathering. 'There's no need to worry, folks. Mr Nogg is a fine fellow and I'm sure he means you no harm.'

'Thank you, Sergeant,' said Abel. Any further conversation was curtailed when a voice called from across the yard.

'Mr Nogg, sir.'

Abel turned to see the unmistakable bundle of ginger hair waving to him. 'My dear Aano Grunt,' replied the pterosaur. 'I received your message. I gather you have a matter of urgency to discuss with me.'

The ape hurriedly made his way through the crowd, and as soon as he was close enough, he held out his long arm to shake hands with the formidable beast towering over him. The crowd hushed, as did Abel himself; he could not remember the last time anyone had actually initiated a cordial gesture such as a hand shake.

The ape looked up, his eyes so utterly lovely and bright brown.

A tear welled in Abel Nogg's eye. To be touched or welcomed amiably meant so much to him. In all his travels through this world and many others, he would often be greeted with animosity at the least, and more often with threats and name-calling, regardless of what disguise he might be wearing. Even when appearing in the guise of the indigenous peoples, he would find himself being persecuted and victimized; the words "book" and "cover" briefly came to mind. He offered his hand, complete with the most perfect, purposeful claws imaginable. Silence held the crowd in awe while the humble orangutan held the hand of Nature's most vicious looking creature.

Aano broke the silence. 'It's nice to see you again, Mr Nogg; thank you for coming so quickly.' To endorse his gratitude, Aano then put his other hand over the top of Abel's in a two-handed gesture. A muttering gradually grew among the crowd as the mallards mumbled words of astonishment and relief in equal measure.

'Perhaps he really is all right.'

'How amazing.'

'Who would have thought it?'

'Well I never, how wonderful.'

'Thank you, my friend,' said the huge pterosaur, 'perhaps there is somewhere we can talk; do you have news for me?'

'Yes sir,' replied Aano, suspecting Abel already knew more

than he was letting on, as if this was all part of a great pre-ordained plan of some sort. He looked around the yard at the caravans, none of them were big enough to house a pterosaur of Abel's conformity. 'What about the storeroom? Perhaps we could fit in there?'

'There is more headroom, fer sure,' Sergeant Uppendown commented. 'We're using it as our dormitory at the moment but I'm sure it will make a fine meeting place.'

'Excellent,' said Abel.

The mallards of Smallbeef parted ahead of him as he hobbled in his ungainly gait towards the storeroom.

Aano called out as he went, 'Mrs Waters-Edge, could you fetch Inspector Orange and bring him to the storeroom to join us?'

'Of course,' she replied, looking to her husband, Harold.

'I'll help you get him across there, my dear,' said Harold.

With so much to talk about, the residents of the caravan park milled about the yard engaging in vibrant discussion about the biggest pterosaur they had ever seen. Those who had recently returned from Fort Bog continued to regale their neighbours with tales of slavery and imprisonment at the hands of the Beasts of Grey. Others extolled the virtues of Punch, the Suffolk horse, who had shown the Bogs the error of their ways, an act which eventually led to their freedom. The atmosphere became somewhat sober when they got to the part of the story where Beeroglad, the Bog leader, paid the ultimate price to ensure the safe return of the select few who had ventured into the world of the humans.

Inside the storeroom, Sergeant Uppendown, assisted by Constables Lou Kinnear and Stan Duprite, hurriedly moved the hay bales to one side to make room before the arrival of Abel and friends. The light in the room dimmed when Abel stood in the doorway, his figure completely blocking out the daylight. The Mounties watched as he stooped and squeezed sideways, forcing himself through the opening.

'Now that I'm in, I'd better hope I don't need to get out in a hurry, eh,' Abel laughed.

'Fer sure, sir,' replied the sergeant, jovially.

Aano followed close behind and waited with fingers twiddling in front of him as was his way when thinking delicately.

Uppendown and his constables made as much room as they could in so short a time, the sergeant then asked, 'Would you like us to leave now, sir?'

'No, please stay, Sergeant; you might well have a valuable thought on whatever it is Mr Grunt has to say.'

'Very good, sir,' replied Uppendown.

'Good afternoon, Mr Nogg.' The voice of Inspector Orange called in a rather muted tone from the doorway.

'Ah, Inspector, please come in, we have been waiting for you,' said Abel.

Al Orange made his way into the room with Marion and Harold steadying him and guiding him towards a convenient hay bale on which to sit. With three large geese of the Mounties, three substantial mallards, an orangutan and a huge pterosaur, things were quite cosy within the storeroom, but on looking around, the aura of every one of them was plain to see, melding warmly with the next and reassuring them that they were all in good company.

Al Orange could not help but cast an eye towards one of Abel's wings in particular.

Abel noticed his regard. 'Do not worry, my friend,' he said.

'I can't help it,' Orange replied. 'I can't look at you without seeing the bullet hole in your wing.'

'Would you ever order your constables to do the same thing again?' asked Abel.

'No, never,' replied Orange without hesitation.

'Then you are a better fellow for it, are you not?'

'But that doesn't alter what I did.'

'Then what would you have me do; should I beat you? Perhaps I should order your constables to do the same to you, hmm? Would a bullet through your wing make you see things differently?'

The inspector looked to the ground in thought. 'No, but that is what I deserve.'

Abel reached out and carefully rested a hand on the mallard's shoulder. 'What you deserve is the chance to lay your dark thoughts and your paranoia aside for good. When you led your party back from the world of the humans you proved yourself worthy of others trust and—'

'But that doesn't change what I did,' Orange butted in.

Abel led the mallard's eye towards Aano Grunt. 'Inspector, cast your mind back to when you were in the world of the humans searching for the one who bargained your soul for the Amulet.'

The inspector sat quietly, difficult memories coming swiftly to the fore.

Abel went on, 'The remainder of your team were waiting for your safe return beneath the hidden arch on the common.'

Both Aano and Sergeant Uppendown joined in the reminiscing, being as they were both members of the said team at the time.

Abel continued, 'They had to decide who would venture out into that dangerous world to find you.'

'Why did they bother?' said Orange, forlornly.

'Because every soul is worth saving,' replied Abel. He gave

Sergeant Uppendown a knowing nod to encourage him to take up the tale. The sergeant returned the nod and then he turned to Inspector Orange, saying: 'One of us had to go out into the open to search for you, Inspector. The trouble wus, none of us birds could go because we would be spotted too easily among the small birds of that world. Punch would have gone but he's a horse and can't speak English, so he couldn't go. That only left Mr Grunt, the orangutan. He immediately volunteered to go and search for you, despite the fact that you had on many occasions done yer best to assault and even shoot him.'

'Why, why would he do that for me?' muttered Orange.

'Yer constables asked the same question. They knew only too well how you had treated him previously – and do you know what Aano Grunt said?'

Orange shook his head, silently.

'He asked every one of us to look up at the trees and imagine how heavy he would be if he carried all his resentment and grudges around on his back. "The trees would never take my weight, and then where would I be." That's what he said sure enough. He said that to carry others bad behaviour around in yer own head is to let them run yer life.'

After two seconds of thoughtful silence, Aano Grunt finished the tale, 'Your life is yours, Inspector, and no one else's; so no matter what others have done to you, you should always do what you know to be right – simple.'

Sergeant Uppendown added one final thought. 'When you were leading us back through the humans' world towards the timbered wall, I wus glad to have you ahead of me, sir; you had spirit and verve despite all that you had been through. Yer constables followed you, hoping for your sake that you would succeed in getting us safely home, not for their sakes but for yours. They may not have said much during the journey, but they were sure willing you on all the way, and you won through.'

'Thank you, Sergeant.' Al Orange sniffed and raised his head. 'That was one of the rare occasions when my head felt light and my thoughts clear.' He settled his gaze in Abel Nogg's eye. 'I don't know what you did, Mr Nogg, but after you gave me my instructions on that day, I felt as though someone had swept through my mind, throwing out all the stuff that didn't belong. I could see clearly for the first time what needed doing.' He shivered visibly and uttered a groan; his head began to drop once again.

'Inspector,' said Abel, 'keep your head up; you know the path you must take, it is the righteous path and worthy of you. Follow it and you will not be alone.'

Aano Grunt sat down next to Orange and patted him on the back. 'I think you should tell Mr Nogg about your dreams now, Inspector, don't you?'

19

Before long, Al Orange was in full swing, regaling his audience with the curious contents of his dreams. He had expected a look of disbelief from those in the room, but rather, every eye seemed to encourage him to continue. Sergeant Uppendown was certainly not about to dismiss the inspector's tale; he himself had been a part of the expedition into the world of the humans and knew only too well of how strange things could get. Likewise, Aano and Harold had also shared in the weird events of late; Aano especially had spent many a quiet night trying to make sense of the humans' behaviour. He was also acutely aware of another presence that seemed to be lurking in the shadows, never showing itself except it seems to Al Orange. As for Abel Nogg, well – he just knew, but he had to let the creatures of this world work things out for themselves.

Having spoken for twenty minutes, Al Orange paused and looked about. Everyone sat silently sorting the inspector's words, stringing them together so that they might stay in the correct order.

'Well done, Inspector,' Abel eventually broke the silence. 'You have done well to recall your thoughts in such detail.'

Orange breathed a sigh of relief not to be ridiculed for such ramblings.

'The question now is what to do next?' Abel added.

'Do you mean you believe me?' said the inspector.

'My dear Inspector, you may have had some failings in your past, but lying was never one of them.'

The others in the room nodded in agreement.

Abel continued, 'You spoke of two men in particular in the room of your dream – think of the one sitting down, are you certain you have never seen him before?'

Al Orange replied immediately. 'I've never seen him in that guise, but there was something about his eyes.' He shivered. 'They were a dirty yellow with large black pupils, but they seemed to give off a certain light.'

'And did you notice a certain smell?' asked Abel.

'Yes,' replied Orange, desperation wetting his eyes. 'Fungus or decay…not very nice to be honest.'

Aano Grunt leaned across and reassured him with a pat on the shoulder.

Abel resumed his questioning in as soft a tone as he could manage. 'And the man who ran with you, the one who showed you the location of the body, what did you make of him?'

'He seemed to be suffering like me, desperate, exhausted and unhappy.'

'Would you trust him to tell the truth?'

'Yes I would, sir, definitely.' Orange's confidence began to waver when he realized that Abel Nogg, the last one you would ever want to let down or cross, was about to stake everything on what he, a mere mallard had told them. 'But this was only a dream, Mr Nogg,' he said, trying to back-pedal a little.

'Believe me, Inspector, those thoughts were put in your head by a malevolent being; one who you have come to know. It is my belief that he has planted such thoughts to lure some of you from this world back into that of the humans.'

Sergeant Uppendown and Aano Grunt spoke up together as their pennies dropped. 'To get hold of the Amulet.'

'Of course,' Harold joined in, remembering how everyone seemed to want to take the Amulet from him when he had last held it. 'But why is it so important to him?'

'I think I know,' said Aano, his intelligence shining through. 'The nasty one, whoever he is, can travel through the timbered wall whenever he wants, but unlike Mr Nogg, he can't bring anyone else through with him unless the Amulet is nearby.'

Abel Nogg nodded. 'Absolutely correct, Mr Grunt. Whoever he is, he will be waiting for your return. I am sure his intention is to follow you back – with all mankind in tow.'

Distress instantly showed on all the faces in the room.

'But we've seen how humans behave, sir,' Bob Uppendown said, his normally calm demeanour showing signs of anxiety. 'Their world is all wrong, totally screwed up.'

Aano replied in defence of the humans. 'Perhaps it's not their fault. Perhaps they didn't have such a nice place to start with; maybe their world has always been bad and they're gradually making it better.'

'I wish that were true,' Abel Nogg replied. 'But the truth is, they started with precisely the same benefits as your predecessors did in this world. They were given everything they needed, their world was in balance just as yours is today.'

Those in the room sat in silence while recalling all that they had seen during their short stay in the humans' world.

Aano scratched the top of his head and said, 'How can a supposedly intelligent breed deliberately spoil their own world – why would they do that?'

Abel replied, 'Of all the animals in your world, Mr Grunt, you are as close to a human being as one can get.'

'Oh no, please don't say that, Mr Nogg; I've seen how they behave – I've seen them up close.'

Abel noticed the perplexed look on the ape's face. 'The

building blocks used to create you are identical to those of a human, with the exception of three, or thereabouts.'

'Well, I'm glad I haven't got the last three, that's all I can say,' Aano replied.

Abel then asked of him, 'Can you imagine raising a club, or other similar weapon, to strike one of the birds in this room, Mr Grunt? To strike them in such a manner as to grievously hurt them?'

'No, please don't say such a thing, Mr Nogg. That's dreadful. How could you even think that I might?' The ape tightened his arm around Al Orange for comfort, while his other hand rested on his own forehead in despair.

No one in the room wanted to be seen to question Abel Nogg's ethics, but to deliberately upset Aano Grunt seemed cruel and unjust. Sergeant Uppendown was about to speak up when Abel moved towards him with a sharp look in his eye, one which did not sit easily with those in the room. They had never known the huge pterosaur to act in such a way before; this was absolutely the opposite of what they had come to expect. Abel drew closer to the goose who remained quite still with his Stetson perfectly straight upon his immaculate black and white head.

'If you cannot do it, Mr Grunt, then perhaps I should do it for you,' said Abel. He stopped two paces from Bob Uppendown, well within striking distance.

The sergeant remained unmoved, not understanding what was happening, or why. 'Please, sir,' he said, 'what is the meaning of this? Tell me what I've done to deserve this.'

'You have done nothing, Sergeant,' said Abel. 'Perhaps I simply want to exert my authority, so that you all know who is boss.' He then turned to Aano. 'Well, Mr Grunt, will you let me strike this goose before your eyes, or will you try to stop me?

And if so, how would you do it?'

Despite being the shortest in the room, Aano knew he would be the one, if any, to stop the pterosaur. *But how?*

The remaining mallards and geese lined up close to the sergeant to show that they stood as one while Abel continued to address the ape. 'Look on the hay bale in the corner.'

Aano quickly went to the shady corner where, lying on top of the bale, he saw a flintlock pistol as used by the Armed Response Ducks.

'Pick it up,' said Abel, showing no emotion in his voice.

'No, Mr Nogg.'

'I said, pick it up, Mr Grunt.' Abel slowly raised his arm as if about to strike Bob Uppendown.

'No, Mr Nogg. I could never fire it at anyone, so why would I pick it up in the first place?'

'If you do nothing then the sergeant will soon feel my wrath against the side of his head; now pick up the gun!'

The birds closed ever tighter together, they would not retreat, yet they knew they could never equal the pterosaur in strength, but they would stand their ground in the hope of somehow reconciling the beast.

Abel raised his clawed hand above the birds' heads. 'To do nothing, Mr Grunt, is not an option. I shall wait no longer.' The birds looked up, their beautiful eyes never losing their sparkle, but quite possibly about to lose their light altogether.

Aano picked up the pistol by the barrel, he could see it was half-cocked and presumed it was loaded. He had accidentally fired it once before when rescuing Inspector Orange, and so he knew of its devastating power.

'Mr Grunt, all you have to do is shoot me. Point it and squeeze the trigger, otherwise your friends will be laid to the ground never to rise again.'

Aano quickly moved towards the pterosaur, still holding the pistol by the barrel. The geese and the mallards wondered what else could be done. They looked to the door, thoughts of making their escape fleeted through their minds.

Abel read their thoughts. 'You might make it,' he said. 'But then you would have to leave Mr Grunt behind.'

Before the birds could reply, Aano squeezed in between his colleagues and the pterosaur. He looked up steeply to find the beast's eyes looking down at him. He turned the pistol about and slipped his finger through the trigger guard.

'So,' Abel said softly, 'you would take a life to save a life after all.'

'No, sir,' Aano replied, 'there is only one who has that right.'

The birds spoke up in perfect harmony. 'That's right, Mr Grunt, you tell him.'

With that, Aano reached forward and took hold of the pterosaur's free hand and placed it around his own which was still holding the pistol, ready to fire. He then raised the barrel to his own temple, and looking straight into Abel's eye of crystal blue he said, 'Now it is you who must squeeze the trigger, you who must choose. If you squeeze, you will lose me and you will lose the love of all those in the room and all those outside as well.'

Every perfect eye in every perfect head waited with bated breath. All stood together, knowing they were right.

Abel Nogg drowned in the beauty of the orangutan's mind. Aano stayed in the eye of Abel, not letting him look away until tears flooded from every eye in the room. The threatening hand above the birds came slowly to rest behind them and caressed them, drawing them closer. The other hand let go of Aano's grip around the pistol. 'Point that away and pull the trigger, please, Mr Grunt.'

Pointing the gun into the hay bale in the corner, Aano squeezed the trigger, a tiny spark ignited the powder in the side cup sending a cloud of smoke into the air. No smoke came from the barrel and no shot ahead of it. 'It wasn't loaded after all,' said Aano.

'Now come here, please,' said Abel, trying to wipe the tears from his eyes with clawed hands that were not really designed for such niceties. With his vast wings wrapped gently around all the birds and the rotund body of the ape, Abel resumed his speech, 'You could have resolved your problem by ending my life and yet you chose to give me the final choice. You proved that you value others before yourself, my friend.' He then released them from his embrace, saying, 'You all proved your love for each other and for life. I am truly humbled before you.'

'Sir?' Sergeant Uppendown queried, obviously bewildered by what had just occurred.

Abel answered, 'When I held my hand above you, ready to strike you, you did not move but stood your ground, Sergeant; why was that?'

It took but a second for the goose to answer. 'Because I am the senior rank here, sir. And to be honest, if I had moved away you might have turned your attention to one of my friends – and I sure wouldn't like that.'

Abel so wanted to smile, but his conformity in his present disguise would not permit such a distortion of his beak. 'My dear Sergeant, more than anything else right now, I hope you know that I would never hurt so much as one feather on your body, or any of your colleagues for whom I have the utmost respect…and love.'

'Then why?'

Abel resolved their conundrum by saying, 'I could have simply told you of the difference between you and humankind,

183

but instead, I let you show yourselves.'

Every bird let out the longest sigh of their lives as realization sank in.

Aano Grunt could not hide the look of doubt on his face – doubt in himself. 'Mr Nogg,' he said, 'I think I've seen my weakness and I don't like it, I don't like it at all.'

'How do you mean?'

'Well, if I was totally truthful and innocent – as innocent as these birds who honour me with their friendship, I would not have had to take the time to think about whether to shoot or not. But I did – I did have to think about it. Does that make me bad?'

Abel replied, 'The blueprint of your design is very nearly the same as that of man – any man. Your recent visit to their world showed you how they respond to anything that shows any sign of being different from them, especially if it challenges their own ideas.'

'But I don't want to be like that,' said the ape. 'I don't even want to think like that.'

Abel took a few moments to look into the ape's eyes once again, carefully moving through Aano's mind on gossamer feet and peering into every corner. 'Don't worry, Mr Grunt…you will never be like that.'

20

One by one each member of Abel's crew squeezed through the doorway and out into the open air. Al Orange felt strangely light, as if a load had been lifted from him. He still could not believe that he had divulged so much of his troubled mind to his colleagues without any intervention from his nasty tenant who would normally shut him down by blinding his mind's eye. *Perhaps Abel Nogg is right. Perhaps I'm just a pawn in my demon's game. Oh, by the Great Duck, I hope I'm not letting them all in for a bad time.*

Abel Nogg was the last to exit. 'My friends, you must get a good night's rest; I shall call on you tomorrow and accompany you back to the timbered wall where I might well have something to show you.' He then looked at Al Orange. 'Inspector, you in particular need a good sleep, be sure to keep Mr Grunt close by.'

'Yes sir, thank you,' Orange replied, casting a hopeful eye in the ape's direction.

A wry twinkle shone in Abel Nogg's eyes when he turned to Aano and casually asked out of the blue, 'Mr Grunt, how do you feel about gorillas?'

'Gorillas?' Aano cupped his chin with one hand and scratched the top of his head with the other. 'Magnificent fellows,' he said, sounding somewhat in awe. 'Don't they dwell somewhere in the middle of Africa?'

'Hmm,' replied Abel, 'In some worlds perhaps; I was just

wondering – that's all.' With that the pterosaur turned and opened his wings whereupon Mother Nature instantly lifted him from the ground and pointed him in the direction of the timbered wall. 'Good night, my friends.' With a gathering rush he accelerated over the treetops and was gone.

***

The light faded over Davidsmeadow as the tide of life began to ebb. An air of peace and stillness filled the streets. Most creatures of the day had made their way home while those inclined to venture out after dark had yet to appear. Inspector Hooter had bid Dana Lethgerk good night after satisfying himself that she was suitably recovered from her ordeal in the alleyway. Making his way back to the station, he glanced fondly at the table outside Café Hero where he had first met her. His memories of that first meeting warmed him as he passed by before turning left at the corner and crossing the road. He was about to enter the police station when Mrs Bottoms-Up rounded the corner having done some last minute shopping. As usual, she had her four newest ducklings in tow, now all of two feet seven inches tall.

'Good evening, Inspector,' Mrs Bottoms-Up called.

'Good evening, Mrs Bottoms-Up. My word, aren't your children growing fast, wonderful, quite wonderful.'

'Thank you,' Betty replied, hoping her youngsters would not say anything to embarrass her before she got them around the next corner. But she was not quite quick enough.

'Good evening, Mr Inspector, sir,' said young Bertie.

Oh no, not again, thought his mother. *Please don't say anything else, Bertie, please.* Betty tried to usher Bertie to her other side, out of sight of Hooter, but that was not going to stop the youngster asking the question:

'Do you know how to make eggs, Mr Inspector, sir?'

Hooter, quite taken aback by the forthright nature of the little duck had to pause to gather his thoughts.

Betty Bottoms-Up blushed. 'Please excuse young Bertie, Inspector, he's just being curious like young ducks are at times; he doesn't really know what he's saying.'

'I quite understand, madam. Don't give it another thought,' said Hooter, hoping that would be the end of the matter.

'But do you?' Bertie asked again.

Bertie's brother then joined in. 'I bet you've made lots of eggs, sir, you being important and everything.'

'That is quite enough, children. You're not to ask such questions of grown-ups, is that understood?' said their mother.

Not capable of stopping at such short notice, Bertie's bill kept opening and closing and the words kept coming out. 'Is making an egg like making a wardrobe?'

Hooter at last felt he could answer without leading himself into another innocent ambush. 'No, of course it isn't,' he chuckled. 'You need lots of tools to make a wardrobe, but none to make an egg.'

'That's like magic, then,' said Bertie, 'making things without any tools.'

'Hmm, I suppose it is,' Hooter replied. 'Not that I've made any,' he added.

'I bet you've made lots of wardrobes though.'

Hooter replied in a sombre tone, 'No, I haven't done that either.'

Betty came to Hooter's rescue. 'The inspector is far too busy for such things, children. Now come along, we must get home before it gets too dark.' She nodded respectfully to the inspector and hurriedly led her troupe down the road and out of sight.

Hooter crossed the road wondering if he would ever know

what it was like to make an egg and have a family of his own. He opened the station door and made his way to his office. His head was in an emotional muddle. *Have I devoted all my time to my job at the expense of having a life of my own? Is it too much to ask to have someone to hold me occasionally and say something nice?* He cast his mind back to his brief time with the lovely Marion Waters-Edge. *Thank heavens we didn't get around to making any eggs, that would have made things very awkward – and now I've found Dana, what am I to do? She won't wait forever. Perhaps it's too late for me to change, I'm sure I'm past my prime and probably couldn't make an egg if I tried.* He sighed and put his cap on the hat stand. 'Constable Howard,' he called.

'Yes sir?'

'Would you bring me a cup of cocoa, please? I think I'm going to have an early night.'

'Of course, sir, right away.' PC Howard busied himself making the cocoa while thinking to himself, Oh dear, The inspector seems a bit upset again. I thought he was getting better, happier and more cheerful, especially since Miss Lethgerk came on the scene. I hope being an adult doesn't mean always being happy then sad, then happy and sad. He returned to Hooter's office where the inspector was now lying on his bed beneath a lightweight blanket.

'Thank you, Constable.' Hooter, took the mug of cocoa and put it on the bedside table.

'See you at reveille, sir?'

'Of course, Constable. Good night.'

After making sure the blue lantern outside the station was lit, Howard closed the door and joined his comrades in the dormitory. James, Thomas, Russell, Peter and Robert were speaking in hushed voices, still discussing the incident in the alleyway.

'Is the inspector all right?' asked Robert.

188

'I'm not sure,' Howard replied. 'He seems a bit low, things on his mind I think.'

'That's probably because he's quite old,' said Robert.

'Maybe.' Howard reached up and turned down the light. 'Goodnight, chaps.'

'Goodnight,' five voices replied in the velvet darkness.

In keeping with much of the town, the police station fell silent. But there were always those who lived for the night by Mother Nature's personal invitation. The owl hooted from the tree in The Square. The tree was now almost bare having drawn the goodness from its own leaves during the autumn and since cast them across the pavers below. The owl turned his head and waited for a reply in the far distance, it was not long in coming. Flying low and straight he made off to meet his soul mate, keeping an eye open should he happen across an unfortunate vole or mouse perhaps. Nature in perfect balance.

The rain had stopped, leaving the town resting beneath quilted skies with stars above in an endless heaven, and creatures below in theirs…Beautiful.

21

The next morning in the humans' world, Kate was sat at a table by the pond. The front page of an early newspaper told of the plight of thousands still suffering throughout the world from drought and disease as famine gathered pace. Page two added to the misery by telling of the suffering of children at the hands of those who subjected them to abuse of all kinds, supposedly in the name of marriage – these children being only ten years of age in far off lands.

'How can this happen?' Kate muttered.

'Good morning, madam.' The young barista interrupted her thought, carefully putting a coffee on the table. 'Shall I make one for your friend?' he asked, looking in the direction of Walter who was now springing down the steps towards them.

Kate looked over her shoulder. 'Thank you, yes,' she replied, keeping her eyes on her handsome colleague.

'Hi,' said Walter, 'Is mine on the way?'

'Of course,' Kate smiled.

'Thank you,' Walter replied, taking a seat opposite her.

Kate slid the paper across the table. 'It's hard not to despair.'

Quickly glancing down at the copy, Walter replied, 'I know, but we are not here to act, but to observe and wait.'

'But sometimes it seems cruel to stand by and watch while so many people with nothing suffer, and others with plenty turn a blind eye'.

'You know what Abel Nogg would say. We are only two – there are millions here who could help, but they choose to see through blinkered eyes. It's their world and they have everything they need for all to prosper, and yet they stand by and blame others – always others.'

The two of them sat quietly while putting their own responsibilities in order.

'Any new ideas?' asked Kate, breaking the silence.

Before replying, Walter looked down, comparing his coffee with Kate's. 'That's sad,' he said light-heartedly trying to raise the mood.

'What is?'

'Well, have you noticed the swirl on top of my coffee is random, but yours is heart-shaped…I think you have an admirer.' Walter gestured subtly with a sideways nod towards the barista.

Kate followed his aim and peered across at the young man behind the counter who just happened to be looking at her at the same time. He turned away embarrassed, with her image indelibly printed on the inside of his head, *She's so beautiful.*

'I wonder how he'll turn out,' Kate mused.

'The barista, do you mean?'

'Yes. He's about to enter adulthood. Can you see his aura?'

'Of course I can,' Walter raised an eyebrow, 'not at all stable is it.'

'That's what I mean; he could go either way from where he is right now. His emotions are all over the place; I wouldn't mind betting he sees everything through his thoughts of love and lust.'

'Aren't most humans like that though?'

'I think so,' Kate replied. 'But lust can be expensive – in more ways than one.'

'Very true,' Walter replied, deliberately staring into Kates

191

eyes and raising both eyebrows, teasingly.

Kate smiled back. 'Don't be naughty.'

'Sorry,' said Walter, gently rubbing Kate's hand. 'So, once we've finished our coffee shall we head back to the timbered wall?'

'I think so,' Kate replied. 'We might have missed something…we might even catch sight of the loner in the trees again. I can't help thinking he could tell us more.'

***

The low cloud that had kept the night's chill off the land carefully took its leave as dawn broke over the timbered wall. The breeze teased the pines and the oaks, helping them shed a few more used needles and leaves in readiness for the season's change. The effect of the breeze was heightened when Abel Nogg slid sideways through the air on stilled wings. He waited for the trees to lean away from the track, thereby affording him just enough room to land without interfering with their branches. *What a patient chap,* the trees thought.

Having landed and folded his wings he hobbled over to the wall and settled on all fours listening to the songs of the birds among the foliage; he could hear the leaves holding conversation with the birds on the trees behalf, as they often do.

***

'I'm getting to know my way around here quite well now,' said Kate, taking care to steer her people carrier around the potholes along the track. She looked across at the firing range which occupied much of the land within the limits of the perimeter track. 'I wonder what takes up that space in the water birds' world.'

'Not a firing range,' Walter replied. 'Somehow I can't imagine a giant duck having a need for such a thing.'

'Hmm, but the Armed Response Ducks did have flintlock pistols.'

'And where do you suppose they got them from? asked Walter. 'No one in their world would make such a thing.'

'I think someone might have left them behind while on a previous visit,' said Kate.

'Yes, but flintlocks?' Walter replied. 'It must have been two hundred years ago.'

Kate pondered for a moment... 'Thankfully, birds like Inspector Hooter and his friends use the power of speech rather than the weakness of violence.'

'Unlike the humans of this world,' replied Walter, despondently.

'Hmm,' said Kate, 'no matter what race or creed, every human on this Earth has the use of a full vocabulary, don't they?'

'Of course they do.'

'So why don't they use it instead of fighting each other all the time?'

'They never seem to learn,' Walter replied.

Kate continued. 'Thankfully, birds like Inspector Hooter and his friends don't see the need for such weapons or they would have reproduced them by the thousands by now.'

'Like the people of this world did,' replied Walter, despondently.

'Can you think of one good thing that comes from weapons?' Kate asked.

'You know as well as I do, Kate; no good ever comes of weapons.'

'But what about your soldiers, don't they carry guns?'

Walter very slowly turned his head to meet Kate's eyes.

'Yes,' he said, 'but they are all fake.'

'Then why carry them?'

'Just to create an illusion, but every one of my squad carries his strength in his heart – like you and I.'

After a brief silence, Kate asked, 'Have you noticed how often the people of this world use the word "but"?' It usually comes before an excuse of some sort. I doubt if they could exist without it.'

Before Walter could add to her comment the timbered wall appeared ahead of them on the left hand side of the track. The trees gave a discrete shimmy on the couple's arrival, nothing excessive, just enough for Kate and Walter to notice. They got out of the car and walked the last few paces to the wall. Their skin tingled. 'Someone else is here,' they said, looking at each other.

The trees rustled, You're getting warm.

Walter kept his eye on the remains of the tin canopy which hung precariously from the timbers. He walked over and reached out his hand, stopping short of actually touching anything. 'The presence is almost tangible,' he said.

Kate watched silently, half expecting something to happen.

'Hello, Kate.' A familiar voice called from behind the wall.

'Did you hear that?' she said, moving cautiously along the timbers to take a peak around the other side.

'Be careful,' said Walter, still studying the tin canopy.

Not sure of what to expect, Kate tentatively put her head around the end of the wall. 'Oh, wow!' she shouted.

Walter raced to her aid, thinking she needed help. Kate had almost disappeared behind the wall when Walter reached out to grab her arm.

'It's all right,' said Kate, 'look, it's someone we both know.'

Walter was not quite ready for what came next. He rounded

the end of the wall and looked along the other side to see a huge pterosaur's head protruding from the timbers. Not just any pterosaur, but the head of Abel Nogg replete with brilliant red face and amazing blue eyes.

'Good morning, my friends,' said Abel.

Utterly flummoxed, Walter leaned backwards and peered along his side of the wall. *If his head is that side, how come his body isn't this side?*

'Are you looking for something?' said Abel, amused at the uncommon look on the captain's face.

'Where is your body?' asked Walter, incredulously.

'It's where it always is, on the other end of my neck just like yours is.'

Walter looked again around the end of the wall. 'Er, no it isn't.'

'Well, yes it is,' replied the pterosaur, enjoying the witty exchange and happy to wait for the penny to drop.

Kate stepped back and also took another peep on the other side. *Nothing.* She walked slowly along the trackside of the wall until she got to where she thought Abel's body should be. The trees rustled, *You're very warm, almost hot.* Standing very close to the timbers, she could feel a distinct buzz, *Oooh, it's right here.*

'Do you mind, that tickles,' Abel called out.

'You're on the other side of the ether aren't you.' Kate could not conceal her amazement at seeing first-hand the workings of the wall; she beamed the most beautiful smile which remained on her face as she returned to face Abel. 'Why don't you come all the way through?'

Abel's head explained, 'If I was to show myself completely, there is a chance that a distant rambler or dog-walker might spot me, and I think the people of this world have seen enough strange creatures for the moment, don't you?'

'So why don't you simply change your appearance, like you did before?'

'I could, but to be honest I only need to talk to you briefly and it didn't seem worth the effort of changing back and forth.'

Walter remained somewhat stunned by such goings-on. He had met Abel in his pterosaur guise previously, but seeing him in such a position, neither here nor there, took a little more figuring out. 'So this is where you move from one world to the next…through this timbered wall?'

'Yes, Captain. This is what I wanted to show you. I can come and go as I please, but others may only pass through if the Amulet, which I currently have in my possession, is present.'

The wonder of such a notion built rapidly in the captain's mind. 'So I could walk straight through the wall right now if I wanted to, because the Amulet is here.'

'Correct,' replied Abel. He knew the captain wanted desperately to try it out.

'May I?' Walter asked, holding his hand out for Kate to accompany him.

Abel nodded. 'I suggest you enter from the track side of the wall and be sure to return in the opposite direction as if you were going back through an ordinary doorway.'

'Ah, right,' said Walter. He and Kate excitedly made their way round to the other side.

'Shall we?' asked Walter, gently squeezing Kate's hand.

'I think we must,' Kate replied excitedly.

Walter slowly reached forward with a pointed finger, not knowing what to expect; Kate prompted him to ease his tight grip on her hand. 'Sorry,' he said. 'He we go.' His finger touched the wall which instantly softened and pulled the pair of them through with the firmness of a mother determined not to let go of her loved ones.

The timbers deposited them carefully in the sand – in the other world. They both stood in silence, taking a few moments to look around and take in what had just happened.

'The birds sound the same,' Kate whispered, listening to a blackbird singing away to its heart's content.

Walter kicked the sand with his boot. 'It feels the same, too.'

They looked along the length of the wall expecting to see one part or the other of Abel Nogg sticking out. 'Where is he?' Walter softly muttered.

'Why are we whispering?' Kate asked.

Walter shrugged his shoulders and gave an endearing smile. 'This is wonderful, the colours are so clear.'

Kate inhaled deeply. 'Mmm, I can smell the pines and the grass; I can even smell the sand, it's fabulous.' Her smile joined his. 'But where is Abel Nogg?'

'Let's think this through logically,' said Walter, straightening his officer's cap. 'We stepped through the wall—'

'Got sucked through to be more precise,' Kate interjected.

'Well, whatever,' Walter continued, 'we came through the wall from our side – the side of the humans, right?'

'Right.'

'And so, we are now standing in the wold of the water birds, right?'

'Right.' Kate could not help but smile her softest smile to encourage the captain's workings.

'Therefore, Abel's head won't be on this side, will it?'

'No,' Kate's smile endured.

Walter concentrated harder as he pictured the wall from above with Abel's abundant body on one side and his head on the other. 'Of course,' he said, taking Kate's hand once again and leading her round to the other side. 'When Abel's head was sticking out in one world, where was his body?'

Kate replied, 'It was still in the other world – the water birds' world.'

'And which world are we now standing in?'

'The water birds'.' Kate took up the narrative. 'So his body will be…' They rounded the end of the wall side by side…'right here, tah dah!'

Sure enough, there, with its neck disappearing into the timbers was the massive body of one very large pterosaur with its long tail swaying to and fro above them.

The desire to touch the incredible creature overwhelmed them both. They were head high to the impressively muscled thigh and so it was there that their hands softly fell. The muscle twitched at their touch, ticklish perhaps. They stroked lightly, the muscle twitched again, but they could hear no vocal response. In the other world however, Abel's eyes were struggling to hold back the tears born of a rather sensual origin, something he could not recall ever feeling, one hand in particular gave rise to an especially intense tingle.

About to stroke the beast for the third time, Kate's antics were brought to a sudden halt when the spade-like end of the tail swept round and came to rest against her olive porcelain cheek. She gasped at the touch, so strong and yet of such obvious tenderness that she was reminded of just who she was touching. 'I think we had better stop,' she said.

'Perhaps we should go back through the wall,' said Walter, 'we can hardly have a sensible discussion with Abel's rear end; even he isn't that clever, is he?'

Walter motioned to step up to the timbers, but Abel's tail quickly pressed against his chest, barring his way.

'Wait,' said Kate.

Walter realized his error straight away. 'Of course, we have to think of this as a normal door. To go back to where we started we must go back in the opposite direction.' The tip of the tail patted him softly on the head, leaving his cap slightly crooked. Kate giggled.

They both made their way to the end of the wall once again and took one last look at the huge body sticking out from the timbers. They then quickly peered around the end timber, *No head*, then back again, *big body*, then back again, *no head*. Having got things set firmly in their minds they stepped up to the wall; the timbers gladly pulled them in and set them down on the other side in the blink of an eye. Running as quickly as they could they rounded the end timber – and there was Abel Nogg's head staring straight at them.

'I'm glad you have sorted out the workings of the timbered wall,' said Abel. 'I trust you now know which world you are in and what you would see if you peered around the end.'

'Yes, thank you,' said Kate, with a hint of embarrassment on her face. 'I'm so sorry,' she added. 'I didn't mean to touch you in such a way, but without a head it's very easy to forget there is someone on the other end.'

Abel might have cut her short with an understanding acceptance, but he so enjoyed the warmth which came with her humility that he indulged his normally hidden feelings and let her finish her apology before explaining, 'This must be a fleeting visit, my friends. I wanted you to see the wall for yourselves. I also need to update you on a certain matter.'

'Good news, I hope,' said Walter. 'We could certainly do with some.'

'Quite possibly, Captain.' Abel then turned to Kate. 'You are acquainted with Inspector Orange?'

'Yes,' Kate replied, 'he's a very troubled soul; if I didn't know better I'd say he had a very unwelcome presence within him. How is he now? Have you seen him?'

199

'He is the reason I'm here,' said Abel. 'He has become very distressed of late and insists that he has been shown the whereabouts of a shallow grave on this very common.'

'A grave?' replied Kate, 'but I thought the missing Bog had been retrieved and returned home.'

'My dear Kate,' Abel's voice took on a solemn tone. 'You also met the pterosaur known as Beeroglad did you not?'

'Oh yes, what an impressive character, very nearly as big as you.' Kate's enthusiasm was plain to hear. 'He took the young constables under his wing in the absence of Inspector Hooter while they were in this world. In fact, I'd say he saved the entire squad from being captured by the police at Heath Pond…him and Aano Grunt.'

'I'm afraid I have sad news, my dear.' Abel held Kate in his eyes for a few seconds to prepare her for what he was about to say. 'It seems that Beeroglad encountered a truly bad individual on the last leg of his expedition here.'

Kate's expression fell to one of sadness while she recounted her last sighting of him. 'The last we saw of him was when he set off from the underbridge on the other side of the common, he was going to Smallbeef to meet Professor Hole; surely the professor didn't cause Beeroglad any trouble?'

'No, he didn't, but somewhere along the way, Beeroglad met his match and was substituted for the corpse in the chest.'

Sorrow filled Kate's heart, her blue eyes wetted to overflowing. Walter put his arm around her, trying to fill in the sequence of events which he himself had not thus far been aware of. 'So Beeroglad was a pterosaur?' he asked.

'Yes,' said Kate, keeping her emotions at bay. 'He was also troubled by thoughts not of his making, just like Inspector Orange, but he had overcome them and vowed to spend the rest of his life helping others…that's what he was doing when he disappeared.' Bolstered by Walter's support, Kate asked, 'Do you mean it was Beeroglad in the chest?'

'Yes, my dear,' replied Abel. 'As soon as the wagon had passed through the timbered wall the chest was opened…to reveal his deceased body.'

'But I saw the missing Bog in that very chest in Art Helkendag's storage unit in Davidsmeadow; I screwed the lid on myself.' Kate cast her mind back to that fateful night. She whispered to herself, 'The room…the mess…a fight perhaps?'

Abel took up the conversation, 'It seems that the missing Bog is still somewhere in this land, the land of the humans. It may well be that the body has been buried on the common to lure another rescue party through the wall to find him.'

'And you think Inspector Orange has been shown where the grave is…in a dream?'

'I am sure of it,' replied Abel. 'That is why I wanted you to see how the wall works. You might be called upon to breach it yourself in the near future.'

Walter had listened to Abel with utmost passion. He had always known of the presence of the ether, but until now had never seen it for real. His inquisitive mind prompted a question. 'Mr Nogg, you emphasized the importance of going through the wall in the correct direction; what would happen if we simply kept going round in the same direction?'

Abel smiled and nodded slowly, accepting the officer's genuine regard. This was one of those moments when he might have entered the mind of the inquisitor to see what was within before continuing further, but he already knew the immeasurable contents of Captain Haker; this was how man once was, how he was meant to be. 'I would dearly love to show you, Captain, but time is not on our side. You will find out what lies beyond the wall in the other direction when the time comes, you may be sure of that.' He then looked to Kate, 'And you too, my dear. I suggest you think of the timbered wall as a door – you come through in one direction and return in the other.'

Neither Kate nor Walter had realized that at some time during the conversation they had joined hands. 'That is good,' said Abel, 'there will come a time when couples such as you will have a place, a special place.' He lingered in their eyes one last time before saying, 'I must go now, but I would ask if you could both be back here tomorrow at midday. Your question might be answered then, Captain. I shall be here with a few friends, and together I hope you will make a plan on which will rest the future of this and other worlds; until tomorrow, my friends, goodbye.' The pterosaur's head immediately slipped back into the timbers leaving no clue as to him ever having been there.

'Wow,' said Kate.

'That was the weirdest thing,' replied Walter, at a loss for words. 'I thought I'd seen pretty much everything there was to see in this world, but that takes the biscuit.'

'Yes but that wasn't altogether in this world was it.' Kate pondered aloud, 'I wonder if Abel's friends will include Inspector Hooter or any of his crew. It would be wonderful to meet them again.'

22

Constables Howard and Thomas returned from their late morning patrol of Davidsmeadow.

'Is all as it should be, Constables?' asked Hooter, calling from his office.

'Yes sir, quite busy but nice,' replied Howard.

'Excellent.' Inspector Hooter appeared in the front office and proceeded to address the entire squad. 'In light of events yesterday in the alleyway, I think it would be a good idea to have some refresher training in respect of apprehending villains, culprits and bounders.'

Constable Russell spoke up on behalf of his colleagues, 'Do you think it was a shortcoming on our part that we didn't catch anyone, sir?'

'Not at all, Constable. I'm quite sure you did everything that could be done. But a little recap now and then is always a good thing.'

The constables sighed collectively. They would certainly not like to think that the inspector felt let down by their actions. Hooter was about to continue when the station door opened and to everyone's surprise and delight, there stood the local bobby with his helmet on slightly crooked as usual.

'Sorry to interrupt, sir, but I thought I should let you know I'm back and ready to resume normal duties in the community, sir.'

The squad shuffled about to make room for the bobby to enter and close the door behind him.

'Excellent timing, Constable,' Hooter remarked. 'We are about to go into the town and undertake some on-site training; I see no reason why you shouldn't join us, do you?'

'No sir, thank you, sir.'

Hooter continued, 'Listen up, Squad, we shall make our way to the alleyway where the incident involving Miss Lethgerk occurred yesterday. So let's have you in tip-top order lined up outside in single file right away.' He then turned to address the bobby but faltered almost immediately, 'Constable…erm,' It was only then that he realized he didn't actually know the bobby's name. 'Er… what **is** your name, Constable?'

The Bobby hesitated in his reply. Reluctant to expose himself to closer scrutiny. 'Um…'

'Come along, Constable, don't be shy.' Hooter encouraged the constable by introducing his squad first. 'Here we have Constables Thomas Thomas, Howard Howard, James James, Peter Peters, Russell Russell and Robert Roberts.' With renewed breath, Hooter continued, 'We also have Constables Lock, Stock and Barrel, but they are not here at the moment, they're out on familiarisation duties.' The Flying Squad waited eagerly, keen to finally know the name of the bobby. 'Well?' Hooter persisted, 'your name can't be any odder than my constables' can it?'

The bobby took a deep breath; the little duck inside him covered his eyes and ears, not wanting to hear the likely hoots of laughter at his expense.

'We are waiting, Constable,' said Hooter, still the epitome of patience.

The bobby caught the eye of everyone in the room one by one, finally coming back to the eyes of the inspector. 'It's…Five Degrees, sir.'

Hooter raised an eyebrow. 'I think you'll find it's a little warmer than that young fella, more like twelve I'd say.'

'No sir, it's Five Degrees.'

The room remained silent. No sniggers, not so much as a titter from anyone.

'Five degrees of what?' replied Hooter.

'That's my name, sir. I'm Constable Five Degrees.'

Hooter rubbed his bill, casting his mind back to the last conversation he'd had with the bobby concerning the odd shape of his head. 'Would that refer to the angle of lean of your helmet?'

The Bobby's bill quivered. 'Yes sir.'

The other constables jostled closer to him, gladly letting their warmth meld with his to offer their support.

'It's all right, mate,' James whispered. 'We all guessed why your helmet is always crooked.'

'That's right,' Russell continued the whisper, 'It makes no difference to us. The fact is we were glad enough to see you when you turned up at the inn that time, and wrapped your bicycle round the Bog; he would have given us a right beating if it wasn't for you.'

The bobby wiped his eyes, and the little duck inside him opened his. *Perhaps I am all right, after all.*

Hooter kept up the momentum to avoid any further dwelling on the subject. 'Now then, Constable Five Degrees, you shall join us as we march through the town to the alleyway for our training session; take up your position at the rear, please.'

'Yes sir.' The bobby's heart swelled with joy. *Marching out with the Flying Squad – me.* His little duck inside clapped his wings encouragingly.

The squad promptly lined up outside the station and waited for the inspector's next order. However, the proceedings were interrupted when around the corner came Mrs Betty Bottoms-Up with her troupe of youngsters bobbing up and down in their own version of a single file march.

'Hup two three four, hup two three four,' sang young Bertie at the front, his cumbersome webbed feet keeping time with his verse.

Hooter was a little reluctant to engage in conversation for fear of what young Bertie might come out with next, but to ignore them would be impolite to say the least, especially as Mrs Bottoms-Up was always a most respectful and diligent mallard.

'Good afternoon, Mrs Bottoms-Up,' said Hooter. 'My word, I do believe they've grown at least another inch since I saw them yesterday, quite wonderful.'

'Thank you, Inspector,' the blushing mother replied while giving young Bertie a stiff looking at as if to say *"don't you say a word, young duck".*

Bertie loved his mum and tried as hard as he could to remain silent, but his bill just would not stop opening and closing of its own accord. 'Good afternoon, Mr Inspector, sir. We are marching like constables,' he said in a very matter of fact sort of way. 'I know all the words, Hup two three four.' The ducklings raised their legs up and down on the spot, in time with his call. 'Hup two three four,' all bobbing up and down trying to impress the inspector.

'Simply marvellous,' said Hooter, relieved at not being subjected to any more innocent questioning by the youngster – but he should have known better by now.

Bertie still thought he hadn't got to the bottom of this egg making business, so he asked, 'Is it possible to make eggs on your own, Inspector sir?'

Betty Bottoms-Up blushed brighter than ever. 'What did I tell you, Bertie?'

The constables were still standing to attention, keeping a perfect straight ahead look. As much as Hooter wanted to, he knew he could not simply walk off without answering the duckling's question, so he answered as comprehensively as he knew how. 'No, young duck, it takes two to make an egg; a Mrs Duck and a Mr Duck, that's how things work.'

'Is that so that one can hold the lump of wood while the other saws it off?'

Hooter looked at Mrs Bottoms-Up, hoping she might intervene, but Bertie hadn't finished, 'I can see how it would be easier for two, especially when it comes to rubbing things to make them smooth – as smooth as an egg, at least.'

'Young fella,' Hooter replied, 'I told you yesterday, eggs are not made of wood.'

'What are they made of then?' asked Bertie.

'They are made from…ducks,' Hooter was sure that this reply had brought an end to the matter.

Bertie stared wistfully at the sky and rubbed his bill for the first time in his life while pondering the subject. 'Made from ducks?' he whispered on youthful chords. His mother looked him in the eye. *Don't say another word, Bertie.* She hoped that somehow her thoughts might find their way into Bertie's mind, but he was still too busy thinking about making eggs from wood.

'But if eggs are not made of wood, why do Mum and Dad spend so much time in the shed together?'

'Home with you, Bertie, and not another word.' Betty turned to Inspector Hooter. 'I'm so sorry, Inspector, all I seem to do when I meet you is apologize for Bertie's behaviour.'

'Don't give it another thought, madam,' Hooter replied, wondering what she and her husband really did get up to in the shed.

'Hup two three four, hup two three four.' Bertie and his brothers and sister were soon out of sight around the corner with a very embarrassed mum in front.

Hooter removed his cap and dabbed his brow. 'Phew.' His squad had remained at attention throughout, finding the episode very amusing to say the least.

Having straightened his cap yet again, Hooter called out, 'Squad, by the front, quick waddle.' Off waddled the squad, in perfect time with each other and helmets precisely upright – except for Five Degrees at the back, but he was smiling inside nonetheless.

The immaculate police procession turned right at the corner and passed Café Hero before proceeding down the High Street and left into the alleyway.

'Squad, halt.' Hooter looked around, there was no one to be seen. 'Squad, stand at ease – stand easy.'

The constables relaxed their stance, casually looking around at their surroundings. Russell and Roberts paid particular attention to the walls and hedges on either side of the alley. *No sign of disturbance, not so much as a snapped twig,* they thought, *so how come the bounder escaped?*

'Gather round,' Hooter called, breaking the constables' train of thought. 'The aim of today's lesson is to make sure we are all familiar with the proper use of handcuffs.'

Seven constables exhibited seven puzzled looks. *Handcuffs?*

'Excuse me, sir,' Constable James spoke up, 'but we don't carry handcuffs.'

'Precisely, Constable,' Hooter replied, 'but after listening to Aano Grunt's recollections of how Inspector Orange arrested him and put him in handcuffs, I thought perhaps we should consider making them part of our normal compliment.'

The constables were not so sure, but they were constables

not inspectors, so they listened with all due diligence while Hooter went on with his training session. He raised a wing to expose a pair of handcuffs hanging from the handle of his truncheon which was in turn securely housed in its holster. Hooter took the cuffs and lowered his wing. 'Here we have one pair of standard issue handcuffs. They can be attached to a villain by simply pushing them against the part of the body you wish to secure; they open and close automatically, and once fitted they can only be unlocked by means of a key.'

Uh-oh, thought the constables.

'Which I have in the bottom of my truncheon holster,' Hooter added.

Thank heavens for that.

'Handcuffs are to be used if you are apprehending an individual who you think is quite likely to try to escape, even if you have explicitly told him not to do so. Is that all clear so far?'

'Yes sir,' came the reply seven-fold.

'Excellent.' Hooter continued, 'Can anyone tell me what the main problem is with fitting handcuffs to a suspect?'

Constable Five Degrees tentatively put his wing up. 'Is it that most suspects we come across don't have hands, sir?'

'That's it exactly, Constable, well done.'

Five Degrees put his wing down feeling very pleased with himself, that being the first time he had answered an official question.

'So?' asked Hooter. 'What are the alternatives?'

'Legs, sir,' Robert Roberts answered confidently, 'definitely legs.'

Hooter replied with a spring in his voice, pleased at the way things were going. 'Wonderful, Constable. Legs indeed are our only other option.'

The constables exchanged glances, *This is a doddle*, they

thought; all except Constable Five Degrees. 'Erm, sir?' he asked.

'Don't worry, Constable. If you cannot keep up we'll recap at the end and answer any questions you may have, all right?'

'Erm, yes sir, but—'

'At the end, Constable, at the end,' Hooter insisted. 'Now, I'd like a volunteer to act like a suspect.'

After a couple of seconds no one had stepped forward, and so, Constable Five Degrees did the noble thing.

'Well done, Constable. Remember, for the purpose of this exercise you must act like a villain.'

'I'd rather be a bounder if that's all right, sir. I think a villain sounds a bit too nasty and I might not do the role justice.'

'Very well,' Hooter replied, keen to keep up the momentum.

'There is one thing, sir,' said Five Degrees, 'what if—'

'At the end, Constable, at the end.' Hooter eagerly stooped down and clicked the cuffs around each of Constable Five Degrees' legs.

'They're not too uncomfortable are they?' asked Hooter.

'No sir, but—'

'Tup, tup, questions at the end.' Hooter now stepped to one side and gestured with a wing. 'There we have one securely cuffed bounder.' He nodded, saying, 'I think you'll agree, Constable, that even with your very best impersonation of a bounder you most certainly will not escape from my custody until I release you.' With a smile in his eye at having given what seemed to be a very comprehensive lesson, Inspector Hooter finished off by saying, 'Well, Constable, get out of that if you can.'

With that, Constable Five Degrees spread his wings and flew off, his legs shackled together but not preventing him from carrying out a typical near vertical mallard take off.

The squad stood in silence. Oh dear, they all thought, surely that shouldn't have happened.

'How far do you want me to fly, sir?' Constable Five Degrees called out, hoping he had done the right thing.

The rest of the squad knew this was not the outcome Inspector Hooter was expecting. They each recalled the time when their inspector resorted to flying with only one wing in order to use his binoculars in mid-air; the resultant spiralling Earthward of the entire squad almost spelled the end of them. On that occasion Hooter came up with a very dubious excuse, saying he was thinking of inventing a helicopter, but of course no one knew what a helicopter was, or did, or even looked like. The constables waited silently for yet another incredible excuse.

'Well, erm, I knew this would happen of course; I'm only surprised none of you spotted the flaw beforehand.' Hooter gazed upward and called out, 'You can come down now, Constable Five Degrees.'

The constable circled and lined himself up carefully, judging his approach very accurately to land in the small courtyard by the side of the tearoom rather than risk his wings interfering with the wall or hedge bordering the alley itself. Not all water birds are capable of landing and taking-off so steeply, but Five Degrees managed very proficiently, hardly needing to alter his step once on the ground.

'Right, well, thank you, Constable, for demonstrating the uselessness of handcuffs. Of course I knew that's what you would do and I'm pleased you didn't let me down.' The inspector promptly unlocked and removed the cuffs.

'Oh, I see,' replied Five Degrees, 'you were one step ahead of me there, sir. For a minute I thought you were just being daft, but you were just testing me, eh, sir.'

'That's right, young fella. You may rest assured I was never in any doubt as to the outcome.'

'Right sir.' Five Degrees stepped back in line with his comrades, relieved at not having embarrassed his new-found mentor after all. The other constables had their doubts.

Hooter held up the cuffs one more time. 'Can anyone think of any other way to secure a bounder using these?'

Thomas offered his thoughts. 'I suppose we could attach one cuff around the leg of the bounder and then attach the other cuff around an immovable object – like a small tree or a post or something.'

The inspector rubbed his bill while mulling over the suggestion. 'But then how would we get the bounder back to the station?'

'We could dig up the tree, sir, and take it with us,' said Constable Peters in support of his fellow constable.

'Can you imagine the looks we would get waddling up the High Street carrying a tree with a mallard shackled to it? No, Constable, I don't think that would do at all. You may rub your bills if that will help,' said Hooter. All seven constables began rubbing their bills, eager to be the one to come up with a sensible solution.

'The thing is, sir,' said Robert Roberts, 'handcuffs must be called handcuffs because they're for cuffing hands.'

'I'm sure you are right, Constable. The truth is, I cannot even remember how or when the perishing things came to be in our possession; I mean, in a land where no one has hands, what is the use of handcuffs?'

Constable James suddenly shivered. 'Oh dear, sir.'

'What is it?' asked Hooter.

'I've just had a nasty thought, sir. What about the humans in the world on the other side of the timbered wall? The cuffs would fit them, right enough.'

'By jingo, you're right. Come to think of it, all the policemen in that dreadful world carried handcuffs on their belts. That can only mean one thing, Constables.'

The constables stood in silent contemplation, waiting for their leader to finish.

'Human beings break the law!' Hooter tried to sound as if he was certain in his reckoning.

'But sir,' said James James, 'I thought they were supposed to be the leading species, the top of the tree so to speak. If they are, then they should lead by example, surely.'

'Constable James, all of us who visited that world saw first-hand how they behave. You saw what they did to me. For no reason they tried to beat me up and when that failed they shot me and locked me in a cell. Who knows what they would have done to me if I had not been rescued? And as for the behaviour of all the adult humans around the pond, shaking their pushchairs at us and hurling very naughty words into the air, why? I think you are right, Constable James. I think handcuffs were invented specifically for human beings; why, I'm surprised they don't all walk around wearing them permanently. The puzzle is, how did the handcuffs come to be here?'

After a little more collective bill rubbing, the inspector brought things to a conclusion. 'I think this is one of those questions that we may never know the answer to, but one thing is for sure, if we are called upon to venture into their world again we must all be sure to take a pair of handcuffs with us as part of our standard equipment – do we all agree?'

'Yes sir,' seven voices replied.

The little duck inside Hooter breathed a sigh of relief that he had somehow managed to turn the training session from what could have been an unmitigated humiliation into a resounding success, having tested and found a possible use for the handcuffs which hitherto had never been considered necessary.

'Right then, Constables, I think we have done enough training for today; you may make your way back to the station and resume normal duties. I shall just conduct a patrol around the town while I'm here. So let's have you in single file. Squad, attention, by the front, quick waddle.'

And so the squad went smartly in one direction while Inspector Hooter went the other, hoping perhaps to bump into a certain beautiful female mallard named Dana.

23

The remainder of the day passed without incident. It was now evening and all was quiet around the town. The constables had conducted their last patrol of the day and had found nothing amiss. Inspector Hooter lay on his bed dozing among thoughts of his past, wondering what his future might bring. *Will it bring companionship – one special bird to hold at the end of the day?* His constables had settled in the dormitory where their collective chatter had subsided into gentle breathing, at peace with their world.

Constable Five Degrees, being the official local bobby, had retired to his flat above the police station, he too lay on his bed after what had been an interesting day for him. Hopefully, his new-found colleagues in the Flying Squad would become good friends; he had always been a bit of a loner, never quite feeling at ease with others due to his odd shaped head. *Inspector Hooter said it needn't be a problem, so perhaps I'm just being over-sensitive.* Now he rested, comfortable with his lot, looking forward to tomorrow and whatever challenges it might bring.

Mother Nature had left the town in silence. No breeze to tease the few remaining leaves on the trees, no clouds to block out the partial Moon. Just peace and quiet.

Constable Five Degrees, although feeling at ease and a little tired from his busy day, found it difficult to get off to sleep. He whiled away the passing minutes by listening as hard as he could, trying to identify even the slightest sound from outside; there really was nothing to hear until the gentle hush of air preceded a fleeting shadow across his window. *Whatever could that be?* He listened for a few seconds more. A faint shuffling could be heard in the courtyard below. He slipped from his bed and reached for his truncheon, *Just in case someone is lost, so I can point the way for them.* He carefully opened the door from his flat and made his way down the outside staircase. The Moon did its best to cast a silvered light across the courtyard, leaving only one corner in shade. Stepping off the bottom step, Five Degrees could see no one, but he sensed a closeness. *Someone is here, I'm sure of it.* Leaving his truncheon in his holster, he moved to the middle of the yard and turned his head almost right around to survey the scene. 'Is anyone there?' he whispered. 'I'm a police duck, so you can come out if you like, you're quite safe.' The feeling of another's presence grew. *Perhaps I should call the others for support.*

A softened gruff voice whispered from the darkened corner. 'Don't do that.'

'What...who?'

The next moment the unmistakable shape of a monstrous pterosaur sidled into the open for the constable to see plainly. 'Don't be alarmed, Constable, it's me, Abel Nogg.' He hunkered down on all fours to make himself as short as he could, although he still towered way above the mallard.

'Mr Nogg, sir,' exclaimed the mallard, surprised and relieved. 'What are you doing here at this hour? Should I fetch the inspector for you?'

'No, Constable, there is no need to wake him, I am quite sure you can deal with my request.'

Five Degrees whispered his reply, 'If I possibly can, sir, of course.' Having become acquainted with Abel during his stay at

Fort Bog, the constable held no fear of the hefty beast standing before him.

'Please, come closer,' asked Abel, holding out an alarmingly clawed hand.

'Oh, right,' replied Five Degrees, waddling quietly forward.

'I do not want to disturb Inspector Hooter, but I would like you to give him a message first thing in the morning. Please ask him to meet me by the timbered wall at noon tomorrow.'

'Certainly, sir,' said Five Degrees.

'I see you're not wearing your helmet.' Abel whispered.

'Oh, sorry, sir, I forgot to put it on in the hurry to get down here.'

Abel raised his arm and gently ran his cupped hand over the mallard's head while admiring the reflective blues and greens making the most of the Moon's light. The mallard made no attempt to back away from Abel's single-handed embrace, in fact he rather enjoyed the affection, something he had not experienced before. Abel's eyes issued a light all of their own, a blueness which danced and whirled hand in hand with the mallard's eyes of soft hazel.

After a minute or so, when Abel had assured himself of the mallard's nature, he gave a gentle squeeze and released the constable from his hold. 'You are a good bird, my friend, and you are in good company here.'

'Thank you, sir.' Five Degrees was not too sure of what had just gone on but he felt strangely sorted, as if everything inside his head had been rearranged very slightly, but nicely.

Abel stepped back a pace and raised his wings. The mallard could not help but gasp quietly at the awesome wingspan.

'Do not forget my request, Constable; Inspector Hooter – the timbered wall – noon tomorrow.'

'Righto, sir.'

Invisible hands lifted the pterosaur above the rooftops and turned him in the direction of Smallbeef. With long, near silent sweeps of his wings he was quickly nought but a memory.

With no one but the Moon for company, Five Degrees took his time to gather his thoughts before making his way back up the stairs and into his cosy lodgings. With his instructions firmly registered, his mind soon floated away, waiting for the sunrise to trigger his inner alarm.

**

A fine late autumn day came to light. A blanket of mist lay over those parts of the land that needed it, like a cold compress soothing the scuffs and scratches sustained through the two previous seasons of sowing, growing and reaping. With her sweetest breath, Mother Nature lovingly blew the mists away over the eastern horizon to be taken up into the air and continue their endless journey around the world; who could say how long it would be before their return to this most hospitable land? But return they would, for they were loved and respected. *If the air and the water are not treated with respect what chance has life got?* That was the birds' mantra.

Within an hour of sunrise all the mallards and geese within Smallbeef had preened and cleaned and eaten. Inspector Orange sat at the table in what was Dick's front room. He had finished his breakfast of porridge and tea, and now he stared out of the window feeling rather bleary eyed after an unusually deep sleep. For the first time in many a year he had slept with no incursion from his demon. *Has he finally left me? Could I really be rid of him? Don't tempt fate you old fool, not yet.*

Aano prompted the mallard from his thoughts. 'Inspector, how did you sleep?'

'Better than I've ever slept before,' came the reply. 'I'm still trying to wake up. I'd forgotten what it was like to sleep alone in my head.'

'That's a good sign,' said Aano, sharing the inspector's view through the front window. Their attention was taken when one very large pterosaur shuffled up the path towards them. 'Here comes Abel Nogg,' Aano grinned nervously. 'I hope he doesn't want to use me to demonstrate any more of his principals.'

'He tested us all yesterday in one way or another,' replied Orange. 'You acquitted yourself brilliantly, though.'

They had no time for any more chit chat as Abel halted outside the front door. He knew he had been spotted and so he waited the few seconds it took for Aano Grunt to open the door and welcome him. 'Good Morning, Mr Nogg, sir. It looks like being a lovely day.'

'It does indeed, Mr Grunt. That bodes well for our activities today, which is why I am here.'

'Ah, I see,' replied Aano.

Inspector Orange leaned forward in his chair to get up. Abel quickly called out. 'Stay where you are, Inspector, I'm sure you can hear me from there and I am sure you need your rest.'

'Thank you, sir.' The mallard let himself back down, glad of a little more time to recover.

'Mr Grunt, would you be so kind as to gather the following individuals in the yard in half an hour. I wish to take you to the timbered wall to show you something.'

'Of course, Mr Nogg; who would you like?'

'Yourself and Inspector Orange, and also Sergeant Uppendown and Harold Waters-Edge...and his son Dick.'

'Will we be gone long?' asked Aano.

'I expect to have you back here by teatime, my dear ape, so I shall see you all in the yard in half an hour, all right?'

'Yes sir, absolutely.'

***

Knock, knock. In Davidsmeadow, Constable Five Degrees tapped lightly on Inspector Hooter's office door. 'Excuse me, sir, are you awake?'

'I certainly am, Constable.' The inspector opened the door almost before Five Degrees had finished what he was saying. 'What can I do for you?'

'I have a message for you, sir; it's from Abel Nogg.'

'Abel Nogg, is he here?' Hooter peered over the constable's shoulder expecting to see the pterosaur squeezed into the front office.

'He was here last night, sir, after lights out. He didn't want to disturb you but he gave me a message for you.'

'I see, well in that case you had better tell me.'

'Yes sir – he said for you to be at the timbered wall by midday today, he will meet you there.'

'Ah, I see, okay.' Hooter gazed at the bobby for a second or two longer. There was something different about Five Degrees, something subtle but definitely different. 'Thank you, Constable, you may go about your routine duties now; I'll have a quick breakfast and then set off for the wall.'

'Yes sir.' Constable Five Degrees turned and made his way towards the door to leave.

'Wait a minute,' Hooter called aloud. The rest of the squad, on hearing the inspector's call, came out from the dormitory to see what was going on.

'What is it, sir?' said Constable James.

Five Degrees stopped in his tracks, thinking he had done something wrong. He waited apprehensively while the other constables jostled into the office.

Without giving any clue as to his concern, Hooter said, 'Constable James, take a look at Constable Five Degrees.'

'Erm, right, sir.' James perused the bobby from top to bottom and then back up to the top. 'Done it, sir. I've looked at him, now what?'

'Take another look, more carefully.' Hooter turned to the others. 'All of you, can you see something odd?'

Constable Five Degrees remained quite still, embarrassed by such close attention. *What have I done wrong?*

The constables looked the bobby up and down once more and then spoke up in unison, 'Nothing odd at all, sir.'

'Exactly,' replied Hooter, 'exactly.'

'Eh?' said six constables.

'Eh,' said Five Degrees.

'Straighten your helmet, Constable Five Degrees.'

Without thinking, the constable reached up to do as he was told, but his helmet was not quite where it would normally be; it felt different. He explored its position, puzzled. 'I think it **is** straight, sir.'

'That is precisely what I mean,' said Hooter, 'your helmet **is** straight.'

'Permission to remove my helmet, sir,' asked Five Degrees.

'Granted.'

Five Degrees removed his helmet while all in the room watched eagerly. He then cautiously ran his wing over his head, feeling its shape as he often would. 'It feels properly round, sir; my head is properly round!' A tear blossomed in his eye. 'It's properly round!'

How can that be? The Flying Squad exchanged looks of amazement while Five Degrees repeatedly put his helmet on and then took it off, then on and off several times to be sure he was not imagining things. 'Oh yes,' he said, 'it's definitely properly round.'

Hooter rubbed his bill with a certain look in his eye. 'You

said Abel Nogg visited you last night?'

'Yes sir, we spoke for about five minutes, that's all.'

'He didn't just speak, I bet.'

A thought entered Five Degrees' mind. The little duck inside him smiled knowingly, *Miracles do happen, with a little help*. 'I think I'll just do an early patrol around the town,' said the young bobby. He stepped out from the station, turning his head this way and that way and looking at his reflection in the shop windows. *Properly straight*, he smiled.

'Wonderful,' said Inspector Hooter. 'Now then, Constables, back to business.'

***

After settling his constables into their routine, and having had his breakfast, Hooter was now flying eastwards at an altitude of five trees. This kept him comfortably below the clouds which were also travelling in the same direction, albeit at a much slower rate. Before long he was passing to the south of Smallbeef. Thoughts of Marion Waters-Edge briefly entered his mind, causing his heart to give a gentle tug as he passed by unnoticed. The open moorland soon came into view, the greens and yellows of the flora had dulled in readiness for the change of seasons, but it still had a welcome familiarity to it. He could not help but compare the land below him to the same land in the humans' world. *Nature is no different in either world, and yet this land is so much sweeter and balanced.*

Onward flew the lone mallard, now getting on in years, philosophizing as he went, grateful for the day in which he was flying. After a few more horizons the timbered wall came into view. The tops of the trees waved gently to welcome the inspector who they knew to be a jolly nice chap. A few minutes later he had landed by the wall, on the side of the common. He took his time to look around, always a nice thing to do, if only to make the flowers feel appreciated; all was as it should be and very nearly silent apart from the faint twittering of small birds on the wing. He slowly waddled his way around the end of the wall onto the track where he then made his way along the verge, halting by the trackside beneath the tin canopy.

He recalled the last time he had stood on this very spot when he and Aano Grunt had returned from the other world with the wagon, only to find that the body they had brought back was none other than Beeroglad. He sighed softly and then, feeling quite alone, he settled down on the grass verge with his thoughts, and waited quietly for Abel Nogg to arrive.

24

Hooter's head had barely settled into his chest when a pine tree sprinkled him with a few loose needles. 'Eh, what?' He lifted his head and looked around. N*othing, No one.* Among the pines stood a particularly large oak of senior years. The tree had met the inspector on several occasions before and felt he knew him well enough, so he took careful aim and let go an acorn with utmost precision. The other trees giggled when the acorn bounced off Hooter's head and rolled across the track.

'Very funny,' mumbled Hooter, looking up to see the oak's branches beckoning him to look higher still. It was then that he realized what the oak was trying to tell him. His heart warmed when he saw the ape, Aano Grunt, hanging upside down from the clawed feet of Abel Nogg, hovering in the sky above him.

Aano called out, 'Good morning, Inspector.'

Hooter cast a quick eye towards the Sun's glow which was partially obscured by the low cloud. 'Good afternoon to you, Mr Grunt, I think you'll find it's about half an hour beyond noon.'

'Oh, right, thank you,' said Aano, not endowed with such precise time keeping abilities as a mallard.

'Honk honk,' the unmistakable sound of a Canada goose announced the arrival of the rest of Abel's crew close behind.

'Oh my word, how wonderful,' Hooter called out. One by one his friends landed on the track which seemed wider than usual thanks to the trees leaning obligingly away.

Aano was first to touch down, hands first and doing a forward roll to right himself. 'It's good to see you again, Inspector.'

'It's good to see you too, Mr Grunt,' Hooter replied.

Next down was Sergeant Uppendown, looking as immaculate as ever in his super sharp Stetson. Inspector Al Orange came in next, topped off with his chequered baseball cap. Lastly, Harold and Dick Waters-Edge completed the ensemble.

The entire crew were quick to sort themselves out and line up ready for Abel's address which they knew would not be long in coming.

'Thank you, everyone – and thank you, Inspector Hooter, for answering my call; you obviously got the message from Constable Five Degrees.'

'Yes sir.' Hooter was hoping to broach the subject of Constable Five Degrees' head, but he put the matter to one side, sensing that Abel had more pressing things to discuss.

Abel wasted no time in beckoning the crew to come closer and gather round, enjoying the closeness of such beautiful creatures. 'I have asked you all here today to tell you a little more about the timbered wall.' He paused briefly before turning to Inspector Hooter. 'Inspector, you asked me a while ago about the importance of going through the timbers in a certain direction.'

'Oh yes, that's right, I did.'

Abel's audience listened wide-eyed, secretly dreading the day when they would have to repeat their journey into the world of the humans.

Abel touched the Amulet which hung around his neck, he then ensured he was within two paces of the wall. 'Inspector Hooter, would you care to touch the timbers and peer through?'

Hooter looked puzzled. 'How do you mean – peer through?

225

I seem to remember the wall pulling me all the way through as soon as I touched it; I didn't have a choice of stopping halfway.'

The rest of the crew muttered in support, 'Yes, that's right, it did.'

Abel replied, 'Ordinarily you would be quite right, Inspector, but for the purpose of this exercise you may imagine that I have had a word with the wall – and it will comply with my wishes, I'm sure.'

Hooter tilted his head and looked at the wall, saying, 'Did you hear that, wall?' He then cautiously waddled forward, stopping with his bill just a feather's breadth from the aged timbers. 'Now?' asked Hooter.

'Now, if you please,' replied Abel.

Hooter's bill touched the wall. 'Ooer,' he mumbled. The timbers pulled him in more softly than usual, giving him the chance to control his movement and bring himself to halt as soon as his head emerged on the other side. 'Ah, here we are,' he said, looking around at his surroundings. Fortunately there was no one within sight of that side of the wall which now had a brightly coloured mallard's head sticking out of it.

The rest of the crew stared at Hooter's back end still sticking out on their side, and for some inexplicable reason every one of them experienced a strong urge to give the softly feathered rump a prod. Aano, being mentally the closest to a human, felt the urge the strongest. 'I don't know if I can resist it,' he said.

'Not now, Mr Grunt,' said Abel, 'I would not want you to cause the inspector such a shock as to make him jump all the way through.'

'No, of course…I'm sorry,' Aano replied, 'I don't know what came over me.'

'Perhaps you would take a look around the end of the wall and tell us what you see,' asked Abel.

Aano started towards the end of the wall but paused. 'Surely there won't be anything there, will there?'

Every bird in the crew tilted his head, puzzled by the ape's assumption. *How odd, but the inspector's head must be somewhere.*

Aano continued to make his way to the end and enthusiastically peeped around the other side. 'As I thought,' he called out, 'no head.'

'No head?' Three mallards and a goose waddled hurriedly to join Aano to see what he was talking about. On peering along the other side of the wall they were indeed greeted with no head – nothing sticking out from the wall at all.

Aano, being the bright chap that he was, continued aloud with his thoughts on the subject. 'Don't you see? His head is sticking out the other side right enough, but in the other world, the one with the humans in.'

Abel Nogg nodded to acknowledge the ape's intelligence. 'Well done, Mr Grunt.' He then addressed the rest of the crew, 'Does anyone **not** understand what Mr Grunt has said?'

The others paused for a few moments with enlightened expressions on their faces. Sergeant Uppendown spoke up on their behalf, 'I think we all see what has happened, sir; Inspector Hooter is at this very moment looking out across the humans' moorland on the other side of the wall. I sure hope no one notices him, I don't think they would take too kindly to a giant duck's head growing from the timbers.'

The group chuckled quietly while peeping from one side to the other in quick succession. 'That's what's happened, no doubt about it,' said Harold Waters-Edge. 'He's half in this world and half in the other.'

Inspector Hooter felt entirely comfortable in the embrace of the timbers as they held him gently but firmly around his shoulders. He spoke quietly to himself while turning his head freely to study his surroundings. 'It's the same time of year as in our world, the flora is beginning to rest, and there are fewer flying insects about. I can't see a single person anywhere, perhaps they don't come out in the colder weather. It's just as well there's no one here, I don't think they would take too kindly to me appearing like this.' It was then that he noticed movement among the trees on the far side of the common. 'A human, a man I think, on his own.'

Hooter's commentary was cut short when Aano Grunt's head popped through the wall and appeared right next to him. 'Hello,' said the ape, grinning with excitement.

'Good heavens, you made me jump, Mr Grunt; I must say you look most peculiar with just your head showing.'

'I can't imagine what I look like on the other side with just my back end sticking out, I hope they don't get up to any mischief,' said the ape. 'I must admit I was very nearly tempted to give your rump a gentle poke, just for fun you understand.'

'Of course,' replied Hooter, making allowances for Aano's almost human sense of humour. *Very strange.*

'Mr Nogg said you were to come back now,' said Aano.

'Okay, but before we go, take a look up there; can you see that man right over there on the top of the rise?'

Aano stretched his neck as if the extra few inches would make a difference over a distance of a mile or so. 'I think I can see him, is he alone?'

'Yes he is, he seems to be wandering around kicking the sand. Thankfully his eyesight is not as good as ours – or mine at least.'

'I think we should go back now, before he notices us,' said Aano.

Without further ado, the wall squeezed them both very gently and returned them fully to their side of the wall.

'It's good to have you back,' said Abel. 'I trust you found your little trip interesting.'

'Oh yes,' Hooter replied. 'It felt most peculiar being held halfway through. For such gnarled looking timbers they have an extremely comforting embrace.'

'Perhaps they just like you, Inspector,' Abel Nogg chuckled. 'Now please gather round in a circle while I tell you more.'

And so, Harold and Dick, Bob Uppendown, Inspectors Orange and Hooter, and Aano Grunt encircled the giant pterosaur, knowing they were about to be enlightened with yet more incredible knowledge.

'Now then, my friends, this might get a little complicated, so if you do not understand anything I say, please speak up immediately.'

'Of course – immediately,' Hooter replied.

'Thank you, Inspector,' said Abel, in no doubt as to who would be doing most of the speaking up. 'I may have mentioned previously the importance of going through the wall in the correct direction.'

'Yes you did, sir; to me anyway,' Hooter keenly replied.

'In reality,' Abel went on, 'it makes no difference. The wall will take you from this world and put you into the next whichever side you approach it from, but, and this is important; in order to return, you must always come back in the opposite direction to that in which you went. Is that clear?'

His audience took two seconds of thought before replying as one, 'Yes sir.'

'I just think you will be less likely to get confused if you always make a point of starting from the track side.'

The birds pondered briefly before Hooter spoke up again, 'How can we get confused if all we do is go through and then come back. When we went through last time we didn't get confused, it all seemed quite logical?'

'Indeed,' replied Abel, 'but you only visited one other world – the world immediately next to yours.' Abel held out his hand. 'I will now ask you to come with me, Inspector Hooter; we shall go through the wall together. If the rest of you would wait here, we shall only be five minutes or so.'

Hooter straightened his cap and stood to attention facing the timbers. 'Ready when you are, Mr Nogg.'

'Thank you, Inspector, shall we go?'

The pair touched the timbers together; Hooter could not help but give another, 'Ooer,' as he got gently sucked in and passed all the way through before being placed carefully on the sand in the world of the humans. Abel stood by his side, scrutinizing the landscape to ensure they were alone.

Hooter spoke up quietly, 'When my head was here just now, I thought I saw a lone man up there on the top of the ridge. I'm sure he didn't see me though.'

'Really, that is very interesting, Inspector. That is approximately where Inspector Orange said the man in his dreams took him. We must bear that in mind, but now I would like you to follow me.' Abel cautiously made his way to the end of the wall and onto the track.

Hooter kept close behind, conscious that he was now in the world which he knew to be rather hostile. 'Are we safe here?' he asked.

'We shall be gone in a few seconds,' Abel replied. 'Stand by my side facing the wall again, please.'

The inspector did as Abel bid, drawing confidence from the pterosaur's closeness.

Abel then asked, 'If you put your head through the wall from here, what would you expect to see?'

Hooter had resisted the urge to rub his bill so far, but he was stumped, and so he repeated the question to himself while resting his bill on an upturned wing, 'What would I see if I looked through from this side, eh? That's a very good question indeed, Mr Nogg. I have a feeling it won't be my world because we would have to go back the way we came for that to happen.'

'Well done, my friend.' Hooter's apparent understanding surprised and cheered Abel no end. 'Why don't you take a peep? The wall will hold you halfway like before.'

'Well, okay, if you're sure,' said Hooter putting his trust wholly in his mentor. He gingerly waddled forward making every effort not to let out another 'Ooer'.

The wall pulled him in and held him as before with only his head and neck protruding on the other side. He had not expected to see what was now laid out before him. His eyes widened so far that he felt sure they were about to fall out. He dared not say a word for fear of giving himself away.

Abel's head promptly appeared through the wall next to his. 'What do you think, Inspector?' he asked, calmly.

'Sshh,' Hooter muttered, 'they mustn't hear us or we'll be for it and no mistake.'

'Really, and why is that?' Abel slowly turned his head to the right and the left, his long beak arcing from side to side. 'Take a good long look and tell me what you see.'

The land certainly reminded Hooter of his own world; the level parts and the ridges in the distance topped by pines and oaks, all very familiar. 'This is obviously the same place but in another world...'he paused to collect his thoughts. Immediately in front of him stood a small settlement comprising single storey wooden cabins arranged in no particular order, and none more than twenty paces square. 'It's so beautiful,' he whispered.

'Do you mean the cabins?' Abel asked.

'I mean everything,' replied Hooter, gulping in astonishment.

'It's so bright and clear.'

The presence of two heads protruding from the timbered wall had so far gone unnoticed, but then a large black individual looked up from his rocking chair on the veranda in front of one of the cabins.

'Perhaps we should go all the way through now,' said Abel.

'What?' said Hooter, alarmed at the thought of being spotted. 'Surely you mean we should go back.' He had barely finished the sentence when the wall pushed as gently as ever, and the mallard and the pterosaur landed ever so tidily on the sand – in yet another world.

25

Hooter now stood in the cool afternoon Sun with his back to the timbered wall. He scanned from left to right at the randomly placed cabins, some with wisps of smoke gaily dancing about the tops of stove pipes. Uncut but naturally tidy grass surrounded each cabin to a point where the trees took over, setting the boundary of the settlement. A manicured pebble track wound its way between the homes, leading the eye to the top of a rise where the pines, oaks, and birch formed a natural barrier from one end of the horizon to the other.

Having given Hooter a while to survey the scene, the hefty creature on the veranda leaned forward and rose from his chair. He immediately settled on all fours with his knuckles resting on the boards beneath him, but still he did nothing to acknowledge the arrival of the two visitors.

'Well?' said Abel to Hooter. 'What are you thinking?'

'I'm not sure,' replied the inspector. 'He's a bit taller than me, six foot I would say, but he looks so strong.'

'He is certainly that.'

'But why have you brought me here, Mr Nogg. This is all very fascinating, but how will this help our cause?'

'I would just like you to talk to him; that is all.'

Hooter remained planted in the sand, reluctant to move away from the wall. Thoughts slowly gathered in his head. *I've never actually seen one before…but I think he's what's called a gorilla.*

The creature on the veranda slowly turned his head in Hooter's direction.

Abel pressed his hand against Hooter's rump. 'Why don't you go and introduce yourself,' he said.

Hooter took a deep breath. 'Right,' he said, 'nothing to be afraid of, just something that looks a bit too much like a human for my liking.'

'Never judge a book by its cover,' said Abel.

'Of course Mr Nogg, I'm sure you are right...' Unseen by Hooter, while he was studying the creature on the veranda Abel quickly morphed from his guise as a pterosaur into something quite different. Hooter turned to face him and continue the discussion. 'Oh my word!' He gagged in shock, for it was not the familiar long beak that greeted him, but a gorilla with a face as black as a velvet night sky and eyes of brilliant blue staring right into him. 'Who are you? Where is Abel Nogg?'

'Calm yourself, Inspector,' said the gorilla.

This was not the same beast that Hooter had come to know, and yet the eyes were most certainly those of Abel Nogg, holding him and peering deep into his mind as Abel was prone to do.

'Mr Nogg? That is you – isn't it?' Hooter bravely stood his ground, gathering every ounce of courage he could muster.

'Yes, it is me with a different cover, that's all.'

'But...how...why?' Hooter struggled to keep up with events.

Abel continued, 'This is not the first time you have seen me in a different guise, my friend.'

Hooter remained speechless, his mind working harder than ever; he seriously considered reaching for the wall hoping it would look kindly upon him.

Abel gently rested a powerful hairy arm on Hooter's shoulder and explained. 'It would make no sense for me to venture into this world looking like a giant pterosaur; I would be rather conspicuous don't you think, seeing as such creatures do not exist here. A gorilla's covering makes far more sense, they are after all the most senior of breeds here.'

Hooter's nerves compelled him to rub his bill to aid his thought.

Abel continued, 'In your world I had cause to meld with the pterosaurs, for they were plentiful, and that was where many of your troubles lay.'

'What about in the world of the humans, surely you didn't take on their appearance, did you?'

Abel's gorilla face, being far more pliable than that of a pterosaur, gave rise to a hint of a smile. 'Yes I did, what is more, I met you on several occasions while you were there.'

'What? But I would have recognized you if I had seen you – no, Mr Nogg, I'm sure you are mistaken.'

'I can understand you not taking much notice of me on our first meeting. From what I remember of it, you spent most of your time with your head in Kate Herrlaw's bosom. All you saw of me was the back of my head – and my chauffeur's cap.'

'That was you...driving me around?'

'Small world, isn't it,' Abel chuckled, his face creasing into a disarming smile. 'Now then,' he nodded in the direction of the gorilla on the veranda. 'I think he has been waiting long enough, don't you?'

'Oh, right, yes.' Hooter waddled boldly but cautiously towards the cabin where the very substantial ape waited on all fours, watching the giant duck's advance. When Hooter got to within five paces, the gorilla stepped down from the veranda, knuckles first, and turned to face him. The situation reminded Hooter of his first encounter with the humans by the pond in Davidsmeadow. *I don't really want another confrontation like that...*

At least this chap isn't carrying any weapons, not that he would need a weapon to put me down if he had a mind to. He gulped a hefty gulp as the four hundred and fifty pounds of muscle moved towards him. Two thoughts entered the mallard's head. *Fight or flight?*

The gorilla had a purposeful look in his eye.

Hooter remained firm, fluffing up his chest.

The gorilla measured the mallard's bearing, noticing the wings twitching by his sides.

Hooter felt he should do something, but could not think what. *I could raise my wings to show I'm unarmed and mean no threat, but the last time I did that I started a riot.* His wings twitched again.

The gorilla noticed Hooter's edginess and wondered if such a movement was a precursor to some sort of aggression.

Hooter's wings twitched yet again, as if they had a mind of their own. He had no idea what to expect next. *I presume gorillas grunt and snort, don't they? But Aano Grunt doesn't, despite his name.*

The gorilla had settled comfortably on all fours at eye level with the mallard. He had done all the assessing he needed and would wait no longer; he moved forward stopping within arm's reach...a very powerful arm's reach.

Hooter was about to open the dialogue when the gorilla beat him to it. 'Do you intend doing something with those wings?' he asked with an extremely upper crust dialect.

Hooter forced his wings tight against his sides. He had not expected such a refined voice to come from such a robust creature. 'Oh – no, not at all, sir.'

'Thank heavens for that,' replied the gorilla, 'for a moment I thought you were going to hit me.'

Hooter replied with a nervous tremor in his voice, 'Oh goodness me, no. Why would I want to do that? The truth is I didn't quite know what to do with them; my breed use their wings in many expressive ways, quite autonomously.'

The gorilla reached forward with one hand. 'How do I shake hands with a creature that has no hands?'

Hooter slowly raised one wing to the horizontal. The gorilla tenderly curled his fat fingers around the tips of the feathers. The two of them shook in mutual admiration, the gorilla being very careful not to squash any feathers. Hooter's heart raced at such a tactile touch from what was an extremely powerful animal.

The gorilla continued his greeting, 'I must say, your colours are all the more beautiful for being magnified.'

'Thank you,' replied Hooter, wondering what he meant by magnified. 'I must say your stance on all fours when you stood your ground was quite breath-taking. I can't imagine anyone taking issue with you, unless they had some sort of predilection for pain.'

'Oh, all bluff really.' The gorilla smiled, putting Hooter all the more at ease. 'I have never had to make a point yet, despite my job.'

'Your job?'

The gorilla focused on Hooter's cap badge and continued, 'I represent the law in these parts.' He smiled again to prepare the mallard for what might be a bit of a surprise. 'I am Gerald Wunfith, Officer in Charge, The Heavy Mob. How do you do.'

'Heavy Mob?' said Hooter.

'That's right. What else would you call a squad made up from individuals weighing more than four hundred pounds each?'

'Do you mean you are a police officer?' asked Hooter, somewhat confounded.

'Why so surprised? Everywhere has a policy or two to uphold, so that is what I do with the help of a few others; I uphold policy. Is that not what you do, or have I misunderstood your cap badge?'

'Oh, yes of course, that is precisely what I do. I am Inspector Hooter of the Flying Squad.'

'A very apt name, Flying Squad. On your wings I dare say you cover a lot of ground extremely quickly. I cannot imagine anything getting away from you.'

'Very rarely, Officer Wunfith.' Hooter enjoyed saying "Wunfith", it rolled off the tongue nice and easily. 'Wunfith, that's an interesting name if I may say. Does it have any provenance?'

'Oh, I'm not sure really, old chap. My mother would know.'

Hooter eyed the gorilla up and down and after making a quick calculation in his head, he said, 'I have a friend who happens to be an orangutan. If I compare you to him I would guess your weight at about one-fifth of a ton. Perhaps that's where your name comes from?'

The gorilla guffawed heartily at such an amusing notion. 'But I did not weigh one-fifth of a ton when I was born, which is when I was named. Therefore I think it unlikely.'

'Hmm,' Hooter rubbed his bill and replied with a smiling eye, 'I see what you mean; you would have been named Gerald Twenty-Pounds if that were the case.'

Gerald could not help but warm to the honest bearing of the mallard. Having composed himself he enquired, 'May I ask what your first name is?'

'Oh, um. To be honest I don't know. For as long as I can remember I have been called Inspector Hooter – strange really.'

Gerald quelled another bout of laughter. 'Well, perhaps you were born with a police hat already on your head and so they called you "Inspector" right from the start.' Another hearty chuckle vented from his handsome black face.

'I don't think so,' Hooter replied. 'I would never have fitted inside the egg if I had a police hat on.'

'Well,' said Gerald, still not entirely sure if the inspector was joking or not, 'that will have to remain one of life's mysteries. A puzzling but lovely one if I may say.'

Now feeling completely at ease in the company of the impressive gorilla, Hooter asked, 'What is your rank, Officer Wunfith?'

'I am a silverback gorilla,' Gerald replied. 'As such I have never felt the need of a rank.'

'But who gives the orders?'

'To be honest,' said Gerald, 'we never seem to disagree on matters to warrant an order being given. After all, we all know right from wrong, so what more is there to say?'

'So you are just Officer Wunfith.'

'Just Wunfith, really. There is a Wunforth, and a Wunthird and so on.'

'How clever,' said Hooter.

'Would you do something for me?' asked Gerald.

'Of course,' replied Hooter.

'Would you spread your wings wide for me?'

Hooter could not understand the gorilla's interest in a mere duck, but he felt no threat from the handsome beast and so he gingerly opened his wings, spreading them as wide as he could.

'I say,' said Gerald, trying not to gawp at the mallard's display. 'That is absolutely amazing, truly beautiful.'

'But I'm a mallard. What else did you expect, surely you've seen a mallard before.'

'Oh yes, many of the local ponds have a healthy indigenous population of water birds, most of which are indeed mallards...but they only stand shin high to you or me. You on the other hand are truly impressive. Who would have thought it? A mallard almost as big as a gorilla.'

239

Such an accolade coming from so formidable a creature as a superb silverback gorilla left Hooter lost for words. 'Well I, erm, well that's to say, erm…thank you.'

'I do hope I haven't embarrassed you, Inspector, my apologies once again.'

Hooter prised his gaze from the gorilla's face and looked about. A scene of peace and tranquillity greeted him in every direction, but then a seed of uncertainty suddenly sprouted inside his head. He paid particular attention to the bushes and undergrowth surrounding the settlement. 'Do you have humans in your world?'

'We do, yes. Does that bother you?'

'To be honest my previous meetings with them have been less than amicable.'

'And why is that, Inspector?'

'Well the thing is, in my world water birds such as me rule the roost. The humans are only twelve inches tall and they never make any effort to meld with society. They don't get along with any other creature – not one.'

'Does that make them bad though?'

'I suppose not, but they're always arguing and bickering with each other, over territory and possessions mainly; very uncivilized.'

Gerald carefully put his long arm around Hooter's shoulder and replied, 'Don't worry yourself, dear friend. There are humans in this world and they are as tall as you and me, but they confine themselves to lands far away from here; they tend to occupy areas not favoured by others. It is where they were put originally and they have stayed there ever since, keeping themselves separate from the rest of society.'

'Do you ever see them?'

'They never migrate if that's what you mean. They have

struck a balance between themselves and Mother Nature. They live mostly in the central lands of a large continent to the south of here called Fricka. It's a few thousand miles away so you need have no fear of them.'

'Do you ever go there to see them?'

'Sometimes groups of gorillas visit their land to make sure all is well. They do not stay long though and they are very careful not to disturb the humans' way of life. It is their land and they tend to it quite happily.'

Hooter's interest in the humans seemed limitless. 'I can't imagine how they survive in the wild. Aren't they all naked and skinny?'

Gerald laughed a fulsome laugh. 'Naked? Of course not. They're covered in hair, mostly dark, although some have been seen with lighter shades, but they are always covered in hair, not as thickly as a gorilla mind you.'

'Fascinating,' Hooter replied. 'Can they climb and swing through the trees?'

'Oh no, Inspector. In that respect they have something in common with gorillas. Their build and weight precludes them from hanging around in trees lest the branches should break. They make nests of foliage on the ground, rather quaint really.'

The two of them paused in thought, taking a good second look at each other. Their auras radiated every colour of the rainbow in equal measure, proclaiming a warm heart beneath the handsome covering of both hair and feather. Gerald glanced across at Abel Nogg who had been patiently taking account of them both. Abel, still in his gorilla disguise, nodded to Gerald, who returned the nod and then turned and looked Hooter in the eye. 'You have been shown this place for a reason, Inspector. I myself am not privy to Abel Noggs plans, but I am sure we shall both be enlightened when the time comes.'

241

Hooter was about to reply with another question, but movement in the trees at the top of the distant rise caught his attention. 'Oh my word,' he whispered into the gorilla's ear.

'What is it?' Gerald whispered back.

'More gorillas,' said Hooter, maintaining a note of calm while the little duck inside him began jumping up and down excitedly. 'You did say they are safe, didn't you, Officer Wunfith?'

'Why should they be otherwise?' Gerald smiled. Together they watched one gorilla, and then two, and then families of the great hairy beasts emerging from the trees.

'There must be a hundred of them,' Hooter gawped.

'Thereabouts,' replied Gerald. 'They occupy the homes here, they will be very interested to see a mallard as tall as them.' He chuckled a refined chuckle.

'Perhaps I should go now,' said Hooter turning to Abel for support.

Abel slowly shook his head in reply. 'Enjoy the moment, Inspector. You are privileged.'

'Right, yes of course, privileged.' Hooter returned his eyes to the slope down which were coming what seemed like a horde of interlopers. Just then a rare ray of enlightenment lit up inside him. 'What am I thinking? This is not my land, they are not the interlopers, I am. This is theirs.' A smile of wonderment lifted his face. His eyes wetted in amazement while he watched the entire community knuckle walking towards him. Some very large males, some slightly smaller females and many adolescents staying close to their mothers.

It was not until the gorillas were halfway down the slope, that one by one they noticed the astoundingly large mallard with his eye on them. 'What is that?' they muttered to each other. On seeing such an unbelievable spectacle, the youngsters reached out and held tightly to their mothers' hands. Those mothers who were carrying babies held them closer to their breast and slowed their walk. They were unsure of the intentions of such a monstrous bird, and were glad to let the males go ahead.

Again the situation reminded Hooter of his first meeting with the humans in Davidsmeadow. *I don't think I could stand another encounter like that. At least these folk aren't threatening me with pushchairs and the like.*

Gerald took a few steps back, leaving Hooter to his thoughts, and curious to see how the mallard would deal with the situation.

The gorillas were now at the bottom of the slope and had all seen the giant mallard standing in the middle of their village, uninvited.

Hooter gulped a very hefty gulp and muttered just loud enough for Gerald to hear, 'There he is, the alpha male, just like in the human world.'

The crowd made its way along the main thoroughfare towards him; one especially well-built male came to the fore, an impressive silverback with a purposeful look in his glistening dark eyes. Walking on his knuckles he looked straight into Hooter; had he stood upright he would most certainly have exceeded six feet in height.

'I don't know why,' Hooter whispered to himself, 'but I think you are all right.' Bolstered by his meeting with Gerald, he decided to stand his ground, puffing his chest up once more, but making no sudden movement that might be misunderstood.

The alpha male stopped five paces from Hooter. With no instruction necessary his entourage dispersed, each member going into his or her own cabin while their leader stood firm. Many gorilla heads soon appeared at the windows to see what would happen next.

Once satisfied that his charges were safely ensconced in their homes the silverback stepped forward, not taking his eyes off of the stranger of many colours.

Hooter thought to himself. I must keep my wings still this time, this fella looks every bit as strong as Gerald.

The gorilla took his time, studying the mallard closely, all the way from iridescent head down to webbed foot. He then looked across at Gerald Wunfith, asking, 'Is this bird for real?'

'Absolutely,' Gerald replied, 'not sure why he is here, but he is a thoroughly likeable chap.'

26

Hooter slowly waddled forward with his wing outstretched hoping for a cordial shake.

The gorilla responded by raising one hand from the ground and introduced himself, 'Matthew Muchmuscle, Mayor of this fine settlement. Pleased to meet you, Mr...?'

'Hooter – Inspector Hooter of the Flying Squad.'

'Flying Squad, eh. How peculiar,' said the mayor. 'Where exactly are you from?'

'Ahem,' Gerald Wunfith interrupted the mayor's questioning and drew his eye towards Abel who was still standing by the timbered wall.

'Oh, I see.' The mayor tapped the side of his nose and gave a wink, 'Say no more.' He then raised both hands high in the air and brought his fingertips down to the top of his head. Within seconds every cabin door opened and gorillas of all sizes ventured out from their homes to get a better look at the giant duck with the amazing plumage.

One hundred gorillas quickly surrounded the celebrity, all with beautiful enquiring brown eyes. One youngster, standing at about three feet six inches tall, looked up at Hooter's head, 'Why are you so big, Mr Duck?' he asked in perfect diction. 'How did you fit inside an egg? Eggs are so small I cannot imagine how you got in there. Do you float? You must be very heavy. Can you fly? Did you come far to get here?'

Gerald Wunfith butted in. 'That is quite enough, Master Nosey. Give our guest a chance to get his breath.'

Those in the crowd chortled at the youngster's innocent inquisition, although they too wondered about such things. *Where could such a duck have come from?*

Gerald stepped in and pulled Hooter close enough to whisper, 'No one here knows of the timbered wall or its purpose, except me and Mayor Muchmuscle. Be careful not to let slip such privileged knowledge.'

Hooter whispered back, 'So you know about it then?'

'Abel Nogg has told me of its importance so that I may keep an eye on it, but I do not know how it works. You are indeed honoured.'

'Sometimes I'm not so sure,' Hooter replied. He then squatted down and lowered his head to look the young inquisitive gorilla in the eye. 'Let me see now,' he began. 'In answer to your questions, young fella; firstly, I am a normal sized mallard where I come from. Secondly, the egg I came out of was about the same size as Officer Wunfith's head, otherwise I would never have fitted in, would I?'

One hundred gorillas chuckled at the stranger's sense of humour. *Comparing Officer Wunfith's head to an egg, how funny.*

'Thirdly, I may be quite large, but I am relatively light when compared to an adult gorilla, my bones are hollow and my wings are very wide as you can see.' Hooter spread his wings wide over the heads of those around him.

The crowd gasped. 'So beautiful.'

'Such wonderful colours.'

'Why, his wingspan is as wide as my house.'

Hooter slowly folded his wings back by his sides, taking care not to sweep anyone's head as he did so. 'As far as swimming goes, my young friend, I prefer not to, but I have had occasion to when my rowing boat once sank beneath me.'

The crowd laughed again. 'He is so funny, a mallard in a rowing boat, whatever will he think of next?'

Gerald interjected once more, saving Hooter from having to explain where he had come from. 'That is all for now, everyone; the inspector and I have a lot to talk about. I am sure you will see him again. Now please go about your business as usual.'

Having watched and listened to Hooter and Gerald, Abel Nogg gestured for them to join him by the timbered wall. The whole affair had been somewhat overwhelming for Hooter, but he had coped well and had gleaned a fascinating insight into this most hospitable of worlds.

'Come, Inspector,' said Abel, 'it is time to return to your own world. Your friends will be worried for you.'

'Of course, Mr Nogg,' replied Hooter.

Gerald stepped a little closer to Hooter and spoke in a hushed voice. 'I have no more idea than you as to why Abel Nogg brought you here, Inspector, but I have no doubt it is part of his great plan. I am equally sure that we will meet again. Until then, my friend, goodbye.'

Hooter stood boldly to attention. 'Goodbye, Officer Wunfith.'

Abel then put his hands on Gerald's shoulders and turned him to face the wall. 'Stand quite still, Gerald, and do not move. This is for your eyes only.' Using Gerald as a make-do screen, Abel released him and took hold of Hooter with one hand while touching the timbers with the other...and they were gone.

The timbers held Abel and Hooter midway, halting their transit while Abel morphed from gorilla back to pterosaur. Hooter could see nothing while within the embrace of the wall, but there was no mistaking the feel of the hand on his shoulder as it changed from strong and meaty, to long, bony and clawed.

27

Its job done, the timbered wall reluctantly released its two charges out onto the track, now in the world of the humans. Hooter had barely straightened himself up when a very welcome voice came from behind him.

'Hello, Inspector; It's lovely to see you again.'

A tingle shot up the mallard's spine when he turned to see Kate Herrlaw standing there. He made no attempt to hide his delight at seeing her again. 'Kate Herrlaw! Oh, my dear, how lovely to see you – and who is this handsome stranger by your side?'

'Let me introduce you to my accomplice,' Kate replied. 'This is Walter Haker, he is an army captain and a good friend.'

Walter's smile barely concealed his amazement at being up close to such an amazing creature as the giant mallard. He offered his hand. 'It's good to meet you at last, Inspector; Kate has told me a lot about you.'

Hooter's bill blushed brightly.

Abel, now fully in the guise of a pterosaur, curtailed their conversation. 'We must not linger here, my friends; the inspector and I are aliens in this land.' He turned to Kate and Walter. 'Do you recall how the wall works, and the importance of travelling through it in the correct direction?'

'Yes,' they replied.

'Good,' Abel quickly reiterated his instructions. 'The

inspector and I are returning to his world. We shall pass through from the other side to land on the track once again. But you, Kate and Walter, are on an outward journey to the inspector's world, therefore it might be better if you set off in an anti-clockwise direction and go through from this side, understood?'

'Absolutely.'

'Through you go then,' said Abel. 'The timbers will look kindly upon you.' Abel and Hooter hurriedly made their way around the end and approached the ether from the other side, touching the timbers together. Meanwhile Kate and Walter, after taking a deep breath, took hold of each other's hand and stepped up from the opposite side.

'Well, here goes,' said Walter, looking into Kate's eyes. The lightest of touches had the hands pulling them in as one, squeezing them together as they passed through. For one brief second they felt the pterosaur and the mallard ooze past them going in the other direction. *Ooh, this is really weird.*

Abel Nogg and Inspector Hooter came cleanly to rest on the track. Hooter staggered with one wing to his head. 'My word,' he said, clearly in a daze.

Abel gestured towards the grass. 'Perhaps you should sit down for a moment, Inspector, until your head clears.'

'Thank you, Mr Nogg, I think that's a good idea.'

Meanwhile, Kate and Walter had also landed softly in the land of the water birds, but on the side of the common. 'Mmm, lovely,' said Kate, taking a deep breath. 'It smells so different, don't you think?'

'Clean,' Walter replied.

Kate took her time to stare right across the common to the trees on the far side. 'I feel no threat here, do you?'

'None – just harmony.' Walter let go of Kate's hand and lifted his head before shouting at the top of his voice, 'Hello!'

'Sshh, you silly thing, you don't know who might hear.'

Walter's call was swiftly answered by a symphony from the trees a mile away. Every bird among their branches sang, twittered, whistled, squawked, cooed and hooted. Their tones raced down the slope to be caught by the pines and oaks surrounding Kate and Walter.

'Wow, how's that for a welcome,' said Kate.

The birds were still singing to the newcomers when a hairy ginger head appeared from among the bushes. 'Hello, there,' he said, his broad apish grin filling his face.

'What the...?' Walter stepped back in shock. 'That's an orangutan. Surely he's not native here, is he?'

Kate's voice broke into a laugh. 'It's Aano Grunt, the local farrier and all round lovely chap.'

Aano stepped into the open for Walter to get a better look. 'I didn't mean to make you jump, sir.' The ape maintained the grin while his eyes were drawn compellingly into Kate's. 'It's lovely to see you again, Miss Herrlaw – just lovely.' His lips pouted of their own accord as they were prone to do whenever his emotions got the better of him. He quickly put his hand to his mouth to cover his obvious delight at seeing the human-looking lady once again. He mumbled through his hand, 'I'm terribly sorry.'

Kate walked lightly across the sand and cupped Aano's head in her slender hands. 'My lovable ginger ape; you never were very good at hiding your feelings.' She kissed his forehead with the softest touch of her lips. Aano's eyes very nearly popped out of his head.

'Ahem,' said Walter, 'I hate to break up your special moment, but shouldn't we find Abel Nogg and Inspector Hooter? They must be here somewhere.'

Aano Grunt gathered his composure and uncovered his

mouth. 'That's what I meant to tell you, they're all waiting around the other side on the track – look.'

Kate and Walter followed in Aano's wake to be confronted by Abel, Hooter, three mallards and an impressive Canada goose wearing a Stetson.

'Wow,' said Walter. 'I don't know why I'm surprised at such a sight, but seeing them close up is just amazing.' His eyes danced from one spectacular creature to the next, their perfect eyes welcoming him to linger. 'Stunning,' Walter murmured, 'utterly, utterly stunning.'

Inspector Hooter, still sitting on the grass and recovering from his meeting with the gorillas, dazedly put a few words of his own together, 'Stunning, yes – they were stunning too.'

'Who wuz?' asked Sergeant Uppendown. 'There seems to be a lot of stunning-ness going on around here.'

Walter beat Hooter to his reply. '**You** are all stunning.' His eyes swept quickly across all before him. 'I'm the only ordinary looking creature here.' He smiled reservedly.

Kate turned to him and said, 'Believe me, Walter, you are not ordinary.'

'You sure aren't, sir,' Bob Uppendown said in support.

It was only then that Walter realized every eye was studying him from head to foot as closely as he was scrutinizing them.

Kate whispered in his ear, 'Don't you see? We are as beautiful to them as they are to us.'

'If you don't mind me saying, ma'am,' said Sergeant Uppendown, 'yer friend and yerself are somewhat different to the humans we saw previously in that other world…yer auras are balanced and right, the way humans are meant to be, but aren't anymore.'

Kate replied, 'I'm afraid you are right, Sergeant; the humans from the world next to yours are very troubled…' she sighed, 'and the sad thing is, it's all their own doing.'

After giving everyone time to make their acquaintances, Abel Nogg took up the discussion, 'Kate and Walter, if you would accompany me onto the common for a moment – I wish to show you something.'

Kate and Walter followed him closely.

'Do you see the treeline at the top of the rise?' Abel's beak pointed at the horizon a mile or so distant.

'Yes,' Walter replied, studying the trees in as much detail as he could. 'If we were still in the humans' world that would be where we saw the man walking with his dog, collecting firewood.'

'That's right,' said Kate, 'his dog wasn't with him on the last occasion though.' She looked around momentarily while getting her facts straight. 'That's also the spot where Walter and I lost track of the footprints left by someone other than the lone man…they simply disappeared into thin air.'

'Almost as if something literally took flight,' Walter added.

Abel listened while the twosome continued their account.

'It was really strange,' said Kate, 'but all the while we were there, we were sure we were sharing the space with others who we couldn't see. I'm sure the trees knew more than they were letting on, but you know how secretive trees can be.'

Abel threw a little light on the subject. 'I have a feeling that while you were up there searching among the trees, some of those who you have just met here were also there, in that very same spot—'

'But in this world, you mean?' said Kate.

'So we were sensing their presence through the ether,' said Walter.

Abel moved on to make his point. 'At the top of the rise, just in front of the trees in the world of the humans, lies the body of the lost Bog. The lone human discovered it with the help of his dog. He in turn told Inspector Orange of its whereabouts in a dream which they seem to have shared on more than one occasion. I am certain we can trust in their account, but I need you to verify the exact location so that those tasked with recovering the body will waste no time in searching.'

Kate and Walter pondered the issue for a few seconds. Walter then replied, 'As far as I can tell from here, that area looks virtually the same as it does in our world.'

'Quite so,' said Abel.

'So, once we have found the grave we could come back here and report to you or whoever, and show them where it would be if it were in this world. Then they would know where to look when they venture through themselves. Erm…does that make sense?'

Kate smiled. 'Not entirely, but I know what you mean.'

Aano Grunt, having much in common with humankind, put his head round the end of the wall to see what Kate was doing. 'Are you going now?' he asked.

'I'm afraid so, Mr Grunt,' Kate replied, 'but we will meet again soon, I'm sure.'

After much hugging and shaking of hands and wings, Walter and Kate bid everyone farewell before taking a deep breath and stepping up to the wall once again. This time Kate reached out deliberately slowly, teasing the wall with her most delicate of touches. Despite their robust appearance the gnarled timbers reacted instantly to her finger tips, pulling them whole-heartedly into its clutches. In little more than a second, Kate and Walter were released onto the track in the world of the humans once again.

They both took a deep breath.

'Phew, doesn't smell the same, does it,' said Walter, blowing

253

out through his mouth.

'No,' Kate replied. 'It's no wonder though, is it? Every day mankind pumps billions of tons of waste into the air and into the water, or buries it in the ground – just to live the dream.'

'The sad thing is,' Walter added, 'so many generations have passed since purer times that they don't realize how things should be.'

'Thankfully, we're not the ones who will reckon them,' replied Kate.

***

Meanwhile, still in the world of the water birds, Abel Nogg held his wings aloft. 'Please gather round, gentlefolk.' The birds and the ape moved closer; Abel then began his address:

'Kate Herrlaw and Walter Haker have returned to the humans' world to establish the exact whereabouts of the missing Bog. When they have found it they will get word to one of us. In the meantime you must all be especially vigilant in respect of strangers in your midst. I fear the one who is behind these troubles is playing a waiting game; his aim is to take possession of the Amulet for his own gains.'

Aano Grunt asked, 'But he could never take the Amulet from you, could he Mr Nogg?'

Abel replied, 'There will soon come a time when I shall hand the Amulet to one of you in order for you to fulfil your task; that is when you will be most at risk from others who wish to spoil your world. You must all be sure to divulge the whereabouts of the Amulet only to those in whom you have total trust.'

'I see,' replied Aano, 'but why can't—?'

Abel knew what the ape was about to ask, and so cut him short. 'As I have explained to some of you before, I can help you and show you, but the doing must be yours. The world in which you live is the way it is because of your actions, not mine. Like all worlds, in the beginning you were given all you could ever need, what you do with it is up to you – unless you are reckoned and found wanting.' Abel then turned his attention to Inspector Hooter. 'Inspector, you will receive word in due course as to your next move, until then you must carry on as normal.'

'Of course,' Hooter replied. 'There is just one thing, Mr Nogg.'

'What is that?'

'Should I keep what I saw through the second lap of the wall to myself – the gorillas I mean?'

'It is up to you who you tell. It will also be your decision if you should visit there again.'

Hooter rubbed his bill while the responsibility of his position sank in. Look out for strangers in my midst…Gorillas I might need to visit again…The Amulet; good heavens, whatever next? Sometimes I wish I was just a constable.

Abel raised his wings and released the crew from his ethereal hold. 'It is time for you all to return to your posts. Trust in each other and above all, trust in Mother Nature – but you already know that, I'm sure.'

The trees leaned away from the sides of the track while the pterosaur rose up on vast wings gathering the air beneath them. Above the treetops he turned and disappeared beyond waving branches, leaving four mallards, one goose and an orangutan with a lot to think about and a lot at stake. And in Aano Grunt's case, a long walk home.

28

With Abel gone, the crew took stock of what they had been told. Like all animals do, they looked up to the sky for inspiration and support. The permanence of the heavens comforted them and the Moon cast its silvered light across the dew-laden grasses to show them the way home. It was only then that they realized how dark it had become.

Looking first at the trees and then at the ape, Hooter asked, 'Can you swing through the trees in the dark, Mr Grunt?'

'I don't think I should,' Aano replied. The Moon picked out his concerned grin. 'I don't think my eyes are as sharp as yours.'

'Hmm,' Hooter pondered the situation. 'The rest of us will be fine as long as we maintain an altitude of five trees or more.' He looked again at Aano while bill rubbing to enhance his chances of coming to a sensible solution. 'Sergeant Uppendown, you have the most impressive wingspan by a considerable margin. Do you think you could fly with Mr Grunt hanging beneath you?'

'I'm not sure, sir. He may be shorter than me, but I'm pretty sure he's a good bit heavier.'

Inspector Orange, who until now had remained quietly in the background, spoke up. 'I can vouch for Mr Grunt's mass.' He lingered in Aano's eyes respectfully. 'Having physically fought him on more than one occasion I can tell you he is no lightweight. I would guess him to weigh at least two hundred pounds.'

'Good heavens,' Hooter remarked. 'What on Earth are you made of, Mr Grunt?'

'I think I'm mostly muscle, water, and solid bones; whereas you, Inspector, seem to be mostly feathers, hollow bones and warm air.' Aano chuckled and grinned broadly, meaning no disrespect. 'I'm certain that even if I had a pair of wings like yours I would still not get off the ground.'

Al Orange spoke up again, 'I will stay here with you, Mr Grunt, until morning.'

Aano replied, 'There is really no need, I will be quite all right. After all, it's not as if we're in the human world, that would be a different matter altogether.'

'Never the less, I would be happy to stay and keep you company,' Al Orange insisted.

'Thank you,' Aano conceded, 'that will be jolly nice, Inspector.'

Hooter wrapped things up. 'That's settled then; Inspector Orange and Mr Grunt will stay here until daybreak and then make their own way back to Smallbeef. The rest of us will set off now; I shall leave you at Smallbeef and continue on to Davidsmeadow alone. How does that sound?'

'That sounds fine, sir,' Uppendown replied on behalf of the rest of the crew.

Hooter looked at Al Orange and Aano in turn. 'I look forward to seeing you again soon.' He then addressed his depleted temporary crew of two mallards and one Canada goose. 'I shall fly point with Mr Waters-Edge and son on each flank, outers high. Sergeant, will you fly tail-end Charlie?'

'Fer sure, sir.' Uppendown angled his Stetson a little forward in readiness.

Once again, the trees intuitively leaned back to give the birds

257

a little more room.

'Prepare to take off,' called Hooter. 'Take off.' With that, he promptly led the way into the air, rising steeply beyond the treetops. Harold followed closely behind, followed in turn by his son, Dick. As soon as the mallards were airborne, Sergeant Uppendown spread his wings wide. The trees, realizing he was going to be a close fit, leaned back a little more as he passed, Mexican-wave style.

'Thank heavens fer those Mexicans,' said Uppendown as he lifted-off after several long strides.

Mexicans? The trees whispered to each other. *Aren't we Scottish?*

Once in the air the birds quickly fell into formation at a height of five trees and disappeared over the distant western horizon.

***

'It looks like being a dry night,' said Aano, admiring the early star in the south-eastern sky. 'Venus, I think.' He then turned his attention to the ferns lining the top of the bank opposite the timbered wall. 'Excuse me for a moment, Inspector, I'm just going to pop up there to gather a few bits and bobs.'

Inspector Orange didn't let on, but he was glad to stay back and remain in Aano's company for the night rather than spend it in Smallbeef without him. He had found a true soul mate in the ape, absurd as that may sound. 'I've heard of your hat-making skills, Mr Grunt. Now I'll get to see for myself.' His eyes dared to let go a sparkle of light from deep within him. Hitherto he would have been too frightened to tempt fate by showing such positivity of thought.

'Not too long, but just long enough,' the ape whispered as he perused the ferns. 'Not too many, but just enough.' He pranced and danced his way back down the bank onto the track, and then, holding the ferns he had picked, he gave a quick twist and a flick. 'Tah-daa,' he said, holding the finished product in the air for Orange to see. 'A hat, just right for keeping the dew drops of my head in the night; I'll make one for you too if you like, Inspector.'

'Thank you, my friend, but I have no need of such a wonderful piece of millinery. I'm able to put my head deep into my plumage beneath my wing, nice and warm and waterproof.'

'Of course, how clever,' Aano replied, trying to put his head under his arm pit. 'It doesn't seem to work for me.'

'That is because you are an ape and I am a mallard. I guess we're just about as opposite as two creatures could possibly be....' Al Orange hesitated. He really wanted to show the ape his true heartfelt feelings but couldn't quite bring himself to.

'I suppose we are,' said Aano. 'I mean, you can fly, I can't. I can climb and swing through the trees and you can't.'

'I can turn my head right around to see what's behind me,' said Orange. 'You can't.'

'I can pick things up with my feet.'

'I can stay out in the rain and not get wet.'

'I can do a forward roll.' Aano grinned. 'Shall we call it a draw?'

'Absolutely,' Al Orange replied. He wanted to continue in respect of his emotions but the little duck inside him quivered nervously at rendering himself vulnerable, so he decided to leave things be for now.

Aano gazed up at the mature oak towering above him. 'I would normally climb up there for the night, but to be honest there's very little cover at this time of the year, what with most of the leaves having fallen.'

Al Orange settled down on the grass at the base of the

timbered wall. He looked at Aano and slowly raised his wing, spreading his feathers to create a perfect canopy. 'You are welcome to shelter under here,' he said.

'Oh my word,' Aano replied, more than a little surprised at the inspector's offer.

The inspector slowly lowered his wing while the little duck inside him sadly lowered his eyes, thinking he had been rebuffed.

'That would be lovely.' Aano grinned. 'If you are quite sure it wouldn't be too intimate.'

'I'm offering you a place to shelter, my friend. Does your kind not huddle in groups in times of need?'

Aano replied instantly, 'Of course they do, but to be honest I can't actually remember being with any of my own kind…but I'm sure I must have been, once. Rather strange really.'

Orange gladly lifted his wing once again and let the ape snuggle beneath what would be his armpit, if mallards had such a thing.

With the inspector's wing gently resting over him, Aano relaxed into the soft grass and the even softer side of his erstwhile companion. The Moon looked down on the unlikely sight as the wall's shadow imperceptibly slid over them while they slept in each other's warmth. *Perfect*, thought the Moon.

***

The pines, the oaks and the birch lined the horizon ahead of Hooter and his followers. Their moonlit silhouettes created a passing foundation for the indigo skies above, teeming with seemingly everlasting cobalt bodies. Beyond the next horizon lay the village of Smallbeef.

'This is where we must part, Sergeant,' Hooter called out.

'Fer sure, sir,' replied Uppendown. 'Have a safe journey the rest of the way.'

'Thank you, Sergeant. It was good to see you again – good night, Mr Waters-Edge, good night, young Waters-Edge.'

'Goodnight, Inspector.' Three voices sang out in the late night air, the trees stretching as tall as they could to try to catch them, a game they always enjoyed playing.

With the Moon and the stars for company, and Venus high above the left quarter of his bill, Hooter knew he would soon be back in Davidsmeadow. Far below him the wily fox crept stealthily among the undergrowth, searching casually for a starter. Above the fox, but still lower than Hooter, the owl soared on silent wings, his mind focussing intensely, and his eyes seeking the slightest movement of vole or mouse beneath the blanket of fallen autumn leaves. Neither fox nor owl were troubled by the monstrous duck cruising overhead, they all knew their place in the great plan despite never having read the book.

Now alone, Hooter's thoughts turned to his new-found companion, Dana Lethgerk. *Could I be so lucky?* Hooter dared to let his mind wallow in his heart's longing. *I lost Marion before I had a chance to show her my true feelings…perhaps that was just as well. I can't imagine what Harold Waters-Edge would have made of me otherwise.* Onward he flew, the wind singing as his wings embraced the air beneath them, Mother Nature's breath holding him aloft. *Oh Dana, you seem too good to be true – so beautiful. But why shouldn't I have a lover in my life; I'm not so old or washed up that someone won't want to be with me…or am I?* Nature's gentle hold on him wavered. His wings lost their natural rhythm when the air beneath him began to fail as if being taken from him by another. 'What on Earth is going on?' Hooter looked up, *Nothing.* He looked to the left, *Nothing.* He looked below him and to the right…and could not believe his eyes. 'What are you doing out here at this time of night?' he called. Never had his heart experienced so powerful a spur. The little duck inside him raised his wings and jumped up and down with joyous abandon. Hooter forced himself to look straight ahead for two anxious seconds before turning his head again to make sure he was not imagining things.

He was not. Just beyond his reach to his right, the most beautiful eyes looked up at him. Eyes of such clarity that they hijacked the Moon's light and sent it like an arrow straight into the inspector's heart, leaving him speechless and overwhelmed. Images of what was unquestionably the most perfectly staggeringly beautiful creature he had ever beheld stormed his emotions. Unknown to him, his tail feathers were wagging of their own accord.

'Hello, Inspector.' Dana Lethgerk married her wingbeats with Hooter's, outwardly flying ahead of Mother Nature's hold. 'I hope I didn't startle you, I had no idea you would be out here.' The darkness couldn't hold back her subtle colours of autumnal glory; white, beige and brown, radiating a translucent light of their own, illuminating the air close to her body. Hooter could not take his eyes off her. This was the first time he had actually seen her fly. The ease with which she kept pace with him bestowed a superior grace throughout her movement.

'Have you been far?' Dana asked, not needing to time her breathing with her exertion.

'Oh, nowhere in particular,' Hooter replied. I can hardly say I've been through a solid wall to see some gorillas; she would surely think me barmy.

'I take it you're returning to your station now?' Dana made a point of directing her gaze into Hooter's eyes as she spoke.

'Yes,' Hooter replied, 'I'm in need of some shut-eye. I've had a very tiring day.'

'I don't suppose you would see me home first, would you?'

Not for one moment would Hooter deny those perfect eyes such a simple request. 'Of course I will, my dear. I can hardly leave you in the dark, especially with the bounder from yesterday still at large.'

High above the trees the two of them flew, one lit by the moonlight, the other by some ethereal means.

The final stand of trees before Davidsmeadow waved a warm-hearted welcome to the inspector.

'I don't actually know where you live,' said Hooter.

'If you see me to the pond, that will be fine,' Dana replied.

'The pond...are you sure? That can be a dangerous place in the dark, I would never forgive myself if you were to fall in the water. The lifeguard is not on duty at night.'

'I promise I'll be careful,' she replied with a kindly smile in her eyes.

The Moon cast its reflection into the flat water of the pond for them both to see.

'There it is, to our left,' Hooter called. 'Follow me down – we can land on the shore, but do be careful.'

The margin twixt water and land was plain to see in the clear night air. Hooter touched down first and quickly stepped to one side, beckoning Dana to descend on his landward side. Her wings caressed the air more gracefully than any angel might. Silently, she lowered herself onto the sand. 'Thank you, Inspector.'

Hooter keenly ushered her away from the water's edge. Memories of his own unplanned excursion into those very waters were still clear in his mind. 'It really wouldn't do for you to end up in there, it's full of fish and the like; no place for a lady duck.'

Dana allowed herself to be escorted from the sand and onto the grass bank where she paused. 'Could we sit for a while,

Inspector, I think the flight has taken a little more from me than I realized.'

'Of course, my dear. Please make yourself comfortable. I won't leave you until you are quite recovered.'

Dana sighed. 'You really are quite the gallant knight.'

Hooter straightened his cap, hoping to conceal his blushing; at least his tail feathers had gotten over their initial excitement.

'This is such a beautiful world, don't you think?' Dana leaned slightly towards Hooter, resting her soft side against his as they sat beneath the slowly changing electric sky. 'Do you think there are other worlds out there, besides ours?' she asked.

Hooter replied dreamily, 'Among the stars, do you mean?'

'Yes, where else would I mean?'

'Oh…I'm not sure really.'

Dana tipped her head to one side, asking, 'Do you mean you're not sure where I mean, or you're not sure if there are other worlds up there?' She waited while Hooter's mind hurriedly tried to sort out an answer. She knew he was thinking carefully before replying.

'I'm still not sure,' he said, hoping she would not press him further on the matter. She slowly tipped her head the other way as if tempting him to expand a little.

He rubbed his bill. 'I suppose there must be life up there somewhere, after all, the stars are endless; so it's daft to think that this is the only planet with life on it.'

'Hmm.' Dana rested her cheek against Hooter's. His hidden place began to stir; never had he been touched in such a way before. The little duck inside him covered his eyes, unsure of where this might lead.

In a voice as soft as down, Dana continued, 'I suppose half of an answer is better than no answer.' She paused to see if Hooter would pick up from where he had left off. He did not.

Instead, he returned her affection by carefully and slowly rubbing his cheek on hers. Her touch was so soft, he didn't want to talk, but preferred to sit looking out across the water at the Moon's reflection smiling happily for him.

'It's getting late,' said Dana, easing away from Hooter's side. 'I must go now, I too need my beauty sleep.'

'Of course,' replied the love-struck inspector. 'Not that your beauty is in jeopardy, I just meant—'

'It's all right, my funny inspector,' Dana smiled. Her eyes cast their blue light across Hooter's face. 'I know what you meant.' She leaned forward and touched her bill on his before turning and taking her leave. 'I shall see you again soon – goodnight.'

'Goodnight, my dear,' replied Hooter.

29

It was a little before midnight by the time Hooter returned to the station and sorted himself out. He settled into his bed with a muddled mind. His chance meeting with Dana Lethgerk had left his emotions up in the air. *What were the chances of that?* He wriggled into the mattress, his head full of images of her soaring effortlessly through the night sky. He rubbed his cheek on the pillow while imagining he was still by the pond with her cheek against his. *So beautiful, soft and warm.* He soon drifted off to sleep while recalling her every word about the stars and other worlds.

***

The dawn sunlight slowly crept through the trees seeking out the timbered wall. Aano Grunt sniffed lightly; the air beneath Al Orange's wing smelt sweet with an earthy quality to it, warmly inviting him to stay beneath the feathered cover for just a while longer. He snuggled a little closer and listened to the mallard's heartbeat while thinking, *The inspector had a quiet night, no bad dreams, that's nice.*

The mature oak, having watched over them through the night, sought another loose acorn to play bombsies with. With utmost precision the acorn bounced off the inspector's bill with a dull thunk.

'What the devil?' Orange looked up expecting to see a squirrel rummaging about the oak's branches, but there was no sign of movement. 'Hmm…bloomin' trees, daft sense of humour if you ask me.'

'Pardon?' Aano emerged from beneath the mallard's wing and issued a long yawn. 'I can see why you tuck your head among your plumage, it really is very cosy – did something wake you, Inspector?'

'Yes,' he replied, still with an eye on the oak. 'The trees seem to think I need help telling the time.'

'Well, I'm sure they're only looking out for you. I always find them to be most helpful, I simply cannot imagine a world without them. Quite apart from being my main way of getting from A to B, they do most of the breathing on Mother Nature's behalf, don't forget that.'

'I know,' said the inspector, setting his cap straight on his head. He looked up at the hefty branches once more. 'Thank you, old fella,' he said. The tree rustled and let a handful of spent leaves float wistfully down in appreciation of the mallard's kind regard.

'There, you see, he likes you really,' Aano smiled.

Al Orange got to his feet and stretched his wings, reaching from one side of the track to the other.

'That really is amazing,' said Aano admiring the textures and colours. 'You must spend ages preening that lot.'

'All part of being a duck,' Orange replied. 'I imagine you must spend some time sorting your hair out, too.'

Aano looked down at his hairy belly, and then at his equally hairy arms. 'I don't think there is anything I could do to make myself look as splendid as you, Inspector.'

'But in your own way you are beautiful,' replied Orange. 'Just not in a bird sort of way. I bet there is a lady orangutan somewhere out there who would positively swoon at your rugged good looks.'

267

Aano instinctively stared at the south-eastern horizon. For some unknown reason he found himself imagining a lush jungle on an island many thousands of miles away. 'Hmm, a lady orangutan,' he sighed.

Al Orange lined himself up with the track. 'We mustn't waste any more time, Aano. Would you like me to circle above you while you make your way back?'

'No, Inspector. I'll be fine with the trees for company; it will be nice to see them again, you go on ahead. I'll see you later in Smallbeef. Thank you for your company in the night, it was quite an experience.'

'Please be careful,' said Orange, noticing the trees leaning away from the trackside for him. He spread his wings and within a few strides he was airborne, rising above the trees to see the western horizon beckoning. The trees resumed their normal stance and waved ever so subtly at the inspector while Mother Nature discretely helped him from behind. The Sun busily warmed the frost laden moorland as the mallard settled into a steady rhythm, feeling buoyed at having had a peaceful night in the company of the most bizarre and dear friend a duck could possibly imagine.

After seeing the inspector safely into the air, Aano loped towards the nearest tree of such girth as to allow him a good grasp. 'Nice tree,' he whispered.

Nice erm, hairy chap, the tree rustled in reply.

And so it was with consummate ease that the ape made his way carefully through the wooded stretch of the common, grinning and thanking the trees for their help as he went along.

***

In Davidsmeadow Police Station, Constable Thomas called out to Inspector Hooter, 'Constables Thomas and Peters going out on morning patrol, sir.'

'Very well,' Hooter replied through his partly open office door. He eagerly tidied his bed, leaving the blanket folded in regulation order before entering the station office where Constable Roberts sat smartly waiting for something to happen.

'Were there any problems yesterday in my absence, Constable Roberts?'

'None, sir. All very quiet.'

'No sign of the bounder who accosted Dana Lethgerk?'

'No, nothing, sir. We patrolled that area thoroughly throughout the day but found nothing untoward.'

Hooter rubbed his bill. 'I shall take a wander down there myself in a while, you never know, something might come to light.'

'Very good, sir,' replied Roberts.

Catching the constable's eye again, Hooter asked, 'Did you happen to see Dana Lethgerk at any time yesterday?'

'No, sir. We went round the town many times, she must have been busy elsewhere, doing whatever it is she does.'

'Of course, Constable. I dare say she will appear somewhere or other today.' Dana's image remained at the very forefront of Hooter's mind, his "police" thoughts having to find a way around them.

The Sun sidled its way across the roof tops, its autumnal path casting long shadows in the town centre, especially outside Café Hero. At this time of the year the chairs here would remain in the shade for much of the day, only brightening up during the latter part of the afternoon if the clouds allowed it, but this would not deter those patrons seeking a social cuppa.

'I'm going out to meet up with Constables Thomas and Peters,' Hooter called as he straightened his cap in front of the station mirror.

'Righto, sir.'

Hooter gingerly opened the station door and peered each way to see if there was any sign of Mrs Bottoms-Up, or more precisely, her young son, Bertie. 'Good, it seems to be all clear,' he whispered. The air in the street felt cool around his legs, sharpening the senses but doing little to clear his head of Dana. He crossed the road and made his way towards the corner; fate seemed to have a way of presenting the Bottoms-Ups just when he least expected it. 'Any minute now,' he muttered. He got to the corner and still there was no sign of the charming but embarrassing Bertie and his lovely mother, Betty. As soon as he rounded the corner his gaze fixed on the nearest table outside the café.

'Hello, Inspector.' Dana sat calmly sipping her morning tea. 'I have an extra cup for you if you would like to join me.'

'Oh, well, yes of course, thank you.' Hooter slid the chair out from the table and sat facing the lady duck with the amazing eyes. 'After your late night flight I wasn't sure if you would be up yet,' he added.

'Oh, I have far too much to do to waste the day sleeping.' Dana poured Hooter's tea and rested her eyes in his while they each sipped dreamily – especially Hooter.

Neither of them said a word, sitting comfortably within each other's eyes until a voice from the next table broke the ambience. 'Hello, Inspector. This is my first cup of tea in my whole life.' It was Bertie, sitting with his sister and two brothers, and of course his mother.

'Oh, my my,' said Hooter, hoping against hope that this would not be a repeat of the previous meetings with the youngster. 'Take care not to spill it, young fella.' Hooter paused helplessly, he knew Bertie was undoubtedly about to come out with another innocent shot from the hip.

'Is that lady your wife?' asked the duckling.

His mother quickly interjected. 'Bertie, get on with your tea and don't be so nosey.'

'Yes Mum. I just wondered—'

'Yes well this is a time for sipping tea, not for asking adults personal questions.'

'Yes Mum.'

Not wanting to see Bertie saddened by his gentle reprimand, Hooter took the time to look the youngster in the eye, saying, 'No, young fella, this lady is not my wife, she is a good friend. It's always good to have good friends, don't you think?'

Betty Bottoms-Up smiled at the inspector for his forbearance in the matter, she nodded to Bertie as if to encourage a polite reply.

Bertie's eyes sparkled. 'Yes sir,' he said. 'Do you think I'll have some good friends when I grow up?'

'I'm sure you will,' said Hooter.

'Will she be as beautiful as your friend?'

Hooter blushed on Dana's behalf. 'If you are very lucky…perhaps she might.'

'And will she smell odd like your friend?'

'Bertie, that's enough!' Betty was mortified at her son's unintended slight. 'I'm terribly sorry, Inspector, and you too, madam.' She turned and said to Bertie, 'You can leave that tea where it is, young duck, we're going home.' Betty ushered all four of her offspring from the table. 'And you won't be coming out again until you learn to keep your bill shut.'

Bertie's young eyes overflowed profusely, his bill trembled; never had his mother spoken so firmly to him before. He only wanted to know about grown-ups and things. Away down the road went the Bottoms-Up troupe. Not waddling lithely with Bertie singing out the time, but with bills dropped and mother at the back keeping the pace as fast as the little ones could manage.

'Sorry, Mum…I only meant—'

'Don't say another word, we'll see what your father has to say when he gets home.'

Bertie did not say another word. Around the corner, bill still quivering, along with his siblings, all very quiet and sad for Bertie.

Hooter and Dana sat in silence, not the easy silence that they were enjoying before Bertie's appearance, but an unpleasant silence. Hooter forced himself to speak up first. 'Children eh. You never know what they're going to say next, or where they get it from.'

Dana replied in an unusually unsympathetic tone. 'Sometimes children need to be put in their place.'

They sat quietly watching the world go by, each taking an occasional sip of tea to soften the impasse.

'Well, my dear,' said Hooter, 'I must be on my way. I have a patrol to finish and I haven't even started it yet.'

'Of course,' Dana replied. 'I'm sorry for being such a sour-puss; I'm sure I'll feel better later. Perhaps we could meet for lunch?'

Hooter straightened his cap. 'One o'clock at the little tea room in the alleyway?'

'That will be fine.' Dana remained seated while Hooter got to his feet and set off around The Square before disappearing from view down the High Street. He kept his gaze focused on those around him, purposely not looking back at his sweetheart who had seemed unusually curt. *Perhaps she just doesn't like children. But what duck doesn't like children? No, I think she's simply having a bad day, females sometimes have those…apparently.*

***

272

In the world of the humans, by the pond on the heath, the breakfast sunshine lay long tree-shadows across the sand and grass. Kate perused the morning newspaper to see what was making the headlines.

'It seems the famines, droughts and diseases all around the world aren't enough for these people to contend with; their leaders are threatening each other with nuclear missiles now.'

Walter replied despondently, 'At this rate there won't be anything left to be reckoned.'

Kate sighed, 'Millions led by a few – never getting it right.'

'Drink up,' said Walter, 'time to move on.'

'You are a hard taskmaster, Walter Haker,' Kate smiled.

'We have places to go and people to see.' He gazed skyward. 'And beautiful weather to do it in.'

'My car or yours?' asked Kate.

'I have my Landrover with me today, we'll take that.'

'Is that with or without a driver?' Kate cheekily asked.

'Without,' Walter replied. 'I am capable of driving myself around, you know.'

Kate smiled the most homely smile. 'Isn't that a bit beneath a captain?'

'Only when it suits.'

Kate then brought things back to more serious matters. 'I take it we're going across the common to look for the grave – yes?'

'Yes,' Walter replied. He reached across the table for Kate's hand. 'We know where to look, so we shouldn't have any problem finding it, and when we do we can simply draw a diagram of its whereabouts to give to whoever comes calling for it.'

'I wonder who that will be. Abel didn't actually mention that bit.'

'No, but I have no doubt he will get word to us somehow.'

'Okay, let's go.' Kate got to her feet; the two of them walked together, though not hand in hand, up the slope to Walter's Landrover and were soon on their way with the low Sun reflecting in their eyes of purest blue.

***

Al Orange had arrived back at Smallbeef, a place he had come to regard as his home. The birds there had shown him love and care which he felt he did not deserve. Their kindness had engendered feelings within him which he had long since abandoned at the behest of his dreadful tenant; now however, he was finding his feet again, keeping his head full of all manner of thoughts based on truth rather than paranoid lies which he had been force-fed for much of his life.

In the meantime, Aano Grunt was barely a quarter of the way back, swinging languidly through the trees, enjoying the intercourse which they so sociably offered. Quite often he would resort to walking when the trees were too sparsely grouped. But as always, Aano would thank them for their help and bid them good day before bounding across the sand to the next stand of trees waiting enthusiastically for his arrival.

'Nice trees, lovely trees,' he would whisper, 'thank you so much.'

What a nice chap, we could do with more like him, the trees would rustle in reply. Aano knew what they were saying, despite their lack of spoken words.

30

Walter stopped the Landrover just short of the timbered wall so as to afford a better view across the common. He and Kate peered into the distance towards the top of the rise where they had previously met the troubled Mr Jones. Walter carefully leaned across the front of Kate with binoculars in hand and peered through her side window. 'Well, if nothing else, our man is a creature of habit. He's up there now, picking up fallen wood.'

'Why don't we drive up there?' Kate eased Walter to the upright position with a gentle push and a wry smile. 'We could get quite close to him before venturing on foot.'

Walter duly snicked the Landrover into gear. 'Okay, let's have a go.'

At little more than tick-over the Landrover made its way without causing any alarm to the local wildlife, the damp autumnal air suppressing any dust that might have risen.

With his trailer full of fallen timber, Jones poured a cup of coffee from his flask while collecting his thoughts. The faint chatter of a diesel engine soon filtered through the trees, waking his interest. *Not the Ranger's usual pick-up*, he thought, *sounds more like a Landrover*. Unsure of what to expect, he walked around to the back of his trailer to meet the visitor halfway.

The Landrover came to a halt and the engine stopped. Kate and Walter alighted and, both smiling, they made the last few paces on foot. 'Hello again,' said Kate, 'you've been busy.'

'Yes,' Jones replied, almost shyly. 'Nothing wrong, I hope.'

'No, we just like to keep an eye on things up here.'

Walter took another step forward. 'When we met you the other day you were with someone else, but he left before we got to speak to him.'

Jones hesitated. 'No, I don't think so. I was here alone.'

Kate thought perhaps her charm might encourage him to open up. 'Mr...I'm sorry, I didn't catch your name?'

Reluctant to enter into a conversation that might be full of tricks, Jones looked towards his car. 'I'm sorry, but I've got to go now or I'll be late for work,' he said.

Kate replied in kindly tones, 'Okay, we'll move our Landrover out of the way for you, but we just want to talk to you.' Her eyes searched for the man's soft spot. 'Please, you're not in any trouble but we think you could help us with our search.'

Jones looked briefly into Kate's eyes, amazed at their blueness. Something familiar jarred his sense of self-preservation. He then noticed the same look in the eyes of Walter. 'Who are you?' he asked timidly. His gaze then fell to the ground. Kate and Walter could not help but notice the look of despair on his face.

'What on Earth is troubling you?' Kate ventured to rest a hand on his shoulder but he backed away just enough to keep out of reach. He looked around at the undergrowth, searching for any tell-tale movement of others who might be listening.

Walter took up the dialogue. 'The fact is, we know someone else was here with you – could you describe him for us and tell us what business he had with you?'

'Describe him?' Jones' struggled to hold on to the tears. 'All I can say is he's everything you would not want in a person.'

'How do you mean?' said Kate, calmly.

Clenching his fists by his sides in a state of extreme tension, Jones continued, 'I don't even know if he **is** a person, or what he is...I just want to be left alone – now please let me pass.'

'Okay, forget the stranger for a minute,' said Kate trying to keep things nice and relaxed. 'Have you come across anything unusual on your travels up here – anything at all?'

Jones didn't reply verbally, but he turned his head and cast his gaze twenty paces away towards the edge of the level ground on which they stood. He remained silent, his eyes doing the talking.

Walter watched while Kate walked into the open. She studied the ground as she went, lightly scuffing the sand until she reached the spot Jones was paying particular attention to. She stopped and turned; Jones discreetly nodded to her.

'We won't trouble you anymore, sir,' said Kate, making her way back to the Landrover, collecting Walter as she went.

Once in the cab, Walter nodded through the windscreen to say farewell to Jones before reversing back along the track, leaving the dejected human to his own company once again.

'I sensed we were being watched from the bushes, did you?' said Walter.

'Yes I did,' Kate replied. 'And I think we know who by, but I don't think it would be in anyone's interest to make the point right now.'

'Do you think that patch of ground is where the grave is?'

'I'm sure of it,' said Kate. 'I could feel it in my feet.'

Having turned his vehicle around, Walter drove the Landrover back towards the main track. 'I think we'll stop at the bottom behind the wall; we can keep an eye on things from there and see what comes to light.'

'Good idea,' said Kate.

***

Jones leaned against the front wing of his old Volvo, wishing so much that he was no longer here. Tears flowed unhindered down his cheeks.

'I thought I told you not to talk to anyone,' said a voice close behind him. Jones knew who it was. He turned to see the man in the hat staring across the bonnet at him.

'You are very stupid,' said the man.

Jones cried out, 'For heaven's sake, can't you leave me alone?'

'Hah,' the man in the hat laughed. 'What has heaven got to do with it? Heaven won't help you here; you should know that by now, you pathetic little man. Oh, and by the way, I use the term "man" as an insult. But you know that already.'

From behind the timbered wall, Walter raised his binoculars towards the top of the rise once again. 'There he is,' he whispered. 'It looks like your friend Helkendag has come out of hiding. He seems to be talking to our loner.' Walter handed the binoculars to Kate. 'Take a look.'

She quickly found the target through the lenses. 'I don't think the atmosphere is very convivial up there, they seem to be arguing.'

***

'Just shut up.' Jones shouted as he made his way around his car to get to the driver's door, but Helkendag stood in his way and was not about to move.

'You will go when I say you will.' Helkendag raised his hand and struck Jones hard on the shoulder. Jones lost his footing and fell backwards landing some ten feet away.

***

'Quick,' said Kate, 'turn this thing round and get us back up there. Helkendag's showing his true colours.'

Walter hurriedly shunted the Landrover back and forth.

**

'What's the matter with you?' Jones shouted. 'I've done nothing to deserve this, just let me go, will you?'

The man in the hat sneered. 'You wretched excuse for a human. Look at you. You ask what you've done to deserve this; I will tell you what you've done. You've done nothing, nothing but try to make your own feeble little way through life. Like most of your kind you are not worthy of this world – the fact is you do not deserve to be here at all.' Helkendag's eyes turned from blue to black, the blackest, dullest black there is.

'Why won't you just let me go?' Jones pleaded. 'I'm no use to you; you said yourself I'm wretched.' He then laughed a self-deprecating laugh while tears waited to show the world his pain. 'I agree, I am wretched. I'm no bloody use to man nor beast. I don't even want to be here, so why don't you just finish me off, eh, end it, I don't care.'

A nasty smile preceded Helkendag's reply. 'You seem to be mistaking me for someone else; I am not the reaper, don't you remember? I have told you many times before, I am man's accuser, unofficially, you understand. Sadly I cannot hand down a verdict, nor can I pass sentence, but as you know, I can make your life utterly miserable until someone with more compassion comes along to relieve you of this tiresome life.'

Jones got to his feet, keeping a good arm's length away from his adversary.

'Tell me,' said Helkendag, 'which is the most unpleasant – having me inside your head, or meeting me in the flesh?'

Jones did not answer, but rubbed his shoulder feeling the

bruise coming to life.

The man in the hat continued to provoke. 'I told you to keep away from here, did I not?'

'Why should I?' Jones replied, sounding rather like a young child arguing vainly with the local bully, a bully whose spite knew no limits.

'Because I said so.' Helkendag removed his hat and placed it on the roof of the car. His full shock of blond hair gave a false impression as to his nature. He continued, 'You have fulfilled your purpose as far as I am concerned. You have shown those who would enquire the whereabouts of the grave, so I have no further use of you, but I dare say your life has some way to run yet although the final decision is not mine. However, I would not want to give you false hope; you can rest assured I shall be with you for many more enjoyable days and nights—'

Jones interrupted, 'I will beat you. There is another much stronger than you, and honest too.'

The man in the hat vented a haughty laugh in Jones' face. 'Oh, listen to yourself. You couldn't fight off a toothless, one-legged dog; don't you remember, you are useless, weak and totally pitiful. Where is this other person you speak of? I assume he is a person, or are you talking of someone bigger than that.' He raised his hands in the air, mockingly. 'Ooh, you don't mean…God, do you?'

'You know who I mean,' Jones replied.

'Then why can't you even say his name, eh, why?'

'I don't need to.'

'Oh, but he would like you to, I am sure of that. He puts a lot of store in that sort of thing…people saying his name.'

'All right…yes, I do mean God; not some phony self-righteous hypocrite like you who only gets pleasure by hurting others.'

The man knew Jones was barely a whisker from falling completely apart, but he would not allow that; he had gotten the measure of man's capabilities and could hold a withered soul on the edge of the abyss for years, or until someone else did indeed come calling. 'There now, that didn't hurt did it? I'm sure God would be heartened by your saying his name, but do you honestly think it will do you the slightest bit of good?'

'I know one thing,' said Jones, 'he is truth and he has never put anything in my head that wouldn't stand the test of time.' He straightened himself, standing as tall as his five feet nine would allow. 'You, on the other hand, know only lies and deceit. You create paranoia in the minds of those who are susceptible for whatever reason. You only attack the meek. If anyone is useless – it is **you**.'

The man replaced his hat and adjusted it to be sure it was perfectly straight. He then stepped forward within reach of Jones once again. Thoughts of retreating fleetingly entered Jones mind, but he had nowhere to go and the truth was, he really did not care what might be about to happen to him. So he stood resolute while the man with eyes of pitch moved closer.

***

It was not easy for Kate to look through the binoculars while being bounced about inside the cab of the Landrover as it climbed the rocky slope. A brief stretch of smooth track afforded her a glimpse of the one-sided encounter up ahead. 'He's going to hit him again,' she said, her heart hurting for the beaten recipient of Helkendag's cruel pleasure.

***

Faster than the human eye could detect, a right-hook caught Jones on the jaw. His feet left the ground and he fell heavily to

Earth, his arms offering no protection from the landing. He felt nauseous, his head swam in the mire of his own cerebral fluid. Even the effort to groan in agony was beyond him.

The man in the hat stood over him, smiling callously. 'I have tired of you but I will accompany you through the rest of your life, you may be sure of that. I doubt however, if you will have the pleasure of my physical company again, but you never know.' He kicked Jones in the side, not hard, but enough to ensure he still had his full attention. 'Just to give you a heads up, the doctor who tends your needs really has no idea of your ailment; in time you will find yourself in the hands of those among your breed who fancy themselves experts in their field of mental illness. You know of course they know nothing, but you will follow their will, I can tell you that much.' He turned and walked off into the undergrowth, saying, 'I hope you like white-tiled walls and grubby ceilings, oh, and electricity – shocking stuff.' His sickening laugh faded into the trees. Jones lay there on the hardened sand, hurting and crying to himself. The trees heard him as they had heard many others before, they being the witnesses to all things in this world. They rustled softly and invited a blackbird to come and sing among their branches. *Perhaps that will help the poor chap,* they thought.

Oblivious to the singing bird, Jones got to his feet and staggered to the car. Throbbing pain raced through his jaw, through his ear and into his head. He pulled the car door shut and turned the ignition key, the car started. He groaned as he put the gear lever into reverse, his ribs adding to his discomfort. With his mind in turmoil he cared not for the trailer as his old Volvo pushed it backwards, twisting and turning from side to side until the front corner of the trailer struck the back of the car as the outfit tried to bend in half behind him. With a rear light now broken, Jones completed the turn and desperately floored the throttle. Much of the wood he had gathered flew from the trailer as it bounced violently over the rutted track at breakneck speed.

Walter was about to turn in when the Volvo with distressed trailer in tow hurtled from the track right in front of him and made off down the road.

'Do we follow him or try to find Helkendag?'

'Helkendag,' Kate replied.

The Landrover relished the bout of off-roading as Walter willed it onward, making light work of the uneven terrain. They pulled up harshly and both jumped out, eager to find the illusive man in the hat.

'Not again,' said Kate, despairingly. 'His tracks go into the trees…and then disappear.'

Resigned to the fact that Helkendag had given them the slip yet again, Walter cast his eyes across the sand. 'Oh well, while we are here with no one around we might as well take a closer look at that patch of ground.'

'Okay,' Kate took a few steps forward and then stopped. Her voice trembled slightly. 'It's here, right here.'

'Are you sure?'

'Absolutely, if you stand here you'll know for yourself.' Kate beckoned Walter to join her with an elegant wave of the hand, stopping him two paces short of where she stood. 'What do you feel?'

'Erm, nothing much, just sandstone beneath my feet I guess.'

'Now step forward, close to me.'

Walter did not need asking twice. Two more steps had him sharing the soft sandy patch.

'That's quite close enough,' Kate smiled. 'Now what do you feel?'

'Ooh.' Walter consciously held the shiver at bay. 'It's actually tangible, in the ground. Definitely right here.'

Kate knelt down and began carefully sweeping the sand to one side. 'I wonder how deep it's buried.'

'Wait a minute, Kate. Don't use your hands.' Walter hastily made his way back to the Landrover and promptly returned with a foldable shovel. 'Now let the dog see the rabbit,' he said, carefully scraping the soft sand away. In less than a minute he stopped suddenly. 'Is that what I think it is?'

'If you think it's the clawed hand of a huge pterosaur, then yes it is,' Kate whispered.

The trees whispered too, secretly glad to see someone trying to put things right, knowing as they did that the deceased flyer did not belong in their world.

'It's not very deep.' Walter continued by hand to remove the loose sand from around the bony hand which would easily equal two of his own in every direction. Two more minutes of delicate investigation convinced the two of them that the creature was quite a bit deeper in the ground with only his hand reaching up to the surface. 'Weird,' said Walter, 'I think I should cover it back up now and get some of my men out here to stand guard until we know what Abel Nogg intends to do with it.'

'I agree,' Kate whispered in reply.

The trees whispered their approval.

After returning his shovel to the Landrover, Walter contacted his company via the radio. 'Hunter from Huntmaster.'

'Hunter in – go ahead, Huntmaster.'

'Hunter, please arrange immediate watch comprising twenty beings to Grid Reference November 352, Whiskey 150. Check.'

'Check.'

'Watches to be relieved every four hours, until further notice, over.'

'Roger, Huntmaster. Four-hourly watches at Ref November

352, Whiskey 150. Twenty beings each, immediately, correct? Over.'

'Correct, Hunter. I shall wait at Reference Point until arrival of first watch, over.'

'Roger, Huntmaster – Hunter out.'

Walter then turned to Kate, who by now was standing by his side with her head resting lightly on his shoulder. 'They'll be here in twenty minutes,' Walter said, his cheek accidentally on purpose rubbing against hers as he turned.

Kate smiled and said quietly, 'I'm pretty sure the body will have to be returned to where it was found in Smallbeef. That's where it was originally laid to rest.'

'So that is where it must be collected from – is that right?'

'Most probably. Abel was quite adamant about that.'

'Will it have to be the same crew who came to collect it last time?'

Kate's eyes lit up. 'Inspector Hooter and whoever else he chooses, I guess, yes.'

'Okay,' Walter concluded. 'My team will stand guard through the night. If we don't hear from Abel Nogg in the morning I'll have the pterosaur exhumed and taken to my garrison for safety.'

Kate nodded. 'I hope you've got a deep freeze – our friend is beginning to whiff.'

31

Sitting behind the desk in his office, Inspector Hooter recounted the events of the last twenty-four hours. He had met the most amazing gorillas in a world which he did not even know existed; additionally, he had been unexpectedly joined by Dana Lethgerk on his journey home through the night. His face took on a concerned look when he thought of this morning's affair with young Bertie outside the café. *I suppose it was a bit rude of him to comment on her smell; I hadn't noticed it before and to be honest I still don't know what the youngster was on about.*

A polite knock on the office door brought Hooter out of his thoughts. 'A cup of tea, sir, just how you like it.' Constable Robert Roberts put the welcome cup down on the desk and then turned to leave.

'Just a minute, Constable,' said Hooter.

Roberts waited by the door. 'Yes sir?'

'It's about Miss Lethgerk.'

'Is there a problem, sir?'

'Have you ever noticed anything unusual about her?'

Roberts thought carefully before replying. 'Well sir, I don't know if it's my place to say, but she does look amazing...I mean her colours, especially her eyes. She's always very polite and thoughtful too.' Roberts leaned further into the room and lowered his voice. 'And to be honest sir, she obviously has a soft spot for you.'

'Hmm…does anything else come to mind?'

After a little more thought Roberts replied with a perceptible note of hesitancy, 'No sir…not really.'

'What does "not really" mean?' Hooter beckoned Roberts to come back into the room.

'I'm sure it's nothing, sir, it's just that things do seem to happen around her – just little things – things that probably don't really matter.'

'Like what?' Hooter found himself rubbing his bill in readiness for Roberts' reply.

'Well sir, for instance, there was the incident in the alleyway when she was accosted by a bounder who we never found.'

'Yes…but that just means we didn't find him. It doesn't mean he didn't exist.'

'No sir, I suppose not.'

'Is there anything else?'

'Not really, sir. I think I'm just being paranoid.'

'Thank you, Constable, that will be all for now.'

'Yes sir.' Roberts closed the door behind him, leaving Hooter with his cup of tea in the solitude of his office.

***

'Honestly, Bernard, I have never been so embarrassed.' Betty Bottoms-Up stood in her kitchen in Smallbeef; her husband stood next to her looking out of the window at their children playing on the grass. Sadly, Bertie was not among them; he was now confined to his bedroom.

Bernard replied, 'Well, you know what children are like, they speak their mind but they don't mean nothin' by it; they don't know any better at that age.'

'But to tell an adult mallard that they smell odd is not acceptable.'

'No, dear.'

'I didn't know where to put my face, really I didn't.'

'No, dear.'

'And as for the lady concerned, Miss Lethgerk, she was mortified – just mortified.'

'Yes, dear.'

'And poor Inspector Hooter, well, all he wanted was a quiet cup of tea with his lady-friend when Bertie pops up and says she smells. It's just not good enough, Bernard, it really isn't.'

'No, dear.'

'Bertie has to learn his manners.'

'Yes, dear.'

'I want you to talk to him. And make sure he listens.'

'Me, dear?'

'Yes, Bernard, you. You are his father after all. He listens to you.'

'Yes, dear. Are you sure he listens to me, dear?'

'Well, he will have to, he certainly does not seem to listen to me; I have told him time and time again not to open his bill without thinking very carefully about what he intends to say. And what does he do?'

'He tells a lady she smells, dear.'

'Exactly, Bernard. That is why you must go to his room and speak with him this minute.'

'This minute, dear?'

'Yes, Bernard, this very minute.'

'Yes, dear.'

Bernard was the sort of mallard who, if he were a human, would wear smart working trousers with braces, and a white shirt with the sleeves rolled tightly up above his impressive biceps, but he could not do that of course, because he was a mallard.

He went to Bertie's bedroom and opened the door to find the youngster sitting on the edge of his bed. Bertie looked up at his dad who he loved very much. His sorrowful eyes let go an innocent tear which joined the others that had already landed on the floor. 'Sorry, Dad,' his bill quivered.

'Now, son, don't worry. I know you didn't mean no harm by what you said. You just gotta learn to think a bit more before you says it.' Bernard sat next to his son and put a wing around the youngster's shoulder. 'I know yer a good lad.' He could not help a brief chuckle getting past his attempt at a serious look. 'But what was yer thinkin' about…telling a lady duck she smells, I mean that's not the way ter behave, is it?'

'No, Dad,' Bertie sniffed. 'But I didn't mean she smells – I just meant she smells different to other mallards.'

'Blimey, Bertie, you ain't knee 'igh to a moor'en; 'ow many mallards 'ave you smelt in yer life, so far?'

Bertie's eyes settled into his dad's, gaining comfort from the fact that he was being listened to. 'I smell you and Mum every day, Dad. And I smell my brothers and sister every day. And I smell Inspector Hooter most days, if he doesn't see me coming first.'

Bernard squeezed Bertie closer. 'I loves you Bertie, because yer honest and that's 'ow I wants yer to stay.'

'Yes, Dad.'

'But do something for me, will yer?'

'Yes, Dad.'

'I wants you ter promise that you'll count ter five before you says anythin' to an adult in future, at least until yer a bit older.' Bernard's eyes sank lovingly into his son's. 'Will yer do that, just fer me?'

'Yes, Dad, I promise.'

'That's fine then, I'll tell yer mother what we've agreed on, an' I'll tell her…I mean I'll suggest to her, that you can come out of yer bedroom and join the others.'

'Thank you, Dad.'

***

Hooter entered the front office and asked of Constable Howard, 'Who is on lunchtime patrol?'

'Thomas and James, sir. They're about to leave now.'

'Excellent, I think I shall join them.'

Constables Thomas and James presented themselves as smart as ever, with helmets perfectly upright as was the way when conducting a walking patrol. They stepped out from the police station and turned left. Inspector Hooter followed them cautiously, hoping not to meet the Bottoms-Up family again. 'Is the coast clear?'

Thomas and James looked both ways. 'All clear, sir.'

'Right, off we go then.' Hooter took up position at the front and led his two constables around the corner into The Square. All three of them immediately scanned the tables outside Café Hero, *Nothing untoward going on.* They waddled smartly onward, nodding good afternoon to those they passed along the way. They soon turned into the narrow alleyway where Hooter's eyes immediately lit up; there was Dana, sitting alone outside the little tea room with a pot of tea for two.

'Listen up, Constables. I shall let you continue your patrol while I discuss matters with Miss Lethgerk – matters relating to the incident the other day, you understand.'

'Of course, sir,' Thomas replied.

Dana spoke softly, 'Won't you sit down, Inspector?'

'Yes, thank you.' Hooter waited until his constables had turned the corner and gone from view before actually taking a seat. He looked at the tea pot.

Dana smiled at him. 'Shall I pour?'

'Yes please, my dear.' Hooter had decided not to mention the earlier mishap with Bertie Bottoms-Up, hoping that the matter would simply fade away. 'It's nice that the rain has stayed away, we've had our share just lately, wouldn't you say?'

Dana paused before replying, intending to keep control of the conversation. 'I'm sure we have, Inspector, but you are waterproof so I can't imagine it bothers you too much.'

'Oh, no, not too much.' Hooter felt awkward now. He wished he had not started off with such a trite remark. 'But it's nice anyway.'

'Relax, Inspector. You seem fidgety; I don't make you nervous do I?'

'No my dear, of course not. The truth is I'm a little embarrassed by the affair this morning.'

'Look, you lovable mallard; it was not your fault and no harm was done, so let's forget about it, shall we?' Dana sipped nonchalantly from her cup, casting an air of calm across the table.

'Wonderful,' said Hooter, 'we shall say no more of it.'

'Good.' Dana held Hooter's gaze. 'Now you can tell me all about your day; it must have been very exciting.'

'But the day is only halfway through.'

Dana reached across the table and ran her wing tip down Hooter's side. 'Then tell me about yesterday; I looked for you but you were nowhere to be seen.'

'Ah, yesterday,' Hooter wavered. He had always made it a policy of his to keep work and social life separate. 'To be honest, Dana, I went out on a regular patrol across the countryside, just to make sure everything was as it should be.'

Dana continued to rub Hooter's side. Something he was not used to.

291

'And was it?'

'Was it what?'

'Was it all as it should be?'

'Oh, yes, yes. No problems. We really are very lucky to be surrounded by such lovely countryside, don't you think?'

'Truly,' Dana replied, now returning her wing to her side of the table. 'I can see you don't want to discuss your work with me—'

'It's not that I don't want to, but I shouldn't.'

'Don't worry, I promise I won't ask you again.' Having finished their tea, Dana rose from her seat and asked, 'Shall we walk a while?'

'That would be nice,' Hooter replied with a caveat, 'But I do think perhaps we shouldn't be seen holding wings or anything that might be misunderstood by the public, if that's all right with you?'

Dana chuckled. 'That's fine, come on, just a little walk by the stream behind the shops before I go.'

'Go?' Hooter could not conceal his concern. 'You don't mean to go away, do you?'

'No, you silly thing; I mean I have to go and do things this afternoon, that's all.'

'Oh, I see.'

'My dear Inspector, I do believe you are letting your feelings show. You must be careful of that or you might start enjoying life.'

Hooter was unsure of how he was supposed to feel. He only knew that the little duck inside him was doing cartwheels and clapping with joy that at last he had found someone truly lovely to share special moments with. But he was Inspector Hooter of the Flying Squad, and as such he had a position to think of, he had standards to maintain. *Yes, but that doesn't mean I shouldn't enjoy*

Around the corner from the tea room they sauntered, Hooter keeping the minimum discrete distance from Dana as they waddled casually by the side of the stream which separated the backs of the shops from the park. On the far side of the park a row of terraced cottages ran like a brightly coloured ribbon from one end to the other. The park itself was blanketed in lush grass which, despite this being well into autumn, still exhibited a vibrant green, painted by Mother Nature personally.

To get into the park the two of them had to cross a narrow footbridge of deeply grained oak planks. Hooter beckoned Dana to go first. 'Thank you,' she said, keeping to the centre of the planks. Hooter followed one pace behind her. When they were halfway across a gentle breeze came upon them, wafting softly in their faces. 'How lovely,' said Dana, taking a long inward breath to savour the scent of the grasses mingling with the aroma from the trickling water beneath them. 'Your world is so redolent of all that is wonderful.'

Hooter also took a deep breath. 'I can't argue with that, but it's not only my world, it's yours as well.'

'To be perfectly accurate,' Dana said, 'it doesn't belong to either of us...or anyone else for that matter. We only look after it while we are here.' The tone of her voice intimated that she was saying nothing that Hooter did not already know.

'Of course,' Hooter replied. 'That is why we must do our best not to spoil it in any way.'

'Do you think you succeed in that?'

Hooter had to pause for a bill rub. 'Hmm, try as we might, we must accept that we are mere mortals, wonderful, but not perfect.'

'You look quite perfect to me,' Dana replied.

'Perfect in body maybe, but we all have the capacity to do

wrong; that is why we need some of us to apply policy and guide each other along the way.'

Dana slowed her waddle momentarily to allow the inspector to come alongside her. She then continued, 'Would you say your world is as perfect now as it was when mortals were first put here? Mortals like you, I mean.'

'Oh, my dear.' Hooter so wanted to put a wing around the beauty beside him to lend some gravity to his response. 'That is a huge question. It's all about striking a balance between yourself and Nature, you know that – I'm sure.'

'But if you really put your mind to it, could you think of a world even more balanced than this one?'

'Yes, I think I can,' Hooter answered eagerly without thinking what he was saying. 'And not so far from here, why I was there only the—' He stopped abruptly. *Have I said too much? I must be careful not to divulge what I have seen.*

'Tell me more.' Dana's voice teemed with enthusiasm. 'Where is such a world? Could we go there? Or are you just speaking metaphorically?'

'I think I've said too much already, my dear – police business, you know how it is.'

'Ah, I see.' Dana leaned a little closer. 'There is no one looking.' She gently rubbed her cheek on his.

'Please, madam, not here. I have my position to think of.'

'Just one more little rub, please.'

So soft was Dana's touch that Hooter barely felt it, but he tingled all the same. The sensation caused him to snatch a light but sharp intake of breath. His nostrils being but a feather's thickness from Dana's cheek took in the scent of something not of a duck. He took another inward sample, more subtle. *Lavender, yes, it's Lavender, with something else beneath, very odd though.* He slowly drew away. 'I really think we should be getting back'.

'Already? But we have so much to talk about. You don't realize how exciting your job is. I simply want to share in it with you; is that so bad?'

'Of course not.' Hooter gave her a gentle hug around the shoulder before adopting the more proper space between them. 'Please try to understand, my dear. I must keep my police business separate from my social life, otherwise I might accidentally compromise myself, or others, and that would be quite dreadful.'

Dana's expression took on a countenance of sadness. 'You don't trust me.'

'Of course I do, but that is how it must be.' Hooter's voice was one of mollification. *This isn't easy, treading the line between responsibility and friendship…not easy at all.* 'I'm afraid I must find my Constables now. I should finish the patrol with them. Perhaps we could meet again tomorrow?'

Dana looked Hooter right in the eye, fixing him to the spot. 'Okay, if you say so.' She turned and waddled slowly away in the direction from which they had come. Hooter watched her cross the little bridge, his heart aching so. The little duck inside him welled up out of sadness for the beautiful lady mallard who only wanted his special friendship. As soon as she was gone from view Hooter continued his way through the park hoping to catch up with Thomas and James somewhere in the town. *Sometimes I wonder if this job is worth it,* he thought forlornly.

32

Early the next day in the humans' world, the Sun reached over the surrounding trees and spread its light across the pond on the heath, highlighting the ripples as they teased the bobbing water birds.

Kate made her way down the slope towards the kiosk. This had become her regular rendezvous point with Walter.

The barista, on seeing her, readied two cups. 'Good morning, madam – your usual?'

'My usual,' Kate replied, 'but hold the other until my friend gets here, thank you.'

'Certainly madam,' said the barista.

Kate sat facing the water with her back to the kiosk. Her coffee arrived with the usual heart motif fashioned in the topping. Kate looked up at the young man and smiled a thank you. He fumbled his reply as usual, 'That's lovely, thank you, miss, madam – no, yes, madam.' He walked away, blushing profusely as only a fully primed juvenile not entirely in control of his diction could, seeking the refuge of the other side of the counter. *Doh, why do I always fluff it?*

Kate wistfully stirred the artwork into the milky froth, wondering what the day had in store. Her mind wandered back a couple of weeks to when she first met Inspector Hooter in the police station. *Things have been anything but dull since he came on the scene.* She rested the spoon back on the saucer and lifted the cup to her lips.

'Hello, Kate.' A voice of perfect clarity spoke close behind her.

She knew the voice, but such was her unpreparedness for it that the mug in her hand jarred, threatening to spill the drink over the table. Overtaking the sequence of events, a hand reached around her and held her wrist steady. The coffee settled, none spilt.

Feelings from deep within her soul raced to the surface, her heart pumping expectantly. She turned around in her seat, she knew who would be there, but she had no idea what guise he would be in. *Surely not a pterosaur, not here,* she thought.

Standing looking down at her was a man of unremarkable appearance, average height, greying blonde hair balding beneath a cream Panama hat. He wore tweed trousers with a matching waistcoat and the sleeves of his white shirt rolled up. Casual but smart you might say.

Kate let his eyes of crystal settle in hers, leaving no barrier to resist his presence. 'Who are you today, Leon – or is it Abel?' she asked.

'Either will do, Kate.' He smiled the smile of a senior gentleman of those parts. 'Do I pass muster?' he joked.

Kate's heart had yet to regain its equilibrium. 'It really is you, I can't believe it. The last I saw of you was your rear end sticking out of the timbered wall. I think I prefer this look…' She paused while recalling in fine detail the magnificent pterosaur that Abel presented in Hooter's world. 'Hmm, I don't know though, perhaps we should call it a draw.'

Just then, Walter appeared behind them. Not realizing who the newcomer was, he asked politely, 'Good morning, may I join you?'

Abel turned and faced him, letting him take his time to figure things out.

'Good Lord.' Walter found himself falling into the uniquely infinite depths of Abel's eyes. His mind emptied as he swam through ambrosia, his thoughts being read and reinforced at the same time until Abel let him go. Walter exhaled long and slow while composing himself. 'Phew…will we ever see the real you?' he asked.

'One day,' Abel replied. 'One day everyone will.'

Walter eyed the chair opposite Kate and looked Abel in the eye. 'May I?'

'Of course,' said Abel.

Walter took his seat. He could not help but hold Kate's gaze for a full five seconds, enjoying the aura given off by the two creatures opposite him.

The barista returned. 'Can I get you anything, gentlemen?' He looked at both men in turn.

Walter replied, 'Two Americanos, please.'

Abel slowly swept his eyes across the pond and along the road behind him. 'It seems quite peaceful now,' he said, watching the children playing on the swings and slides while their parents chatted casually to each other. 'You have both moved among these people for many generations.' He shared his eyes between Kate and Walter in equal measure. 'Would you say they are better for all the generations that have gone before them – or have they learned nothing?'

Walter and Kate both knew the answer without the need to ponder or tally mans' account. 'They have learned nothing,' Kate replied mournfully. 'They have been blessed with more gifts than any other creature that has ever been in this world, yet they still have an innate desire to do wrong, either in person or vicariously.'

Walter joined in. 'It's not as if they accidentally do wrong,' he sighed. 'They actually make an effort to deliberately commit bad deeds. The only thing they have learned is how to kill more effectively.'

Abel reached forward and took Walter's hand. 'Do not vex yourself, my friend; remember you are here to observe, and in exceptional times such as these, to offer help.'

'Yes, of course, I'm sorry, sir.'

Kate held Walter's other hand, saying, 'You haven't been here as long as me. As time goes by you will learn not to let things get to you, otherwise you would go quite mad and be no good for anyone.'

'But isn't that like accepting that things can never be put right?' said Walter.

Abel answered, 'People ask why God allows such dreadful acts to take place in his world. But I tell you they do not take any responsibility for their own actions. They have been blessed with the ability to know right from wrong…and they know compassion. There is no reason on this Earth why they cannot live in harmony, not one morsel of an excuse for not doing so. But many of them would rather expend ten pounds of effort to do wrong, than one ounce of let, to live in peace.'

The atmosphere at the table had become one of sadness, not what Abel had intended, so he changed the subject. 'We must talk of today's events, there are matters in urgent need of your attention.'

'The grave?' Kate replied.

'Indeed.' Abel held their attention totally. 'Inspector Hooter and whoever else he chooses, will collect the body in the next day or two.'

'Oh my,' Kate replied in a worried tone, 'that is so dangerous for them.'

'At least the body will be ready for them this time,' Abel said, reassuringly. 'Thanks to you they won't have to go looking for it.'

The worried look on Kate's face preceded her request. 'Is there no way that you, or we, could intervene just a little more?' She looked achingly into Abel's eyes and continued, 'Perhaps we could take the body down to the timbered wall for them, then they could simply pull it through without having to set foot in this world.'

'No, Kate,' Abel replied compassionately. 'You know as well as I, that those who misplaced the body must return to the place where they left it and take it from there – continuity is important. Strictly speaking, Inspector Hooter should have at least one of his own constables accompanying him, but by way of grace that condition has been waived.'

'I know,' said Kate, sighing anxiously. 'But I had to ask.'

Walter asked, 'Is it okay to keep the body where it is, on the common?'

'No, Walter,' Abel replied. 'You are to keep it among your garrison until the time is right.'

'Certainly, sir, I'll arrange that right away.'

'You should also keep some of your team at the timbered wall, further information will come through in due course.'

'Yes, sir.' Walter retired to his Landrover to make the call.

Abel then asked of Kate, 'Have you seen much of the suited man in the hat?'

'No,' said Kate, 'he seems to have been otherwise engaged of late. I'm concerned that we might end up in a confrontation with him, and to be honest I don't think Walter or I would be able to stand up to him.'

'Concentrate on that which you can influence. In the meantime I shall take a look around and get the measure of things.'

'If he really is who we think he is what chance has mankind got?'

'All is never lost, Kate. As long as something exists, then it has a chance to redeem itself.'

'Does that go for The Dark Angel as well?'

Abel faltered, unable to reply positively.

Walter returned to the table. 'All arranged, sir. We'll stand ready for your word.'

'Thank you, Captain.' Abel rested a hand on each of their shoulders. 'I shall go now, but you will hear from me in a day or two at the most. Until then, my friends, let love lead your hearts.' Abel turned and made his way up the slope to the road, disappearing behind a hedge – gone.

***

Inspector Hooter had spent a restless night in the solitude of his bed in the police station. His thoughts had wrestled with the notion that he could have a life beyond that of a police officer. *If I can't make it with Dana I can't make it with anyone; that much I do know.* He rose from his bed and preened himself in front of the mirror which hung above his wash stand. *Look at me, I'm not getting any younger. Time is passing me by and so is any hope I have of finding a partner.* He straightened the feathers beneath his wings, twisting his shoulders to ensure they felt just right. *And Dana shows a genuine interest in my work, perhaps we could find a happy balance between my responsibility as an inspector and that of a loving husband.* His heart warmed at the prospect of having such a beautiful mallard to come home to after a hard day's work. *Perhaps we could even have a home of our own – no more sleeping on station. I could actually go home each night and maybe switch off for a few hours in the company of a wife of my own.* He smoothed the feathers over his perfectly rounded head. 'That will do,' he muttered. 'That's about as good as I'm going to get.'

Constable Peter Peters called in the direction of Hooter's office. 'Constables Peters and Howard going out on patrol, sir. Will you be joining us?'

'No, Constable. I have things to think about here, perhaps I shall venture out a little later.'

'Righto, sir.'

Hooter watched from the front window of the station as Peters and Howard made their way up the road. No sooner had they rounded the corner when Mrs Betty Bottoms-Up appeared. Hooter shrank back from the window, not wishing to be spotted, but he wanted to see that young Bertie was with them. Sure enough, the youngster followed close behind his mother while his siblings followed equally close behind him. However, there was none of the usual jollity about the troupe's demeanour, rather, they waddled in silence, Bertie keeping his bill firmly shut as his father had advised. As Bertie passed by the police station he couldn't resist a quick look across to see who might be watching. He caught a glimpse of the inspector shying away from view. The youngster returned his gaze to the front without acknowledging Hooter's presence. *Sometimes grown-ups can be really odd*, he thought as they followed in Constables Peters' and Howard's footsteps around the corner and out of view.

***

A few miles to the south of town, Constable Five Degrees cruised at a height of four houses which is generally considered to be somewhat less than four trees, a mature pine being the datum. He was still getting used to the feel of his helmet, now able to adjust it in accordance with regulations. 'Thank you.' He spoke quietly into space as the air rushed smoothly past his ear holes, his feathers reducing the wind roar to little more than a distant hush. 'Thank you for thinking of me, and thank you for blessing me with…well, with a straight head.' His eyes drifted skyward as he gave thanks, knowing that he was being heard.

He began to climb higher as he approached Harting Down, one of the many undulations that formed the South Downs. Being a young adult mallard of similar age to those in the Flying Squad, he managed the climb with no problem. He always enjoyed this particular part of his patrol, the countryside being so varied as to always present something new to marvel at as he crested the hill. On this occasion the southern horizon remained shrouded in far off mists, the Sun taking its time to mop them up. Sometimes he would increase his altitude by another four trees to see the true horizon presented by the sea in the very far distance. But this time his tour was curtailed when a gruff voice startled him from behind.

'Good morning, Constable. A fine day to be out and about.' Abel Nogg came alongside, Mother Nature supporting him on stilled wings.

'Oh, Mr Nogg, you made me jump,' said Five Degrees.

Abel's eyes smiled while he looked at the constable's helmet. 'The regulation forward tilt I see, perfect.'

'Thank you, sir.'

'Could I ask you to land for a moment? Wherever is convenient for you.'

Without question, Five Degrees banked smoothly to the left, and having lost most of his height, he presented the underside of his wings to the oncoming air and adopted a vertical body to land with only one step required on the ground. Abel marvelled at the inherent skill of the young bird, a gift which although untaught and natural, was never taken for granted. The pterosaur floated down with his vast wings spread wide, giving

303

Mother Nature plenty to hold on to. He immediately folded his wings and settled on all fours next to the mallard. Five Degrees stood in wonderment, not noticing his bill agog.

'Your bill,' Abel prompted.

Five Degrees closed his mouth, leaving only his eyes wide open.

'Wonderful isn't it,' said Abel. They both stared at the surrounding countryside from their vantage point high on Harting Down. The sky had brightened to leave the finest wisps of high cloud to float in Natures arms. Small birds swooped and darted about the valley below, while rabbits chatted idly in the lea of the hedgerows, sampling the grass and dandelion. 'Just wonderful,' Abel repeated to himself.

'Sometimes I have to say it out loud,' said Five Degrees. 'Just so I know I'm not dreaming. Mind you, it's not so good for some animals.'

Abel turned his head and looked the mallard in the eye, wondering what he might be about to come out with; he could see a lot of Inspector Hooter in the young bird.

Five Degrees continued, 'I mean, I don't think I would want to be a vole – or any small animal come to that. There's always something out to get you, for dinner.'

'That is true.' Abel carefully opened one wing and swept it across the sky. 'You must consider the world as a whole, as one living breathing entity.'

Constable Five Degrees relaxed, knowing he was about to be loved by words.

Abel added, 'It was created in perfect balance…everything happens for a reason…a reason guided by Mother Nature to keep the world healthy and prosperous. The vole or the sparrow might be taken, but it is not a waste or a loss if it remains part of this world, which it does.' He sighed and then carried on,

'Remember this, my friend; nothing in life ever stays the same. That a creature might die today does not mean he will not see another day – he will, you will, but you will not be a mallard forever. If everything disappeared when it died, then most of the world would have disappeared by now, but it is still here, is it not?'

The constable remained transfixed by Abel's lesson. The pterosaur's words seemed to be reinforcing that which he already knew, a wisdom so deeply entrenched and ancient that they formed the very substance from which his soul was made.

'The important thing is,' said Abel, 'you must try to leave this world in as good a state of health as you found it; Mother Nature asks nothing more than that. If you accept that the world itself has a soul then you will find it easy to understand how important it is that it should be treated with love. Your soul yearns for love – as does the world's.'

Abel stroked the mallard's back tenderly with a straightened hand so as not to hurt with his claws. 'Perfect,' he said again.

Five Degrees felt strangely emboldened by Abel's regard. He was glad to have been reminded of the true importance of being an animal.

'Now.' Abel's voice took on a more sober tone. 'It would be of great help to me if you would take another message to Inspector Hooter, right away.'

'Of course, glad to.'

'Could you ask him to be at the timbered wall, mid-morning, the day after tomorrow?

'The timbered wall, mid-morning, the day after tomorrow; yes sir.'

'Tell him the time has come. He will know what you mean.'

'The time has come, yes sir. I'll set off right away shall I?'

'If you would, please.'

Constable Five Degrees adjusted his helmet in readiness, giving it one extra squiggle just for the sake of it. With wings spread wide he was about to take a couple of long strides when he felt an invisible hand support him from beneath his rump. Up he went with the least effort, the hand releasing him as soon as he reached four trees high. 'Ooh, how odd,' he remarked, never having experienced anything quite like it before.

Abel looked up and waved to him, thinking silently, You will make your life count, my friend, do not worry.

The trees rustled excitedly as the mallard headed north, his colours seeming even more brilliant than usual and his helmet badge catching the Sun's rays and sending them into the trees to tickle their tops. *What a thoughtful chap*, the trees whispered to each other.

33

In Smallbeef, the afternoon Sun gently warmed Al Orange's back while he sat on one of the hay bales in the yard. Aano Grunt, having eventually returned from the timbered wall, joined him for a welcome cup of tea. 'Shall I pour?' he asked, bringing his arms down to his sides.

'That would be nice,' Al Orange replied. The word "nice" had been excluded from his vocabulary for a long time, but thanks to Aano he was coming to grips with his troubled mentality. He knew that for some reason the evil one who had for so long occupied his mind had left him; for how long he did not know, but he was grateful for the respite which gave him time to see things in their true perspective, helped in no small part by the philosophy of Aano Grunt.

Now sitting opposite the inspector, Aano duly poured the tea. 'Ah, lovely,' he said, pouting his lips and taking a long sip. 'I never really fancied tea before I came here, but I must say it's very refreshing, almost as tasty as water.'

Orange comfortably settled in Aano's eyes; that was another thing that had changed recently – the ability to look others in the eye. 'For as long as I live,' Orange said, 'you will most certainly be the oddest looking, oddest thinking, oddest doing creature I will ever know.'

A look of concern creased Aano's forehead. 'Is that good?'

Orange chuckled. 'Yes, Aano, that's very good.'

'Top up?' asked Aano, reaching for the teapot again.

'Please,' Orange replied.

Before Aano had reached the pot, Orange rested his wingtip on top of the ape's hand, stroking the haphazard hairs which seemed to have no particular order to them. 'You are a special friend…Aano.'

Appreciation poured forth from Aano's bright brown eyes. 'And so are you.'

They sat a while in silence, recalling the animosity that had prevailed between them in the past, all due to the inspector's attitude. Their peaceful pondering came to an abrupt halt when the trees rallied to announce an airborne arrival. Moments later Abel Nogg landed vertically in the centre of the yard, his wings casting long shadows across the ground. He folded his wings and hobbled over to Aano and Al Orange. Many of the residents came out from their homes for another chance to see so impressive a creature.

'Good afternoon, one and all,' called the pterosaur.

The inspector and the ape rose from their straw seats to acknowledge Abel's presence.

'I need a quiet word with the two of you,' said Abel. 'Perhaps over by the lean-to where it's quieter.'

'Certainly,' said Aano leading the way with his arms automatically rising above his head.

The ape and the mallard settled down inside the lean-to. Lucky, the donkey, lay in the corner, his feet nicely on the mend thanks to Aano tending to him in his role as farrier.

'I won't come in,' said Abel, hunching down as low as he could in the doorway. 'I would like you, Mr Grunt, and you, Inspector, to be at the timbered wall the day after tomorrow by mid-morning. Inspector Hooter will also be there, as will the Suffolk horse and a wagon.'

Aano gulped, he knew what that meant. 'Just like before,' he said. 'I take it we are to go through the wall again to complete our mission.'

'You are indeed.' Abel looked around and noticed Sergeant Uppendown keeping a discreet distance on the far side of the yard. 'Ah, Sergeant Uppendown, could I have a word, please?'

'Fer sure, sir.' The Mountie promptly made his way to join them.

'Mr Grunt and Inspector Orange are travelling to the timbered wall the day after tomorrow. I think it would be good if you were to join them. Your discipline and stout demeanour will prove useful, I'm sure.'

'Fer sure, sir. Glad to,' replied the Mountie, looking as smart as ever in his perfectly dimpled Stetson hat.

'You all know what to expect,' said Abel casting an eye across the three of them. 'Hopefully, this time, your mission will be concluded without any interference from others who seek to spoil your world'

'Will we be gone long?' asked Al Orange.

'Most of the day I would think,' Abel replied. 'In the meantime please do not mention this to anyone, it is important that as few folk know as possible.'

Orange, Aano and Uppendown looked each other in the eye and then replied as one, 'Yes sir.'

'Very good,' said Abel, 'I shall see you at the timbered wall, farewell until then.' With that he stepped away from the building and, with wings held wide, rose silently and eerily into the sky with no apparent effort. The trees hurrahed and reached as tall as they could in the hope of the slightest touch as the beast passed over them.

***

Mid-afternoon in Davidsmeadow saw the Sun casting a cool light across The Square. Inspector Hooter rounded the corner from the police station, hoping to meet Dana once again. He felt things had become a little strained of late and wanted to put matters right. He was sure in his mind that Dana was the one for him. He was equally sure that if he let her slip from his life now, he would never get another chance of finding a partner with whom he might share his twilight years. *I wonder how old she is. She certainly looks younger than me, but not by much I think.* With his heightened emotions held in abeyance, the tables outside Café Hero came into view. *There she is, how wonderful. I must keep my cool this time.* True to form, Dana sat at the same table on the pavement with a pot of tea ready and waiting.

'Hello, my dear,' said Hooter pulling his chair out from the table and making himself comfortable in the gaze of his beautiful would-be companion.

Dana's eyes seemed bigger and brighter than ever, if that were possible. 'I wasn't sure if you would be here today, Inspector,' she said.

'Oh, I can always find time for you, Dana.'

Dana poured the tea while continuing, 'You seemed very pre-occupied yesterday, as if you have more important things on your mind.'

'Oh, you know how it is, my dear, police business and all that.'

Dana's eyes glistened as she replied, 'Ah, police business, eh. It seems to me that your job might prove to be something of an issue if we were to become more than just friends.'

Hooter's heart skipped a beat. His resolve to remain calm began to melt away.

Dana added, 'If you cannot trust me, Inspector, I'm not sure that we will have much of a future together.'

'You mustn't think like that, please.' Hooter immediately found himself wrong-footed. 'Of course we can make things work, we just need to agree on where the line is drawn between work and play.'

'You mean I must agree with **your** idea of where the line is drawn, don't you?'

Hooter stumbled over his reply. 'But…well.' He took a sip of tea in the hope of something worthwhile coming into his head. Oh how he wanted to rub his bill.

'Don't worry, my lovely inspector.' Dana reached across the table and rubbed his shoulder. 'I won't put any pressure on you, but I don't think it's a very good foundation for a lasting relationship if one side can't trust the other.'

'But that simply is not true,' Hooter retorted firmly. 'If it were true then I would certainly not let on that I shall be away for a couple of days on the other side of the common, undertaking a rather dangerous mission would I?'

A look of concern briefly washed the colour from Dana's eyes. 'A dangerous mission – but why you?'

'Because I have unfinished business to attend to; business which I alone am qualified to conduct – with a few of my colleagues of course.'

'But at your age you should be letting the younger ones take the risks. Why can't they go instead of you?'

'Because it is my job; that is what I do.'

Dana quickly sorted her thoughts. 'I could come with you.'

Hooter shook his head. 'No, my dear; I can't possibly take you, it would be far too dangerous. I would never forgive myself if any harm should come to you.'

'But that would be my choice…you are not responsible for my well-being.'

'But I am a police officer. I am responsible for everyone's

well-being, especially yours, my dear.'

Dana would not relent, 'Please promise me you will give the matter some thought. I might be very useful to you; I am quite fit you know.'

'That may be, but I have my orders.'

'Orders are there for guidance, surely.'

'Not these orders. The one who gave these orders is not to be questioned.'

Once again Dana paused for thought. 'And who is this individual who would have a mallard risk all for him?'

'But I'm not risking all for him – I'm risking all for the sake of all those in this world.'

'I think perhaps you are being a little melodramatic, Inspector.'

Hooter shook his head with more conviction than before. 'Believe me, I'm not. There is an evil presence at work in our midst and it has fallen to me and a select few to do what is necessary to put things right. It was after all, my constables who inadvertently caused the problem in the first place, not that they knew what they were doing.'

'What on Earth do you mean?' Dana tilted her head to one side to further amplify her interest. 'What could your lovely constables have done that was so bad?'

Hooter knew he should not divulge the presence of the ether and should certainly not mention the location or the workings of the timbered wall, but how else could he possibly explain recent events? Silence hung in the air above the table, neither Hooter nor Dana knowing how to progress what had become an intriguing tale.

'Well, Inspector, if you feel you cannot tell me more, I do understand; it is your job after all to ensure the safety of everyone…even at the expense of your own personal life.'

The little duck inside Hooter's stomach dropped his head. The love that had grown within him, bringing him hope of a meaningful companionship seemed to be at odds with everything he had come to believe in. *I mustn't tell her more; Mr Nogg said I shouldn't tell anyone who didn't need to know…but I trust Dana implicitly, so why shouldn't I share my load with someone I care for and who cares for me?* But the inspector's sense of what was right had become obsessive, giving him no leeway to feed his own avian needs. The little duck inside him sank to his knees with an aching heart at the probable loss about to be suffered.

'I am so sorry, my dear Inspector,' said Dana, 'I know I've caused you a conundrum, believe me I don't mean to. Why don't we sleep on it, perhaps we could meet in the morning for an early cuppa?'

'Yes,' Hooter replied eagerly, glad of the chance to give his brain a rest. He rose from his seat and rounded the table to ease Dana's chair away for her.

Dana's eyes sparkled the most intense blue imaginable. 'I shall see you in the morning then.'

'Yes, my dear, goodbye for now.' Hooter turned and retraced his steps to the police station, not feeling like completing his patrol of the streets of this fine old town. His little duck silently wept into his heart.

***

Inspector Hooter had been in the station for two hours, it was now late afternoon. Never before had he faced such a conflict of emotions. He cast his mind back to his brief liaison with Marion Waters-Edge, an affair which was halted before it even got off the ground when her husband returned after a year-long absence. *But Dana is different. I feel a real connection with her, but I must not let her presence interfere with my police duties or decisions…Oh*

313

dear, what am I to do?

A knock on his office door suspended his troubled course. 'Come in,' he called.

Constable Five Degrees entered and promptly stood to attention as if to further enhance his straightened head. 'Good afternoon, sir.'

'Good afternoon, Constable. To what do I owe the pleasure of your company?'

'Well sir, while I was on patrol over Harting Down I came across Abel Nogg.'

Hooter immediately sat up in his chair and leaned forward, his interest well and truly gathered. 'Was this just a chance meeting?'

'I don't think so, but it's hard to tell with Mr Nogg, isn't it.'

'That's very true, Constable. Do go on, what did he have to say?'

'He asked me to give you a very important message – you are to attend the timbered wall, mid-morning, the day after tomorrow.'

'The day after tomorrow, eh.' Hooter rubbed his bill.

'Mr Nogg also said to tell you "the time has come", he said you would know what he meant.'

'Oh yes, Constable, I know what he means. Was that all?'

'Yes sir, is there anything I can do to help, sir?'

'No, Constable. This is something only I can resolve, thank you, you may go now.'

'Yes sir.' Five Degrees turned and left the room, closing the door quietly behind him.

Hooter slowly slipped back in his chair and let out a long breath. 'Thank heavens, at least I can get this matter over and done with once and for all…maybe then I can think more clearly about my own life and my own future.'

That night Hooter slept lightly, his thoughts skimming like a squat pebble over flat water. Images of Dana would flash before him, only to disappear in less than a second. Likewise, the timbered wall would suddenly loom as large as life towering above him, pulling and pushing him from one world to the next. Giant humans tormented him by waving pushchairs in his face and raising rifles to their eyes. Gorillas looked curiously at him and put their arms around him to embrace and comfort him. And so he tossed and turned all night, bouncing like the pebble across his own mind, never holding on to anything long enough to make any sense.

Dawn eventually came to his rescue, reaching in through the office window. At first it diluted the darkness to a charcoal, and then to a translucent grey through which he could make out the shapes of the furniture in the room. The blackbird, tit and robin heralded the coming of the new day with a symphony of Nature's own doing, no manuscript required, just the joy of seeing another day. Hooter slid from his bed, yawning as he got to his feet. His head immediately filled with images of Dana Lethgerk, replacing all the miscellany that had accompanied his thoughts in the night. *I must let her know that I won't be here for a while, I do hope she understands.*

34

Early morning in Smallbeef. It had been decided that Aano Grunt, Inspector Orange and Sergeant Uppendown would aim to arrive at the wall by dusk on this day, thereby avoiding any rush as might be the case if they left things until the next morning. It was also decided that, rather than swing through the trees, Aano Grunt should make his way riding Sergeant Uppendown's own horse.

It was to that end that Aano stood on a hay bale by the side of the fabulous dark brown, almost black, Hanoverian mare. A look of slight apprehension veiled the ape's face as he took hold of the reins in one hand and carefully placed his foot in the stirrup. With the lightest of pressure he sprang gently up into the saddle. The horse remained quite still while the sergeant adjusted the stirrup length to account for Aano's rather short legs.

'At least the bow in yer legs fits nicely around the horse's girth,' Uppendown said with a chuckle in his voice. 'With such short stirrups you almost look like a race jockey.' The sergeant instantly wondered why he had said such a thing, being as he had no idea what a race jockey was, nor did anyone else judging by the bemused looks on their faces.

Aano spoke up chirpily. 'I must say this saddle is more comfortable than sitting on the flat plank of the wagon.'

'Fer sure, Mr Grunt, my mare will make better progress this

way, too.'

The horse turned her head and settled amiably in Aano's eyes. She had never had an ape on her back before, but she instinctively felt his convivial nature through his legs fitting nicely around her sides. Aano leaned forward and gave a long stroke down the side of the horse's neck. 'You are truly beautiful, madam,' he said. 'I hope I don't cause you any discomfort.' The horse issued a short muffled neigh in reply.

'I think you two will get along just fine,' said Uppendown. 'From what I've heard, you learned very quickly while in the company of Sergeant Jolly recently.'

'Yes,' Aano replied, 'but my excursion was cut short when I got arrested by Inspector Orange; at least I know that won't happen again.' Luckily, the inspector was out of earshot and so did not have to apologise yet again for his previous bad behaviour.

'I guess you had better get going, now,' said Uppendown stroking the hind quarters of the horse. 'She will happily canter much of the way with a short trot or walk to break the routine. She has a smooth action so hopefully you won't suffer too much from saddle bum.'

By now Inspector Orange had joined them and looked up at Aano sitting tall in the saddle. 'We shall leave here at around midday, Aano,' he said. 'We'll most probably catch up with you before you get to the wall, but if not, we'll see you at dusk…take care, my friend.' He dared to pat Aano softly on the thigh before moving a pace backwards to give the mare room to turn and move off without stepping on anyone's toes.

Keeping a light hold of the reins, Aano replied, 'Goodbye then, see you soon.' He felt quite grand aboard the immaculate horse which was adorned with blue and gold numnah and a rich dark leather saddle. The mare too felt strangely privileged to be carrying such an extraordinary creature on her back. Their auras melded warmly as they went at a brisk walk up the road, heading towards the common where the track would take them onward to the timbered wall, and the next episode in what had become something of a saga.

'I hope he manages okay,' said Al Orange, distinctly worried.

'Don't worry, sir,' Uppendown replied, 'he's a natural with horses, and my mare is especially kind; she'll get him there all right.'

***

Sitting at his desk in Davidsmeadow, Inspector Hooter had finished his cup of tea. He sat staring at the wall opposite. Many thoughts whirred around in his head. *I don't know what the matter is with me anymore, I just don't feel entirely in control of my own destiny. How I wish things could go back to the way they were before the Bog went missing. If only my constables hadn't buried him in the wrong place.* He knew his constables were not to blame; they had all been duped by someone rather nasty, someone who had not yet finished with them, or so Hooter thought. *I'm not even sure if I'm going to come through this in one piece.* He stood up and put his cap on – perfectly straight of course. He then took his prized binoculars from the hat stand and placed the strap around his neck. *I don't know why I bother with these either, my eyes aren't in the right place to see through them – sometimes I think this whole world is all wrong.*

Constable James, at the station desk, could not help but notice the doleful expression on the inspector's face when he emerged from his office. 'Is everything all right, sir?'

Hooter hardly heard the constable's enquiry. 'What? Oh, yes, Constable. Everything is all right, thank you.' He then opened the station door to leave without saying where he was going, or why.

'Excuse me, sir,' James called. 'Are you going out on patrol?'

Hooter stopped and turned. 'Oh dear, what am I thinking of? Yes Constable, I am just going to conduct a quick patrol of the town centre.' After a brief bill rub he added, 'Please inform the rest of the squad that I shall be leaving here mid-morning. I have been summoned to the timbered wall; more than that I cannot say, but I expect to be away for a day or two.'

'Would this be in connection with the missing Bog, sir?'

'Yes it would, Constable, but I have some business to sort out in the town before I leave, I shan't be long.'

'Right sir.'

Hooter closed the door behind him and waddled across the road in the direction of The Square. He would normally keep a lookout for the Bottoms-Up family, hoping to avoid them, but today his mind was on more important things. The Bottoms-Ups were now a mere trifle, almost a welcome distraction, but there was no sign of them anyway. Around the corner he went. One by one the tables came into view outside Café Hero. Not at the first, not at the second – but then there she was, sitting with perfect posture as always, a pot of tea for two ready and waiting.

Dana's eyes met his and drew him to her from a range of twenty paces.

'Good morning, Inspector. I hope you are well today.'

'Good morning, my dear. Yes, thank you, I'm quite well.'

'Only quite well? Oh dear, I hope I'm not the cause of your woe.'

'No, no. I think I'm just a little tired, nothing a good night's sleep won't put right.'

Dana poured the tea and then she sat looking attentively at her beau. She knew Hooter had something on his mind. 'Well?' she enquired.

'I have received my orders in respect of the matter we

discussed yesterday.'

'I see. And what precisely do these orders say?'

'All I can tell you is that I shall be leaving here mid-morning today to give myself plenty of time to get to where I am required to be.'

'And where are you required to be?'

'As I said yesterday, I have unfinished business on the other side of the common.'

'The common is a big place, can't you be a bit more specific?' Dana casually took another sip of tea.

'No, my dear. It would make no difference if you knew anyway.'

'Then why not tell me? If it will make no difference, what harm will it do to share your concerns with me?'

'That is not what I meant. I meant it will not help in any way if you knew where I was going, therefore I must keep it a secret – I shall be back in a couple of days and hopefully I will be able to explain everything then.'

After the final sip of her tea, Dana arranged the crockery tidily in the centre of the table, saying, 'Very well, my brave inspector, until then.' She leaned forward and touched her bill on his. The faint smell of lavender hung in the air with a hint of something else in the background.

'If you are leaving mid-morning, you had better get back to the station; I'm sure you have things to sort out before you set off.'

'Yes, you are quite right as usual. I look forward to seeing you again soon.' Hooter rose from his chair. His little duck sat in the bottom of his stomach with his head buried in his wings.

***

Aano had found the rhythm of the Mountie's mare and

found himself flexing his back nicely with the horse's action. An easy canter soon had the landscape passing by at a fine pace.

'This is the life,' said Aano, sharing his thoughts with the horse.

'Tuffets of straw, grasses more green.

Rabbits-a-hiding, not to be seen.

Sienna's and umber's reach for the sky.

While distant horizons beckon the eye.

How marvellous.'

The mare huffed softly in peaceful accord, *What a nice chap, odd, but nice.* But then her ears suddenly rotated and pointed forward. Something or someone was standing in the middle of the track about fifty paces ahead. On sensing the horse's concern, Aano stretched up as tall as he could, peering over the horse's head. It did not take him long to realize who it was. 'How odd?' Aano muttered, keeping a calm note so as not to cause the horse to worry unduly. 'We have a long way to go yet, so why would Abel Nogg be waiting for us out here?'

Aano need not have fretted over the mare's constitution, she had met the pterosaur on previous patrols with Sergeant Uppendown and she knew him to be of a majesty beyond reproach. The pterosaur focused on the mare's eyes and she welcomed him in. In her eyes Abel Nogg found love and strength in equal measure as the horse slowed to a trot and then to a walk. Her entire face smiled while together they shared ethereal thoughts and memories. She came to a halt with her nose almost touching Abel's formidable beak. She took several short intakes of breath through flared nostrils, enjoying his closeness.

'Perfect,' Abel whispered. The mare blew in his face, sweetly, their eyes let go in perfect accord.

'Hello, Mr Nogg,' said Aano. 'I didn't expect to see you until we got to the wall.'

Although Abel had hunkered down on all fours he was still easily at eye level with the mounted Aano; he lingered in the ape's sparkling brown eyes as he began to explain, 'It is important that I talk to you here, where no one else is witness.'

Aano pouted his lips, not as a sign of affection but more of thoughtful anticipation, wondering what Abel could possibly want with him in the middle of nowhere.

Abel continued, 'You know you will be going through the ether very shortly, most probably tomorrow.'

'Yes, Mr Nogg.'

'And you know the passage through the wall is only granted if the Amulet is within two paces of its timbers.'

'Yes, Mr Nogg.'

'I must place a responsibility upon you, my friend.' Abel raised his right hand, the Amulet hung from his clawed fingers. 'You will be the keeper of the Amulet for the duration of your quest, you must keep it safe and not let it fall into the hands of any who would misuse it.'

A concerned frown creased Aano's brow. 'I remember the problems Inspector Orange had when he carried the Amulet, it caused him no end of grief.' Despite his unease, Aano took the stone by the string; he then unfastened the pouch which he wore around his middle to carry the mobile phone that Kate had given him previously. 'It will be safe in here,' he said, dropping the Amulet in and replacing the phone on top to conceal it.

'Those who might try to relieve you of it know that if they force it from you, the Amulet is rendered useless; only if you actually hand it to them will it maintain its power over the timbered wall.'

'And I must be within a couple of paces of the wall for it to work,' Aano confirmed.

'That is correct, Mr Grunt. In your case you might use your overall arm-span as a guide.'

'Yes, of course,' Aano replied, daring to let the reins lie on top of the horse while he stretched both arms out wide.

'Above all else, Mr Grunt, you must not relinquish the Amulet until you are safely back in this world – whatever provocation might be set upon you.'

A little gulp made its way down Aano's throat. 'You can rely on me, Mr Nogg, sir. I won't let you down.'

'It will be the creatures of your world who will be let down, not me, my friend.'

'Right – yes.' Aano took up the reins once again. The mare readied herself.

Abel concluded, 'We shall meet at the wall with the others. Do not mention the Amulet, or the fact that you have it, to any others in your party, understood?'

Slightly puzzled, Aano replied, 'Right sir, it will be our secret.'

'Farewell then, my friend. I shall see you soon.' Abel stepped to one side and the horse set off at a walk with the contrasting bright ginger ape aboard. Their vibrant colours seemed all the more brilliant set against the autumnal shades around them.

The trees whispered as the duo passed them by, *Jolly well done, and good luck.*

Before rounding the distant bend, Aano turned to see Abel Nogg still standing on all fours watching him and the horse until they were out of sight.

***

In Davidsdmeadow Police Station, Inspector Hooter finished a light snack of pellets and tea before summoning all his squad into the main office. Quite a squeeze, but they never minded being close to each other.

323

'Listen carefully, Constables, I have something very important to tell you.' He looked around the room and then asked, 'Has anyone seen Constable Five Degrees?'

'He's out on one of his rural patrols, sir,' James answered.

'Hmm, never mind; he already knows what I am about to tell you, it was he who gave me the message in the first place. I have had word from Abel Nogg.'

As soon as the constables heard Abel Nogg's name they knew what was coming next.

Hooter continued, 'I shall be leaving very shortly. I shall be going to the timbered wall, and I'm sure you all know why – as Mr Nogg so succinctly put it, the time has come. I shall be meeting up with a select few, although I do not know who exactly. I can only assume that with their support I shall be venturing into the world of the humans once again. Let us hope that this time we are successful in returning the missing Bog's body to its rightful place of rest.'

'How long will you be gone, sir?' asked Constable Thomas.

'A couple of days I would think. So I have put your names in my cap. Whichever name is drawn from it, that constable shall assume the rank of Leading Constable until my return.'

Hooter lifted his cap in the air. 'Constable Roberts, if you would do the honours, please.'

Roberts reached up and took one piece of paper from the cap and handed it to Hooter.

Hooter read the name aloud, 'Constable Russell, you are the lucky one.'

'Thank you, sir,' Russell replied, somewhat shocked at the unexpected promotion.

'I have no doubt that with the help and support of your colleagues you will manage splendidly.'

Russell cast a fleeting glance around the room. Every eye

sparkled lovingly in return. 'Thanks, mates. Oops, I mean Constables.'

Inspector Hooter tipped the remaining pieces of paper onto the office desk and placed his cap back on his head, adjusting it with a slight forward tilt in readiness for his flight. 'I know I can rely on you all to do your duty. You all know where I am going and the perils that await....' After a brief pause he concluded in a broken whisper, 'Perhaps a little prayer in my absence would be nice.' He then made his way to the door, concealing a tear doing its best to escape his eye, from there he waddled out into the open without looking back. With wings spread wide, almost touching the buildings to either side, he rose impressively into the air and quickly disappeared over the roof tops.

The constables stood in silence, seeking comfort in each other's eyes. It all seemed to have happened so quickly. They had never seen their beloved inspector so emotionally taxed before. *Is it his romantic involvement with Dana that has upset him so? Or does he have a bad feeling about his mission?*

35

Sergeant Uppendown studied the clouds above Smallbeef. He knew the Sun was somewhere up there, almost immediately overhead. 'Round about noon,' he said.

'We should be on our way,' said Al Orange.

'Fer sure, sir,' replied Uppendown. 'Sergeant Jolly is taking over my responsibilities in my absence...so I guess we are about ready.'

And so without further ado, the two of them took to the air and headed east in the wake of Aano Grunt and the Hanoverian mare.

***

Inspector Hooter maintained an altitude of five trees; with the shrouded Sun to his right he cruised comfortably along, knowing that he had plenty of time to reach his destination by dusk. He was sure others would also be making the journey although he did not know exactly who they would be, or their timings. He had only put one horizon between his tail and Davidsmeadow when he became aware of another pair of wings gaining on him. Without turning his head or breaking his rhythm he assessed the situation. *They're not mallard's wings...or a goose's, they don't sing in the right way.* The next moment the long beak of a pterosaur came alongside him, followed by the head and long neck. It was Abel Nogg.

The pterosaur took care to keep a comfortable distance away to avoid their wings conflicting with each other. 'Good day, Inspector, would you be so kind as to land on the track below? I have to ask something of you.'

Hooter descended swiftly, lowering his rear end and holding the air in fully spread wings to land almost vertically on the track. He immediately brought his wings to his sides and stepped to one side to watch Abel land eerily silently in front of him. They both took time to look around to be sure they were alone. The occasional rabbit and crow were of no concern, being totally untrained in the art of the English language.

'I see you are wearing your binoculars, Inspector.'

'Yes, I don't know why I bother though, I've never managed to see a thing through them; my eyes are in the wrong place.'

'I have another use for them – a very worthy cause.'

'Oh?' Hooter displayed his endearingly puzzled expression.

'Would you hand them to me, please?'

'Certainly, sir.' Hooter lifted them over his head and gladly passed them to the pterosaur. 'I don't really care if I don't get them back,' he said despondently.

Abel held the glasses in one hand while in the other he produced an Amulet. 'You know what this is, I'm sure,' he said, dangling the stone by its string.

'Oh yes, sir,' Hooter replied. 'It's the Amulet for passing through the timbered wall.'

'For the duration of this mission I need you to take charge of it,' said Abel. 'You must relinquish it to no one, not at any cost, no matter what duress you might suffer.'

'I quite understand, Mr Nogg.' Hooter was now resolved to the fact that there were most likely extreme difficulties lying ahead.

Abel then unscrewed one of the larger lenses of the

binoculars and, holding them vertically, he carefully dropped the Amulet together with its string into the opening before screwing the lens back in place. 'There, that should keep it from prying eyes.' He then carefully slipped the binoculars back over Hooter's head and let him adjust them to hang comfortably against his ample soft chest. Abel then added, 'You are well versed in the workings of the Amulet and the timbered wall, Inspector, but let me reiterate one very important point; the Amulet will only work if it has been freely given to the holder. If this stone is taken from you by force it will have no effect on the wall whatsoever. Do not forget that.'

'Yes, Mr Nogg, I mean no, Mr Nogg, of course.'

'Do not give it up at any cost and do not let anyone else know you hold it, not even your closest friends. To do so might put their own safety at risk.'

'I wouldn't want that, sir.'

'I know, Inspector, and I know I can rely on you to the bitter end.'

Hooter did not like the sound of that last remark. *To the bitter end?*

'You must be on your way now, Inspector. I shall see you again soon, at the wall.'

'Of course, Mr Nogg, goodbye then.'

It took but a minute for Hooter to get airborne and get his bearings before heading east towards the wall and his friends who were either ahead or behind him, he was not really sure. His flight path kept him two miles to the north of the South Downs, running more or less parallel to them. Unknown to him, a pair of eyes peered over the crest of those hills, too far for some to see, but not for eyes as black as pitch.

***

Sergeant Uppendown and Al Orange had maintained a steady cruise for their entire journey, their bills level pegging all the way, also at a height of five trees. 'We're nearly there,' Uppendown called. 'Mr Grunt and my mare have done well to stay ahead of us.'

Orange squinted, focussing on a hint of colour half a mile ahead. 'If I'm not mistaken, Sergeant, that's them up ahead. I'd know that ball of ginger hair anywhere.'

'I guess yer right, shall we join them fer a break?'

'Why not? We have plenty of time.'

Aano Grunt paused from his lyrical waxing when the mare's ears once again displayed an interest by rotating like radar scanners sweeping the skies for the incoming airborne bandits. But there were no bandits, just two distant shapes closing quickly on her. She huffed softly. Aano deferred to her superior sense of presence and patted her on the side of her neck. 'Lovely girl.'

In less than a minute, Orange and Uppendown had caught up with them. 'How yuh doin',' called the sergeant. 'I hope the mare's been behavin'.'

Aano looked up and could not help but marvel at the incredible beauty of two huge colourful birds flying in perfect unison with each other. 'She's been absolutely wonderful,' he replied. 'It's amazing how much horses flex when they get going isn't it.'

Orange called out, 'Would you like us to stop for a breather with you?'

'Okay,' said Aano, 'we're nearly there, but it would be nice to stop for a chat. We've got plenty of time, after all.'

The horse came to a halt without Aano giving any instructions, four-square and facing straight ahead as per her training. 'She makes me feel rather shoddy,' Aano said light-heartedly. He sat for a few moments admiring the horse's neatly flowing dark mane and her superb muscular form glistening in the otherwise lacklustre light. He could not help but look down at his own covering of hair. 'Oh dear me,' he sighed. 'I don't think I could ever compete with you, you lovely thing.' He patted her again. She huffed softly.

Orange and Uppendown had landed and made their way over to Aano and the horse. The horse instinctively side-stepped to the edge of the track to where a convenient hefty tree stump stood. 'My word, how thoughtful,' said Aano as he slid from the saddle using the stump as a footstool. He stretched and bent up and down several times, touching his toes and raising his arms above his head. 'Ooh, that's good.' He then walked over and put his arm around the inspector. 'How are you feeling now?' he asked.

'Surprisingly good,' Orange replied. 'It's as if a huge weight has been lifted from my mind. I don't understand why or how, but I feel so alive again – and so light.'

'That's wonderful, Inspector. It seems your nasty old tenant has given up on you. Perhaps he knows when he's beaten, eh?'

Orange was reluctant to tempt fate, so he declined to answer. Instead, he waddled to the front of the horse and shared her eye, a loving and knowing eye. 'It's strange that a creature so steeped in ancient knowledge and ethereal strength should not have been blessed with the gift of speech,' he said.

'She seems to manage very well without it,' said Aano.

The grey woollen clouds looked down upon the four of them; four beautiful creatures providing a most pleasing focal point, and so in return the clouds gladly opened their formation to let the mild sunshine cheer the common light.

'How wonderful,' said Aano. The mare huffed in agreement.

***

Maintaining a brisker pace than usual, Hooter had almost caught up with the others. The South Downs to his right continued their unbroken procession, guiding him on his course. Unfortunately, they also guided another flyer on the other side of their slopes, a flyer with sinister eyes easily keeping pace. No light reflected in the eyes, their dullness concealing an insatiable appetite to do harm for harm's sake. As surely as eyes can smile, so these were grinning sickeningly.

There they are. Hooter's heart warmed when the forward horizon drew closer to reveal his friends on the track half a mile ahead. He stilled his wings and glided with the air whistling softly beneath them, gently bringing him lower. By the time he reached his friends he was no more than two trees high. 'Hello, everyone,' he called while banking sharply to circle the group.

Aano waved his long arms in the air. 'Inspector Hooter, how wonderful.'

With a few backstrokes Hooter landed on the track a thoughtful distance from the horse so as not to startle her, although in truth she was of such bearing as to not be worried by a giant mallard at all, especially one wearing a police officer's cap.

Three large birds and one orangutan exchanged heartfelt greetings, glad to be in each other's company again. Hooter also took the time to waddle over to the mare and give her a soft feathery stroke on the side of her well-muscled neck, for which she was most appreciative; she expressed her sentiments by depositing a wet kiss right on top of Hooter's cap. 'Thank you,' said Hooter. He looked into the horse's eye and happily lingered a while. 'Beautiful,' he said, thinking of another horse with whom he had become rather close to in the past and would soon be meeting again.

Al Orange gazed along the track in the direction of the

timbered wall. 'Not far now, Mr Grunt. You should get there in less than half an hour, I would be happy to shadow you if you like.'

'No, don't worry, Inspector. I'll be fine with this lovely horse; you stay with Inspector Hooter and Sergeant Uppendown.'

'Fair enough.' Orange looked to Hooter and Uppendown. 'Are we ready, then?'

'Ready, sir,' Uppendown replied, tilting his Stetson slightly forward.

'Me too,' said Hooter, also adjusting his cap.

The three of them lined up in single file in the centre of the track. With wings spread wide, Inspector Orange took to the air first, climbing impressively steeply for an older mallard. Inspector Hooter followed closely behind, matching Orange's effort. The two of them circled while Bob Uppendown took a few extra strides before lifting from the ground. Once airborne he quickly climbed and joined them at a height of three trees.

Hooter called out, 'Into formation, starboard line-out, outer high.'

Al Orange slipped back one length to Hooter's right and slightly higher, Uppendown then took up the same position relative to Orange.

'Away we go,' Hooter called.

The three of them accelerated powerfully, keeping their wings in time with each other, although Uppendown needed to trim his a little to prevent himself pulling away. The trees marvelled and cheered as the accomplished flyers whistled overhead, two dressed in splendid blues, greens and fawns with white collars, and the other in sharp black and white top with a soft buff underside. *What posh chaps, so thoughtful, too,* the trees rustled.

The Hanoverian walked elegantly over to the tree stump and stood quite still. Aano thanked her and hopped up onto the stump before taking the reins and springing up into the saddle, taking care to land without a bump for the horse's sake. With his feet in the stirrups and the reins correctly held in his hands he gently squeezed the horse's sides with his legs, not so much to tell her to walk on but just to let her know that he was ready. The horse duly turned and continued at a leggy brisk walk.

'No need to rush,' Aano said quietly. 'Let's enjoy the countryside while we can.'

The horse huffed agreeably, loving the easy contact between her and the ape.

The rhythmic cullip cullop of the horse's shoes on the track lulled Aano into a dreamy stare. He had become very comfortable aboard the Hanoverian and found himself gazing wistfully along the road ahead, leaving the horse to do the thinking. This worked fine until the horse stopped suddenly and planted her feet firmly on the ground. Something had caught her attention to her right. She hardly needed to turn her head, her peripheral vision being a strong point. She seemed to be concentrating on the distant hills, or more precisely on the gap between two of the hills.

Aano deferred to the mare's better instinct. 'What is it, girl?' He sat tall in the saddle trying to follow the horse's gaze, not an easy task with her eyes set in her head differently to Aano's. He could see nothing worthy of note, but the horse had definitely seen something. *Perhaps something fleeting between the two hills*, Aano wondered.

The horse did that thing that horses sometimes do when vexed. She turned her lips inside out, tasting the air and blowing through her nostrils. There was nothing to be seen, but she knew all was not well. Aano, having very flexible lips, copied her as best he could. He could not actually turn his lips inside out like she could, but he managed a very impressive pout, taking in long breaths to savour the air. *Hmm, she's obviously smelling something I'm not.*

The horse reverted to the norm, Aano followed suit. The horse then cautiously walked on, waiting for Aano to gather up the reins and set his legs to her sides. As soon as he had done so, she picked up the pace to a working trot, keeping her eye on the landscape to her right as she went.

'Good girl,' Aano whispered, glad of her inherent sense of self-preservation.

Down the track they went, eagerly anticipating the company of their friends once again.

36

Hooter, Orange and Uppendown had arrived at the timbered wall and settled down on the grass verge, waiting for Aano to arrive. What little sunlight filtered through the blanket of cloud failed to infiltrate the pines, oaks and birch, leaving the visitors in cool dappled shade. Inspector Hooter made a point of keeping himself and the Amulet a safe distance from the wall to be sure that no one should accidentally be pulled through. *I must not let on that I am the one holding the Amulet,* he reminded himself.

The trees held their branches still so that any additional visitors would be heard in advance. Like all trees all over the world, they and their forebears had witnessed many an incredible sight in their lifetime, bearing witness to much of life's doing and undoing. The three water birds sat silently while thinking to themselves and wondering what might lie ahead in the immediate future. Being at the heart of the animal world, they never took tomorrow for granted when they still had today to contend with; today would always be enough.

The towering pines collectively shushed above the silence. *Someone is coming.*

Uppendown extended his neck, looking back along the track expectantly. The lithe clip-clop of a horse in brisk trot could be heard drawing closer. Uppendown's expression turned from imminent relief to one of concern when he saw the anxious look on his mare's face, the whites of her eyes clearly showing.

'Hey there, girl.' The sergeant steadied the horse, stroking her warm neck to comfort her. 'Have you had some sort of trouble?' he asked.

Aano relaxed into the saddle and replied on the horse's behalf, 'Not really, although I'm not sure that we weren't being followed or shadowed from the far side of the Downs.' He joined Uppendown in stroking the mare. 'I couldn't see anything, but something certainly caught her eye.'

'Hmm,' Uppendown paused. 'She's a sharp girl this one; she wouldn't worry over nothin', that's fer sure.'

From where they were resting, the Downs were hidden from view by the high bank and mature trees flanking them. Hooter waddled along the track to a clearing and peered across the open common. The Downs were barely visible in the late afternoon mist, and from where he stood they were a good two to three miles away. *Nothing out of the ordinary as far as I can see, but the haze doesn't help.* He returned to the others. 'It seems all quiet out there now, but perhaps we should take turns to keep watch, until dark at least.'

'Fer sure, sir,' said Uppendown, holding the horse steady while Aano slid from the saddle onto a handy domed clump of grass. 'I'll take my horse along to the stream and let her drink; I'll keep a lookout while I'm there.'

'Wonderful,' said Hooter. 'It will be dark in about an hour, perhaps we should forage a while for food, and then we can settle down for the night; we have a big day tomorrow.'

Orange and Hooter delved cautiously into the undergrowth along the verge, the odd grub or late berry would suffice their immediate needs. Aano was content to sit on the clump of grass, chewing on a tasty ball of greenery that he'd fashioned from the shrubbery. Ferns were still plentiful but he always found them rather bitter and sometimes gave him an upset tummy, so he reserved them for his millinery skills which, from the look of the clouds above, might come in handy later.

The last vestige of light saw three water birds, one orangutan, and a beautiful horse gathered together by the timbered wall. They each surveyed the immediate area, looking for just the right spot on which to settle. The steep banks to each side would help shelter them from the elements while the trees whispered lullabies to them as they dozed – trees like to do that. Bob Uppendown decided he would nestle among the hefty clumps of soft grass opposite the wall, they would provide support and warmth. Two clumps along, Hooter did likewise, and another two clumps along Al Orange did the same. All were close enough for comfort, but each within their own space. The Hanoverian stood a few paces away on the grass verge with a simple rope cordon keeping her secure. That left only Aano Grunt; he had already created his hat of ferns and was now standing beneath the mighty oak trying to decide which bough would offer the most comfortable resting place. 'There,' he whispered, 'half a tree high, perfect.' With the ferns held in his mouth, he took care not to hurt the oak as he calmly made his way up to his chosen bough. The tree rather enjoyed the feel of the ape's well-padded hands and feet. *Not as ticklish as bird's feet,* he thought.

And so the chosen few settled into their make-do nests, hoping for a peaceful night. The pines wished they could speak, they sensed a less welcome visitor moving among them, one they had witnessed before in this very part of the woods. They looked down upon Inspector Orange in particular and worried for him. *Oh the poor chap.*

The party had soon slipped into a surprisingly deep sleep. The clouds had returned in strength, barring the Moon from the common. Nothing stirred. Even the trees remained still, unable to see their neighbours in the unusually black night. Al Orange had sunk into the grassy mattress with his head resting on his chest rather than beneath his wing. For the third night in a row he felt as though a weight had been lifted from him, his soul unshackled from the pit of despair through which he had waded hopelessly for so long. He looked forward to getting back to full health to join his constables once more, and had vowed never to take up firearms again, nor to use his truncheon for anything other than pointing the way to those who might enquire. He was a new duck – a rather mature new duck, but new on the inside at least.

But then, without warning, horror smacked him in the face. Any dreams that might have been about to show their light within him were quickly stifled when a firm hand clenched around his bill. The hand lifted him forcibly to his feet. Such was the grip that he was unable to raise even the slightest murmur for help. He opened his eyes wide to see a black silhouette barely visible against the unearthly darkness. The silhouette was human shaped.

No, please, no. Al Orange panicked, trying to twist his head free of the vice-like grip which immediately began hauling him away along the track, his heels digging into the unyielding ground, failing to overcome the pull of his attacker.

Those who might have been within earshot slept on, cocooned by an unnatural veil of blackness. The intruder came to a halt when he reached the distant bend in the track where the bushes lived in dense groups. He released Orange with a firm push sending the mallard stumbling onto the trackside verge. 'Hello, Inspector,' said the deep voice.

Orange straightened himself up, perspiring nervously. His voice failed to break through the gagging lump in his throat. His soul caved in; utter despair welled up from his belly trying to vacate the sickening pit in which he was surely drowning.

'Oh dear,' said the voice, sneeringly. 'My apologies for upsetting you. Your voice will come back in a few moments. When it does you won't shout out, will you? If you arouse your friends I might have to silence them – permanently, and I'm quite sure you don't want that.'

Very slowly, the lump in Orange's throat shrank. His voice returned, hoarse and painful. 'By the Great Duck, I thought I had seen the last of you, you—'

'Now, now, let's have less of the bad manners if you please,' the voice interrupted.

Orange stared wide-eyed into the darkness, gathering what meagre light he could. The figure before him stood slightly taller than him, wearing the familiar wide-brimmed hat which he had come to despise.

'Why are you here?' said Orange. 'You can't hurt me anymore, I've gotten wise to you. I know who I can trust and I know whose entire entity is built on lies and deceit.'

'Well now,' the voice replied, 'you make quite a few points there. Let me deal with them very briefly. Firstly, I am here because you are going to get something for me. Secondly, I think you will find that I can still hurt you an awful lot. Thirdly, your pathetic intellect will never be wise to me…and what was the fourth point?' he mocked. 'Ah, yes, you inferred that I lie to you. That is very upsetting to me, all I have ever done is try to guide you along the way so that—'

'Nothing you have ever said to me has come true, nothing.' The inspector's voice had lost its tone, his chords barely managing a loud whisper a response.

The man in the hat snapped sharply, 'Enough of this. I shall tell you what I want and you will oblige, is that understood?' He tipped his head slightly to one side to encourage a quick reply.

'No,' Orange said on his breath. 'I will do nothing for you, now go and leave me and my friends alone.'

The man smiled a handsome smile, many would find his looks endearing and charming, but you know what they say about books and their covers. 'How have you been, lately?' he asked, almost glibly.

'What?'

'Have you been feeling better of late?'

'Without you in my head I have been able to live again, to see again and to feel again.'

'Precisely,' said the man. 'It felt good didn't it? Life without me blocking your view of the world, always behind your eyes and always in your thoughts.' His voice began to rise in volume. 'Always screwing you up and making you feel sick of your own existence,' he hollered. 'Always wishing you could curl up and die!'

Orange pleaded in pain. 'Stop it, stop it, please.'

'Oh, I will stop and I will leave you alone, just as soon as you get the Amulet from Inspector Hooter and hand it to me – that is all you have to do.'

Tears silently rolled down the inspector's chest, falling unhindered into the grass and hurriedly soaking into the soil from where they had first come to life. 'But I know why you want it now,' Orange retorted, 'and I won't have any part in your nasty plans.'

'Oh dear, that is very unfortunate, Inspector.' The man moved closer and put his face up to the end of Orange's bill. The mallard recoiled at the smell of decay, he stepped back until the bushes pressed against his rump. The man continued, 'You might not care much for your own life, but what about the lives of your friends?'

'What do you mean?'

340

'It's quite simple. You get me the Amulet, then I leave you alone…if you don't get me the Amulet, then your friends will get very hurt – fatally so.'

Al Orange struck out with his bill, aiming for the man's throat; he was never going to be fast enough. The man leaned to one side faster than Orange could see.

'That was a very silly thing to do,' said the man. His hand wrapped around the mallard's bill again. Holding it tighter than ever he began to twist his grip.

Orange tried in vain to resist, but his head was being twisted to an unnatural angle. The tendons and muscles in his neck screamed in agony, creaking and cracking at the base of his skull. His eyes bulged, staring into the black orbs beneath the wide brim of the hat.

The hand released its grip so suddenly that the most intense pain shot through Orange's neck at being thrust back into its normal position.

'Do not try to talk, Inspector, or nod your head. I shall leave you now, but unless you want me as your lifelong tenant you had better do as I asked. Before this mission is over I shall have the Amulet – it that understood?'

The inspector could not reply, his neck trying to rearrange its inner workings.

The bushes shook violently as the man in the hat walked through them, not caring for their presence or their right to be there. Orange stood alone with his life in pieces yet again. He listened to the trees shivering in the distance, betraying the man's escape route, then he turned painfully and began to waddle back towards the others who had remained blissfully unaware of the vile interloper who would mess with his head at will.

He tried not to groan as he sat back down among the grassy

tussocks. Sleep would elude him for the remainder of the night while he tried to clear his head and figure out his options.

The clouds moved on, heading north, taking with them the cold air from the continent, and images of an evil presence. The Moon, having tired of waiting for the clouds to let him in, had also retired for the night leaving only the stars to cast their light of millennia over the land below.

Al Orange closed his eyes, wishing they would never open again, but he knew they would as surely as he knew he had no options.

37

The dawn brought an end to a desolate night. The local birdlife began their twittering among the trees while the rabbits set about sampling the day's offerings beneath the bushes and hedges, always keeping a lookout for raptors.

Aano Grunt was first to open his eyes; he particularly enjoyed the first drink of the day, especially when poured from his upturned hat of leaves. *Mmm, dew drops and rain drops, the perfect cocktail.* He took his time to sip the water without spilling any. After licking his lips he took a furtive look at his companions below. Uppendown and Hooter were still dozing, but Orange was awake. *My word, he looks rather bleary eyed. I'll give him a few minutes to sort himself out, perhaps he had a restless night.*

The oak tree had enjoyed the ape's company, a warm bodied soul resting in his care gave him a sense of purpose. *Birds are one thing,* he thought secretly, *but an ape in my arms, that's something to tell the pines about.*

Bob Uppendown woke next, extending his neck to take a slow look all around; everything seemed as it should. He smiled up at Aano who in turn waved back, still comfortably ensconced in the care of the elderly tree.

Hooter soon followed suit, opening his eyes and taking a long stretch from head to foot, finishing with a purposeful wag of his tail feathers. 'Good morning, everyone.'

'Good morning, sir,' replied Uppendown.

'Good morning,' Aano called, rising from his perch.

Inspector Orange said nothing, unable to see through the fug that had returned with a vengeance. Total despair swamped his entire body. He felt as though he weighed a ton. His head hurt and he could see no thought of any sort within his mind – the man in the hat had been true to his word.

By the time Aano had descended the tree and conducted a rudimentary reshuffle of his hair, which made no discernible difference to his appearance, Al Orange had got to his feet. However, unlike Uppendown and Hooter, he made no attempt at preening.

'Oh dear me…oh no,' Aano said quietly. He recognized Orange's demeanour, he had seen him in this state many times before but had hoped he was now free from such depressive forces. The touch of Aano's arm around his shoulder had the mallard bursting into tears, unable to hold on to what dignity he had left, his eyes pouring forth his pain.

'It's all come back,' Orange wept openly. 'I can't go on anymore, he's inside my head again.'

Uppendown looked on, bewildered and embarrassed, he had never seen a grown bird in such a state of mental distress. He had heard Aano's account of Orange's troubles, but to see it displayed so openly came as quite a shock. Hooter had witnessed his fellow inspector battling with his inner turmoil on previous occasions, but was still very alarmed to see him in such a dreadful condition. 'The poor chap, whatever can have brought this on?'

'There, there, Mr Orange, sir.' Aano gently pressed his forehead against the mallard's temple. 'Don't worry,' the ape whispered, 'you are not alone, share your troubles with us, we will listen.'

Orange could barely talk through the sodden blubbering

issuing from his bill and his nostrils and his eyes. 'He won't let me…he won't let me talk of him.'

'Let's take a little walk, shall we?' Aano slid his hand down the mallard's back, guiding him along the track while Uppendown and Hooter looked on, each with a worried expression.

'I really thought he was getting better,' said Hooter.

Uppendown replied, 'It's as if something hit him in the night while we were sleeping, but how come none of us saw anything? Weird fer sure.' He tipped his hat to the back of his head. 'Perhaps Mr Grunt will find out what the trouble is.'

Walking down the track, Aano fondled the pouch on his waist belt to ensure the Amulet was still safely tucked away. When they reached the stream he stopped but Al Orange waded straight in until the water came up to the top of his legs.

'By the Great Duck, how I wish I could simply wash away what is in me.' He stared down at the sparkling water rolling over the large pebbles in the stream bed. His wobbly reflection stared back at him, but when he stared more intensely he saw something else in there; beyond his own image he could see another. The ripples in the water masked any detail, but he knew it was neither his nor Aano's reflection. 'Who are you?' he whispered into the water.

'Eh?' said Aano, wondering who the mallard was talking to, but before he could enquire any further he watched in disbelief as Inspector Al Orange lay down, completely immersing himself in the world's gift to all living things. The water swirled and danced about the troubled soul that had laid itself at its mercy. Sunlight speared the waters, passing through the mallard and lighting the pebbles beneath him. Aano stood gobsmacked. The stream was barely thigh deep and yet the water covered the large mallard entirely, depriving him of air. Aano continued to stare helplessly, held by an invisible hand, not able to move from the side of the stream.

In the next moment the waters jettisoned Al Orange from their hold as if firing him from a catapult. The mallard sprang into the air and opened his wings to guide himself to the water's edge. His demeanour had turned from pathetic and pitiable, to one of bellicosity and strength. He breathed long and deep, his chest becoming engorged with a lifetime's worth of suppressed hatred for the one who had constantly depressed him and tormented him. He turned and waddled forcefully back onto the track, pushing Aano aside, though not harshly. With eyes glaring he engaged in a forced march straight up the middle of the track. He passed Uppendown and Hooter without acknowledging them. Aano followed closely behind, casting a concerned and confused look in their direction. The two birds tagged along wondering what could possibly happen next.

'Inspector, what are you doing?' asked Aano, with some apprehension. 'Where are you going?'

Orange ignored the ape's question, focussing instead on the bushes ahead; the bushes where the man in the hat had accosted him during the night.

'Please, Inspector Orange, you're worrying me now,' Aano pleaded. 'What on Earth is the matter?'

Uppendown and Hooter kept pace, saying nothing.

Aano reached forward and took hold of Orange's tail feathers to slow him. 'Can't we talk about this? I mean—'

'Do not worry, my friend,' Orange replied in a stern voice while keeping his attention fixed straight ahead. 'I have a point to make and an argument to settle.'

Hooter, Uppendown and Aano could not help but notice Orange's colours, exceedingly bright and vibrant; his metallic blues and greens dazzled and his bill shone bright yellow. 'What could possibly have happened to him?' Hooter exclaimed.

Aano, while trying to keep up with Orange, turned and replied, 'He went into the water…I thought he was just going in to have a wash…but then…'

'What, what happened?' asked Hooter, trying to catch his breath, such was his exertion in keeping pace.

'I don't know,' Aano replied through a nonplussed grin. 'The water somehow completely washed over him and something held him down. He didn't struggle at all though, and then something lifted him from the water and he landed back on the bank.'

'Oh boy,' said Sergeant Uppendown, 'and I thought things couldn't get any weirder.'

Al Orange was taking no notice of the conversation going on behind him, he was on a mission and nothing was going to stop him. He continued at a firm unduck-like gait until he reached the bushes where he had met his intruder a few hours earlier. He stood firmly in the middle of the track and opened his wings as wide as he could, they spanned from one verge to the other. *How marvellous*, the trees whispered as they discretely leaned inward in the hope of having a little touch of his rejuvenated plumage. Aano, Hooter and Uppendown stopped a couple of paces behind, not wanting to interrupt whatever it was he was doing. *He's clearly doing something*, they each thought to themselves.

Without wasting another second, Inspector Alan Orange, while keeping his wings at full extension, shouted at the top of his voice. 'I am still here, do you hear me? I am still here, you nasty pathetic piece of work.'

The trees, having witnessed the assault the night before, shivered nervously while trying to keep hold of the few leaves they still had. Orange went on with his verbal retaliation. 'You cannot hurt me anymore. I have seen everything you are not. I now know you are nothing – nothing, do you hear?' He paused briefly for breath. 'Here I am,' he held his wings higher still and fluffed up his chest to present an unmissable target for whoever might take offence at his outburst. 'Here I am, come and do your worst, you vile heap of stinking putrefaction.'

'Please, please.' Hooter tried to intervene. 'You mustn't use language like that, it really isn't very nice, you'll upset the trees.'

Orange continued staring into the undergrowth. 'Nice? Not very nice? Hah!' He laughed hysterically. 'Believe me, the one to whom I speak is not very nice at all. I don't know of any words that come close to describing the degree of vileness and decay that he strives to instil into any unsuspecting creature, with the sole purpose of destroying all that is good in them.'

Hooter was speechless, not knowing what or who Orange was referring to. But the trees knew.

Aano spoke in a low voice, 'This is difficult to explain, but I think Inspector Orange has gone through some sort of enlightenment. He seems to be facing his nemesis head on, as though he doesn't care what happens to him anymore.'

The sound of approaching hooves from further down the track silenced the discussion. Their eyes veered from Inspector Orange to stare at the distant bend, the same bend where one hundred horses had thundered their way to reckon mankind's previous wrongdoings.

'Only one horse,' Aano whispered, 'pulling a cart or a wagon, I think.'

Their nerves hung on their breath, hoping that whatever was about to come upon them would at least be benevolent.

38

The crew need not have worried. Their eyes lit up when around the bend came the superbly muscled Suffolk Punch known to them all. He had a four-wheeled wagon in tow, a sturdy affair clattering effortlessly across the hardened gravel. Hooter looked curiously at the driver, as did his colleagues. *A human? Surely not in our world. How can that be?*

Al Orange briefly returned his attention to the bushes, he had not quite finished his rant. He mumbled under his breath, 'I have not finished with you, I know you are in there.' He then turned and joined the others in their study of the man on the wagon. *Another man in a hat.*

The wagon stopped next to them; they all stepped away, not trusting the human sitting atop the plank seat. None took their eyes off him.

The man sat in silence, looking in turn at each of the party. A more perfect collection of eyes he could not imagine. His gaze finally came to rest on Hooter, he smiled an easy smile at the mallard and waited for a response.

A tiny seed of familiarity grew within Hooter's mind. His eyes smiled back and then he whispered tentatively, 'Mr Nogg…is that you?'

The others stared curiously. 'Mr Nogg?' they all whispered on mystified breath.

'Good morning, my friends.' The tension within the group

evaporated instantly, Abel Nogg's unmistakable tones putting them at ease. He jumped down from the wagon, his descent eerily restrained by an invisible third party.

Of them all, Inspector Hooter had experienced the most contact with humans; he had actually seen Abel Nogg in human guise before, although he did not realize it at the time.

The man before them most certainly looked like a human, but he did not smell like one. He waited while the group studied his tweed trousers and waistcoat, and his white shirt with sleeves rolled up, all topped off with a cream Panama hat. His blond-grey hair sat easily on his collar and ears. 'I apologise if my appearance alarmed you, but that seat was just too uncomfortable for my pterosaur guise, so I had a quick change just for the journey.'

'I know what you mean,' Aano replied, 'it's not much better for me when I sit on it.' The ape recalled his last trip racing across the common with an army of grizzled mercenaries in hot pursuit.

'That sure is somethin', sir,' said Uppendown, tipping his Stetson to the back of his head. 'What a disguise.'

'I can quite understand you all being disturbed by my appearance, but I assure you there is no need for alarm; it really is me under here.' It was then that Abel Nogg noticed the fiery look in Al Orange's eyes. 'You look troubled, Inspector.'

Orange's chest rose and fell fully while he gathered his composure. His voice still had an excitable tremor to it when he began, 'There was someone in the water – just now, in the water with me.' He paused while Abel's eyes held his, knowingly and lovingly.

'Calm yourself, Inspector Orange, you have been through a lot. Whatever you found in the water must have been in you all along; you simply needed help in finding it.'

Aano put his arm around Orange again, squeezing him gently. 'I'm sure things are going to work out fine.'

The entire party was taken by surprise when a wood pigeon popped up in the back of the wagon and perched on the side. 'Vroo croo,' he said, which in tone sounded rather like hello. The birds chuckled to each other.

'Isn't that the carrier pigeon from Smallbeef?' said Bob Uppendown. He waddled closer and studied the pouch hanging from around its neck, noting the initials SB embroidered in the cloth. 'Yep, that's the one sure enough.'

Aano added, 'He must be the chap who went missing when we sent him with a message for you, Mr Nogg.'

'He is indeed,' Abel replied, smiling. 'When I found him he was about to become breakfast for a Perigrine.'

'That's always a worry,' exclaimed Hooter.

Abel continued, 'I – erm, asked the Perigrine if he would consider letting him go just this once. Thankfully he did.'

'Coo, croo,' said the pigeon, endorsing Abel's account of events.

Abel held out his hand and the pigeon hopped onto his finger. 'He seems to have lost his passion for flying at the moment, so he rides around in the wagon, keeping close to others where he feels safe.'

'How wonderful,' said Hooter. 'I'm sure he will return to Smallbeef when he's good and ready; these things take time to get over.' He stroked the little pigeon with the very tip of his wing. 'How quaint.'

Abel turned to Al Orange. 'Inspector, do you mind talking to us about your troubles?'

Orange looked in turn at Hooter, Uppendown and Aano. 'Okay,' he replied. 'I think it only right that they know what is following us.'

'Well done, Inspector. I know it is not easy for you,' said Abel.

'They already know much of what has happened,' said Orange, 'especially Aano Grunt, he stood by me throughout my ordeal.'

'Quite so,' Abel replied. His voice, while seeming perfectly natural in a huge pterosaur, seemed at odds with his untrustworthy human guise, but the birds knew his appearance was only skin deep.

Inspector Hooter spoke up for the group, 'We know from what you have told us before, Mr Nogg, that there is a nasty presence in the human world who wants to enter our world and mess it up like he has others.'

Al Orange raised his voice above those around him. 'He is here now. He visited me last night while you were all asleep.'

'But how?' exclaimed Hooter.

'You all slept through the darkness, the clouds pressed down on you all, keeping you in place. All except me.' Orange's eye wetted but he forced himself onward with his account. 'He held me by my bill, hard and tight.'

The others gasped in disgust. 'That's a dreadful thing to do to a duck,' they muttered.

'He dragged me by my bill to the bushes here....' Tears now rolled down the mallard's cheeks, down his neck and over his chest to fall once more onto the gravel. 'He was in my head,' he sobbed.

Aano moved to comfort him. Orange motioned for him to stay where he was. 'No, Mr Grunt, thank you, but I'm all right.' After a deep breath he continued, 'I cannot describe how it feels to have him inside me – inside my head, staining my mind and soiling my eyes so that I see everything as though I were looking through his eyes, not mine.'

'You poor duck,' whispered Hooter, now close to tears himself.

'He threatened to stay with me for the rest of my life if I don't do as he asks.'

A few moments of silence preceded Hooter's obvious question. 'And what **did** he ask?'

Orange gave Hooter a knowing look and chose his words carefully so as not to give away the identity of the current holder of the Amulet, believing it to be Hooter. 'He wants me to find the Amulet and give it to him.'

Hooter somehow maintained a poker face, also not wanting to give anything away. Meanwhile, Aano Grunt looked on, discretely feeling the Amulet concealed within his phone pouch. *Oh dear me, I must keep this a secret or we'll all be in bother.*

Uppendown asked, 'When you were shouting into the trees just now – wus that yer reply to him?'

'Yes, Sergeant. I won't cower to him anymore. If he wants the Amulet, he won't get it from me.' Al Orange wiped his eyes. 'I would rather be dead than live with that on my conscience again…and in any case, whatever it was that happened to me in the stream just now was far and away the stronger power – and it was true and felt so good.'

Abel Nogg butted in. 'You must remain strong in your hearts, all of you. That will not be the last you hear or see of the bad presence, and remember, he too can appear in many guises.'

Hooter thought aloud for all to hear. 'We must stay alert at all times until we are all back safely with the missing Bog.'

'I must talk to you now about the mission, my friends.' Abel led the way back to the timbered wall with the pigeon still perched on his finger; the mallards and the goose followed right behind him with Aano and Punch sharing an amiable eye at the rear.

When they reached the wall the pigeon hopped off and made himself comfortable on top of a post at one end of the ancient timbers. The rest of the team gathered round to hear what more Abel had to say.

'Inspector Hooter, why don't you make your way through the wall and pop your head out the other side like you did the last time we were here?'

'Will I stop halfway through again?'

'Quite possibly.'

'Right then,' said Hooter, but then a thought suddenly occurred to him. *How can I pass through the wall without giving away the fact that I have the Amulet on me?* His concerns were quickly assuaged when Abel stepped a little closer and escorted him to within reach of the timbers to give the impression that it was he who held the Amulet and not Hooter. Aano Grunt, thinking that it was in fact he who held the treasured stone, stayed a little further back, relying on Abel's permanent intercourse with the ether to get Hooter through.

Hooter took the last step alone. Invisible hands welcomed him in, holding his cuddly plump figure while easing him part way through. Once again he was held with his rump sticking out in his own world while his head appeared through the timbers staring into the world of the humans. *My word?!*, he thought, being careful not to make a sound, for there, standing right in front of him in the sunlight were two soldiers with their backs to him. Hooter studied them while still in the wall's embrace. *They seem quite young, in some sort of sand-coloured battledress, I think. I mustn't let them see me. I wonder why they are there?*

Silently, the hands drew him back into his own world and released him onto the track where his friends waited anxiously. 'My word, that was most peculiar,' he said. 'There are two soldiers standing right by the wall, on the other side.' He couldn't resist the urge to waddle to the end of the wall and peer around the end, knowing that there would be no one there. *No one.*

'The soldiers you saw are friendly,' said Abel. 'They follow Captain Haker who you met recently. They are waiting for you to give the word, and when you do, they will go and collect the missing Bog and deliver him to the professor's 'Dig' in Smallbeef, from where you must transport him back here.'

Hooter rubbed his bill, ably abetted by Orange and Uppendown rubbing theirs. 'I can't help getting this awful sense of deja vu,' said Hooter.

'If you think about it,' said Abel, 'your previous mission into the other world was a success in so far as you did return the coffin to its rightful place; it was unfortunate that its contents had been switched without your knowledge. That will not happen this time.'

'So, are we to start right away?' Hooter looked to Abel for a hint.

'I would suggest you wait until dark before venturing through the wall, but you might let the soldiers on the other side know your schedule.'

Aano added his thoughts on the matter. 'Instead of cutting straight across the common like we did last time, why don't we follow the track all the way round? It will be a longer distance, but it might be just as quick because the wagon won't keep sinking in the sand.'

Hooter replied, 'Hmm, I think that might be a good idea, Mr Grunt. It will be easier for Punch to pull the wagon too.' Hooter took a long pensive look at the timbered wall, he could sense the timbers waiting for him to step up again. With both Abel Nogg and Aano Grunt standing close by, he waddled forward once again. He had barely touched the timbers when the hands pulled him in like an amorous lover, embracing him wholeheartedly before depositing him fully on the other side, right behind the two soldiers.

Sensing a presence, both soldiers turned instinctively. 'Whoa!' exclaimed one.

'Wow, what an amazing sight,' said the other. 'The captain said to expect you, but it's still a shock to see you in the flesh – or should I say feathers?'

Hooter cast an enquiring eye over the two of them in return. The first thing he noticed was that there were no guns on display. 'I must say you are both very smart, very smart indeed.' He stretched his neck to peer around each of them as best he could. 'Yes, very smart. Abel Nogg assured me that you are here to help me in my mission.'

'That's right, sir,' replied the one with stripes on his uniform, finding it difficult to take his eyes off the incredible sight before him. 'Every feather is perfect, every colour and every texture, just perfect.' He extended his arm to touch the amazing mallard. 'May I?'

Hooter watched as the soldier's hand approached. 'Why would you want to?'

'I have never seen anything like you before,' replied the soldier. 'We have emu's and the like, they are about your size but they're not anything like as finely detailed as you.' He very gently ran his hand down Hooter's folded wing. 'So smooth and soft.'

'I hope you don't mind if I don't want to touch you in return,' said Hooter. 'Most of my experiences with humans have been rather unpleasant.' His mind drifted for a second, 'There is one in particular though, very lovely…but I don't really know if she is human anyway.'

The other soldier looked uneasily out across the common.

'We had better get on with the matter in hand, Inspector, before anyone sees you.'

'Of course, Corporal…you are a corporal aren't you?'

'Yes sir, corporal will do fine.'

'Well now,' Hooter explained, 'my party and I intend to cross via the timbered wall just after dusk today, with a wagon in tow. We shall head straight for Smallbeef using the perimeter track as far as we can. The horse pulling the wagon will be the limiting factor as far as our speed goes, but he knows the way and will make good time I'm sure.'

'Okay, Inspector. We'll make sure the cargo is in Smallbeef all boxed up and ready to go. It won't be left alone at any time, so no one will be able to tamper with it.'

'Excellent,' said Hooter. 'May I ask the name of your officer in charge?'

'Certainly, sir. It's Captain Haker – Walter Haker.'

'Walter Haker…that's fine, thank you.' With that, Hooter bid the soldiers farewell and turned about. The soldiers watched him soften and disappear into the gnarled timbers. The hands wasted no time in pulling the mallard back into their company before very carefully placing him on the other side, in his own world. He promptly shook himself from head to foot before being greeted by his friends once again.

'Welcome back, Inspector,' said Abel. 'I trust you have liaised with those on the other side?'

'Yes,' Hooter replied, quizzically. 'I confirmed that they are indeed Captain Haker's men.'

'Well done, you need have no doubts as to their loyalty.'

Hooter rubbed his bill, thinking slowly to himself. *Walter Haker, Kate Herrlaw*. He jiggered the letters around in his head. 'Hmmm, must be a coincidence.'

Abel smiled liberally. 'In time, Inspector, in time,' he

responded, as if reading his mind.

Aano Grunt put his hand up and asked, 'What is the plan now, Inspector?'

Hooter cast his gaze towards Abel Nogg, who in turn gestured back. 'It is your show, Inspector; it must be your doing that resolves the situation, not mine.'

Al Orange, Bob Uppendown and Aano Grunt moved in closer; Punch cullomped his way forward to stand at the back of the group, still with the wagon hitched up. It was only then that he noticed the rather beautiful Hanoverian standing in the lea of the bushes within the rope cordon. *Ooh I say*, Punch thought, *I wonder if she's spoken for.*

'Ahem,' said Hooter, noticing a certain look in the Suffolk's eye. 'If I can have **all** your attention.' He was not sure why he bothered about Punch listening or not, being as he could not understand English words anyway, but he knew the horse had a way of feeling the words and their meaning. 'We shall leave here and go through the timbered wall just after dusk today. We shall all travel in the wagon to avoid any mid-air collisions with the dreadful obstructions that criss-cross the land on the other side. We will only fly as a last resort. Captain Haker's men will have the Bog ready to go when we get to Smallbeef.' Hooter gave Abel another brief look, asking, 'I take it they will help us load the body onto our wagon if needs be?'

'That will be quite in order, Inspector.'

'Thank you. As soon as we have the body on the wagon we will make our way briskly back to the timbered wall and safety. We will do as Mr Grunt suggested and use the perimeter track to make it easier for Punch. The chances of anyone being out there in the dark are very slim; as far as we can tell, humans have very poor night vision anyway.' He looked hopefully at his squad. 'Any questions?'

'It almost sounds too easy,' said Sergeant Uppendown.

'It does, doesn't it,' Hooter replied, thinking he must have forgotten something.

Aano tried to reassure everyone, saying, 'We had problems last time because we were running late and ended up travelling back in broad daylight with an army of very bad men chasing us with guns. This time we should be able to get in and out without being noticed.'

'Fer sure, Mr Grunt,' said Uppendown.

'You seem to have everything in hand, Inspector,' said Abel. 'I shall take my leave of you now.' He looked down at his arms before going on, 'I don't think these will be much good for flying.'

'Can't you pop into the bushes and pop back out as a pterosaur, or doesn't it work like that?' asked Hooter.

'I could,' Abel replied while keeping his eye on the Hanoverian which seemed to be listening in on the conversation in much the same way as Punch would. 'I quite like the idea of riding her back to Smallbeef, if that would be all right with you, Sergeant – I take it she is yours.'

'She is, sir. You would actually be doing me a favour if you were to take her back, otherwise there would be no one here to care for her while we are away.'

'Excellent.' Abel walked over to the mare who huffed softly at his approach. He untied the cordon and handed the coiled rope to Hooter. 'You might need this, you never know.' Abel soon had the mare tacked up, having given her several pats and strokes as he went along. Unlike Aano, he had no need of a fence or stump to stand on in order to mount; he simply stood next to the horse and with a barely perceptible flex of his thighs, he rose up into the saddle. Punch looked on; he had experienced Abel as a rider in the past and well-remembered the interaction

359

between the two of them. He also recalled the unearthly way in which Abel would mount and dismount without causing any strain on his back whatsoever.

The mare waited until she was sure Abel's feet were properly in the stirrups and his hands had a comfortable hold of the reins; she then turned without being asked and walked steadily down the track. 'I shall see you all soon, my friends,' Abel called, hardly concealing his anticipation of the ride ahead. The crew watched as the horse picked up the pace to a brisk trot and disappeared around the distant bend. They all remained silent along with the trees as the sound of metal shoes pounding the gravel suddenly sped up, becoming faster and faster until one step blurred into the next – then silence. Horse and rider were gone.

39

Aano Grunt set about unhitching the wagon, all the while pondering the conundrum of the Amulet. *I'm sure Inspector Orange thinks Inspector Hooter has it. Why would that be?* He continued removing the harness, giving Punch the occasional pat on the shoulder. 'Good boy.' With the harness removed, he took a brush which had been thoughtfully placed in the wagon and began brushing Punch all over, something Punch always enjoyed; that done, the ape then led the horse down the track a little way to the stream for a welcome drink.

'There's something about that ape,' said Bob Uppendown. 'He has an amazing aura, and it always rubs off on whoever he's with.'

The two mallards and the goose watched from the rear as the Suffolk horse and the orangutan ambled down the track, their colours melding softly as they exchanged thoughts.

The wood pigeon remained contentedly perched upon the post next to the wall. He tipped his head and eyed up the senior oak with its wonderful array of stout branches towering above him, all offering good grip and a comfortable resting place. *Perhaps I'll venture up there later, if things go well,* he thought. *I'll stay here for now though.*

Hooter waddled over to the wagon to look in the back. 'Well I never,' he said, 'there's a sack of pellets, cereal, some carrots and bananas in here. And a water container too.'

'That'll be Mr Nogg's doing,' said Uppendown.

By the time Aano and Punch had returned from their trip to the stream, the tail-board of the wagon had been lowered and the food and water set out.

'My word,' said Aano, 'a buffet, how wonderful.'

'Help yourself,' said Hooter.

After handing a carrot to Punch, Aano expertly stripped a banana and savoured the luxury. 'Mmm, perhaps one more,' he said, after offering Punch another carrot.

***

In Davidsmeadow, Constables Howard and Thomas were on a late afternoon patrol of the town. So far there had been nothing worthy of concern, as was usually the way in their world.

'That was a strange affair,' said Thomas.

'What was?' Howard replied.

'That business in the alleyway.'

'Hmm, well, we can't win 'em all.'

'No, I suppose not, but it still seems a bit odd. I can't think where the bounder could have hidden and us not find him.'

'Perhaps that's the trouble,' said Howard.

'What is?' replied Thomas.

'SBT,' said Howard, confidently.

'SBT…what's that?'

'Well, we've never actually had any Specialized Bounder Training, have we?'

'No, I suppose we haven't.'

'When was the last time we lost a culprit?'

Thomas thought carefully before replying, 'It must have been when Punch the horse and Dick Waters-Edge escaped near Smallbeef.'

'That's right, and we actually had them surrounded at the

362

time; it doesn't say much about our training does it?'

'But we've all got our Constable Qualification,' replied Thomas.

'Hmm, but what did we do to earn that?'

'Oh be fair, mate,' Thomas replied defensively, 'we had to learn to point the way with a truncheon…and not every duck can bend his legs up and down while saying 'ello, 'ello, 'ello – that takes a lot of practice that does.'

'Perhaps you're right, Tom,' said Howard, reflecting in more detail. 'Our formation flying is way more disciplined than any others, too.'

'Well there you are then,' said Thomas, rather pleased with his vindication of his profession, but that didn't stop him rounding off by saying, 'That still doesn't explain how the bounder in the alleyway disappeared.'

Howard smiled. 'Well anyway, I made up the bit about the Specialized Bounder Training, I don't think there's any such thing.'

The mood turned rather more sombre when Thomas said, 'Did Inspector Hooter seem morbid to you, when he left earlier.'

'He was a bit, but I thought he was just tired.'

'Perhaps,' Thomas replied, 'but he's never asked us to say a prayer for him before.'

'No, that's true.'

'I just thought he seemed resigned to something going wrong on his mission, as if he'd lost hope.'

'I must say, I wish we could all have gone with him,' said Howard. 'I bet we could keep him safe.'

'We didn't do a very good job on our last mission. We were all there by the pond on the heath, and the inspector still got taken prisoner.'

'I see what you mean, it's as if something or someone is always behind the scenes messing things up for us; not just the humans, but someone else…weird.'

They continued their patrol, eventually arriving back at the police station just as the light began to fade. Inside the office they found all their comrades, including Five Degrees, chatting idly among themselves, discussing what problems their inspector might encounter and when he would most likely return. After a while they ran out of opinions, the group finally coming to an apprehensive silence.

Constable Russell, being the Temporary Senior Constable, stared at the ceiling and began to utter a prayer, quietly saying, 'Dear Great Duck, our Heavenly Father….' The rest of the squad immediately joined with him, all with heads held high. 'You are the God of all that has ever been, of all that is and all that ever will be. Guide us this day by your closeness. Forgive us our failings and show us your road that we might avoid the wrong one. And most of all right now, Great Duck, stay with our Inspector Hooter and his crew and keep them safe. Please. Amen.'

'That'll do it,' said James.

'Yes, that'll do it, all right,' said the rest of them.

***

By the timbered wall, Hooter could put it off no longer. The day was gone and dusk was upon him. 'Mr Grunt, would you get Punch harnessed up to the wagon, please. It's almost time.'

'Of course, Inspector, right away.' Aano applied the gentlest fingertip on Punch's chest which had the horse reversing steadily towards the wagon until he was close enough to be strapped and clipped into place.

As soon as Aano had finished harnessing Punch, he jumped

up into the wagon to give the birds a welcome hand in emptying it, leaving only an assortment of ropes and odds and ends in the back beneath the tarpaulin.

'There, that should do it,' said Hooter. He motioned for Aano to close and fasten the tail-board. 'If you would be so good as to take up position at the front, Mr Grunt, you are by far the most experienced driver here.'

Punch huffed in agreement.

Although not totally dark, the Sun had long gone over the horizon, leaving a palette of greys and silvers to dress the flora. Hooter then suggested that Al Orange be first up into the wagon.

'I have a question,' said Orange in reply.

'Oh, what's that then?' Hooter replied.

Everyone stopped what they were doing and listened carefully.

Orange asked, 'Unless someone here is keeping secrets, we don't have the Amulet – so how are we going to get through the wall?'

'Ah, um,' Hooter replied uncomfortably. He rubbed his bill, desperately hoping a handy thought would enter his head. It did not.

Aano Grunt, feeling for the inspector's predicament, spoke up, 'Perhaps we should assume that Mr Nogg has entrusted one of us with the Amulet, with strict orders to keep its possession to ourselves.'

'Ah yes, well done Mr Grunt, I'm sure that's what has happened. So whoever has it, must say nothing.'

Sergeant Uppendown could not conceal his puzzled look. 'There is one problem with that, Inspector.'

'Yes, I know,' Hooter replied, realizing what the sergeant was about to say. 'How can the keeper of the stone take up position by the wall without giving away his identity?'

'That's no problem,' Aano piped up once again. 'If we all stand by the wall together, then we won't know who the wall is conceding to, it could be any one of us.'

'Excellent, Mr Grunt, very clever,' Hooter beamed. They all agreed with the ape's reckoning, saying nothing more as Aano took hold of Punch and stepped forward. The rest of them accompanied the wagon keeping close to either side.

Aano could not help giving Hooter a sideways look from his vantage point. Hooter returned the look, each thinking they were the one with the ancient key. Inspector Orange also cast a knowing eye in Hooter's direction, but said nothing. Sergeant Uppendown looked at all of them in turn, without a clue as to who had what. As for Punch, he just knew this was where he had to be and that he could not be in more trustworthy company.

40

Five brave souls stood line abreast, their nose, bill or chin an inch from the timbers that longed to hold them once again. The pigeon remained on the post, 'Coo, coo croo,' he said, which as far as anyone could make out meant something like au revoir which meant something like see you later.

'This is it, then,' said Hooter in a hushed tone. All eyes looked along the line to see him slowly lean forward the last inch. The timbered wall wasted no time in hauling all five plus the wagon into its heart. To hold so many beautiful creatures in one go sent the most intense thrill racing through every fibre of the wall's body. Within seconds the timbers reluctantly released the crew, easing their grip slowly to allow each of them time to find their footing in the world of the humans.

Hooter whispered, 'Is it my imagination, or is it slightly darker here?'

Looking skyward, Sergeant Uppendown replied, 'I think yer right, sir. The cloud cover is about the same, but the air seems less transparent.'

Punch steadily hauled the wagon away from the wall and into the night air where the crew took a few moments to take in their surroundings.

Inspector Orange rallied their thoughts. 'This is no place for star-gazing, the sooner we get on our way the sooner we will be back.'

'Fer sure, sir,' said Uppendown.

Aano had sorted the reins and deposited himself on the plank seat. 'If you would all like to climb aboard, Punch and I are ready to go.'

Each bird took his turn to leap into the back of the wagon.

The Moon struggled to keep the crew in its sight. The clouds were many and varied in their constitution, all going about their business which in this instance was to be somewhere else; to that end they continued their slow labour across the sky, getting little help by way of Nature's breath. The Moon took every opportunity to cast its light through whatever gaps appeared, but in the main, Punch was left to see as best he could in the darkness.

'At least the track is quite well maintained', said Aano. He relaxed his grip on the reins, wondering if Punch could see any better than him. The rock steady rhythm of the horse's substantial hooves on the track reassured those on board, but they each bore worrying thoughts of what might lie ahead if things were to go wrong as they had done before.

Many native eyes watched the unlikely spectacle pass along the track; rabbits, badgers, foxes and deer moved aside as the wagon approached. The horse was no surprise to them, even the ape sitting up front did not seem too out of place, but the giant birds in the back needed thinking about. An owl paced the wagon from a height of one and a half trees, he recalled seeing such ducks in the air only a few weeks previously and couldn't help but admire their aura.

Other eyes trailed the party's progress, unseen and silent.

Onward went the horse with stalwart constitution. Hooter and Uppendown cast their minds back to their very first excursion into this world; that too was under the cover of darkness, but on that occasion they were in the air and out of the line of sight of those around them. This time they were on the ground, closer to the irregular roar of traffic on the road to their left. Thankfully, the trees did a sterling job of screening them from view as the humans hurtled past in their speeding cars and lorries, seeing nothing but white lines and deadlines and unnatural demands brought about by their own insatiable appetite for unnecessary spoils. High above, when the clouds permitted a view into the heavens, the vapour trails could be seen striking rips into the sky with Mother Nature following behind rubbing out the lines that did not belong there.

'This is all so wrong,' said Uppendown.

Inspector Orange replied without having to ask what the sergeant was talking about. 'You would think that whatever breed took the lead role, they would know when things were not right. You only have to breathe to know the air here is bad, and yet they do nothing to make it better.'

Hooter responded quietly. 'The problem is, those who purport to be the senior race here, have actually been here the least amount of time, and quite frankly they don't seem to have learned a thing about the world they live in. They don't bother to learn from the other animals.'

'Selfish,' said Orange. 'I don't know what else you can call it. When someone does something which they know is harmful to others but continues to do it because they like it, that's selfish.'

Hooter rubbed his bill. 'I've always wondered why Mr Nogg rates the humans of this world so highly. He reckons they're the most intelligent creature of any world.'

Aano had been listening intently from the front. The others found themselves casting an eye in his direction whenever the term 'human' was mentioned. 'I don't know why you all keep looking at me,' he said, concerned that they thought less of him because of his similarities to other humanoid forms. 'The only thing I have in common with a human being is that my head is on top and I walk upright…well, sort of. And I have hands and feet and fingers and thumbs.'

'And your eyes are in the front of your head,' said Orange.

'And you're a similar shape,' said Uppendown.

'And you have teeth like them,' said Hooter.

'Yes, but my brain isn't like theirs,' Aano replied rather desperately.

Hooter stopped rubbing his bill. 'I wonder what Mr Nogg meant when he said you share nearly all of your DNA with humans.'

'What **is** DNA?' said Orange.

'Perhaps it's something you eat,' Hooter mused.

'I don't think so,' said Aano. 'I think I know the names of all the things I eat, and I have never eaten a DNA.'

'What if it was in a sandwich? You might not notice it then,' said Hooter.

'Don't worry, old chum,' Sergeant Uppendown said, coming to the ape's rescue. 'When Mr Nogg tested you in the barn he said you would **never** be like them.'

'That's right, he did. So that's that,' said Aano, drawing a line under the issue, but he could not help silently scratching his head…*DNA?*

'How did we get onto the subject, anyway?' asked Orange.

'I was saying how I wondered why Mr Nogg rates the humans of this world so highly,' Hooter replied.

'Beats me,' Orange retorted sternly. 'Let's face it, none of us has seen anything remotely good in the way they behave in this world or ours.'

The group sank into a thoughtful silence while pondering the matter. The discussion had at least passed the time while Punch steadfastly hauled them ever closer to Smallbeef and the missing

Beast of Grey.

It was not long before they came to the gate where they would leave the track for the road into the village. Punch came to a halt by the gate and waited for further input from Aano.

'So far so good,' Hooter whispered, sensing he and his party were now very close to the human settlement.

'Can I make a suggestion?' asked Aano.

'Of course, Mr Grunt,' replied Hooter.

'As clever as Punch is, I don't think he knows how to tip-toe. I remember the last time we came down here, his feet made quite a racket on the hard road and I'm sure people heard us passing by.'

'Oh dear, yes you're right,' Hooter said. 'But there's not enough grass for him to walk on.'

Aano cupped his chin for a moment before grinning a hushed reply. 'I kept the empty sacks that our food was in – they're under the tarpaulin.'

'And?' queried Hooter.

'Well, if we cut the sacks in half, we will have one for each foot,' Aano replied.

'One what?' Hooter tipped his head to one side thoughtfully.

'One bootie,' said Aano. 'It will only take me five minutes to fashion them.'

'Over to you then, Mr Grunt. Can we do anything to help?' asked Hooter, still not quite sure of what the ape had in mind.

'No, Inspector. I can manage, thank you.' With that, Aano jumped down and took the sacks from the back of the wagon. The clouds obligingly parted company with each other to allow the Moon to subtly illuminate the ape at work. Aano looked about the ground carefully. 'Excellent,' he said, picking up a sharp handy sized flint. With this he began a tear in the sack and then he pulled the sack into two with his bare hands.

His colleagues gawped at such a show of strength. 'Incredible,' they whispered.

Using the flint again, he cut a length of rope equal to the length of one of his arms. He then unravelled the rope to provide four separate strands. The birds looked on in awe. Aano then took one length of the thin rope, which was now more like thick string, and one piece of the sack cloth to the front of Punch who had been patiently waiting, four-square. His eye settled comfortably in those of the ape as he approached.

'I don't suppose you could lift one of your feet for me, could you?' Aano ran his hand down the horse's front right leg. Punch helpfully lifted it from the ground, standing quite happily on the other three. Having folded the cloth, Aano wrapped it beneath and around the hoof, finishing off above the ankle. He then made light work of tying it in place with the length of string. 'Not too tight, but just tight enough,' he said kindly. Punch huffed softly in reply. The hoof returned to the ground with barely a sound.

'I see, how wonderful, Mr Grunt; horse booties.' Hooter's eyes smiled, glad of the support of such an intelligent and tactile friend.

In a matter of minutes Aano had shod all four of Punch's feet with sack cloth booties. The horse raised and lowered each foot in turn, demonstrating their efficacy for all to see. Aano put his arm around Punch's neck and gave him a hug. 'Thank you, old fella,' he grinned. Punch turned and planted a wet kiss on top of the ape's head.

'Thank you,' said Aano. 'Shall I open the gate now?'

'Yes, if the coast is clear,' replied Hooter.

The metalled road lay deserted in both directions, the Moon casting a cold light over its surface. Aano opened the gate and climbed back aboard the wagon. Without being asked, Punch moved off, he knew which way to turn, this being his home territory in his own world. He rather enjoyed the muted, softened feel of his new shoes, but kept his pace to a steady walk not wanting to risk displacing one. 'Clever horse,' whispered Aano. Punch huffed.

Hooter remarked, 'I do hope none of those dreadful horseless wagons come upon us, we must all listen very hard and speak up if you think you hear one approaching.'

Orange and Uppendown remained silent, one with his head facing forward and the other with his head facing to the side, that way their hearing would cover all directions.

After one hundred paces Punch turned into Shortmoor Road, this would lead him to the 'Dig' in Smallbeef, now only half a mile ahead. The clouds then joined forces once again, barring the moonlight from the village and more importantly from the horse that went on hushed hooves.

Unlike Punch's last visit to these parts, no voices spoke into telephones and no curtains twitched. The locals remained fast asleep, oblivious to the aliens in their midst.

It was not long before Aano whispered over his shoulder, 'We're here.'

Punch pulled the wagon onto the grass before coming to a halt by the side of the Dig which was now partially filled in. Aano immediately leapt from his seat and made his way to the back of the wagon where he lowered the tail-board.

No sooner had the three birds jumped down and straightened their plumage when four figures emerged from the shadows. One of them whispered, 'Inspector Hooter?'

Hooter said nothing until he could make out the shapes walking slowly towards him. He was relieved when he recognised the one at the front as the corporal he had spoken to the day before. 'Yes, Corporal, it's me,' Hooter replied, 'it's good to see you again.' He offered a wing in friendship.

The young soldier was not too sure of how to shake hands with a giant duck, but he responded likewise, gently grasping the feathery tip. 'Thank you, sir, what can we do to help?'

Hooter looked around in the meagre light. 'You do have the coffin, don't you?'

'Yes, sir.' The soldier nodded to his fellow squad members who promptly made their way to what looked like a bush, barely ten paces away. Within a few seconds they had discarded the camouflage netting to reveal the back of a lightweight lorry with one coffin resting in the back.

Hooter breathed a sigh of relief. 'Excellent,' he said in a low voice. 'I don't suppose you could carry it to our wagon for us, could you?'

The soldiers gladly set about sliding the coffin from the lorry onto their shoulders while Aano guided Punch in a series of back and forth shunts to get the wagon turned around, ready for the off. 'This is really clever, you know,' said Aano, glad of the chance to practise his horse control skills. Using nothing more than his fingertip against Punch's chest, the horse would respond by moving backwards until the finger let go. Punch always enjoyed communicating with the ape with his bizarre expressions and very polite manners – and the occasional carrot.

The four soldiers waited patiently with the coffin resting on their shoulders while Punch made the final push to get the wagon in just the right place. The coffin was then slid reverently into the back and the tail-board closed without a sound.

'Thank you so much for your help, Corporal,' said Hooter, shaking his hand again.

The soldier replied, 'Captain Haker said we were to escort you back to the timbered wall, Inspector.'

'Oh, I see. That's very kind of you. I must say it would be

quite reassuring to know you are with us, just in case we run into some sort of trouble.'

'That's fine, sir. Shall we get going then?'

The birds quickly launched themselves into the air to land in the back of the wagon one by one. Aano had returned to his seat and took up the reins while the soldiers promptly rolled up the camouflage netting and loaded it into the back of their lorry along with themselves. The corporal and his driver closed their cab doors and the driver turned the ignition key and pressed the starter button – nothing. He turned everything off and tried again – still nothing.

'She's dead, no lights or anything,' said the driver.

The corporal quickly jumped down from the cab and made his way over to the wagon. 'I'm sorry, sir,' he said to Hooter. 'The lorry won't start; I'm sure it's something simple. If you give us a few minutes we'll have it going in no time.'

Having no comprehension of combustion engines or electronics, Inspector Hooter asked, 'Would a carrot help?'

Aano Grunt could not conceal an embarrassed grimace, he at least knew that the workings of a horseless carriage did not rely on such reliable and simple things as a carrots. Uppendown and Al Orange were not so sure though.

'Er, no, sir,' the corporal replied courteously. 'Unless you know something we don't, I'm afraid a carrot won't be of much help.'

The other soldiers had alighted from the lorry and busied themselves by torchlight, removing metal covers from the side and beneath the unnatural machine to try to find the cause of the problem.

'I really don't want to stay out here longer than is really necessary, Corporal,' said Hooter, growing more anxious with every passing minute.

'I understand that, sir, we shouldn't be too long.'

Hooter rubbed his bill, ably assisted by Uppendown and Orange rubbing theirs.

The clouds closed ranks once again, swathing the land in an inky blackness with no shadows. This time they had arrived with reinforcements, enough to shield the sky for the next hour or so.

'I really think we should get going now, Corporal,' said Hooter, anxiously. 'Under the cover of such darkness we will be very hard to spot once we are off the road and back on the common.'

The corporal reluctantly agreed. 'Very well, sir. We'll catch up with you as soon as we get this fixed.'

'I'm sure we'll be fine,' said Hooter. He turned and gave Aano a nod. Aano gave the reins the gentlest shake. Punch instantly pushed his impressive chest into the harness. They were on their way at last, back to their beloved homeland, their mission completed.

41

Up the road went the heavy horse on muted hooves. Those in the wagon kept a sharp eye out for the merest hint of a headlight in either direction, not really knowing what they would do if one was to come upon them. But fate looked kindly upon the warm hearts, leaving them to travel unhindered as far as the gate which would let them back onto the common where humans rarely went after dark.

They breathed a sigh of relief when after a few minutes they were back on the track with the gate closed behind them. *No chance of being spotted by one of those horseless carriage things now*, they all thought.

Underway again, they each nurtured thoughts of soon being back with their friends, in a land full of respectful souls in balance with the world. A land where each and every living thing lived within its means. *Soon be there, now.*

The trees gently rustled as the wagon passed, wishing the birds, the ape and the horse a safe journey. 'Nice trees, lovely trees,' Aano whispered in reply.

They were about halfway along the track when Punch's ears pricked up. *Has he heard Captain Haker's soldiers catching us up?* The trees ahead leaned inward to slow the wagon's progress and shivered harshly to get the crew's attention. Punch huffed loudly with his ears pointing straight ahead.

Staring beyond the horse's head, Aano muttered under his

breath, 'A man in a smart suit and a wide-brimmed hat…Oh dear. Oh no.'

Punch came to a standstill of his own volition.

'It's him,' said Al Orange, his eyes narrowing with contempt.

With some apprehension, Hooter spoke up, 'Right, well, we had better see what this chap wants.' Hooter, Uppendown and Orange jumped down from the wagon and stood to either side of Punch, adrenaline gathering momentum in their hearts.

Hooter took a deep breath. 'May we ask what your business is here, sir?'

The man silently and calmly adjusted his tie before replying, 'I have business with you.'

'With us?' said Hooter.

'You, Inspector Hooter – with you in person.'

'Me? But I don't recall any plans for a meeting with you out here.' Hooter clutched at whatever words came into his head, playing for time and hoping that Haker's men would soon catch up. 'I don't believe we've been introduced,' he said. 'May I ask your name, sir?'

The man in the hat was about to reply when Al Orange got in first. 'It's Helkendag,' he said with a most un-duck-like look in his eye.

Uppendown asked, 'Do you mean he is the guy you were telling us about?' The one who's been giving you all yer troubles?'

'Yes,' replied Orange. 'By The Great Duck, no good shall come of this.'

Aano Grunt, having shared many troubled times with Inspector Orange fidgeted expectantly on his seat. Punch turned his lips inside out to better assess the situation like horses do. He quickly resumed his normal expression and coughed at the scent of decay coming from up ahead.

Helkendag stepped forward to be sure of being heard by all. 'You know full well what I want, Inspector. You have the Amulet on your person and I want it – so give it to me, please. It's that simple.'

'But what makes you think I have it?' asked Hooter.

'I am not known for my patience, so do not try me. I saw a certain pterosaur give it to you yesterday afternoon. So unless you have since given it to someone else, I think you will find it hidden in your binoculars.'

'Oh.' Hooter struggled for a reply, his thought process deserting him. 'Erm, yes, that's what happened. I gave the Amulet to someone else.'

Helkendag stared with pinpoint accuracy into Hooter's eyes. 'Who?' he demanded.

Hooter was clearly floundering. Aano, now being pretty certain that the Amulet in his pouch was false, spoke up in the nick of time. 'Me,' he said, 'the inspector gave it to me.'

All eyes now fell on the orangutan. Hooter and Orange were especially bemused. *Why on Earth did he say that?*

Aano Grunt continued, 'Inspector Hooter gave it to me yesterday for safe keeping; it was rattling about in his binoculars and annoying him, so he gave it to me.'

Hooter could not begin to keep up with the ape's quick thinking, but he knew Aano sufficiently well to accede to his plan, whatever that might be.

Helkendag shifted his gaze past the horse and into Aano's eyes.

Keeping one hand on the pouch at his side, Aano went on, 'I don't really think I should hand it over to you though, at least not until you explain why you want it.'

Helkendag recognized a certain intellect in the ape's bearing. 'I have embarked on a noble cause, my dear ape.' His tone seemed to extend a degree of conciliation, hoping to draw on Aano's sense of compromise. 'The Amulet is vital to me if I am to succeed.'

With one hand still on his pouch Aano rested his chin in his other hand, pondering and studying the eyes of the human form who would have him believe that no harm would come from handing over the stone. 'Could you expand your request a little, Mr Helkendag? What exactly do you want to do with it once you have it? And how long would you want to keep it?'

'I do not have time to discuss at length with you, Mr...?'

'Grunt – Aano Grunt.'

'Mr Grunt, I need the Amulet right now. Then I shall let you go on your way.'

Aano paused deliberately slowly, he too hoped the friendly soldiers would soon arrive to lend their support. 'But if I give you the Amulet, how will we complete our journey?'

Helkendag drew a deep measured breath. 'I shall ensure that the Amulet will be close by when you arrive at the timbered wall. I shall be there in person to conclude my task.'

'But you have not stated what your task is, Mr Helkendag,' Aano replied.

Helkendag, while not one to let emotions affect his actions could not help but admire the ape's rationale, or his apparent strength of character. However, he was also aware of the soldiers who would soon be on the scene. 'You will see for yourself what my intentions are when you arrive at the wall. Now will you please hand the stone over – right now with no more stalling?' His eyes dulled from bright blue to India ink. 'I will not ask again.'

'Hmm,' replied Aano. 'I don't understand. If your cause is a just one why can't you say what it is? How long would a few words take to say?' Aano knew from previous discussions with

Al Orange and Abel Nogg that the man had no good intentions for either this world or that of the water birds. He thought he would try one more attempt at playing for time. 'You do know, don't you, that if the Amulet is taken forcibly from its present keeper then it won't work—'

'Shut up!' Helkendag snapped, his patience was spent. 'The next words you utter had better be "here you are, Mr Helkendag, here is the Amulet".' His left hand shot out from his side, grabbing Inspector Hooter by the neck; his hand clenched tightly around the feathered muscles. Hooter gagged for breath. Horrified silence beset the group. The trees trembled among themselves; was this to be another of those terrible moments in history which they had no choice but to witness?

Punch hauled himself forward with the wagon in tow. He stopped with his muzzle an inch from Helkendag's face trying not to recoil from the fetid air between them. Helkendag's eyes instantly blinked to reveal the black orbs of no reflection.

Punch had seen such eyes before in his confrontation with Beeroglad, but Beeroglad did not have the overwhelming aura of the man standing nose to nose with him now. Helkendag fired his stare into the hazel eyes of the horse, expecting the animal to step back in shock. But so deep is the soul of such a wonderful creature as a Suffolk Punch that the horse stood firm, staring straight back, confounding Helkendag's efforts.

'Do not mess with me, horse,' the man grumbled.

English was not understood by Punch, but he had heard the words before and had suffered as a result. Still he would not be moved.

Hooter was in a bad fix, struggling to breathe.

'All right,' Aano called out. 'Let the inspector go and I will give you the Amulet.'

Punch huffed and pushed his face right into Helkendag's to

show he had no fear of the unwelcome aggressor. Helkendag released Hooter's neck from his grip. Hooter gasped and coughed.

'Give it to me now,' said Helkendag.

Aano unclipped the flap on his pouch and felt inside for the Amulet. 'Here you are,' he said, holding it aloft for all to see. 'But before I give it to you, you must assure me that you will only use it for a good cause.'

'I can assure you it will be for a very good cause...in my opinion.' Helkendag held out his hand. Aano dropped the Amulet into his palm which instantly shut tight.

Punch exhaled long and strong into Helkendag's face, the two of them stood firm, their eyes locked. Helkendag's black orbs thundered through Punch's mind where they would normally wreak havoc with no compassion. Punch was ready and waiting. A myriad souls from every horse that had ever been, rose up from within him, swirling around and not giving the hardened mind of the invader a chance to take hold. Never had Helkendag experienced such strength from a mere mortal. Caught off balance, he staggered backwards before regaining his stance.

Punch grumbled deeply from within his belly and shook his head to let his mind rest.

'No one dares to face me and gets away with it,' growled Helkendag. 'But I have what I came for. I shall leave you now.' He looked once again at Punch, not quite letting his eyes touch those of the horse. 'We shall meet again – my friend,' he said, sarcastically, 'when I have more time.' He turned his back on the group and walked away down the track. His silhouette soon disappeared into the darkness. The sound of wings distorted the silence, quickly fading into the distance and gone. The trees did not bother waving farewell.

'Sheesh,' Bob Uppendown sighed. 'I'm sure glad that's over. But where does it leave us?'

Hooter wanted to reply, but the pain in his neck got the better of him. 'Ah, ooh,' he said, carefully turning his head each way to realign his muscles.

'You were very brave, Inspector,' said Aano. 'To be touched like that by a human must have been dreadful.'

'He isn't,' Al Orange muttered.

'Pardon?' said Aano. 'Who isn't what?'

'Helkendag isn't human,' Orange replied loudly. 'He might have the appearance of a human, but only when it suits him – rather like someone else we know.'

The trees broke from their silence and waved their tops in relief when a pair of headlights appeared around the distant bend. The lorry stopped behind the wagon and two soldiers jumped down from the cab to be joined moments later by the two in the back. The corporal immediately enquired, 'Inspector Hooter, is something wrong, why have you stopped?'

Hooter gave a little cough and explained in a croaky voice how his party had been stopped by Helkendag who now had the Amulet.

'I see,' said the soldier, rubbing his chin with a gloved hand.

Hooter rounded off his account by saying, 'I must admit I am a little confused now.' He turned to Aano and asked, 'Where did you get the Amulet from, surely you didn't take it from my binoculars, did you?'

Aano gave one of his inimitable grins. 'Of course not, Inspector, I would never steal. I haven't quite worked everything out yet.' He rubbed the top of his head and continued, 'Abel Nogg stopped me on my journey yesterday and gave me that Amulet, saying that I should tell no one I have it. But the thing is, I'm sure I wasn't quite close enough to the timbered wall when you passed through it for the first time yesterday. For the second trip I was, but not the first, I was caught on the hop, you see. And that is what made me wonder if the stone I had was a dummy whereas yours is the real thing.'

'I do hope you are right, Mr Grunt.'

'Yer quick thinking saved Inspector Hooter from a beating, fer sure,' said Uppendown.

The corporal asked of Hooter, 'Would you mind just checking that you still have the Amulet in your possession, sir?'

'Of course, good idea,' replied Hooter. He struggled, as large birds sometimes do, to undo the lens of his binoculars. Aano lent a hand by unscrewing it for him. Hooter then tipped the glasses up – the Amulet fell out into his upturned wing. 'Oh, how marvellous.'

'May I?' asked Aano, carefully taking the stone and turning it in his hand. His smooth fingertips delicately ran over the mirror-smooth finish. The rest of the team waited anxiously for the ape to give his valued opinion. 'Hmm,' said Aano, 'it certainly looks and feels like the real thing.'

The birds let out a long sigh, glad of Aano's knowledgeable support.

Aano then replaced the stone in Hooter's binoculars and popped them back in the fine case which hung as always around the inspector's neck.

'I think you should be on your way now,' said the corporal. 'It will be a relief to get you all back through the wall, safe and sound.'

'Of course,' replied Hooter, 'let's all mount up and get going.'

The soldiers quickly boarded their lorry while the birds got comfy in the back of the wagon with Aano up front, reins in hand. Punch stood ready, waiting for Aano's signal. Inspector Al

Orange sat silently, not saying anything, but in his head were thoughts of treachery. He did not know by whom, but he doubted the accuracy of Aano's account of things. A little duck paced up and down in his stomach while his mind refused to settle.

The wagon moved off with the army lorry close behind. In the coffin in the back of the wagon lay the body of the missing Bog, now rather aged and withered, sorely needing to be returned to its place of birth.

42

It was approaching midnight in Davidsmeadow. Constable Five Degrees lay on his bed staring at the ceiling. Every now and then he would stroke the top of his head and think how marvellous it was. He had taken a real liking to Inspector Hooter and his slightly haphazard ways. He liked how, no matter what else was going on in the inspector's life, he would always find time to comfort others.

The moonlight slid imperceptibly around the room while Five Degrees wondered where Hooter was now, hoping he was not getting into any trouble. He whispered under his breath, praying that the inspector would be looked upon kindly by the heavens and soon be back with his constables and friends. But the little duck inside Five Degrees could not sleep, sensing things were not quite as they should be. Eventually, Five Degrees got up from his bed and put the kettle on for a night-time cuppa and a digestive.

He peered from his window and noticed the light from the window below spilling out into the station yard. *Perhaps someone else is having trouble sleeping as well*, he wondered. He returned to his bed and sat on the edge. *I'm so lucky to have friends like the Flying Squad and Inspector Hooter. I really don't want to lose them.* Voices from downstairs in the office tickled the quiet of his room. He opened the door onto his outside staircase and listened carefully to the voices wafting through the open fanlight below. *It's the constables, it sounds like they're all up.* Taking care not to spill his tea, he made his way down the outside staircase and paused by the back door of the station. He knocked, not too loudly. The door promptly opened inward to reveal all six constables, plus those of the ARDs, gathered in the station office, each with a cup of tea nearby.

'Hello, mate,' they all said in unison, as was often their way. 'Come in – can't sleep eh? Like the rest of us,' said Robert Roberts.

As soon as Five Degrees stepped over the threshold the warmth of the room hit him, not the warmth of a fire, but the warmth of nine convivial hearts welcoming him into their company.

'Do you want a top up?' asked Robert, pointing to the tea pot on the table.

Within minutes, Five Degrees felt as though he had known the squad for all his life, chatting and exchanging thoughts with them while sipping his tea. Inevitably, the conversation soon got onto the subject of their inspector, all of them showing a look of concern.

'I don't know why,' said Five Degrees, 'but I can't help worrying about him. I know I don't even know where he's gone or what his mission is – but I just get this feeling, you know?'

'We know what you mean.' replied Thomas. 'We've been through so many scrapes with our inspector, but no matter what he comes up against, he always seems to get by.'

'He must be very skilful and knowledgeable,' said Five Degrees.

'Hmm,' the nine replied, looking at each other. 'Not sure really.'

'Well,' Constable Russell interrupted, 'as Constable-in-Charge, I think we should all get back to bed and try to get some shut-eye. We've still got our patrols to do tomorrow, and by the end of the day the inspector will be back here with us. Then we'll all feel better.'

Twenty minutes later the Flying Squad and the ARDs were drifting off to sleep in their dormitory; Constable Five Degrees, however, lay sharing his thoughts with the ceiling in his flat. *I think I might just take a trip out across the common tomorrow, on my own…no harm in that.*

***

In the world of the humans, the wagon was only a few minutes from the timbered wall. The clouds had gone their own way leaving the Moon to light the way ahead. Aano recognised the trees as he passed them. Some would give a discrete wave to wish him well. Aano would whisper under his breath, 'Nice trees, lovely trees.' Those in the wagon had remained silent for the last leg of their journey, trying to fathom Helkendag's motives.

'That's strange,' exclaimed Aano, drawing their attention to a silver glow rising up from the trees around the next bend. Everyone on the wagon stared wide-eyed at the unnatural light filtering through the trees. 'That must be right next to the wall,' Aano added.

Onward went the horse with ears aiming forward and eyes and nose keenly searching the track ahead. Around the bend the timbered wall came into view, one hundred paces distant.

Punch braked the wagon to an urgent stop. The birds in the back fell forward. Aano sat confounded by what he saw ahead. The army lorry stopped behind them, leaving its headlights on. Hooter and his team straightened themselves up and peered to either side of Aano, who remained quite still, his heart beating anxiously.

'What on Earth?' Hooter whispered, not knowing what to make of the spectacle.

'Humans!' Al Orange muttered alarmingly. 'I knew we were asking too much to be let alone.'

'There must be hundreds of them, fer sure,' said Bob Uppendown, his normally calm tones sounding distinctly worried.

'But what are they doing here?' asked Hooter.

The crew gawped at the sprawling masses spreading from the timbered wall in every direction across the common with no regard for the flora or fauna beneath their feet. Floodlights on masts washed the land with cold light, painting all beneath them in mono-chromium hue.

'They all seem to be holding something in their hands,' Aano remarked.

'Mobile phones,' said one of the soldiers, three of whom were now standing by the side of Punch.

'Aah, of course.' Aano patted his pouch, feeling his oversized phone which Kate had given him on his previous mission.

'Why do they all need one?' asked Hooter. 'They're standing right next to each other anyway. Surely they could just talk to each other normally.'

The corporal replied, 'Who knows who they've been talking to? I think that's how all these people came to know of the wall…and your journey through it.'

Al Orange muttered very slowly and deliberately. 'My friends, I think we are doomed to failure again…and I know who is behind it.'

No sooner had his words uttered forth when Helkendag appeared from among the crowd. 'Hello again, Inspector. I hope you had an uneventful trip. You are just in time to witness the sharing of your world with these good people.'

'But you can't do that, Mr Helkendag,' Hooter retorted, 'you promised us that you would only use the Amulet for the good of others.'

Helkendag smiled a cynical sneer. 'Yes, Inspector, I did. And that is precisely what I am going to do.'

'Then what are all these humans doing here? They mustn't see how the wall works – they simply mustn't.'

'Oh come now, Inspector; whatever happened to share and share alike?'

'Yes, but that does not include other worlds,' Hooter insisted.

'Says who?' Helkendag replied.

Al Orange leapt from the wagon to land within reach of Helkendag. He stared into his eyes and yelled, 'To call you an unearthly swine would be to insult a pig, you are not even equal to a pig's rear end, you evil b—'

'Stop it, Inspector!' Hooter shouted, his ears hurting from such profanities. 'Don't let him get the better of you.'

Aano Grunt jumped down from his seat and wrapped his long arms around the enraged Al Orange, easing the mallard back a pace to punctuate the assault, temporarily at least.

By this time three of the soldiers had made their way to the wall. With their backs to it they faced the sea of mobile-phone lights which gave the illusion of a thousand fire flies floating gently on the night air. The corporal raised a megaphone to his mouth and called out, 'Listen, everyone. You have no business here. This is army land and you are bound by my instructions.' The human hoard mellowed to a dull muttering. The corporal continued, 'You are all to disperse and make your way home by whatever means you got here. Please do it now.'

One thousand voices roared in reply. 'No! No! Noooooooo.'

The corporal spoke urgently into his walkie-talkie, 'Driver, get on the radio and give our grid reference, – from me, request urgent support for crowd control. Approximately one thousand adult civilians.'

'Roger,' replied the driver. 'Did you say, one thousand?'

'Correct – send it.'

Inspector Hooter tried again to reason with Helkendag. 'You know that those from one world can never find peace in another; that just cannot happen.'

'Give me one good reason why not,' Helkendag replied, his sneer seeming endless.

Hooter responded, 'Because that is not how the world was created; these people have their world and we have ours. Surely one world is enough.'

Helkendag raised his eyebrows. 'Is it though?'

'Of course it is.' Hooter's voice had found a new stance, sounding more authoritative and certain. 'This world was created with everything that every creature could possibly need to live and prosper; there is no need for them to look elsewhere for material gain. Our world has nothing that this one hasn't.'

That told him, the trees rustled to each other, impressed by the mallard's perfectly correct account of things...and trees should know.

'Need?' replied Helkendag. 'What has need got to do with it?'

Hooter answered, 'We all behave according to our needs,' he said. 'That is what determines the balance of all things.' The little duck inside him had found a new strength from deep within. 'Mother Nature provides everything according to our needs.'

'And what if she doesn't?' said Helkendag, certain that the bumbling inspector would soon run out of logical thought, or thoughts of any kind.

'But that's preposterous,' Hooter replied boldly. 'Mother

Nature knows best; she always knows best and always does the right thing. All she asks is that we show due respect to her – that's all she asks.'

Helkendag smiled condescendingly. 'But therein lies the problem, Inspector.'

Hooter, Orange, Uppendown and Aano stared at him.

Helkendag went on, 'Mother Nature seems to have lost her way in this world; the fact is she doesn't provide what the people here want anymore.'

'But that simply cannot be true,' Hooter replied, his voice now taking on its familiar innocent, almost naïve quality.

Al Orange weighed in with his thoughts on the matter. 'It's no use,' he turned his head through a full arc, high and low, and then he took a deep breath. 'This world has been pillaged and abused. We have all noticed how everything is out of balance here. It even smells wrong and the air is heavy with stuff that should not be here at all.'

Helkendag countered, 'Then how can you blame these people for wanting to leave here and come back with you to your world.'

'But sir,' Bob Uppendown spoke up, 'this world is essentially the same as ours, how come they want to leave it; I sure wouldn't want to leave my world again.'

'Is your world riddled with toxins and deadly viruses?'

'Well, no it's not, sir,' replied the Canada goose.

'Is there a desperate shortage of water to drink in your world?'

'No sir.'

'Are your countries governed by those who pursue unfair rights over others, killing and pillaging in the name of what is right, when they know in their hearts that it is not?'

'Absolutely not, sir.'

'In your world does one-third of the population have everything while the other two-thirds die through neglect?'

'Of course not, sir; what would be the point of that?'

'Do you rob and steal from your neighbour?'

'Please, sir, don't say such things,' Uppendown tipped his hat to the back of his head, feeling uneasy at the thought of doing such a thing.

'Do you have individuals who grow, reap and sell destructive drugs to the vulnerable just for their own financial gain?'

'What? I don't even know what that means,' replied the Canada goose.

Helkendag continued his relentless labour while Hooter's squad listened in disbelief that any one of the points he made could possibly be true. *How can he dream up such dreadful acts?* Then Helkendag asked, 'And what of the children in your world?'

'How do you mean, sir?' Uppendown replied.

'Do your children die by the thousands every day for want of a penny, when their leaders spend billions on weapons capable of destroying the world a thousand times over?'

'I can't believe such people exist,' said Uppendown, struggling to get his head around such notions. 'Why do you say such awful things, sir? None of this could ever really happen, so why imagine it?'

Helkendag laughed aloud for all to hear. 'My poor innocent bird, ask any of the thousand who are here in front of you. They will tell you everything I have said is happening right now in this very world – and I have barely scratched the surface.'

'Well I'm sorry, Mr Helkendag, but I simply refuse to believe that one person who has more than they need would stand by while others die for want of a drink or a biscuit.'

'You will believe it when you see it first-hand.'

'How do you mean?'

'It's quite simple, Sergeant.' A broad smile grew on Helkendag's face. 'All these lovely humans will be going through the timbered wall so that they can live with you and your kind. Won't that be nice?' The trees shivered violently when he laughed louder than ever. 'If you ever wondered what a virus was, you'll soon find out. If you ever wondered what hell was like, well…it won't be long.'

Hooter, Orange, Uppendown and Aano looked to the Moon, its silvered light reflecting in their tears. Punch stood four-square, but his head had dropped and his eyes also let go his tears to land in the sand while eyes of the purest blue gazed down from on high, unseen, hurting and loving at the same time.

All in the party now knew Helkendag's presence to be a portent of badness in the extreme.

43

Standing at the base of the timbered wall, looking out across the common, Helkendag held the Amulet high. He turned it between his fingers to let the moonlight catch it and show its perfect beauty, simple but faultless.

'You mustn't do this,' Hooter pleaded.

'Oh, but I must,' Helkendag laughed, intoxicated by lustful revenge on one who until now had always bettered him.

Hooter waddled forward with Uppendown and Orange by his side, putting themselves between the wall and the hoard of humans. Punch could do nothing to help, the wagon prevented him from getting any closer to lend his weight to the cause. Aano however, hurriedly forced his way through the crowd to join his friends, *I must talk to Inspector Hooter, quickly, before it's too late.*

Standing with his back to Helkendag, Hooter faced the crowd who had begun chanting loudly, 'Through the wall, through the wall.'

'Look at them, they're behaving like humans,' said Al Orange. 'Their herding instinct brings out the worst in them.'

Helkendag was unworried by the birds' attempt to fend off the surge that was about to happen. 'You can do nothing now, Inspector, you should move to one side otherwise you will surely be trampled under the weight of a thousand eager souls.'

'Through the wall, through the wall!' chanted the crowd.

'Please, please, stop it.' Hooter called out passionately, raising his impressive wings to emphasize his position. 'Don't let this man fool you,' he shouted at the crowd. 'No good will come of this.' The humans were not listening. They had been groomed, duped and coerced over many months via the aerial highway, their smartphones promising them a world free from all that was wrong in theirs.

'You will not stop them now, Inspector,' Helkendag shouted. 'Look at them, they are hungry.' He then turned and without the need of a megaphone he addressed the fermenting mob. 'Listen to me, my friends.' His voice thundered across the land. 'You are just a few paces away from a new world, a world that will soon be yours.' He raised his voice higher still. 'I trust you will embrace it as you have done in previous times – do not let me down!'

Hooter, Uppendown and Orange turned and were about to wrestle Helkendag out of reach of the wall and so render the Amulet useless.

'Wait, wait,' Aano Grunt called out.

'Not now, Mr Grunt,' Hooter replied desperately. 'Help us get Helkendag away from here.'

'You don't understand, Inspector. Listen to me,' Aano pleaded, struggling to be heard. He wriggled himself into the centre of his three friends, rather like a rugby ball in a scrum, and then he frantically muttered for their ears only. 'Don't you see, the Amulet I gave Mr Helkendag is a dud.'

'A dud?' replied all three birds, their conversation being drowned out by the simmering chanting of the crowd. 'Through the wall, through the wall!'

'Are you certain? asked Hooter. 'How can you be so sure?'

'There's no time to explain now, but you must trust my reckoning. Don't get involved in a fight with this man, he will cast you aside with great force; just ask Inspector Orange, he should know.'

'He's right,' replied Orange assertively. 'By the Great Duck, I hope you are right about the Amulet, Aano.'

Hooter separated himself from his colleagues and looked Helkendag in the eye, an eye that seemed to be growing darker with every passing minute. 'If you won't listen to reason, Mr Helkendag, we have no choice but to let you proceed with this dreadful act, but on your own head be it.'

With that, Aano immediately took control, pulling Hooter away and leading him and his friends back to the wagon where Punch waited patiently. Hooter, still unsure of Aano's reckoning, protested. 'But how are we going to get back through the wall if the Amulet is a fake? And how can we stop all these people following us?'

'I don't know, Inspector, but I think we are better off over here out of the way until we see what unfolds,' Aano replied.

After a few brief moments of silent thought, Bob Uppendown said, 'If yer right about the Amulet being no good, I don't think Mr Helkendag is gonna be too pleased with us when he finds out.'

'You're right there, Sergeant,' Orange replied anxiously. 'We can't get to the wall from the common and we can't stay in this world for long without being caught, and we all know what that—'

'That's it!' Hooter interrupted. 'Not from the side of the common. Quickly, we haven't a second to lose, everyone into the wagon.'

Without query or pause, the crew did as Inspector Hooter bid. He himself remained on the ground next to Punch. The others had never seen such a look of command on Hooters's face. Aano sat ready with the reins in his hands, although he didn't really know why he bothered with them, Punch always seemed to pre-empt his requests faultlessly.

The corporal turned to Hooter and asked, 'Do you have a plan, sir?'

'Yes I do, Corporal. And it's thanks to Abel Nogg.'

'In that case, sir, be on your way. We'll stay here and do our best to stop others following you.'

'Thank you, perhaps we'll see you again one day – but I hope you'll understand if I say I hope we don't, not in this world anyway.'

The corporal smiled and stepped back with his colleagues.

'Shake those reins, Mr Grunt,' Hooter called, 'follow me.'

Punch jerked the wagon into life following Hooter down the track until the timbered wall and bushes screened him and his crew from the hoards on the other side. With his nose just a whisker away from Hooter's tail he enjoyed the sweet smell of beautiful plumage. His whispers willed him to stay close to the inspector. As soon as the wagon was completely hidden from those on the common, Hooter looked over his shoulder. 'Brace yourself, everyone, we're going through from this side.'

Through from this side? But that's the wrong way, surely we should be going back in the other direction. Before anyone could ask if Hooter knew what he was doing he turned to his left with Punch right on his tail. Every fibre among the ancient timbers reached out, longing to hold the mallard once again. Aano, Uppendown and Orange shut their eyes tight. Aano hoped he had gotten his facts straight and that the Amulet in Hooter's possession was indeed the real one. *Otherwise we're in real trouble.*

And so, hidden from view, Hooter touched the wall. His eyes widened as always when the timbers pulled him in – him, the horse, the wagon and its precious cargo. All with wide, beautiful eyes, except for the Beast of Grey in the coffin whose eyes had

398

yet to see a new light.

The entire crew and wagon were gently extruded from the timbers and carefully placed on the sand. It was night, like the world they had just left behind. The air was clear and the sky sparkled while the Moon looked down on them, five souls longing for home, only one of them with the slightest idea of where they were.

***

Unaware of Hooter's departure, Helkendag stared at the Amulet that Aano had given him. He held it high above his head for the baying crowd to see. This would be his crowning glory, the moment he had dreamed of and schemed for. 'Here it is,' he shouted, casting his powerful voice right across the common, the trees in the distance catching his proclamation and stifling it to keep it within the natural depression of the land.

'Through the wall, through the wall!' the crowd chanted impatiently, sensing something wonderful was about to happen to them– their chance of a new beginning.

***

Punch gently nudged Hooter's rump to move forward a few paces to allow him to get the wagon safely away from the timbered wall. Having done so, Aano let go of the reins and jumped down. Uppendown and Orange did the same. Standing line abreast with the horse in the centre they all stared out into the crisp moonlit landscape.

'Where is this place?' asked Al Orange on a whisper.

'Are we safe here?' said Uppendown.

'Are we alone?' wondered Aano.

'I have been here before,' Hooter replied.

'Really?' The crew looked at him quizzically.

399

'This is where I came yesterday when Abel Nogg had me going back and forth through the wall, remember?' explained Hooter. 'He said he wanted me to see this world just so that I would know it was here.'

'He's a very clever chap, that Abel Nogg,' said Aano, his arms slowly rising past his head, as was their way.

'He is,' replied Hooter. 'Mr Nogg explained that as long as you keep going through the wall in the same direction, round and round so to speak, you will pass into a different world each time. That is why we are supposed to go back in the opposite direction to get back to where we started, quite logical really.'

The others had never associated the word "logical" with the inspector before, but his demeanour had changed during the course of the night and he now seemed somehow different, more certain and decisive; they were glad of his leadership right now and hoped that whoever lived in this world would look upon them with a kind heart.

'I think we're about four and a half hours from sunrise,' said Hooter studying the Moon and the stars. The others stood quietly perusing the cabins and the scenery rising towards the wooded hilltop in the distance.

'Who lives in those cabins?' asked Aano.

'Creatures rather like you,' replied Hooter.

'Like me?'

'Well, something like you.' Hooter concentrated on the cabin nearest him. The chair on the veranda on which Gerald Wunfith had sat was now empty. No sign of life anywhere. 'I think they must all be asleep, so we must keep our voices down, until morning.'

'Erm, sir?' said Uppendown. 'To get back to my earlier question, are we safe here?'

'Yes we are, Sergeant, but I must warn you to prepare

yourself for a bit of a shock when you first set eyes on the inhabitants here.'

'Why is that, sir?'

'Because…they are absolutely magnificent gorillas, as tall as us, but very muscular and heavy – the males especially.'

'Gorillas.' Aano seemed excited. 'How wonderful.' He recalled Abel Nogg's question to him a day or two earlier. *How do you feel about gorillas, Mr Grunt?*

'Would they be related to you?' asked Hooter.

'Hmm,' Aano replied, 'Not directly, no. But they are part of the great ape family. They are the biggest and most powerful without a doubt.'

'Have you met any before?'

'No, Inspector, they originated in a different part of the world to me.' Aano scratched his head, pondering. 'I must admit it doesn't seem to make any difference anymore where someone came from, everything is jumbled up, don't you think?'

'I suppose so,' Hooter replied, 'but we all know that it doesn't matter where anyone comes from; all that matters is how we all behave.'

The crew listened to Hooter's rationale with ease, he was most certainly sounding more authoritative by the minute. *How strange*, they all thought.

***

Back in the world of the humans, the crowd had become more excited, almost frenzied. They had been summoned by their smart phones, by someone they did not know, to be part of a new movement. "The first to enter a new world" they were told. The fact that they did not know the sender of such an unlikely offer mattered nought to them, there is always a plentiful supply of wanting souls susceptible to devious minds.

With the Amulet held high, Helkendag felt triumphant. At last his ultimate quest to subvert the powers that set the universe in place had come to fruition. He had the Amulet and he had one thousand humans from all walks of life in the palm of his hand. Within the next minute he would unleash them and let them infiltrate the world of the water birds, to spread like a disease, spoiling and raping Mother Nature as they had done in their own world for so long.

He was about to give the word, when a convoy of lorries appeared along the track. Sand coloured, each with twenty-one young soldiers aboard with eyes of crystal blue and warm hearts – and no guns. The convoy stopped and the engines silenced. The door opened in the lead lorry; Captain Walter Haker jumped down. 'Corporal,' he called out. The corporal at the scene promptly met his captain halfway. 'Where is the wagon?' asked Haker.

The corporal replied in a low voice, 'They passed through the wall from the other side, sir. Inspector Hooter assured me he knew what he was doing. He said Abel Nogg had told him.'

Captain Haker cupped his chin in his hand. 'That sounds about right. And you saw them all go through?'

'Yes sir, all of them, so weird. But we did as you asked, sir. We kept our distance while making sure no harm came to them. None of these people here saw where they went.'

'Well done, Corporal. Now we shall have to see what unfolds here. This looks pretty unpleasant. Explain, please.'

'Yes sir. It seems that the man in the suit standing up front has a stone, an Amulet he calls it. All the people in the crowd believe the stone to be a key which will let them pass through this timbered wall into a new world. The man has promised them a new start. As you can see, sir, they're getting very worked up, I don't think they're going to wait much longer.'

'Thank you, Corporal. We must assume that Inspector Hooter went through the wall in the direction of the next world along, just to get out of harm's way.'

Walter's arrival had not gone unnoticed. Helkendag recognised him as the young man who had become acquainted with Kate Herrlaw. *So you would try to stop me, would you? With your band of followers, just like Hooter and his constables. You laughable fool.*

Walter looked straight at Helkendag, fixing his eyes on him. Helkendag ignored his presence, nothing was going to stop him now. He raised both hands into the air, waving them to stir the crowd into a final crescendo.

'Through the wall, through the wall, through the wall!' they yelled, ever louder.

'Now is the time.' Helkendag's voice boomed above them. 'Your time!' He stepped aside. His eyes morphed into the hardened black orbs with which he so often tormented his hosts. 'Through you go, through you go!' he howled wildly.

Perfect eyes of blue crystal watched from behind the Moon as the human mass surged forward. One thousand souls forcing their way towards the timbered wall.

The human horde was inches from the timbers when Helkendag yelled, 'Just touch it, just touch it and it will yield.' He laughed hysterically at his work. 'At last, at last.'

The first row of humans reached out with their fingers. The weight of nine hundred and ninety bodies pressing against them from behind would not be stopped. The timbered wall braced itself. The eyes watched from behind the Moon. Ten pairs of desperate hands pressed the timbers. The timbers did not recognise them, nor did they recognise the stone in Helkendag's hand.

'Push, you idiots, push!' Helkendag screamed.

The front row had no option to push, first with their hands, and then with their entire bodies as the weight of the entire mob compressed them against the unyielding timbers. Ten people squirmed down the face of the wall, writhing. Twenty more piled into them, then thirty. The surge was unrelenting, nothing could stop the tidal force of those who so wanted to leave their world, crushing those ahead of them.

Helkendag screamed with rage, 'I have been deceived!' He glared at the Amulet. 'I have been given a fake.' His eyes remained as black as pitch as he watched the bodies piling up, deformed and agonized, against the face of the wall. Eventually those at the back the crowd began to slide back like a wave retreating from the beach, a beach strewn with human flotsam. 'That ape – that ape! I shall find him and when I do he will be sorry. To think he could fool me and walk away will be his undoing.' The veins in Helkendag's neck swelled in anger. 'That stupid Inspector Hooter, I shall have him as well, they will regret this day. By all the despair I can muster, they will be done with!' He thrust the Amulet into his trouser pocket and stormed off into the bushes.

44

The sky to the east of Inspector Hooter began to lighten. One by one the local birds in the trees proclaimed the impending arrival of a new day, another chance to revel in their own existence. A gentle breeze teased the sleep from the trees while their silhouettes grew in strength like a developing photograph, their colours not yet apparent.

Punch had spent the night in the lea of the bushes which were always glad to offer shelter to passing travellers, rare as they were. The rest of the crew had spent the last couple of hours hunkered down in the back of the wagon with a spare tarpaulin draped over them to add to the oneness of the occasion.

Punch was the first to wake. The events of the previous night instantly came to the forefront of his mind – all the bright lights and the man in the hat stirring the humans into a frenzy. He shook his big head from side to side to get things in their right place, and then he rose to his feet, flexing and stretching his muscles, completing the process with a soft fluffy huff.

Aano was next to open his eyes. *I've gone blind!* he thought in panic, but then he realized his head was still beneath the tarpaulin. He very slowly slid the cover from his face and stared up at the opaque sky which itself was still in the throes of coming to light. He lowered his sight and gazed out over the edge of the wagon at the strange and yet familiar landscape. He could make out the shapes of the cabins more easily now, with loosely manicured paths winding between them. He lay contentedly sharing his body heat with his friends until he realized it was not one of their wings resting across his chest – but an arm, a hairy arm. As far as he could see it had a very large hand, black and chubby, on the end of it, and was most certainly not his, being ginger as he was. Struggling to keep his fretfulness at bay and not wishing to alarm anyone else, he very slowly turned his head to the right. Two sparkling eyes were looking straight at him. He gulped. 'Er…hello,' he said.

'Good morning,' replied the large gorilla's head.

Aano tentatively asked, 'What are you doing under our cover, if I may ask, sir.'

The gorilla preceded his reply with a broad smile, his white teeth lighting up in contrast with his perfect black complexion. 'Well now,' he said quietly, 'while it might be true that this cover is yours, I think you will find that it and your wagon and all its contents are actually in my land…or at least in the land which I police.'

'I see,' Aano replied, sensing there was more to come.

'And therefore,' the gorilla added, 'I think it reasonable that I should ask you what you are doing under your cover in this land where you do not ordinarily belong.' The gorilla's excellent diction was not lost on Aano, who was now unsure as to whether he should continue the dialogue with the impressive ape or wake the rest of the crew for their support.

The gorilla seemed to sense Aano's dilemma. 'By all means rub the top of your head if that will help,' he suggested with another smile which put Aano more at ease.

The gorilla cast his eye across the tops of the other heads in the wagon which were still dozing, though coming close to waking. The Sun had not quite shown itself, but the air was most certainly brighter. 'Shall we walk a while? We can let your friends wake of their own accord.'

Aano very carefully lifted the tarpaulin and the two great, but very different apes, climbed down from the wagon while Punch looked on from the side-lines.

'He is a very handsome horse,' said the gorilla.

'He is indeed, amazingly strong too…and he has a beautiful mind,' Aano replied. 'I love thinking with him.'

'I can see why you would,' said the gorilla, sharing Punch's gaze.

They wandered a little further away from the wagon keeping their voices low. The gorilla's bulk was easily twice that of Aano, and yet the orangutan felt comfortably at ease by his side.

Aano began, 'I shall try to explain how we came to be here, although I'm not altogether sure of the facts myself.'

'Before you start, let me introduce myself; I am Officer Wunfith. I represent the law in these parts, being a member of the Heavy Mob as I am.'

'Ah, I see,' Aano replied. 'My name is Aano Grunt, and I am a farrier by trade. I look after the horses and donkeys in our world, the world of the water birds.'

'I dare say the birds are glad of your dexterity, I cannot imagine them being too good with their hands, seeing as they do not actually have any.'

'No, that's right, but they manage amazingly well. Would you believe the two mallards on the wagon are also police officers?'

Wunfith quickly put two and two together. 'Would one of them be Inspector Hooter of the Flying Squad?'

'Yes, he would.' Aano too was quick to figure things out. 'So this is where he came a few days ago, when Mr Nogg was explaining more about how the timbered wall and the ether works.'

'Correct, my friend. I did not know at the time why Abel Nogg brought him here, but I have a feeling you are about to enlighten me.'

The two of them sat on the edge of Gerald's veranda, comfortably close. Aano continued, 'We were almost home, we had the coffin on the wagon and all we had to do was…' he paused suddenly. *I wonder how much this chap knows about the timbered wall. I must be careful not to say too much.* He sat in another quandary, unsure of how he could avoid divulging the wall's secret.

The gorilla put his arm around Aano's shoulder, saying, 'If you are concerned about giving any secrets away, let me say that I know of the passage through the wall, but I have never personally experienced it. Abel Nogg discussed the matter with Inspector Hooter the other day when he was here. Do not tell me more than you are comfortable with, my friend. It is enough that I know it is possible to pass through the ether if a certain Amulet is close by…please go on.'

'Oh, right, well when we arrived at the timbered wall late last night we were horrified to find it illuminated by dazzling lights, there were a thousand or more humans ganging up to come through the wall with us.' Aano took a quick breath before continuing, 'Anyway, the man in the hat was there; the bad man in the hat. He held the Amulet in his hand, he was goading the humans on, really whipping them up angrily. But he didn't know the stone he held was probably a dud which I'd given him. As far as I know, Inspector Hooter has the real one hidden about his person.'

'You still have not explained quite how you came to be here though,' said the gorilla.

'That was the surprising thing,' Aano went on enthusiastically. 'Inspector Hooter, in a moment of inspiration,

408

which I have to say he does not often have, suddenly became very authoritative. He decided we could not pass through in the direction of our home because the humans were in our way and would follow us. So he led us around behind the wall, hidden from view, and brought us through in the opposite direction which he recalled from the meeting with Abel Nogg the other day.'

'Are you saying he brought you here seeking refuge from the man in the hat?'

'Not so much that, but we couldn't stay in the world of the humans because they are a very angry breed and treated us badly on our last visit. They chased us with helicopters and grizzled men with guns, all very scary.'

Officer Wunfith offered his hand which Aano gladly shook. 'Do not worry, my friend,' said Wunfith. 'You and your friends are welcome to stay here until you decide what to do next.'

***

Daybreak in the world of the humans saw the last of the ambulances and army lorries taking the broken bodies and the broken hearts away from the timbered wall. Ambulances crewed not by paramedics or technicians, but by young men in battle dress and berets, all with a glint in their eyes. No one would be left behind, and no mobile phone left intact to tell the ridiculous tale of how they were duped into believing they might pass through a mystical wall into another world. Ahead of them was a twenty mile journey at the end of which waited a hospital of Victorian origins, where the dead, the dying, and the able bodied would be treated accordingly. In time they would be returned to society, but their memories would not go with them.

Kate Herrlaw and Walter Haker sat in the Landrover on the common. The rain beat like a rampant snare drum on the cab roof. 'Do you think Mother Nature knew these clouds would be needed?' Kate asked.

'Nothing happens without a reason,' Walter replied while the heavy raindrops removed the evidence of one thousand pairs of feet in the sand, rejuvenating the flora, helping it to stand tall once again. 'You would hardly know they had ever been here.'

'We know who is to blame for this,' said Kate, 'and I doubt if he is going to let things be.'

'You're right, Kate.' Walter sighed. 'Inspector Hooter was so close to getting through to safety. Do you agree with my reckoning? He needs to come back in the opposite direction into this world.'

'Yes, and then he has to go round again to get back into his own world. Two laps of the wall and he'll be safe.'

'All we can do is leave a contingent of my men here to keep an eye on things while we see if we can find Helkendag.'

'We must try to keep him occupied,' said Kate, 'just long enough for Hooter to get away.'

'Don't put yourself at risk,' Walter replied. 'Remember we are only here to watch and take account, we've probably done more than we should already.'

'But we can't abandon the mission now, there's too much at stake.'

'I know….'

They watched as the rain stopped. The clouds moved away to the north, leaving the Sun to cast its warmth over the freshly painted heathland; another masterpiece in the making.

***

Hooter, Orange and Uppendown awoke together. The tarpaulin fell from their faces revealing a brightening sky promising a fine day ahead. Their eyes lingered in each other's for a few seconds.

'Follow my lead,' said Hooter, casting the cover to one side and jumping from the wagon with a little help from his wings. Uppendown and Al Orange promptly followed, the three of them performing a quick shake and preen, not the full works, but enough to pass muster.

The land around them grew brighter by the minute as the Sun rose above the trees to the east. The three birds scanned the scenery from one side to the other. They could see no sign of movement at first, but then a curtain in one of the cabins twitched, then another until many gorilla faces peered from the cabin windows at the bizarre sight. *Three giant birds*?

It was not until Aano waved to them from the shadow on the veranda that they noticed the very large gorilla sitting next to him. 'My word,' said Hooter, 'it's Officer Wunfith, how wonderful.'

Al Orange winced at the sight of a creature every bit as large as a human and of very similar design. 'Are you sure he is safe?'

'Oh yes, he's the one who spoke to me the other day, when Abel Nogg brought me here.'

'He looks mighty impressive, fer sure,' said Uppendown.

Wunfith joined Aano in hand-waving, beckoning the threesome to join them on the veranda. Many more gorilla faces peeped from behind the curtains, but none appeared in the open.

'Follow me,' said Hooter to his team of two standing right behind him. 'Let's keep it smart, we must present ourselves in a good light.'

The three of them had another quick shake and stretched a few inches taller before heeding Hooter's order. 'By the front, quick waddle.'

The gorillas at the windows now pulled their curtains fully

open to see the three giant colourful birds marching in single file towards their own Officer Wunfith, who had now gotten up from the veranda and stood firmly on all fours with his police officer's helmet perched on top of his very handsome head.

'Good morning, Inspector,' said Gerald sharing his gaze between the three equally impressive birds. He lingered a little longer on Sergeant Uppendown, him being somewhat taller than the mallards and looking rather cool in his immaculate Stetson hat. 'Absolutely super,' remarked Gerald.

Having never heard a gorilla speak before, Bob Uppendown and Al Orange both raised a surprised eyebrow at Gerald's precise enunciation.

'Good morning, Officer Wunfith,' replied Hooter. 'It's good to see you again, although I must admit I didn't think we would be meeting again quite so soon.'

'Me neither, Inspector. Mr Grunt has been telling me of your plight, a nasty affair altogether.'

'Let me introduce my colleagues,' said Hooter. 'This is Inspector Orange, leader of the Armed Response Ducks, and this chap is Sergeant Uppendown of the Royal Canadian Mounted Police.'

'Splendid,' said Gerald, 'pleased to meet you.' He continued through a barely concealed wry smile, 'You know, I still can't get over the fact that you talk.'

Al Orange, in no mood for inane small talk, replied bluntly, 'What did you expect us to do – moo?'

'Well, erm, no,' Gerald replied, rather taken aback by the mallard's brusque attitude. 'I thought you might quack though.'

Orange's impatience was clear in his voice. 'Quack? Why on Earth would we quack? We have our whistles if we want to make a quacking sound.'

Gerald apologised, 'I really am most terribly sorry, Inspector;

I meant no disrespect. It's just that all the water birds in our land either quack or tweet.'

Orange, still suspicious of the similarity between the gorilla and a human form, found it difficult to endure what seemed to be little more than a cheap joke at his expense. Gerald sensed the tension in the air. He extended both arms and turned his palms uppermost. 'Please accept my humble apologies, Inspector Orange. That was a foolish and thoughtless thing to say, but you see, we simply do not have water birds the likes of you in our world – and they certainly do not have names.' Gerald paused while rubbing the top of his helmet. 'At least I do not think they have names. I mean, they don't actually speak, unless you count their quacking, so who knows?'

'Fair enough,' said Orange. 'To be honest I was expecting nothing more than a grunt and a snort from you, until you opened your mouth. You speak excellent English, Officer.'

'Grunt and snort, eh,' replied Gerald. 'I cannot imagine why you would think such a thing, but then, we do come from different worlds…shall we start again?'

'That's fine by me,' said Orange, much to the relief of Inspector Hooter.

By now, gorillas stared from almost every window of every cabin. Gerald Wunfith raised his hand above his head and twirled it round and round a few times. The faces immediately disappeared from view and went about their daily routines.

'Make yourselves comfortable while I put the kettle on,' said Gerald, promptly disappearing inside his cabin.

And so, ten minutes later, the three giant water birds, one orangutan and a stout gorilla sat on the veranda supping tea while discussing Hooter's options and the need for him and his crew to return to their own land as soon as possible.

45

From behind the cemetery wall adjacent to the police station in Davidsmeadow a pair of very blue eyes waited patiently. They had been there since before dawn, keen not to miss a certain young officer who would soon be setting off on his patrol.

Constable Five Degrees had decided to venture across the common on one of his routine beats in the hope of coming across any sign of Inspector Hooter. He himself had never had any dealings with the timbered wall and as such was at a loss as to where the inspector might have headed. *All I know is – he went east.*

'Good morning, everyone,' said Five Degrees, putting his head around the open office door.

'Good morning,' replied Constable Russell. 'Are you going out on patrol?'

'Yes,' replied Five Degrees. 'I thought I would have a look beyond Shortmoor.'

'Okay, mate – oops, I mean Constable,' replied Russell in his temporary position of authority. 'When do you expect to be back?'

'Hmm, I'll do a broad sweep so I doubt if I'll be back much before dusk.'

'Okay, but be careful; see you later.'

The constables watched as Five Degrees adjusted his helmet to effect a slight forward tilt as per flying regulations. He could not resist another little tweak, the straightness of his head still being a thing of wonderment. Out in the street, with his wings narrowly missing the buildings to either side, he rose swiftly into the air and circled the town once to get his bearings. He then accelerated away, using the South Downs as his guide.

The eyes by the cemetery watched him disappear beyond the roof tops.

Cruising comfortably at an altitude of five trees, the constable took his time to admire the beauty of the land below. *So many shades of green, mauve and yellow.* The trees were always glad to see the young constable on the wing. They would wave their tips discretely in the air to acknowledge him. He in turn would rock from side to side to return their regard. *So beautiful.* The village of Smallbeef came and went beneath him. He recalled his first meeting with Inspector Hooter in the little caravan park there. He especially remembered falling off his police bicycle in front of everyone, and how Hooter had insisted that he kept riding it rather than fly on account of him not having had any formal flying lessons. *I wonder where that bicycle is now,* he mused, not knowing the full story of the missing Beast of Grey.

The air suddenly became restless around him; he trimmed his attitude to compensate for the unexpected turbulence before looking to his right…'Oh my,' he exclaimed.

'Hello there, young duck.' Dana Lethgerk had stealthily gained on him without being noticed. 'I hope I didn't alarm you.'

'Oh, no madam.' Five Degrees was sure to maintain a proper manner in the company of this most beautiful mallard. He had seen her about the town and knew of Inspector Hooter's interest in her. He had also heard the other constables talking of her and her unusual ways. Flying at a safe distance to his right in the clear morning air her beauty was plain to see. Her colours, though subtle, were indeed perfectly toned, and her plumage immaculate. But it was her eyes that shocked him. *Incredible, I've never seen any like them before. Now I know what the others were going on about.*

'I think perhaps you should keep an eye on where you are going, Constable.'

'Oh, yes madam, of course.' Five Degrees composed himself and enquired, 'May I ask what you are doing way out here, madam?'

'If I said I was out for a morning flight for no particular reason, would you believe me?'

'Er, no, madam, not really.'

'Then I shall be truthful with you.' Dana's voice competed with her eyes to reach that place a young male knows of, but rarely finds. 'I had a feeling someone from the police station would set off today on the trail of Inspector Hooter. Like you, I am worried for his safety, I would be so grateful if I could accompany you on your search. I promise I won't get in your way.'

'I can't possibly let you do that, madam. The inspector would never forgive me if any harm should come to you.'

'But I would only be following you. I'm sure another pair of eyes would be most useful.'

Five Degrees tried to think of a good reason to bar Dana from continuing without sounding officious. 'Well, madam, I can't actually let you join my patrol, but the law says you are free to fly wherever you want as long as you do it in a peaceable way.'

Dana fluttered her eyes in Five Degrees direction and winked. 'I promise I will behave myself. I shall keep myself to myself, but we might just end up in the same place, if that is all right with you?'

'Hmm, okay, madam. But you must promise me that at the first sign of danger you will turn about and make your way home without any argument.'

'Of course, Constable, thank you.'

The eager young constable continued on his way across the common in the rough direction of the timbered wall. Dana Lethgerk followed a safe distance behind, her eyes scanning all around as she went. If Hooter was nearby, he would surely not go unnoticed.

***

'That's settled then,' said Gerald Wunfith, still sitting on the veranda. 'As I understand it, you cannot return to your own world without first going through the world of the humans, correct?'

'Correct,' replied Hooter.

'And even though you would only be in their world for a few minutes, you would feel more comfortable making the journey under the cover of darkness.'

'That's right, too. The humans don't venture out much after dark, so there is less chance of us bumping into any of them.'

'Then you must use today to rest and gather your strength, my friend. You are quite welcome to use my cabin to lie up in. And please feel free to roam wherever you wish. The countryside is beginning its preparations for winter, but it is still perfectly beautiful to walk through.' Gerald gazed at the cabin across the way and caught the eye of a female gorilla tending to her herbaceous border. He called out to her, 'Excuse me, my dear.'

The female put down her garden fork before elegantly knuckle walking over to the group. 'Good morning, Gerald—I mean Officer Wunfith.' She had a certain glint in her eye and a

417

charming smile.

'Ah yes, my dear.' Gerald failed to conceal his obvious affection for the female who, being very hairy and mostly black, was extremely attractive, even to the water birds' eyes. *Beauty comes in all shades and shapes.* 'Let me introduce you, madam,' said Gerald. 'This is Inspector Hooter who you saw the other day when he visited us. And this is Inspector Orange – this is Sergeant Uppendown – and this fine looking chap is Mr Aano Grunt.' He then paused for a second while taking the female's hand to present her...'And this, my friends, is Miss Velvet Warmheart.'

'How do you do, madam,' the foursome replied. 'Such a beautiful name,' Hooter added, 'very apt if I may say.'

Miss Warmheart responded with a wave of her hand, 'Oh, I am sure you say that to all the lady gorillas you meet.'

'Erm, actually you're the first we've ever met, but perfectly lovely all the same.'

Gerald regained the conversation. 'I don't like to impose on you, my dear, but our guests will be with us for the day and I was wondering if you might see to their needs, you know, tea and the odd snack to sustain them – if it's not too much trouble.'

'Of course,' replied Miss Warmheart in a sublimely soft and clear voice. 'It would be my pleasure.' She could hardly take her eyes off the birds who looked all the more magnificent up close. The birds in turn found her appearance truly striking, considerably smaller than Gerald, little more than half his size, but her colouring was razor sharp; a jet black face with a satin finish, and glossy black hair over most of her body apart from her front upper torso, which was very nearly as perfect as her face in respect of complexion. 'I'll get you a fresh pot of tea,' she said. 'Perhaps you would like some cereal, grain and mixed leaves for breakfast?'

'That's very kind of you, madam, if it's not too much trouble,' replied Hooter, doffing his cap politely.

She smiled and headed for her cabin, moving lightly on all fours with her hair flowing gaily in the morning breeze. Gerald's voice rumbled beneath his breath, 'Wonderful woman, perhaps one day…?'

'Is she your intended?' asked Al Orange.

'I live in hope, Inspector. I live in hope.'

Ten minutes later, Gerald had set off on a short patrol of the settlement while Hooter and his team sat at a table by the side of Velvet Warmheart's cabin, admiring the spread before them. Bowls of cereal and grain, and dishes of various leaves and fruit surrounded the pot of fresh tea. *Gosh. How perfectly proper.*

'Please help yourself, everyone; if there is anything else I can get you please give me a shout. I shall leave you to enjoy your breakfast in peace.'

'Oh please, madam,' Hooter spoke up, 'we would very much enjoy your company if you can spare the time.'

'Thank you, Inspector. That would be lovely,' she replied, pulling out another chair.

The mild autumnal sunshine comforted the party while they enjoyed each other's company. Very different breeds and very different colours enjoying the moment gifted them by Mother Nature, and all truly grateful for it.

Many of the residents had headed off towards the trees at the top of the rise and the pastures beyond. Those who had remained at home went about their business as usual, but none needed much of an excuse to pop outside for an enquiring glimpse of the amazing birds.

Aano was thoroughly enjoying his bowl of salad when one particular gorilla caught his eye. 'My word,' he said, taking care not to point. The gorilla in question was delivering a keg of water to a neighbour, walking on three limbs with the keg under one arm. 'He's almost my colour,' Aano mused, 'how odd.'

'Ah yes,' said Velvet, 'a gorilla from different roots. He's not quite as deep orange as you, Mr Grunt, but close.'

Al Orange added with a chuckle, 'His hair isn't as wayward either.'

'I wonder who his hairdresser is,' Aano joked. 'I doubt I could ever look so suave.'

Velvet looked Aano in the eye. 'Do you not have someone special to help you groom?'

Aano sighed. 'I'm afraid there is no one else of my breed where I live, or at least not that I know of.'

'How sad.' Velvet ran her hand over Aano's head, starting from his brow then over the top and down the back of his neck. 'I have no doubt you would look truly wonderful if you had someone to spend a little time with you.' She smiled sublimely. Aano grinned back, trying desperately not to pout.

'Ahem, anyway.' Hooter thought it best to interrupt the proceedings. 'Officer Wunfith will be back in a minute and perhaps he will give us a little tour of the surroundings, just to pass the time, so to speak.'

'I'm sure he will,' Velvet replied, leaving Aano's hair to point in all directions.

'Oh my!' A distressed cry came from the hedge where Punch had been standing. 'Something has eaten my shrubs,' exclaimed Mrs Muchmuscle, the mayor's wife. Everyone looked over to see the tops of many of the plants missing. Punch snorted through his nose, trying to look nonchalant and innocent, but the head of what looked like a hyacinth hanging from the side of his mouth gave him away. 'You naughty horse,' cried the lady gorilla.

Aano leapt to his feet and bounded towards the shrubbery. 'I'm terribly sorry,' he said. 'In all our excitement at meeting you all, we completely forgot about Punch's breakfast.'

'But he's eaten half a bush,' said the mayor's wife. 'Where does he put it all?'

They both cast an eye at Punch's more than ample belly. Punch huffed again as the last flower disappeared between his lips. *Where's the evidence now?*

Although saddened by the disappearance of her plants, Mrs Muchmuscle instantly succumbed to Punch's twinkling hazel eyes when they reached in and touched her heart. The horse then leaned over for good measure and planted a big kiss in the centre of her head as he was prone to do. Aano was about to apologise again on Punch's behalf, but Mrs Muchmuscle reached up and simply touched the horse's lips with her chubby hand, saying, 'You are a very naughty horse.' She then smiled warmly. 'How would you like a nice big bucket of cereal and a carrot?'

Punch knew the look in the gorilla's eye was a kindly one. As much as he wanted to give her another kiss on the head, he thought better of it and vented a hearty huff instead.

***

In the world of the water birds, the air had begun to cool in the mid-afternoon Sun. Constable Five Degrees had zig-zagged his way through the air between Smallbeef and the timbered wall which, to his relief, could now be seen in the distance. Dana Lethgerk had remained true to her word, following him without interrupting.

Despite his diligence, Five Degrees had found no sign of Hooter's whereabouts. He did a sideways slide in the air to look Dana in the eye. 'I don't think I'll go any further for the moment,' he called. 'I'm going to land on the track down there to have a little think.'

'That's fine, Constable, I shall follow you down,' said Dana.

The trees by the timbered wall gave a silent hoorah with the most subtle of waves. Their movement stirred the pigeon who was now resting high in the oak's branches, waiting for the return of the wagon and crew.

Landing almost vertically, Five Degrees quickly moved to one side. Dana landed immediately behind him, making a delicate descent with utmost precision.

'Coo croo,' said the pigeon, recognising the mallard in the police helmet, but he was not familiar with the other mallard who looked almost too perfect. 'Croo,ooo,' he added, cautiously. The trees too were a little unsure as to the nature of the beautiful stranger's appearance.

'Hello, matey,' said Five Degrees, 'are you waiting for someone?'

'Vroo – vroo croo,' replied the pigeon, landing on a lower branch.

'Ah, I see – I think.' The constable rubbed his bill while pondering the pigeon's reply.

'Do you actually understand pigeon?' asked Dana.

'Just a little. They don't have many words; it's not so much what they say as the way they say it.'

'You are a mallard of many talents, Constable Five Degrees.'

'That's why I love my tours out here in the countryside. I get to meet all the other residents and each time I meet them I learn a little more.'

The pigeon blinked agreeably, 'Croo.'

'The light will begin to fade in an hour or so,' said Five Degrees, looking to the west. 'I'm concerned about you flying in the dark, madam, what with you not knowing the terrain as well as I do.'

Dana replied wide-eyed. 'If we set off right away and go directly home we might make it before it gets too dark, but to be honest, Constable, I feel rather tired after our convoluted journey getting here.'

'I see,' replied Five Degrees.

'I'm sorry,' said Dana. 'Perhaps you were right after all, perhaps I should not have come along with you, but I only wanted to help find the inspector.'

'That's all right, madam, don't worry. I've spent many a night out here with the trees for company, we'll be quite comfy between the tussocks on the verge. We can head for home at first light in the morning.'

'Thank you for your patience, Officer,' Dana replied.

'Croo, croo vroo,' said the pigeon, nervously. Five Degrees didn't quite get that one.

46

The Sun was now one hour away from touching down on the horizon. The clouds were few and far between, allowing the early evening light unfettered access to the land below.

The pigeon had remained perched in the oak tree while Five Degrees and Dana nestled among the long grass on the verge. Five Degrees, being unaccustomed to socialising with females, waited for Dana to strike up a conversation, which she duly did.

'I'm surprised we haven't come across Inspector Hooter by now. Is this not the most likely route he would have taken?'

'I couldn't say, madam, being as I don't even know where he went.'

'Hmm,' Dana pondered the matter. 'But just supposing he had visited this neck of the woods…is there another route home from here?'

'None that make sense,' Five Degrees replied. 'Perhaps we'll pick up his trail in the morning, things always look different on the dawn.'

'I'm sure you're right, Constable. I think we should both settle down and get a good night's sleep.'

'Good night,' said Five Degrees.

'Good night,' said Dana.

The pigeon said nothing.

***

In the world of the gorillas, Gerald Wunfith was giving Hooter and his crew a guided tour of the local area. They stood among the trees at the top of the rise where many gorillas tended the undergrowth around them, ensuring the trees' cast-offs were settling nicely on the ground in readiness for the forthcoming winter.

'Food and cover for the small creatures who live here,' said Gerald.

'Absolutely,' replied Hooter, 'it's nice to see things being looked after.'

Gerald continued his oration. 'Keeping the land healthy ensures that all creatures are able to live by Mother Nature's laws. Everything has its place and is happy to live within its own environment. It is only when their world is interfered with unnaturally that they have to venture further afield to make ends meet.'

'I know what you mean, Gerald,' said Hooter. 'There is a world close to this one, inhabited by humans the size of you, where foxes and rats live in the towns, I ask you, foxes and rats – in towns.'

'Really?' exclaimed Gerald. 'Why on Earth would a fox or a rat want anything to do with a human?'

'To be honest,' Hooter went on, 'when I was last there I noticed a lot of unwanted food and detritus left in bins behind buildings. Very strange. So of course the animals soon realize there are easy pickings to be had. That is when things go awry.'

Gerald rubbed the top of his head. 'Unwanted food?'

'Yes, hard to believe isn't it,' Hooter replied.

Gerald sounded disbelieving. 'But why pick something if you are not going to eat it? That is quite ridiculous.' He cupped his chin in his hand. 'Do you mean they actually go to the trouble of growing something, nurturing it and feeding it and picking it –

and then throw it away?'

'I'm afraid so,' Hooter lamented. 'I don't think I should tell you any more, for fear of upsetting you.'

'Oh come now, Inspector, I am a great big gorilla, I think I am able to keep my emotions under control, don't you?' He put his muscular arm around the mallard's shoulder to encourage him to expand on the issue.

Hooter hesitated.

Al Orange, having no such qualms about telling it how it is, spoke up: 'The inspector is not just talking about plants, Gerald.'

Gerald's bottom lip dropped in anticipation.

Al Orange continued, 'Would you believe they raise animals of all kinds in the most induckane ways. And when the animals are only a few months old they slaughter them, butcher them, wrap them – and then they throw most of them into large metal containers behind shops and bury them in mass graves together with all manner of rubbish, unwanted and unseen.'

Hooter wept while adding, 'And then they build houses on top of them.'

Gerald too, wept. His pure black complexion glistening through the droplets as they ran down his cheeks. 'But why can't the superior breed stop them?'

'Hah,' Orange laughed cynically. 'They **are** the superior breed.'

The sight of a massive silverback gorilla crying openly beneath his police helmet was more than the group could bear. Two mallards, one Canada goose and an orangutan joined him in his sadness. The earth beneath them soon became wetted from their tears; tears not for the meek who suffer, but for mankind and his ability to **make** them suffer. The trees held a minute's silence, listening to the gentle sobbing within their shade. *Oh, the poor chaps.*

Velvet Warmheart had laid the table with a tempting variety of cereals, berries and fruit, and a pot of tea. She knew the visitors would be leaving soon and wanted to be sure they had a decent meal to see them on their way. She cast her gaze towards the distant trees and could see many of those who had been tending to the flora returning home. Mothers, youngsters and a few adult males walking down the slope on all fours, chatting to each other and musing over the strange giant ducks who had come upon them from who knows where.

Eventually, Gerald came into view with Hooter and his party by his side. Velvet immediately noticed Gerald's distressed expression; he walked as though he weighed a ton, his arms and legs having lost their natural spring.

'What is it, Inspector? Has Gerald had an accident?' asked Velvet as soon as they were within earshot.

'No, my dear. I'm afraid it's all my fault. I said something which upset him terribly. I'm so sorry.'

Gerald had wiped the tears from his eyes before being seen by anyone else; it would not do for others to think he was a softy, but Velvet could see the hurt in his eyes. How she felt for him. She reached up and embraced him in a fulsome hug. 'There there, Gerald. Tell me all about it, then you will feel better.'

Gerald's voice wavered in reply, 'No, my dear, I do not think I could bear to repeat what the inspector has told me.' He reluctantly took her hands from around his waist. 'No one else must ever hear of what I have learned, it is simply too horrific.' He looked at the table and changed the subject. 'Let's all sit and enjoy our meal together. I must say, Miss Warmheart, you have done us proud as usual.' The two gorillas lingered in each other's eyes while the rest of the team took their seats and began to pick from the many bowls of Nature's offerings.

Gerald had regained his composure, heartened by the

understanding nature and discretion of Hooter and his friends. He sat opposite Velvet and delicately chose from the various dishes, sneaking the occasional glance across the table at the beautiful female who he hoped would one day be his wife.

***

Meanwhile, the pigeon had been enjoying the company of the oak which had provided a very comfortable perch from where he could watch the world go by, or at least one tiny part of it. He kept an eye on Constable Five Degrees who was slowly but surely drifting away among his own thoughts. Dana remained quite still, calmly turning her head all around to see that there were no interlopers about. The pigeon too remained perfectly still, apart from the occasional blink, like pigeons do. He had thought of offering a coo or two to the oak to show his appreciation, but he decided it might be better to remain as silent as possible; something in the air abraded his senses. Being a beautiful wood pigeon with a relatively small head did not preclude his brain from equalling any other when it came to self-preservation, so he sat beautiful and silent in the arms of the mighty oak.

Five Degrees sank deeper into the soft bedding offered by the tussocks of grass. His eyes closed and his mind rested lightly on the delicate surface of his consciousness. Dana very slowly got to her feet, keeping one eye on the young constable. He did not stir. She made her way across the track towards the timbered wall. The pigeon peered through a half-open eye, quite still.

The trees had something to tell, but they had no choice but to stand and stare silently as Dana made her way towards the aged timbers. They had seen her before, in different clothing.

***

Velvet had gone indoors to make a fresh pot of tea, leaving Gerald to entertain their guests. The conversation was most convivial, care being taken not to mention the behaviour of the humans again.

'Perhaps when your present dilemma has been sorted, you might visit us again,' said Gerald.

'Thank you,' Hooter replied. 'It would be nice to think we have friends in such far off places.'

Al Orange joined in. 'It's strange to think that our worlds are only a few steps apart and yet the journey from one to the other is incredibly perilous.'

'Only the part through the human world,' said Aano, cupping his chin thoughtfully. 'I wonder if it would be possible to move from this world directly to ours without the need to travel through the other.'

'That is something we might think about once we're in the safety of our own land,' Hooter replied. 'For the moment we must concentrate on getting back with the wagon and coffin.' He cast his eye skyward. 'It will be dark enough within the hour for us to make our move.'

***

The pigeon in the oak tree remained silent, remembering his last meeting with Abel Nogg who had saved him from the clutches of the peregrine. On that occasion Abel had held him and spoken to him, not in words but in thought and touch.

Dana didn't concern herself with the pigeon, it was after all just a pigeon, but she watched Five Degrees more carefully, satisfying herself that he really was fast asleep. She then stepped up to the timbered wall. The timbers immediately yielded their resolve, taking the fulsome mallard into their fibres and depositing her in the sand in the land of the humans. With her back to the wall, Dana stared out into the half-light, the flora showed no sign of the previous night's disturbance. Mother Nature had washed and swept as necessary. Dana then promptly made her way around to the other side of the wall, paying particular attention to the ground as she went. Although the heathland had been restored to its former glory, the gravel track was not quite so pristine. Signs of wagon wheels and hoof prints could still be seen. *Ahaa, so this is where you went.*

***

Velvet Warmheart had returned with a fresh pot of tea. She sat back down opposite Gerald who looked across at her with eyes that scarcely concealed his passion. The others around the table enjoyed sharing in his emotions while they picked at the fare laid out before them. They continued chatting idly about nothing in particular, knowing that they would soon be on their way once again, hoping that the trip through the world of the humans would be less fraught than the previous one.

The easy, almost languid atmosphere was suddenly shaken when Aano, halfway through another banana, blurted out, 'Who is that!'

Everyone around the table followed Aano's gaze towards the timbered wall. At first a bright yellow bill emerged from the shadow, followed by a pair of crystal blue eyes and a smooth softly coloured neck. It soon became obvious that it was a female mallard, but such was her natural beauty that many gasps of amazement uttered forth when she eventually stepped fully into the open. She took but a moment to shake herself from top to bottom, settling her plumage perfectly. She then gazed across the grass at those sitting at the table some thirty paces away, her eyes pausing when they saw Hooter staring back at her.

'Dana?' Hooter could not believe his eyes.

430

'Inspector?' Dana's voice exposed her relief at having found him.

'Who is this?' asked Gerald Wunfith. 'What is her business here?'

'Is it all right if she joins us?' asked Hooter, more than a little embarrassed.

Gerald paused for thought. He was not entirely comfortable with unexpected visitors and was concerned that his land might become a regular stopping off place for every waif and stray who happened by. He replied cautiously, 'Very well, Inspector, ask her over.'

'Thank you.' Hooter turned and called, 'This way, my dear.'

Dana waddled elegantly across the sand onto the grass, passing Punch on the way. The horse vented a hefty huff as she did so, not so much an expression but as a means to clear his nostrils of something in the air. Dana noticed the horse's eye, sparkling hazel – and knowing.

As she approached the table, all the males of whatever breed rose to their feet.

'Let me introduce my close friend,' said Hooter. 'This is Dana Lethgerk from Davidsmeadow, in the water birds' world.'

'Pleased to meet you, madam,' replied two mallards, one goose, an orangutan and two gorillas.

'Take a seat, please,' said Velvet, motioning towards the seat next to her.

Dana replied, 'Thank you, Miss…?'

'Velvet Warmheart.'

'What a wonderful name,' replied Dana. 'Very apt if I may say. Your hair is quite exquisite, so black and beautiful.'

As soon as Dana had made herself comfortable, Hooter asked, 'How did you find your way here, my dear. How did you get through the wall, is Mr Nogg close by?'

'My dear Inspector,' Dana chuckled, 'one thing at a time, please.' She attempted to answer Hooter's query while all eyes rested easily on her. 'I accompanied Constable Five Degrees on his patrol, he was keen to find you. I think he is worried for your safety, Inspector. When we came to the other side of the timbered wall he decided to rest up for the night before continuing the search in the morning.'

Throughout Dana's explanation, Punch's nostrils failed to rest.

'Yes but how did you think to come through the wall? And for that matter, how did the wall allow you passage?'

'That part I do not know,' Dana replied calmly. 'Curiosity got the better of me, and I just had to have a closer look. I only touched it lightly, and the next thing I knew it simply sucked me in and put me down here.'

'I see.' Hooter rubbed his bill. 'I can't imagine how that happened, my dear, but I'm glad you made it unharmed. I can only assume Mr Nogg is working behind the scenes somewhere, he moves in mysterious ways you know.'

'I'm sure he does,' replied Dana, looking at the faces around the table for any expression of doubt.

It had not occurred to Inspector Hooter, but Uppendown, Al Orange and Aano each wondered silently…How come she didn't mention passing through the humans' world as well? And why didn't she question who Abel Nogg was?

'The truth is, ma'am,' said Sergeant Uppendown, 'we will all be goin' back very soon; as soon as the light begins to fail.'

'That's right,' said Hooter, 'no time to get too comfy…I don't suppose you noticed anyone else on the other side of the timbers before you passed through, did you?'

Dana looked wistfully into the sky. 'No, Inspector. Only Constable Five Degrees, and he was asleep.'

'Strange, very strange,' Hooter replied.

'If we are to set off soon,' Dana asked, 'could we…I mean you and I, take a stroll while your team are preparing themselves?'

Hooter looked to Aano. 'Would you get Punch harnessed up, Mr Grunt. And if you, Sergeant, could ensure the load is secure. I shall be back in a few minutes.'

'Fer sure, sir.'

Velvet cleared the table while Punch and the wagon were being readied for the off. Gerald remained seated with Al Orange, mulling things over quietly.

Hooter and Dana made their way onto the path between the cabins where they offered their wings to the breeze and within a couple of strides were both in the air. Many gorillas' eyes stared in awe at the magnificent sight as two giant colourful mallards took flight in the direction of the trees at the top of the rise. It took but a minute to race up the slope. Hooter landed first, stepping to one side to watch Dana present her wings at full span with open feathers, landing almost vertically beside him.

'This is nice,' said Dana, 'do the gorillas tend to it? I can't imagine Mother Nature keeping it this tidy.'

'Hmm, I think the gorillas tinker to give a helping hand.'

'I see, a helping hand, eh….' Dana paused thoughtfully. 'Like the one that helped me through the timbered wall.'

'Well,' Hooter replied, desperately resisting the urge to rub his bill again. 'There is no reason why you should not know now, my dear, but the wall only allows passage to certain individuals.' He urgently tried to think of how he could explain further without divulging the existence of the Amulet.

'Certain individuals?' Dana queried.

'Erm, yes, but I cannot say more than that, my dear. If you recall, we did agree to keep police affairs out of our relationship.' Hooter hoped Dana would not pursue the matter further.

'As I recall,' Dana replied, 'it was only you who agreed, I didn't have much choice in the matter.'

'Never the less, I cannot say any more on the subject. Suffice it to say that we shall shortly be passing back through the wall to get home. You will of course be coming with us.'

'Will I?' Dana replied impertinently.

'But of course you will, this is not our world. We shouldn't be here at all, really.'

'Then why are you?'

'That is a long story, perhaps one day when things are different, I might be able to tell you more.'

'But why can't I stay for just a little longer? I could follow on in a day or two. The gorillas here seem very hospitable.'

'No, my dear. You must come back with us to be sure of securing your return passage.'

'But I came through unaided, so why I can't return unaided,' Dana replied, trying to corner Hooter into having to explain further.

Hooter looked into her eyes of perfect blue. She knew his resolve was weakening. 'Please,' she said, humbly.

Hooter questioned his own reasoning. Mr Nogg said I was not to let anyone know unless I trusted them totally. But I do trust Dana totally.

'Please?' Dana repeated. 'If you trust me, what harm can it do to include me in your inner circle?'

'Very well, but this will have to be quick, the others will be wondering where we've got to.'

Dana's eyes smiled while she put a comforting wing around Hooter's shoulder encouraging him to continue with his explanation.

Hooter began, 'In order for anyone to pass through the timbered wall, a certain Amulet must be within a couple of paces of the timbers, otherwise it remains impenetrable.'

'My word,' said Dana. 'An Amulet, you say?'

'Yes, a polished stone with very special powers. Only one exists.'

'Then how did I get through? I don't have the Amulet.'

'That is what puzzled us, my dear…there is only one other person I know of who can pass through without the use of the Amulet, but I didn't think he was anywhere near here.'

'Perhaps he was hiding nearby when I touched the timbers, would that explain it?'

'Ah yes, that might.' A look of relief spread across the inspector's face.

'Where is the Amulet now?' Dana asked, her sense of curiosity unrelenting.

'Um,' Hooter stumbled over his words, but he could see no reason not to tell Dana, after all, he hoped that one day she would be his wife with all the trust and loyalty that marriage entails… 'I have it,' he said.

'You have it on your person?'

'Yes, my dear.'

'My word, that's an enormous responsibility. I can understand you being protective of it.' She gently ran her wing over the top of Hooter's shimmering blue head. 'Could I see it? It must be amazing to behold.'

'Oh no, I'm afraid I can't do that.'

'But if I am to return with you, I shall see how it works anyway, won't I?'

'Hmm, well yes, but—'

'Well there you are then, my darling, what harm can it do if you let me see it for just a few seconds?'

Again, Hooter thought of his future with the beautiful mallard into whose eyes he was most assuredly sinking. But then Abel Nogg's last words muscled their way firmly to the front of his head. *You must relinquish it to no one, not at any cost, no matter what duress you might suffer.*

Hooter replied, 'I'm sorry, my dear, but it simply would not do. I gave my word that I would not give it to anyone…so that is how it must be.' He then prised his eyes from hers and gazed up at the sky. The Sun was almost down on the western horizon, the cooling light well on the wane. 'I think we should join the others now, my dear,' he said while admiring the clearing sky.

Dana's muscles clenched throughout her body. Hooter's gaze was still elsewhere when Dana's eyes flashed from blue to black – a black not of this world. 'Give me the Amulet, now, Inspector.' Her voice took on an edge of imminent consequence, deep and coarse.

Hooter turned, having only half-heard her while wistfully staring skyward. His heart shuddered violently against his chest, hurting his throat and causing him to gag on his words. 'What on Earth!' he cried aloud. 'What's happening? Dana, my dear, what—?'

'Shut up!' Dana shrieked, her eyes hard and black. 'All you had to do was give me the Amulet, you stupid duck.'

'But—'

'I said shut up!' Dana lashed out, striking hard against the side of Hooter's head. Her wing, though of feathered appearance, struck him beneath his chin like a honed metal bar, lifting him from the ground to land on his back with no feeling in his limbs. He stared up in horror at his exquisite love, now towering over him, slowly but surely morphing into something awful.

436

'If you will not give it to me freely, then I have no further use of you,' she growled, her voice deepening with every irate breath.

'But what about us?' Hooter whispered painfully. 'All the lovely words we exchanged, our hopes of a future?' The sight before him turned his stomach, the little duck inside him drowning in the bile of despair.

'Look at me, Inspector.' Dana had lost the colour from her bill, her plumage began to fall to the floor in clumps. 'Look at what you have been holding to your heart, the cheek you touched with your bill.' As she spoke, her bill stopped moving with her words, it had become opaque and disengaged from her face.

Hooter tried to turn away, but his neck lay limp on the floor unable to lift his head.

'Not very pretty is it.' Dana's bill finally became dislodged and fell to the ground to shatter into a million pieces. The front of her face was now open and hollow like a dank cave.

Hooter could contain himself no longer, he vomited at such a repulsive sight. He could feel nothing from the neck down, apart from his heart pounding and his little duck slowly drowning in his stomach. Tears poured from his eyes staring blankly into oblivion.

In less than a minute, the creature before him had shed its entire outer covering and stepped out of the festering pile – and straightened his hat.

Hooter stared in total despair through drowning eyes to see the man in the hat standing there, immaculate. 'You…Helkendag…it was you all along. Behind everyone's troubles, always you.'

'Well done, Inspector. You finally caught up.' Helkendag sniggered. 'Did you honestly think that a duck as beautiful as your Dana could ever love you? You are worthless and pitiful.'

Hooter had lost the little duck inside him, he could feel nothing now, just the fading thump of his heart. He laboured to get his words out. 'If I am worthless...' he struggled for breath, 'so are you...I may be a worthless old mallard but I've thwarted your plans to spoil another world....' His eyes became fixed, staring. 'My world...Mother Nature's creation...not yours.' He lay dying at the base of a pine tree while the nearby bushes rustled in the wake of the fleeing Helkendag.

47

Hooter's crew had readied the wagon and were sitting at Velvet's table, trying to make sense of the mysterious Dana Lethgerk.

'How could she just turn up like that?' asked Bob Uppendown.

Aano replied, 'The inspector was clearly enamoured by her presence.'

Al Orange stared across the grass at the timbered wall. 'Those timbers don't let just anyone through, we know that much.'

'That's right enough, fer sure,' replied Uppendown.

Aano added more with a concerned grimace on his face. 'Mr Nogg told us that only in his presence would the timbers let others pass through without the use of an Amulet….'

'Yes,' replied Al Orange, 'but what about Helkendag? We know he can pass through at will, and we know he wants the Amulet.'

'That's right, too,' said Aano. 'And remember Mr Nogg told us the evil one can change his appearance whenever he likes….' The ape shivered at his next thought. 'The smell,' he mumbled.

'The smell?' said Uppendown.

'Yes,' Aano replied. 'Punch noticed it too. Decay, musky, not nice…it came from Miss Lethgerk when she sat at the table.'

The three of them jumped to their feet. 'Quickly,' they

shouted to each other, 'We've got to find Inspector Hooter and warn him.'

Gerald Wunfith, being the local police officer would not be left behind. He leapt to his feet and, taking Velvet Warmheart in his hand, led the troop in leaps and bounds through the village and up the slope. Many of the residents joined them en-route. Aano jumped onto the wagon and shook the reins urgently. Punch instantly leaned his weight into the harness and had the wagon following in close pursuit of the others.

***

The trees whispered a soft lament to the mallard lying among their shadows, his neck broken and his heart failing. He could hear wings approaching but could not turn his head to see who it was. *Are they angels? Have I earned their attention?* They were not angels, they were Al Orange and Bob Uppendown who had flown ahead of the posse.

'There he is,' called Orange, 'by the trees.' They landed in the most urgent of fashions. Punch, having caught up with the galloping gorillas whinnied and cantered past them with Aano shaking the reins fervently, feeling as one with the powerful Suffolk.

'Don't try to move, sir,' said Uppendown to Hooter.

Al Orange grumbled under his breath, 'Where is he? He must be near.' He stared eagerly into the bagatelle of trees looking for any sign of Helkendag, but there was none.

Uppendown squatted next to Hooter who could do nothing to acknowledge his friends' arrival. Only his eyes moved from one to the other to proffer any sign of life.

The sound of heavy hooves and wagon wheels soon drew near. Aano jumped down from his seat before the wagon had even stopped and ran to Hooter's side. 'Inspector, what's happened?' The ape's heart sank when he saw the inspector's plight.

'We need to get him onto the wagon right away,' said Uppendown.

'Wait.' Velvet Warmheart's kindly voice called out as she and Gerald came over the rise. 'Please,' she said softly, 'let me see.' She knelt down beside Hooter and very carefully gathered his head in her arms, his neck offering no assistance. Tears welled up in Velvet's eyes as she held him tenderly to her warm breast.

Hooter's fading thoughts took him back to when he first met the beautiful Kate Herrlaw. She had also held him in such a way after rescuing him from the clutches of the human policemen. He raised his eyes to meet Velvet's. 'Thank you,' he said with a broken voice.

All eyes fell upon the brave and lovable inspector as he whispered, 'Thank you for not letting me die alone.' He took a feeble breath to expend a few more words. 'I didn't give it to him...the Amulet...I still have it.'

Velvet softly stroked the fine feathers over Hooter's perfectly round head to soothe and comfort him. Hooter's eyes smiled at Bob Uppendown, and then at Al Orange and Aano Grunt, and finally at Punch the horse. Punch responded by easing forward and planting a delicate wet kiss on top of Hooter's head. Hooter could no longer speak, but Punch read his mind and huffed quietly.

And then...Inspector Hooter of the Flying Squad fell asleep inside. His eyes remained wide open, perfectly beautiful with the light of the setting Sun reflecting in them, but he could see no more. He had passed away. The trees stood in silent respect while those in their shade wept openly for the mallard who had touched them all with his simple, sometimes naïve but always honest outlook on life.

The tears continued to flow while Gerald, helped by two of his neighbours, carefully wrapped Hooter's body in a soft cloth and gently placed him in the wagon next to the coffin containing the Beast of Grey.

Many hurricane lamps swung from gorillas' hands as the procession made its way back down the slope. Gorillas of all ages and sizes lined the pathway as the wagon wound its way between the cabins.

Aano eased back on the reins; Punch halted in front of Velvet's home. Encircled by lamps they said their farewells in sombre tones, rubbing wetted cheeks and whispering words of solace.

And so, with a shake of the reins, Punch hauled the wagon towards the timbered wall on the final leg of its journey, with Al Orange waddling to one side and Bob Uppendown to the other. Inspector Hooter would at last escort the missing Bog back to its world of origin.

Within a whisker of the wall, Punch pouted, his muzzle touched the timbers and his eyes widened as always and the timbers keenly took him and his party in.

The gorillas would never forget the day the giant mallards came to visit. Gerald Wunfith wondered what had become of the one they called Helkendag. He knew such evil existed in all worlds, but was quite sure his own kind were above such influence. *But what about the humans who live in the jungles many miles to the south?* He wondered.

***

Now through the wall, Punch pulled the wagon sharply to the right. This was the world of the humans. It was dark, flashing lights cruised across the sky. The smell of industry weighed heavily in the air. 'Keep going, fella,' Aano whispered, not

442

wanting to dwell in this very odd world. Unknown to them, kindly blue eyes watched from the undergrowth as the wagon screwed the gravel beneath its wheels turning tightly around the wall to make another pass from the other side. It was only then that a question entered Aano's head. He spoke aloud so that his friends might share his thoughts. 'The Amulet is still in Inspector Hooter's binoculars…right?'

'Right,' replied Orange and Uppendown.

'And they're still around his neck, right?'

'Right.'

Aano then asked, 'How far is it from the back of the wagon to Punch's nose?'

'Six or seven paces at a guess,' replied Uppendown.

Aano went on, 'So when Punch's nose touched the timbered wall the Amulet must have been much further than two paces away.'

'That's right.'

'So why did the timbers carry us through? It just doesn't make sense.'

'Who cares, as long as we can get through let's keep going,' replied Orange, forlornly.

Having circumnavigated the wall again, Punch was now in position for the final pass, just a few steps from safety. 'Forward, boy,' said Aano, 'good fella.' Punch once again did the business, touching the timbers with his soft pink lips. The wall savoured the gentle touch of the heavy horse and welcomed him through with a hefty squeeze around his substantial torso.

At last they were through, in their own world once again. They all breathed a long sigh of relief before gazing longingly into the wagon at the curvaceous mound beneath the tarpaulin.

'Vroo croo,' said a familiar voice. They all turned and, looking through heartbroken eyes, noticed the pigeon perched on a post, welcoming them back. His eyes blinked slowly. 'Vroo, vroo coo,' he added, warmly.

'Hello to you too, Mr Pigeon,' replied Aano, pulling gently on the right hand rein. 'Would you like to hop on?'

'Vroo,' replied the pigeon, squatting down on the post as if to say, 'No thank you, I'll stay here for now.'

A voice from among the tussocks then called out, 'What? Who? Identify yourself.' Constable Five Degrees emerged from his sleep into the moonlight.

Aano greeted him in saddened tones with none of his usual cheery spirit. 'Hello, Constable, we're Inspector Hooter's crew. We've just returned from his mission to recover the missing body of the Bog from the human world.'

'So that's what the inspector was up to,' Five Degrees replied. 'Do you have the Bog in the wagon?' He waddled keenly towards the wagon and peered over the side. The coffin shape was plain to see beneath the cover, but then the constable's gaze fell upon the rounded shape next to it. He turned and took stock of those standing before him. *Inspector Orange...Sergeant Uppendown...Mr Grunt.* He then returned his attention to the cargo. *No...no.* 'Please don't say...' The moonlight once again reflected in the tears of all present.

'I'm sorry, old chum.' Uppendown put a wing around the young constable's shoulder.

'But how did he die, was it an accident?' Five Degrees sobbed.

'He wus a very brave mallard,' Uppendown explained. 'The bravest. But he wus up against the most evil creature you ever could imagine.'

'But who...?'

Teardrops dripped from the end of the sergeant's bill, joining with those of Five Degrees on their way to the ground.

Aano relieved Uppendown by continuing. 'We were followed here by the inspector's friend, Miss Lethgerk. We should have realised as soon as she came through the wall who she was, but we didn't. And by the time we did it was too late. She had got him alone and killed him.' Aano wiped his eyes with a chubby finger.

Five Degrees' eye glazed over as it dawned on him that he had inadvertently brought Miss Lethgerk to the wall. 'But she couldn't possibly be so nasty, she was beautiful and kind.'

'Books and covers,' Al Orange muttered. 'Books and covers.'

'But why?' Five Degrees mumbled, his voice hardly making it into the world.

'He was after the Amulet.' Aano replied. 'He was going to let the humans through into our world, and he needed the Amulet to succeed.

'Surely you mean, she, not he.'

'No, constable. He was in disguise. Who knows what he is really. But he certainly wasn't beautiful and kind.'

'Oh dear, he didn't get the Amulet did he?'

'No, the truth is we don't know who has it.' Aano rubbed the top of his head, thinking hard. 'We think all the ones we have are duds. But there must be one somewhere, and it must be close by. It's a real mystery…'

Having listened to the conversation, Punch decided it best to move on. He vented a profound huff and took it on himself to ease his chest into the harness. At a respectful walking pace the party set off towards their lovely village of Smallbeef, Hampshire, in the lea of the South Downs in their world, the world of the water birds. The pigeon remained on top of the post, his heart aching for those who cried, and for the plump feathered soul in the back of the wagon. 'Vroo croo,' he sighed.

'Vroo… vroo,' he suddenly exclaimed, wide-eyed and

alarmed, when a hand emerged from a nearby bush and took hold of him tenderly. The other hand then reached forward and took something from the pouch which still hung from the pigeon's neck. 'Thank you, my friend,' said a soft gruff voice. 'Your job here is done, if you are quick you might catch up with the wagon and go home.'

The hand lifted the pigeon high in the air and released him. Away he flew with the Moon reflecting in his eye. A hopeful eye.

***

The night was over. Mother Nature threw a splash of purple across the dawn sky above the gorillas' cabins.

Velvet Warmheart slipped the tea cosy over the pot to let it stew. Her subdued eyes wetted while her thoughts dwelt heavily on the demise of the lovable Inspector Hooter. She sighed, dabbing her eyes with a pretty embroidered hanky.

Knock, knock. A thoughtfully quiet wrap on her front door had her making her way to the window. She discretely eased the net curtain to one side to see a handsomely built silverback with a small case in hand, waiting on her doorstep. She opened the door and was immediately taken by the good looks of the caller.

'Good morning, madam,' said the perfectly groomed gorilla, standing on all fours. 'I believe you have a cabin to rent?'

'Oh, erm, yes, that's quite right, sir,' she replied, still wiping her eyes.

'I would be most grateful if you would let it to me, madam. I have travelled a long way to get here and would be glad of a chance to rest my weary head.'

The aura about the caller was plain to see – to another gorilla.

Gerald Wunfith had now ventured out from his cabin,

wondering why his tea was late. He could not help but notice the impressive build of the male standing on Velvet's doorstep – **his** Velvet's doorstep. He straightened his police helmet and knuckle walked purposefully across the path to Velvet's home. 'Hello, hello, hello,' he said in his perfect diction. 'What may I ask is going on here, then?'

The stranger turned and nodded politely. 'Good morning, Officer. I was just asking this good lady if I might rent your spare cabin for a while.' He looked Gerald up and down and added, 'I must commend you on your appearance. Very smart indeed.'

'Thank you,' replied Gerald, looking to Velvet for her approval regarding the letting of the cabin. She gave a kindly nod.

'You are very welcome to stay, sir,' said Gerald. He in turn looked the stranger up and down, also impressed by his turn out. 'Might I ask what it is you do, sir?'

The newcomer smiled endearingly, 'I am an observer of sorts,' he said.

'Let me show you to your cabin,' said Gerald. 'If you ask nicely, the good lady here will possibly make you a nice pot of breakfast tea to settle you in.'

The stranger nodded to Velvet and doffed his imaginary cap. 'That would be very much appreciated.' He turned and followed Gerald to the cabin, which was only two doors along. As they knuckled walked smoothly across the grass, Gerald asked, 'Your name, sir?'

'It's Hew – Hew Kaartrel.' He stopped and turned to Gerald, offering his hand. The two duly shook in mutual accord.

'I'm Gerald Wunfith, custodian of the law, Heavy Mob,' Gerald replied, smiling.

Gerald opened the door of the cabin. 'Make yourself

comfortable, my friend.'

'Thank you again,' replied Hew Kaartrel.

Gerald closed the door, saying, 'Don't forget, tea on the terrace in five minutes.'

Hew was indeed a sturdy and handsome silverback, quite possibly slightly more robust even than Gerald. Now alone, he put his case on the bed and opened it. There were very few items within. He took a toothbrush and placed it in the washroom along with a large hairbrush. He then looked again into the case and smiled at the two remaining objects. A fine pair of binoculars and a dented brass hooter. 'Marvellous,' he said as he read the engraving on the side of the horn. "Nothing Stays The Same".

Printed in Great Britain
by Amazon